Beneath the Swaying Willow

Amily D'Nas

Royal Lime Press, LLC

Cover design by Dina St Andrew

Cover images: (weeping willow tree branches hanging down over picket fence) Based on original photograph by Amily D'Nas Copyright © 2023

Library of Congress Control Number: 2024901109

ISBN 979-8-218-34369-9 (trade paperback)

ISBN 979-8-218-34443-6 (ebook)

First edition published in Ft. Lauderdale, Florida, USA in 2024 by Royal Lime Press, LLC

Printed in the United States of America

In memory of my father, and all courageous veterans of the United States Armed Forces like him, who defended the freedoms of others yet struggled to find inner peace upon returning home.

Disclaimer

This novel contains sensitive adult topics.
Reader discretion is advised.

Prologue

Russ' soul radiated with joy as he held Nora's hands and gazed into her sparkling green eyes. Her golden hair, adorned with a crown of daisies, glistened in the sunlight as her white dress flowed freely in the breeze. Off in the distance, a rumble of thunder roared out its unsettling warning and a sudden feeling of uneasiness washed over him. Looking up he could see the once clear sky turning foreboding shades of deep grey and black, harkening a sense of gloom and uncertainty on their sacred day.

"What's happening?" Russ asked, gripping her hands tighter as thunder surrounded them and a pelting rain began to fall.

"I have to go now," she said, smiling wanly and letting go of his hands.

"Don't go. Stay here with me," Russ pleaded.

"It's not safe for me here," she whispered, lowering her gaze, turning her back to him and calmly walking away.

Russ turned and realized he had mistaken machine-gun fire coming from the neighboring trees for heavy rain. When he looked back again, Nora was gone. The crown of daisies now lay at his feet on the mud-soaked ground. Russ stood paralyzed with disbelief, surrounded by a sea of his fellow GIs bodies, bloodied by bullets and shrapnel.

"No!" he screamed.

Gasping for breath, Russ sprang up and opened his eyes to find that all of his buddies around the hootch were sound asleep. *It was just a bad dream,* he told himself as he rested his head on his pillow, keeping his eyes wide open and fearing what was to come.

1

1970

Nora Thompson let out an exasperated sigh as she caught a glimpse of her unsightly scar in her car's rearview mirror. The fresh and obvious flaw, just above her right eyebrow, had been drawing unwanted attention in recent weeks. It was ugly, just like the events that transpired on campus leading to her injury. The raised, red line that remained on her forehead, and the swelling waves of civil unrest throughout the nation, served as constant reminders that the world was an imperfect place.

Fumbling with the radio's dial, she adjusted the knob, settled on a familiar folk song and turned up the volume in hopes of drowning out the strange sound emanating from the car's rear quarter. Her late grandfather's once prized possession was now her primary means of transportation and time had transformed it into a jalopy of sorts, with its rust, flaking mint-green paint and the sudden, strange wobble in its rear tire reflecting its true age.

She became lost in her thoughts as the old clunker crossed the town line into Swanset. Her vibrant green eyes were drawn to the familiar weathered salt boxes and simple ranch style houses in the mill town. They were homes of factory workers, aging residents who had survived the Great Depression, and others who had been robbed of their dreams and accepted lack and hardship as their due lot in life. Returning home was always a tradeoff, a simple exchange of noise from all the anti-war protesters on campus for her mother's constant bitching. Relieved to have wrapped up another college semester, she was ever hopeful that her older sister, Emily, would surprise the family and show up for Christmas.

As her stomach let out a loud growl, she realized she had missed lunch in the midst of packing up her dorm room for the long winter break. With the wobble in her back tire intensifying, she pulled over to the side of the road, turned on her hazard lights, and stepped out onto Old County Road. Struck by a burst of frigid air, she fastened up the buttons on her wool coat and came to realize that the mini skirt she put on earlier that morning was not the best fashion choice as it was nearing the end of December. She adjusted her knit scarf snuggly around her neck, and pushed a loose strand of long, golden hair behind her ear as she leaned over to inspect the tire.

"Great! This is just great," Nora said, noticing the tire getting flatter by the second and giving it a swift kick with the toe of her brown, suede, knee-high boot.

Running her hand along the tailfin, she walked around to the back of the car and popped open the trunk to find a full spare tire whose day to shine had finally arrived. The steel X-shaped lug wrench felt frozen to the touch as Nora picked it up and momentarily twirled it in her hands, pondering what to do next and nervously biting her lower lip. Cold, tired and hungry, she glanced around the empty stretch of road and thought it best to get a move on and walk the one mile to her parents' house before the sun went down. The rumble of an approaching car grabbed her attention and she turned to see that a polished black muscle car, with a gleaming chrome bumper, had pulled over behind her.

"Do you need help, miss?", a fit young man, wearing tan corduroys and a partially open sherpa lined denim jacket, asked as he stepped out of the car and made his way over to her.

"Yes, my tire went flat. I have a spare, but I don't really know how to change it," Nora replied as she pointed to the deflating tire, taking notice of his square jawline and piercing blue eyes.

"I can help you with that. I work at a gas station across town and cars are kind of my thing," he said, glancing into the open trunk where the white-walled spare tire, jack and lug wrench sat.

"Thank you. They're not my thing, that's for sure," Nora joked, relieved to have been rescued.

Nora watched as the stranger jacked up the car and popped off the tire's hubcap. He then knelt, loosened the lug nuts, and placed them inside the overturned hubcap one by one, as he removed them. She observed the setting sun hitting the back of his head and illuminating his light, wavy hair.

"Ah, look at that spike. No tire would stand a chance against that," the stranger said, taking the flat tire off and pulling out a large, rusted nail.

"Wow! You saved the day."

"Well, I saved you from needing to get a tow at least. Besides, I couldn't just drive by and leave a beautiful damsel in distress stranded."

"Thank you. I was on my way home for my college break and almost made it. I'm Nora by the way," she said, feeling a rush of warmth in her cheeks.

"These things happen at the most inconvenient times. I'm Brant," he said, a broad smile lighting up his boyish face as he offered out his grease laden hand.

"I'd gladly shake your hand, but I think you need to wipe it first," Nora said.

"Oh gee. What was I thinking?" he asked, shaking his head and rolling his eyes.

"You obviously weren't. Here you can use this. It's seen better days," Nora said, giggling and unwrapping the scarf from her neck.

"I can't wipe my hands on your scarf. Hold on. I have a rag in my car," he said, turning and running back to his car.

Nora studied his athletic build as he wiped his hands on a terry cloth towel and walked back to where she was standing.

"Okay, let's try that again. I'm Brant Judge," he said, extending his now clean hand.

"I'm Nora. Nora Thompson," she said, accepting the handsome stranger's hand and feeling a surge of positive energy take hold of her.

"It's nice to meet you, Nora Thompson," Brant said, nodding his head.

Nora stood enamored, her shyness taking over and making her unable to think of what to say next.

"Where do you go to school?" he asked.

"I attend Bridgegate. I'm studying to be a science teacher," she said, realizing she sounded like a square.

"Right on! I can see you as a teacher, but they may make you wear something more conservative," Brant said with a smile, pointing to her skirt.

"What's wrong with my skirt?" Nora asked, as her forehead wrinkled.

Feeling the skin around the still-healing scar pull taut, she soothingly rubbed it with her fingertips.

"Nothing really. It's just that I attended St. Patrick's Academy for high school and the girls there weren't allowed to show that much leg without getting sent home," Brant replied, his eyes looking down at her toned legs.

"Oh," Nora replied with a giggle. *Think of something else to say to him,* she thought to herself.

"How about yourself? Are you enrolled in college too?"

"No. I'm working at the gas station to earn a few bucks until I'm able to start my training at the police academy. The chief says it shouldn't be too much longer as a few of the veteran officers are retiring next year."

"That's a very noble profession," Nora replied, picturing what he would look like in a uniform, as she pushed another loose strand of hair behind her right ear.

"If you don't mind me asking, what happened to your forehead?" Brant asked, his gaze settling upon her scar.

"It's okay, a lot of people have been asking me about it. I was walking to my dorm a few weeks ago and passed what was supposed to be a peaceful anti-war protest. The campus police showed up when it started to get rowdy and some of the students began destroying property. I tried to scoot around it, but before I knew it, I was in the middle of all this fighting and got hit with a sign that one of the protesters was swinging at the cops," Nora said.

"Yikes, that's rough. I'm sorry that happened to you."

"It makes me feel ugly," Nora confessed, looking down at the ground.

"Don't ever let a silly little scar make you feel ugly. Sure, scars leave a mark, but I think they tell a story in a way. They remind you of where you've been and how far you've come. One day you'll see what I mean. Besides, even with a scar you're beautiful," Brant said, looking her directly in the eye.

"You're kind," Nora said, feeling as if she were transported to another place for a moment as she became lost in his eyes.

"Now be sure to take it slow on your way home. Your father can drop off your tire to be patched at the garage on Read Road. They're open 'til seven most nights. Just let the manager know you're a friend of mine and he'll take care of you," he instructed as he tightened up the nuts on the spare one last time and replaced the hub cap.

"Groovy. Thanks so much. What do I owe you?" she asked.

"Nothing at all. . . except. . . it would be really cool if I could have your phone number," he replied after a moment's hesitation.

"I have a boyfriend," Nora confessed, not wanting to mislead him.

"Some boyfriend, leaving a pretty girl like you stranded," Brant chuckled, appearing to study her.

"He's away. He got drafted," Nora said after a brief pause, looking down at the dirt on the toes of her boots and reminding herself of her promise to wait for Russ to return.

"I suppose that explains that. Maybe in another lifetime."

"Thanks again. It was cool of you to pull over and help me out," Nora said, hypnotized by his gaze and sensing a mutual attraction between them.

"Anytime," Brant replied with a smile.

"Good luck at the police academy too, in case we don't see each other around."

"Thanks, and who knows, maybe we will. Remember not to speed or I'll have to pull you over and write you a ticket," Brant replied, his smile widening, exposing his perfectly aligned teeth.

"You wouldn't," Nora joked, being subtly flirtatious and flipping her hair back as she stepped away.

"You never know. You just never know."

"Well, see you later, alligator," she said, smiling back at him as she opened her car door and got back in.

"Peace," Brant called out, holding up his right index and middle fingers into the shape of the letter V.

Peering into the rearview mirror, she ignored her scar and watched as Brant gave her a wave goodbye and slid his hands into his jacket pockets as she drove off. Moving further away, she tried to focus on the road ahead but found herself unable to stop looking back at the image of him reflected in the mirror.

"Maybe in another lifetime," Nora said, catching herself reiterating his words aloud, following the bend in the road and losing sight of the handsome stranger.

2

After another long, grueling day spent tracking the enemy deep in the jungle, PFC Russell Ayers took a seat on the trunk of a fallen tree, wiped beads of sweat from his forehead, and quenched his thirst with a large gulp of stale water from his canteen. While scanning the flora around him for movement, he waited for the rest of his company to catch up with him on the trail back to base camp and saturated a bandana with the last of his water. He draped the bandana around his forehead and over his military buzz cut, tying it behind his head to cool himself down while keeping his eyes open in anticipation of an ambush from the Viet Cong who he, and other American GIs, referred to as Charlie. The temperatures had exceeded one hundred degrees all week long and Russ was looking forward to getting back to the hootch and dabbling in the smorgasbord of illicit drugs in order to numb his mind and burn off the stress of combat.

"Hey, Ayers, got anything you're willing to trade today?" Johnny Davis, who had been a few paces ahead of him, asked with his C-rats in hand.

"Shit, I don't know. Maybe this can of meat for some smokes," Russ replied, quickly rummaging through the contents of his rucksack.

"You're going to have to do better than that. I'm starving and cigarettes are a hot commodity out here. Throw in the chewing gum and some of that canned cake and you've got yourself a deal."

"Deal," Russ said, shaking Johnny's hand and accepting the cigarettes from him.

"It was another scorcher out here today. North Philly ain't never seen a summer this hot, that's for sure. Hell, I bet it's snowing there as we speak," Johnny stated, popping a stick of spearmint gum into his mouth.

"I bet you're right. You really like that canned cake, don't you?" Russ asked his friend and point man, the two having met after Russ joined his unit's headquarters northwest of Saigon a few months prior.

"Hell yeah, Ayers. This pecan cake is the best. It keeps my sweet tooth happy while out here in the boonies," Johnny joked.

"You're too much," Russ replied, laughing as he flipped open his lighter.

"Keep your eyes open, Ayers. I need to take a leak," Johnny said, opening the fly of his fatigues and turning to face a nearby tree.

"You know I always have your back, Davis," Russ replied, continuing to keep a look out for the enemy as he lit his cigarette.

Taking a long drag, he thought back to the previous July when he had been shipped out, without a unit, on a civilian airplane chartered by the U.S. military. Letting the smoke fill his lungs, he recalled arriving midday at the United States Airforce base at Cam Ranh Bay in his starched khakis. As he exhaled and watched the smoke expel from his mouth, he remembered getting smacked in the face with the horrific smell of raw sewage and jet fuel as the plane's door opened. It had been nothing but oppressive heat, ambushes, explosions and fallen soldiers in body bags since the day he landed.

Like himself, Johnny Davis had also been drafted by the Selective Service. Russ, having witnessed violence and discrimination of Black GIs in Vietnam, had confided in Johnny that it rubbed him the wrong way. It didn't matter to Russ what color Johnny's skin was and vice versa. They were true brothers-in-arms, with no racial barrier between them. The unlikely pair had developed a strong bond and knew they could rely on each other in the bush and tunnels of Vietnam. They also managed to humor one another with jokes and silly antics, providing one another with temporary distractions from the living hell they were caught up in.

"So, I got a letter from my Vanessa in yesterday's mail call. She sent me this picture. Look at her. She is fine, yes, she is," Johnny said, breaking Russ' train of thought and handing him a picture of his girlfriend back home in Philadelphia.

"She's something, Davis," Russ replied, studying the picture of Johnny's voluptuous, dark-skinned girl.

"Have I ever shown you a picture of my girlfriend?" Russ asked.

"Your girlfriend? I thought I knew everything about you by now, but you never told me that you have a girl back home too. Why didn't you tell me about her before?"

"I like to keep some parts of my life private, Davis, but since you're sharing I figured I would too. I thought maybe I'd miss her less if I didn't talk about her but that's not the case. She's my high school sweetheart. Look at her," Russ said, pulling a photograph out of the pocket of his field jacket.

"Woo wee! Ain't she something? Look at those green eyes. How did a little grunt like you manage to get a girl like that anyway?" Johnny asked jokingly.

"Very funny, Davis. Thoughts of her are the only thing getting me through this tour," Russ said, taking back the photograph of Nora that he always carried with him and kept close to his heart.

"Don't you worry, I won't tell her about your time in those girlie bars in Saigon as long as you keep sending those cans of cake my way, Ayers," Johnny said, laughing again and patting him on the back.

"I'll be sure not to tell Vanessa about what you've been up to either so long as you keep sending those smokes my way," Russ fired back, patting Johnny on the back.

"Davis! Ayers! You guys will never guess what I found," Harry Blake excitedly stated, appearing from the trail with a few other guys from their company.

"Heck, I don't know, Blake. Maybe you've found yourself an exotic hooker, like the ones in those girlie bars in Saigon. Ayers and I were just discussing that, weren't we?" Davis blurted out, giving Russ a wink.

"I wish, Davis, but no. Little Spud, do you want to take a guess?" Harry asked, directing his question to Russ who he had nicknamed 'Little Spud' because of his short stature.

"I don't know. A weapon? Maybe one of Charlie's knives?" Russ asked.

"Wrong again. Boys, I found myself a tunnel entrance," Harry informed them.

"Where?" Johnny and Russ asked in unison.

"Just back there about thirty yards or so. I dropped my canteen as we were trekking along and when I bent down to pick it up, I noticed a bunch of loose vegetation that looked a bit out of sorts. As I got closer, I noticed it was covering an entrance hole. I bet that's where Charlie disappeared to," Harry said.

"Good eye, man, but we've got to get back to the hootch before sundown. Ayers and I will check it out first thing tomorrow," Davis replied.

"I can't wait to see what tomorrow will bring," Russ said, exhaling one last puff of his cigarette smoke into the thick jungle air, picking up his rucksack and slinging it over his shoulder, grateful for having survived another day of his twelve-month tour in the foreign land of Vietnam.

3

Nora let out a dry cough and felt her chest tighten as she pulled up to her family's pristine home, knowing that its manicured shrubs and crisp white paint served as a mere façade for all the problems tucked neatly inside its walls.

After turning off the ignition, she opened the car door and stepped out.

"Here we go," she said aloud, grabbing her knapsack and overstuffed bag of clothes in need of laundering from the back seat and heading toward the front door.

She gingerly turned the doorknob, wiped her suede boots on the doormat and carefully peered down the hallway in anticipation of her mother's usual, cold-hearted welcome.

"It's about time you arrived. We've been waiting for you so we can have dinner. Where have you been anyway?" Viviane scolded.

"It's nice to see you too, Mom," Nora replied.

"Please close that door, you're letting all the cold air in. And take off those filthy boots so you don't traipse dirt through the house," Viviane ordered.

"There she is!" Mr. Thompson exclaimed, emerging from the living room, peering over the rim of his reading glasses and hurrying over to help her with her bags.

"Hi, Daddy," Nora said, embracing him.

"I was starting to worry about you," Richard Thompson told his daughter.

"Sorry I'm late but I had a flat tire," Nora replied, removing her boots.

"Oh no. Why didn't you call?"

"There were no payphones around, but a nice guy pulled over and changed it for me. He works at the gas station across town and said you can bring the tire there to be patched."

"That was nice of him. Come in and get warm. How are you feeling?" he asked, brushing her hair aside, looking her scar over and planting a kiss on her forehead.

"I'm fine. I don't want you to worry about me."

"Nonsense, I always worry about you. It's my job. Besides it gives me something to do other than listen to your mother. She's been complaining that dinner is getting cold for an hour already."

"Gee whiz. Really?"

"You know how she gets. I can't blame your sister one bit for not sticking around, but you better not ever leave me," Mr. Thompson said under his breath, leading her into the dining room.

"Don't worry, Daddy. I won't," Nora softly replied as she slid out a chair, smoothed her skirt and sat down at the dining room table.

She studied the tabletop, set with crisp linens, spotless flatware and sparkling crystal drinking glasses and was reminded of how Viviane's materialism and unrealistic expectations had driven her older sister away. The house felt empty without her there, but Emily, who yearned to be an individual and rejected societal norms, had grown intolerant of Viviane's demands, consumerism and rigid world views. She was a true flower child and split soon after graduating high school, embracing the hippie counterculture and hitchhiking her way across the country to San Francisco with others like her during the Summer of Love. The last time she called, Viviane told her she wasn't welcome to come back home until she changed her ways, and no one had heard from her since.

"Nora, for goodness sake, stop your daydreaming. Please take your elbows off the table and pass your father the saltshaker as he asked," Viviane scolded.

"Sure. Here you go," Nora said, smirking.

"Nora, I almost forgot to tell you that Josie called for you earlier. She said she just arrived home from Boston yesterday," Mr. Thompson said.

"Okay, thanks for letting me know, Daddy," Nora replied, smiling and looking forward to getting together with her best friend since second grade, Josie Henson.

"That Henson girl should mind her manners. I don't understand why she feels the need to call as soon as you arrive home. What did she want anyway, Richard?" Viviane complained.

"How am I supposed to know, Viv? She didn't call to speak to me after all, she asked to speak to Nora."

"I'm sure it must be more boyfriend trouble. That fast girl has had more boyfriends than I can count," Viviane rambled.

"Maybe you should stop counting," Richard said.

"She has a name, Mom, and boys aren't her only interest. Josie is smart and was offered a full scholarship in case you forgot. We haven't seen each other since Columbus Day weekend, and she probably wants to get together for a sleepover," Nora replied.

"Maybe time away from her was exactly what you needed. I'm just glad her ways haven't rubbed off on you young lady," Viviane stated, pointing the tines of her fork in Nora's direction.

From across the table Nora watched as Viviane neatly sliced into her petit filet and sipped red wine from a long-stemmed glass. She thought of how her mother had grown even more suffocating since Emily left, as if hoping to mold Nora into a child she could brag about and serve as a reflection of her own old-fashioned views. Nora though, was determined to live life on her own terms and escape the monotony of her stifling little town.

After helping clear the table, Nora plopped down on the couch next to her father, already exhausted from Viviane's incessant nagging, yet knowing she was still luckier than most. She cherished the time with her father who had started his own insurance company with nothing but a dream, a desk, and a few friends as clients. It was now a thriving business in the neighboring city of Weaver Falls. Nora was her father's daughter for certain, a dreamer just like him, paying little attention to the small-minded thinkers in her sleepy little hometown situated along New England's southern coastline.

"You're just in time. The world news is about to start," Richard said, placing his arm around her shoulder.

"I'm sure it will be all bad news," Nora stated, feeling melancholy and leaning her head on her father's chest.

"Now, now. Let's wait and see. It can't be all bad after all."

As the evening news began Nora closed her eyes without responding, dreading what the latest report would reveal. Everywhere she turned she was reminded of the dangerous place, halfway around the world, where Russ now was. In preceding months, she had been avoiding picking up the newspaper as each day brought more devastating news to her hometown and the country at large. The constant barrage of stories in the local and national newspapers, about American soldiers who had gone missing or were killed in action, were too disturbing to read. She thought back to the previous December when the Selective Service held its Vietnam Draft on national television for the entire country to see. Nora and her friends at Bridgegate, like students at other college campuses around the country, watched the live coverage intently from the television in the student union building. Other students, who were against the government's involvement in Indochina, chose to protest the war just outside the building's entryway. Families throughout the nation, from coast to coast, had nervously listened in. Mothers around the United States gripped their rosary beads while silently praying their boys would not be taken away from them. Fathers across the nation cracked open cans of beer to share with their sons, admitting to themselves their boys were now men in the eyes of the government. As fate would have it, Russ hit the lottery that day when the little blue ball numbered 004, corresponding to his February birthday, was drawn. The feelings of impending doom that had been plaguing him for months had been officially validated and not long after, he had been sent to bootcamp, advanced individual training and, eventually, deployed to Vietnam.

"The first account of American prisoners of war held in POW camps was released by the government of North Vietnam today. The partial list, containing three hundred sixty-eight names, is considered by Hanoi to be the closest thing to an official count," the newscaster reported.

As the broadcast continued, Nora squirmed in her seat and tightly clasped her hands, causing her knuckles to turn white. Concerned for Russ' safety, she closed her eyes and thought back on the night before Russ' deployment which had been beset with dread, as they were both aware of what was at stake in the reality of being sent into combat. They had urged each other to stay strong and agreed to write often. During their long, final embrace, they promised each other they would pick up where they were leaving off upon his return, sealing the promise with a tearful, goodbye kiss. She tried to keep her eyes closed as the news report continued, unable to block out the reporter's well-modulated voice.

"Daddy, I just can't watch this anymore. It makes me nervous thinking about Russ," Nora finally blurted out, shielding herself from the images of the American GIs in combat flashing across the television screen.

"I know, but you can't bury your head in the sand either, Nora," Richard replied, turning toward her and placing his hands on top of hers.

"What if he doesn't make it home?" Nora asked, her eyes welling up.

"Don't think like that, Nora. Russ is going to be just fine."

"You don't know that for sure. I'm afraid I'm going to open the newspaper one day and see his picture on the front page with some horrible headline," Nora replied, wiping a tear from her cheek.

"You're right, we don't know for sure, but I have something that may help. This came for you today. I intercepted it before your mother could get ahold of it. You know how she likes to be in everyone's business," Mr. Thompson said, handing her a piece of mail.

"It's from Russ!" Nora exclaimed as she recognized the white envelope with a border of alternating red, white and blue parallelograms around its edges and the word "Free" written in its upper right-hand corner in place of a postage stamp.

She studied the handwriting on the envelope's exterior with the return address sender and location of *"PFC R. Ayers, APO San Francisco 96383"*.

"The news is just about over. Why don't you go to your room and read your letter in private? That way your mother doesn't see it and you don't have to sit here with me feeling worse about things. Remember to call Josie back too," Mr. Thompson said, kissing her forehead again and nodding his head in the direction of the staircase.

"Thank you, Daddy," she said, before kissing his cheek.

Nora eagerly got up from the couch and, with the letter in hand, made her way over to the staircase as the tail end of the news report faded off behind her.

4

R uss knelt, peering down into the opening of the tunnel's shaft, with sweat dripping down his temples and a burning cigarette dangling out the corner of his mouth.

"These smokes you traded me taste like stale crap, Davis," Russ said, knowing they would have to do, as he tried to remain calm and waited for instructions to descend.

He and Johnny were two of only one hundred Tunnel Rats currently serving in Vietnam. Both had bravely volunteered for the dangerous job which required them to rely primarily on their auditory, tactile and olfactory senses to gather reconnaissance. They were trained to detect and destroy any enemy presence in the pitch-black underground labyrinth. All the two needed to communicate in silence was a blink of an eye while out on the trails or a tap of a finger when down inside the darkened tunnels. Each trusted the other with their lives.

Just after sun up, the company traversed their way back to the tunnel entrance discovered the previous day, twenty-five miles northwest of Saigon, on a search and destroy mission. Russ and his buddies knew they were vulnerable to attack as they hiked their way through the unbearable heat and humidity, scanning the flora and looking out for trip wires and booby traps along the way. When an ambush came, it didn't matter where you were from, what your name was, how much money you had, or the color of your skin. It was all about working together as a team and looking out for one another. After only a few weeks of combat, looking over his shoulder and watching out for his buddies had become the new norm for Russ. In Vietnam, he had learned survival was the name of the game.

"What are you waiting for? Get down here and make sure you've got your flashlight on your person this time too," Johnny Davis said, popping his head out of the hole in the ground.

"Hey, I thought you were hiding down there so we wouldn't see that messed up haircut of yours," Russ replied.

"Ayers, it ain't my fault that Army barber only caters to you White folk. He doesn't know shit about cutting Black hair. I'll be growing out my 'fro as soon as I leave this hell hole."

"So, tell me what we've got here," Russ said.

"Well, this tunnel is even tighter than the last one," Davis stated.

"Really?"

"Tighter than my crib back in Philly. I'll be happy to go back to living in the hood after dealin' with this shit," Davis replied.

"Man, you're something else," Russ said with a smile.

"Okay listen up. So, when I went down to scope it out, I could see that this one seems to go on for a while. There's an open room on the left. I already stepped inside it to check it out. It's not booby trapped. No punji sticks or scorpions at least, and no VC. Just a few rats running around and bats hanging on the ceiling. I'm glad you volunteered to come down here with me 'cause this looks like a long one. It's got lots of zigzags, and we've got a shitload of explosives to set up. After about twenty feet the tunnel branches off into a T and that's where all the ziggin' and zaggin' begins. Stay behind me and we'll start setting up on the right side at that first bend. I'll go a few feet ahead of you to check for Charlie, so you'll be clear to place the charges. Ready?"

"Hell, Davis, I was born ready," Russ replied, trying to psych himself up for their latest underground mission.

"Okay, lower him down boys. Remember, lights out, Ayers. Here we go," Davis said before disappearing back into the tunnel.

Russ tried to put his fear into the back of his mind as adrenaline and the speed he had popped earlier that morning coursed through his veins. His buddies grabbed his ankles and lowered him down, headfirst, into the tunnel. He knew he had to keep his head clear and stay focused, listening, feeling and smelling his way through the pitch blackness, all while remaining as quiet as possible, crawling on his hands and knees through the dark tunnel.

With acute senses, Russ and Johnny bravely moved forward along the straight, narrow section of tunnel floor. They were tasked with rigging up explosives, which were to be later detonated, in this newly discovered section of more than one hundred and thirty miles of the tunnel's complex.

Stretching from Saigon to the Cambodian border, the tunnels allowed VC guerillas to navigate the jungle undetected and it was Russ' job to help destroy the complex. The coolness of the hand-carved clay and ferric soil walls provided a bit of relief from the oppressive heat above ground and the two agreed it was the only good part about being in the tunnels. Russ, trying to stay focused, suddenly felt something scurry across his hand, up his arm and over his shoulder before jumping off him. *Damn rodents. That felt like a big one,* Russ thought as he kept moving on without hesitation.

After traversing a few feet further, he felt along the side of the textured wall with his open palm. When it began to curve, he knew this was the first righthand turn Davis told him about. Just as he was about to turn the corner, he heard a subtle movement to his left and ceased his crawl. *Keep your flashlight off and don't make a sound,* he reminded himself as he waited in darkness, sniffing the tunnel air, as a wild animal would do. He listened intently for the faintest of sounds. Suddenly his nasal passages were overcome with the smell of spicey sweat. The enemy was near, and Russ reminded himself that nothing mattered but the kill and making it out alive. He was not about to take pity on Charlie. If he did, he knew he could end up being captured and taken prisoner of war or, even worse, returned home to his parents, Martha and Fred, zipped up tight in a body bag. There was no room for error. He felt the sides of his face bulge as his muscles tightened. With his teeth firmly clenched he remained still and silent. Just then, he felt someone pounce onto his back. This time, instead of being a rodent, it was Charlie, expressing his warm, fetid breath into his ear and tightening a choke hold on him. Without hesitating, Russ reached for his pistol, pointed it upward, and pulled the trigger. The arm around his neck instantly went limp as the lifeless body slumped onto the tunnel floor beside him. It wasn't a silent kill like most of his previous kills with his knife had been. The other VC would surely now know their enemy was down in the tunnel and would descend on them like flies if they didn't find a way out. The gunshot left an almost deafening, high-pitched ringing in Russ' ears, replacing the sound of the VC's breathing he had heard just seconds earlier. Russ forged ahead, determined to do whatever he needed to stay alive. *Just get yourself and Davis out of here,* Russ thought to himself.

"You okay, Ayers?" Davis asked, having backtracked to the spot where Russ was, leaning in and cupping Russ' ear with his hand as he spoke.

"Let's get the hell out of here," Russ replied, overcome with a familiar feeling of dread.

As the two made their way up an ascending branch of the tunnel, they noticed scattered rays of sunlight up ahead.

"Here's a way out. Hoist me up. I'll make sure it's clear. If it is, I'll go out first and then I'll pull you out," Davis said, pointing up to the exit now directly above them.

"I've got you," Russ said, hoisting him upward.

Davis ever so slightly lifted the hatch that was camouflaged with vegetation and looked around.

"Looks clear. I'm heading out. See you on the flip side," Davis said as he flung the hatch wide open and made his way out of the tunnel and into the daylight.

Russ then thought he heard rustling overhead and assumed that Davis was getting back on his feet.

"Davis?" Russ called out.

Receiving no response, Russ felt his heart begin to race.

"Davis, you better not leave me alone down here."

Through the high-pitched ringing in his ears, he heard muffled sounds followed by a thump. *What the hell is that?* Russ thought as something fell into the hole.

"Davis? What did they do to you? No!" Russ cried out, realizing that it was Davis' severed head and dog tags that now lay on the tunnel floor beside him.

"God no! He was my friend. He was my brother," Russ yelled up toward the open hole before falling to his knees.

As the rest of his company made their way through the bush and toward the exit hole where Davis' decapitated body lay, Russ could hear a rapid exchange of gunfire erupting between them and the Viet Cong, followed by a loud explosion. He felt as if he had left his own body and was in another dimension, unable to fully comprehend what was happening around him.

"You were my brother, Davis. You were my brother," Russ cried out in anguish, sitting on the tunnel floor and gently cradling his friend's severed head.

He then carefully closed Davis' eye lids, as if to tell him that he could finally rest. Davis' warm blood ran through the fingers of his trembling hands, becoming tacky and saturating the front of his T-shirt. Davis had given his all, but Russ knew it was now time for him to make his journey home to Philadelphia, and to his Vanessa, as another casualty of the Vietnam War.

A haze of dust particles filled the air around him as Russ' company came to his aide and hoisted him out of the tunnel. Russ rubbed his eyes, staring in disbelief at the freshly killed bodies whose parts were strewn across the jungle floor from grenade blasts and the firefight that had ensued. He felt his chest tighten as he studied himself, counting his limbs and digits on his hands. He began frantically scanning the ground around him, checking to be sure that none of the scattered, bloodied limbs were his. Russ gasped as his breathing sped up and he was unable to control the flow of air in and out of his lungs, feeling as though a part of him had died alongside his friend, deep within the tunnel walls. Russ felt his head grow dizzy and his legs become heavy.

"Ayers, are you okay?" Russ' commanding officer called out.

"I need to finish the mission, Sir. I need to finish the mission!" Russ yelled, wandering aimlessly.

"Ayers, get your ass over here and help pick up these bodies."

"But. . . Sir. . . I can't. I need to. . . I. . . need. . . to finish the. . . mission," Russ repeated, walking in circles and growing more confused with each step.

"Ayers? Ah, shit. God damn it! Where's the medic? Find him and have him sedate Ayers. He's losing his mind. I want him on a Huey, taken the hell out of here and flown to the Evac hospital," the officer called out to another foot soldier while Russ continued mindlessly meandering about, unable to fully comprehend what was happening around him.

5

"I get the feeling your mother doesn't like me much," Josie Henson said, placing her overnight bag down on the shag carpet in Nora's bedroom.

"Don't worry about her, Jo. She's miserable and doesn't like anyone," Nora replied, shaking her head and rolling her eyes.

"Are you feeling better since you had your stitches removed?"

"I guess so. I just hope this scar fades. I hate seeing it every time I look in the mirror."

"All scars fade in time, Nor. Now I want to hear all about the letter Russ sent you," Josie eagerly said.

"Shh. Viviane doesn't know that he wrote me. I had to hide his letter from her. She never liked Russ and keeps trying to convince me to go out on a date with Dr. Perkins' nephew, Chip," Nora replied, closing the bedroom door behind her and securing its lock for privacy.

"Viviane just doesn't quit. Remember how Chip followed you around like a lost puppy at your parents' cookout over the summer?" Josie asked.

"Don't remind me. I'm still trying to forget about that."

"What the heck does Viviane have against Russ anyway?"

"I suppose he doesn't live up to her high standards because his parents are factory workers or something. She has delusions that I'm going to marry a doctor so she can brag to her friends in the garden club and at the hair salon."

"That's too bad. Well, let me hear what Russ had to say."

"Okay, but come closer so you can hear me. You know how my mom likes to eavesdrop," Nora replied, carefully removing the letter from its envelope and reading aloud softly as Josie listened intently.

Dear Nora,

The days are long, and I don't want to bore you with details of my time here, but I'm finally able to get a few free minutes to write you. I received the care package you sent, and it really brightened my day. Your homemade cookies arrived all broken, but I shared them with the guys in my company and they all agreed that they were the tastiest thing they've eaten in weeks. Thanks for sending the T-shirts, socks and chewing gum too. My friend Johnny Davis from Philly has his eyes on the gum, but I plan to use it as a bargaining chip to trade him for some smokes later. I wish I could get you a present for Christmas, like a nice necklace or something, but there aren't any stores out here in the jungle. You won't believe it Nor, but Johnny and I were lucky enough to get selected to go to the USO show. They are even issuing us clean uniforms and transporting us to the base the day of the performance. It should be good fun, but Christmas won't be the same without you. I'll try to write more often but the heavy monsoon rains here can cause the helicopters to get grounded and the trucks are sometimes unable to navigate the washed-out roads, so the mail gets delayed. For now, I'll keep the picture that Josie took of you close to my heart, in the pocket of my field coat. I hope you always keep me close to your heart too. Merry Christmas Nor. Love, Russ.

"Awe, that was so sweet, Nor," Josie said, wrapping her arms around her.

"I hadn't heard from him in over two months. I worry about him, Jo."

"Of course you do. Its normal to worry."

"It seems like the war is all I think about most days," Nora replied, wiping tears from the corners of her eyes.

"I don't like seeing you like this, Nor. You're going to make yourself sick if you don't do something to take your mind off things."

"I can't help it, Jo."

"Well, you should get out more. I was going to ask you if you'd come out bowling tomorrow night."

"Bowling? Since when do you like to bowl?" Nora asked, raising an eyebrow and knowing that Josie had never wanted to go bowling in all the years she had known her.

"Since I met Dennis Blake," Josie said with a wide grin.

"Wait! Who is this Dennis guy and what happened to Glen?"

"I broke up with Glen a few weeks ago. I hear he's now dating that redhead, Brenda, that he works with at the record store. I was so busy studying for my finals that I forgot to tell you. It's no big deal really. Glen has no ambition, and I was getting bored with him anyway."

"And this Dennis guy?" Nora asked.

"I met him when I was waiting in the checkout line at the convenience store when I was home for Thanksgiving. I was holding a bottle of cola and it was so cold that it slipped right out of my hands. Luckily it didn't break. Dennis was standing behind me and leaned down to pick it up at the same time I did. We bumped heads, both started laughing and ended up meeting for a cup of coffee the next day at Swanset Diner."

"Far out," Nora replied, always entertained by Josie's stories.

"We're just having fun. He went to a private high school and will be getting his volunteer corps assignment soon. He's a conscientious objector and is trying to avoid going to Vietnam. His older brother is serving there now. Besides, I don't want to be tied down after what happened with Glen and I'm going to be busy with my transfer to Westlock."

"It's going to be so cool having you close by. My roommate Becky was asking about you before I left campus. We want you to come hang out with us at Bridgegate again."

"Becky was cool. What was her last name?" Josie asked.

"Lieberman."

"That's right, Becky Lieberman. I'll remember it now. You're both in that new co-ed dorm, aren't you?"

"Yes, and this year we are in a double instead of a triple. And I know what you are thinking."

"What, Nor? Westlock is an all-girls school, so I have to be able to meet guys somewhere after all," Josie said with a smirk.

"Don't worry, you'll have plenty of guys to hang out with when you visit us at Bridgegate. They're your type too."

"I know. When I visited you last spring, I met a lot of dreamy guys. They were so earthy in their beaded bracelets and leather sandals. I would have liked to transfer to another co-ed school, but I couldn't pass up the offer from Westlock. I like that they provide a challenging curriculum for women."

"You'll have the best of both worlds, Jo. You'll be attending a college where you'll be educationally nurtured, and your best friend will be nearby in a coed dorm where you can visit and learn things that Westlock can't teach you," Nora joked, poking Josie with her elbow.

"Very funny, Nor. What about you? You said you get lonely. Don't you ever find yourself attracted to anyone?"

"I don't know, Jo," Nora said, shrugging her shoulders.

"It's okay to be curious, Nor."

"I promised to wait for Russ, but I guess I do get curious. . . sometimes," Nora admitted, thinking back to the handsome stranger who had changed her flat tire.

"You don't think Russ has been an angel, do you?"

"What do you mean?" Nora asked, cocking her head to the side.

"I mean it's a well-known fact that the bars American GIs hang out at in Saigon are crawling with hookers. Think about it, Nor. Russ and all those other guys don't know if they are going to make it home or not. Any hot-blooded guy would find what they're selling hard to resist under the circumstances, don't you think?"

"I suppose so," Nora replied, biting her lower lip and pondering Josie's revelation of the recreational activities of American GIs in Vietnam.

"Russ can't expect you to just sit home night after night pining away for him. You need to get out more, Nor. Say you'll come out bowling tomorrow night. Please?" Josie pleaded, looking at her with her brown, doe-like eyes.

"I don't know, Jo," Nora replied, not wanting to believe what Josie had said was true yet knowing that her friend was well read on the happenings in Indochina.

"Would you rather sit home and hang out with Viviane on a Saturday night?" Josie coaxed.

"Okay, okay. I'll go. It sounds like fun," Nora replied, knowing that anything would be better than a night stuck inside the house suffocated by Viviane's negativity and watchful eye.

$$6$$

"He's starting to come around. Get me another IV. We need to keep him hydrated," the Army nurse called out.

Through his heavy half-opened eyelids, Russ could see the blurred outlines of movement around him. The far-off sound of a Huey's chopper blades was getting closer, stirring him awake. *Where am I? Why can't I move? Davis... oh my God, Davis... his body was on the ground... and his head... was missing... his head was in my hands.* Russ became agitated as pictures of the aftermath of the bloody attack flashed through his mind.

"No, Davis! Charlie is out there! Don't go!!" a panicked Russ Ayers screamed, thrashing in the hospital bed, his hands and feet in restraints.

"Whoa there, soldier. It's okay. You're safe. My name is Lt. Peggy Wallace and I'm an Army nurse," she said, tenderly placing a hand on his shoulder.

"I have to hide. I have to get out of here!" Russ screamed again.

"You're safe and in a United States Army hospital at the Cu Chi base camp. No one is going to hurt you," the nurse assured him, placing her hand on his forearm to still his restlessness.

"They're going to kill us. They killed Davis... and what about the rest of my buddies? There were bodies everywhere when I came out of the tunnel. Please... you have to let me go. I need to help them. I have to finish the job," Russ pleaded.

"Can I get some help over here? I've got a restless one. Bring over some sedatives too so I can make sure he doesn't break free of his restraints."

As Russ forced his eyes fully open, the blurriness dissipated and gave way to a clear view of his surroundings. He glanced around to see he was just one of many GIs lying in the camp's hospital. He observed nurses hurrying around the ward handing off supplies, lifting patients into their beds, urgently hooking up IVs, changing dressings and assisting doctors with their rounds to tend to the wounded.

"You must settle down. I'm here to help you. We have a lot of wounded here today and I need your cooperation," his nurse informed him as she hung a new bag of saline on the hook beside his bed.

"Where am I again?" Russ asked, trying to grasp what she was saying.

"You are in the Twelfth Evac Hospital in Cu Chi. You were airlifted out on a Huey yesterday along with a few of your buddies."

"I remember there was heavy fire. . . the VC killed my friend Davis. . . but I don't remember much else."

"I was told that your buddies lifted you out of the tunnel. You were in shock and incoherent so the medic in your platoon sedated you. You're going to spend some time here with us for evaluation. Don't worry, we'll take good care of you. Oh, and the food here is much better than those God-awful C-rats."

"But I have to get back into the tunnels."

"Not today, soldier. Your orders are to rest up for a few days. I gave you a bit more sedative to help you relax. Is there anything else I can get you?"

"My field jacket. I have something. . . a picture. . . in my pocket. I need it."

"Okay, I'll go look for it. What's the picture of?" the nurse asked.

"My beautiful green-eyed girl."

"She sounds lovely."

"She is. She really is," Russ replied, his eyelids once again growing heavy and his body beginning to surrender to the sedatives.

"Good afternoon, Private Ayers," a soothing voice called out.

Who's that? Where am I now? Russ thought to himself, fighting to stay awake and unsure of how many minutes or hours had passed.

Through half opened eyes, Russ saw an Army chaplain standing at his bedside. A stole, with embroidered crosses adorning its ends, was draped around the back of his neck and hung down over both sides of his chest. He had a rolling cart with him holding a chalice, host container and a cross.

"I'm Chaplain Thomas Leonard. I'm here to offer combat stress support and communion, if you would like to receive it."

"Sure. It can't hurt. . . can it?" Russ groggily replied.

"Are you of the Catholic faith?"

"Yes, Sir."

"I understand you lost some friends yesterday."

"Yeah, man . . . I mean, Sir. I'm having a hard time putting the images out of my mind."

"That's understandable."

"Chaplain?" Russ asked, feeling tears begin to pool in the corners of his eyes.

"What worries you?"

"I've taken so many lives. . . and broken the commandments. I don't know if God will ever forgive me. . . for what I've done down in the tunnels," Russ confessed, trying to force his eyes to stay focused on the chaplain, unsure whether he was dreaming or not.

"If you seek forgiveness, the Lord will surely hear you, but first you must learn to forgive yourself. Shall we pray?"

"Yes," Russ replied, closing his eyes and finding himself still in restraints and unable to clasp his hands together in preparation for prayer.

"Almighty God, we ask you to have mercy on us in this hour when we feel confused, low in spirit and with heavy hearts. We ask that you bless and protect Russell and make him an instrument of Thy peace. Comfort him, give him strength, and fill him with your divine presence so that he may walk in your ways in these uncertain times. We pray also for Russell's brothers in arms who gave their lives in dedication to their country. May they have eternal rest in Thy arms amongst angels and all the company of heaven. Amen."

"Amen," Russ softly replied, thinking of Davis once again.

After praying together, Russ watched as the chaplain prepared the eucharistic meal on his makeshift communion table. He then bowed his head again in honor of the sacrament which he was about to receive.

"The Body of Christ," the chaplain stated.

"Amen," Russ replied, allowing the chaplain to place the host in his mouth and feeling it become pasty as it melted into his tongue.

"The Blood of Christ."

"Amen," Russ replied, feeling a sense of peace wash over him as the chaplain brought the chalice to his lips.

Russ sipped the sacramental wine from the offered cup and, having accepted the gift of grace and the chance to preserve himself from future mortal sins, succumbed to sleep, allowing his body a much-needed respite.

7

Nora wrapped her old scarf loosely around her neck, fluffed her hair and pulled the leather strap of her pocketbook over her shoulder. She then hurried out the front door into the brisk winter air before Viviane had time to ask any more questions.

Raising her hand to shield her eyes from the blinding headlights, she made her way down the driveway to the idling car, unable to see anything but its gleaming chrome bumper and knowing that Josie was somewhere inside.

"Hey, Nor. Come in on this side. I'm so glad you could come out with us," Josie said, after stepping out of the car's passenger side door and waving her over.

"Hi! Thanks for inviting me out. Viviane is driving me crazy," Nora replied.

"This is Dennis who I've told you about. Dennis, this is my best friend, Nora Thompson," Josie said, placing her hand on the upper arm of the curly haired young man standing beside the car.

"Hi," Nora said.

"Que pasa?" Dennis replied, giving her a nod and holding the door open to allow the girls to climb in.

Nora slid into the backseat and maneuvered her way directly behind the driver's seat. Josie let out a flirtatious laugh while climbing in next to her after Dennis pinched her butt. He then folded the seat back into an upright position and took a seat up front next to the driver.

"Here in the driver's seat tonight is your bowling partner. Nora, meet Brant Judge," Josie announced as Dennis slammed the passenger side door shut.

The young man behind the wheel turned around and Nora's eyes grew wide, unable to believe what she was hearing and seeing. She sat, momentarily frozen, as she realized she was sitting inside the black muscle car that belonged to the handsome stranger who had changed her flat tire just a few days prior.

"So, we meet again. How's that tire of yours?" Brant asked with a smile.

Nora smiled back as a rush of heat filled her cheeks.

"Wait. You two know each other?" Josie blurted out.

As he backed out of the driveway, Brant gave a quick synopsis of his and Nora's first encounter. Nora glanced to the side and noticed Josie raising her eyebrows.

"Why didn't you tell me about that?" Josie whispered through gritted teeth, nudging Nora with her elbow as Brant continued his story.

"Because there was nothing to tell," Nora whispered back, knowing that she had purposely withheld her attraction to Brant Judge from her friend.

"Are you blind, Nor? I mean seriously, look at him," Josie whispered, confirming that she was not the only one who found him to be easy on the eyes.

"Isn't that right, Nora?" Brant asked, seemingly oblivious to the conversation going on in the back seat.

"That's exactly what happened," Nora replied, perking up and impressed with his recollection of their initial meeting.

Josie and Dennis soon became caught up in an exchange of silly banter while Brant drove through town. Nora found herself nervously chewing the inside of her lower lip and, as the car came to a stop at a red light, her eyes locked with Brant's in the rearview mirror. She caught herself shyly smiling, guiltily having thought of him more than once since the day her tire went flat.

Once at the bowling alley, the group laced up their shoes and made their way to their designated lane. The sound of rolling bowling bowls, crashing pins and the aroma of fried food filled the air. Nora watched as Josie, Dennis and Brant took turns rolling their bowling balls down the lane, offering helpful tips along the way.

"Okay, Nor, you're up," Josie called out.

"Don't laugh at me. Remember this is my first time playing," Nora nervously told the group, afraid to embarrass herself.

"Remember not to step over the line," Dennis instructed.

"I won't."

"Just aim for the middle pin, Nor," Josie suggested.

Stepping forward, Nora slid her fingers into the large holes of a polished green bowling ball, feeling herself tense up and surprised by its heavy weight.

Don't make yourself look stupid, she told herself as she raised the ball up, took a step forward, brought her arm back and released the ball out of her hand.

Nora and her friends watched as the ball went airborne and came crashing down onto the hardwood lane before veering off down the gutter. Nora heard Josie giggling and Dennis erupting into a loud fit of laughter behind her. She felt her cheeks become hot as embarrassment coursed through her veins and she reluctantly turned around. There she saw Brant, looking down at his bowling shoes, with his hand over his mouth and his shoulder slightly jerking, as if trying to fight back laughter.

"That. . . wasn't good," Nora said.

"No, it wasn't, unless you were playing fast pitch softball. Since you're on my team, I think I should give you a few more tips before we go on," Brant said, seemingly not wanting her to feel discouraged.

"Okay," Nora meekly replied, appreciating his offer to help her once again.

"Come stand beside me," Brant instructed.

Nora stood stoic. *Did I hear him right? He wants me to stand next to him.*

"Come on over here. I promise I won't bite," Brant said.

Feeling intimidated by his athletic physique and the thought of being close to him, Nora walked over to where he was standing as Josie gave her a wink.

"Give me your hand," Brant ordered.

"What?" Nora asked, feeling butterflies in her stomach.

"I said give me your hand. Don't worry, I don't have grease on my hands this time," he said as he held up his hand and pressed his open palm against hers, as if comparing them.

"So, it looks like the bowling ball you chose was too big for you."

Nora felt the smoothness of his skin touching hers and the warm feeling that she had the day she met him washed over her again.

"See? You have small hands. Let's find you a different ball. You need to choose a ball with smaller holes so you can get a better grip."

"Oh," Nora replied.

"Here, try this one," Brant instructed, handing her a smaller ball with purple marbling.

"That feels better," Nora said, after sliding her fingers into the holes and feeling its lighter weight in her hands.

"Great! Now, it's also important to keep your swing relaxed and not put too much muscle into it. Like this," Brant said, picking up a ball with his biceps engaged, carefully rolling it to demonstrate and knocking down all the pins in one fell swoop.

"That was what you call a strike, right?" Nora asked.

"Yup. You catch on quick. Now come over here again for a minute."

Nora returned to where he was standing, still holding onto the purple marbled ball.

"It's also important to line up your shot. So, you need to focus and picture it in your mind. Close your eyes."

"Why?" Nora asked.

"Just trust me. Now close your eyes for a minute. Picture the pins in front of you and the ball being released from your hand. Can you picture it?" Brant asked, cupping his hands over hers as she held the ball.

Nora stood with her eyes closed, visualizing all the pins lined up and waiting to be knocked down. "Yes. I think so," Nora replied.

Her heart rate suddenly sped up as the heat from his hands warmed hers. She began picturing the sun dancing off the back of his dusky hair the day they met. As he spoke, his breath brushed the side of her face and she tried to remain focused on what he was saying. Having forgotten how nice it felt to be so close to someone, she allowed the back of her head to rest up against his muscular chest.

"Now open your eyes."

"Okay," Nora softly replied, finding herself not wanting him to let go.

"Remember, bring the ball to your chest, keep your swing relaxed and take your time lining up the shot. Then release the ball on a downward swing. Try not to overthink it. Ready?"

"Ready," Nora replied, still unsure of herself.

"Let's see what you got, Nora Thompson," Brant said, smiling and stepping back.

"Okay, here I go."

Nora took a deep breath in and then exhaled. *Focus*, she told herself as she stood with the ball held up near her chest. After a moment she did just as Brant had instructed, lining up her shot and releasing the ball on a downward swing. She watched as the ball rolled down the middle of the lane, picking up momentum as it went, and headed for the ten pins arranged in a triangular formation. Nora clasped her hands as the ball continued along its trajectory and headed straight for the pin at the top of the triangle. She stood in disbelief as the ball made contact, knocking down all the pins in a sweeping crescendo. Nora jumped up and down and ran over to Brant. Excited to have succeeded, she found herself instinctively wrapping her arms around him.

"Oh my gosh. I did it!" Nora exclaimed.

"Now that's how you roll a strike," Brant said, his smile wide.

Nora basked in the exchange of positive energy between them but quickly found herself releasing her embrace and stepping back. As if guilty of something, Nora looked away and pushed her hair behind her ears.

"Great job!" Josie yelled.

"She's got potential," Dennis admitted.

"Beginners luck maybe," Brant said.

"Maybe it's because I had a great teacher," Nora replied, her eyes meeting his once again.

The group finished off their night of bowling with orders of hotdogs, French fries and fountain beverages in the bowling alley's concession area and shared a few last laughs before heading out to the parking lot.

"Hey, I have to work in the morning. Nora, do you mind if Brant drops Josie and me off at my house first so I can get my car and take her home myself?" Dennis asked.

"Not at all," Nora replied, the feeling of butterflies in her stomach returning.

Josie nudged her with her elbow and looked at her with a sly smile.

"You kids be good now, you hear? Nora, why don't you come up front?" Dennis asked as the car stopped in front of his house and he opened the passenger's side door to let himself and Josie out.

"Goodnight, Nor. I'm glad you came out with us. Thanks for driving, Brant," Josie said, giving Nora a hug.

"Thanks, Jo. I had fun tonight," Nora replied before settling into the front seat and closing the door.

Silence filled the air and Nora once again felt her heart beating faster. She found herself not knowing where to look, afraid to glance in Brant's direction, and at a loss for words.

"Looks like it's just you and me," Brant said, looking over at Nora.

"Do you remember how to get to my house?"

"I do. Do you want to go home now or hang out for a little while?"

Nora shrugged her shoulders and looked down at her lap. *What would Russ think if he knew I was alone with him? Stop it, Nora! You're not doing anything wrong,* she told herself.

"It's up to you. I mean its early still, but I'll take you home now if you want," Brant said, not taking his eyes off her but seemingly able to read her body language and sensing her uneasiness.

"No!" Nora heard herself blurt out.

"No what?" Brant asked, looking puzzled.

"No, I don't want to go home yet. My mother is driving me crazy," Nora found herself saying.

"Okay, well that's a good reason. Do you want to just drive around for a while then?"

"Sure. Sorry, my mother is just always so hard on me."

"Why?" Brant asked, as he pulled the car away from Dennis' house and turned the corner onto Main Street.

"She's old fashioned. Ever since my sister took off to California, all my parents' attention has been turned onto me. They're worried I'll turn out like Emily," Nora said.

"Why did she split?"

"Because my mother is too rigid and she wasn't free to be herself."

"Well, how about you?"

"What about me?" Nora asked.

"Can you be your true self? I mean, do you know how to just let loose and be free spirited?" Brant asked as he stopped at a redlight.

"I don't know. I do wish I could be more like Josie and my sister though," Nora replied, aware that her mother's strictness had stifled her.

"You don't know? When was the last time you allowed yourself to do something spontaneous or out of the ordinary?"

"I'm not sure. I'm always trying so hard not to let my parents down, and worrying about my boyfriend in Vietnam, that I can't remember."

"From what I can see, you have a good head on your shoulders, but you need to live a little."

Nora smiled and watched as he turned the steering wheel and proceeded down Riverside Drive. As Swanset Bay came into sight, she knew that he was right. With all the tension at home, the bad news everywhere she turned, and the war protesters on campus, she hadn't been able to recall the last time she had fun. Tonight was different though, both fun and exciting, and it wasn't over yet.

"Do you mind if I pull over for a few minutes?"

"Okay," Nora replied, biting her lip and unsure of what he had in mind.

After pulling into the empty parking lot of Swanset's now frozen town beach, Brant turned off the engine, leaned his arms over the steering wheel and gazed out the windshield.

"What are we doing here? And what are you looking at?" Nora meekly asked, leaning over the dashboard and looking up toward the sky just as he was.

"Once the clouds move out of the way you'll see it. Just wait," he said, not taking his eyes off the sky.

"What are we looking for, a spaceship or something?" Nora joked.

"Keep watching," Brant instructed.

Nora continued to keep her gaze focused on the sky and soon saw the clouds shift, giving way to a bright winter full moon. She felt her body become energized and her eyes widen as the moon emerged and sat low in the sky, its light illuminating the bay and dancing in the water at the beach's shoreline.

"There you have it. Look at that Nora Thompson. Isn't that something?" Brant asked, admiring the glowing orb.

"It sure is," Nora replied, transfixed by the celestial beauty in front of her.

"It's like a giant, glowing bowling ball, isn't it?" Brant asked.

"It's just beautiful," she said, catching herself smiling and overcome with renewed energy.

"I like coming here when the moon is full no matter what time of year it is. Did you notice the clouds were blocking the moon at first, but as soon as they moved out of the way it was able to shine bright?" Brant asked.

"Yes, I noticed that," Nora replied, feeling warm and loosening her scarf.

"The clouds can dim your brightness if you let them. It's up to you to push them out of the way so that your true self can shine through, just like the moon."

"I never thought of it like that before," Nora softly replied.

"So, if you were given a chance to do something spontaneous, anything at all, what would it be?"

"Well. . . I guess I'd. . .," Nora hesitated, trying to push aside the clouds inside her mind.

"You'd what?" Brant asked, his gaze appearing to study her.

Nora thought hard momentarily and, unable to resist his charms, found herself leaning in toward him and spontaneously pressing her lips against his. She then felt his hands cup the back of her head, pulling her closer, the warmth of his breath and the passion of his kiss setting her aglow.

8

1971

With his eyes closed, Russ retraced the events that transpired since his arrival in Vietnam. His thoughts led him back to the day of his release from the Twelfth Evac Hospital when he was sent back into combat, pumped up on pep pills dispensed by the military, just like the foot soldiers who had come before him. In the weeks that followed, his platoon was subject to more ambushes and more lives were lost. Back inside the tunnels, he began going on solo missions, using his hand-to-hand combat skills to mercilessly kill more Viet Cong as a means of avenging his point man's death. He now found himself inside the Twelfth Evac Hospital again, as ordered by his officer, for further evaluation and treatment.

"Ayers, did I just hear you say that your little sister was here with you?" the officer had asked with a sideways glance after overhearing a conversation Russ was having back in the hootch.

"Yes, Sir. I see her when I'm in the tunnels," Russ had adamantly replied.

"Is that so?"

"Yes, Sir."

"And do you care to elaborate as to how it is exactly that she came to arrive here in 'Nam and why no one else has seen her, Private Ayers?"

"I don't know, Sir," Russ replied, scratching his head.

"Either you've been smoking too much or you are cracking up. Which do you think it is?" the officer had asked.

Ann Marie had been killed in an automobile accident the snowy winter of 1961 at the tender age of eight. His parents had never been able to fully recover from the tragedy, but Russ knew she was his angel now as she appeared to him when he was underground, guiding him in the right direction as he traversed the complex in search of Viet Cong.

As he opened his eyes and sat up in his hospital bed, Russ outstretched his arms. He found himself free of restraints yet trapped once again by the images that continued to cycle through his mind. *It wasn't supposed to be this way. Davis and I were supposed to go to the USO show. We talked about flying home on the Freedom Bird, but the Viet Cong squashed those dreams,* Russ thought. Images flashed in his mind of his fellow soldiers' maimed and bloody bodies, some already dead and others hanging on to what little life remained in them after walking into a trip wire or being ambushed by enemy fire. Russ rubbed his eyes as images of his own hands, sticky with the semi-coagulated blood of Charlie and of his friend and fallen soldier, Johnny Davis, consumed his thoughts. Images of body bags, filled with the remains of those killed in action lined up to be taken home to grief-stricken families, followed. A constant barrage of gruesome flashes of the horrors of the seemingly unwinnable war rotated in and out of his head. He needed to shut his mind off and craved something that would do just that.

Since his arrival in the Cu Chi district, his battalion officer had consistently increased pressure on him to perform his tasks, wanting daily body counts from the jungle floor, but even more so from the underground. He was expected to take out as many Viet Cong and destroy as many tunnels as he could and, like other soldiers, was routinely supplied by the military with speed to help him get the job done. Before long, Russ began popping speed like candy to help increase his alertness and aggression. Much to the battalion officer's approval, he managed to get quite a few kills since he arrived there last summer, two or three dozen, maybe more, he had lost count.

His first kill was the hardest to process, having had to wrestle and slice the throat of a VC he found lurking in the darkness during one of his early expeditions into the underground complex. He recalled the feeling of the knife in his hand as the blade penetrated Charlie's flesh and cartilage, severing both carotid arteries. His battalion officer praised him for the kill, but Russ did not feel worthy of praise for taking another's life. He was restless with guilt and, with hands tightly clasped, begged for God's forgiveness as he knelt beside his crisply made military bed once back in the hootch. That night Russ took his first hit of heroin, as suggested by his officer, to prevent him from cracking up. His heart rate slowed and his mind became drowsy after the heroin's initial euphoric rush took hold of him. Soon each kill began to feel like a release from the intense pressure of war. Nothing mattered in that environment except the kill and getting out alive. *It's them or me*, Russ would remind himself each time, as if to justify his actions.

"Hello, Private Ayers. I'm Dr. Connors. How are you feeling today?" a tall man asked as he approached Russ' bedside with a medical chart in his hands.

"Like hell warmed over, Doc," Russ replied.

"I'm sure you are. You've been through a lot out there."

"What kind of doctor are you anyway?"

"I'm a psychiatrist."

"A psychiatrist? There are a lot of things I need, Doc, but a shrink isn't one of them."

"Sometimes talking to someone can help. Would you like to talk?"

"Why? That's not going to do any good. I've been going over things in my head. Over and over and over. It's like I'm itching out of my skin and my brain won't shut off."

"That's called ruminative thinking. It's your mind's way of trying to cope with the stress of war. It can be unhealthy if it's dominating your thoughts."

"Can you give me something to make it stop?"

"It would be better for you to learn how to process your emotions and gain a better understanding of how to deal with your feelings, instead of just medicating yourself."

"With all due respect, Sir, I've been self-medicating since high school. It's easier than dealing with reality, especially here. This place they call Vietnam. . . it's a miracle anyone makes it out alive. Hell, look at you in that nice clean shirt. I bet you never had to kill anyone."

"You're right. I haven't."

"Then please, Sir, quit your babbling and give me some pills. That's how I've survived for as long as I have in those living hell holes. In a few days, I'll be back down there again."

"What have you been using since you've been here?"

"Gee, Doc, really? Drugs are everywhere. I've been using whatever I can get my hands on. Weed mostly. I pop speed whenever I go into the tunnels to help me stay alert. Back in the hootch I've smoked skag a few times, but I've never shot up with it. I don't want to become addicted like some GI junky."

"You should try to stop using heroin and self-medicating before you head home. That's the best advice I can offer you. You're experiencing combat fatigue and I'm going to give you something that's been helpful to other GIs. It's called chlorpromazine. It's powerful and will help get you through. I should warn you that within the next few months Operation Golden Flow will go into effect."

"What the hell is that?"

"Golden Flow? It's Nixon's campaign against drugs. Starting June twenty-second, we'll be required to take urine samples on all GIs before they return home to check for narcotics. GIs who test positive will be detained for detoxification," Dr. Connors informed him.

"Detained? That's exactly what I don't need. I'll lay off the narcs for thirty days when I become a short-timer so my piss will be clean. Just give me that medication so I can get through this living hell," Russ replied, craving a pill or a hit of anything that would give him immediate relief from his symptoms.

"Coming right up," Dr. Connors replied before turning and heading toward the hospital's dispensary window.

Russ closed his eyes for a few moments to try to still his mind. *I just need to survive for a few more months and then I'll be home free,* he thought, dreaming of the day when he could leave this godforsaken land and return to life as he knew it back home in Swanset.

9

Nora adjusted herself in the sturdy oak chair as she sat in a quiet corner of Bridgegate's library, with her nose in a book, preparing for her midterm exams. She stretched out her arms to loosen her stiff shoulders, let out an audible yawn, and checked the time on her wristwatch. Two hours had passed and, needing a break from studying, Nora turned and looked out the window. Off in the distance she caught sight of coeds outside protesting the war, marching through campus with handmade signs with catchy slogans such as, "Shaft the Draft," "Peace & Love," and "End the War in Vietnam." Her concentration had been disrupted by the muffled sounds of the protesters' loud, repetitious chants seeping through the library's closed, mullioned, second story windows, making her long for life as she knew it before things became complicated.

Nora thought back to her days at Swanset High when she first met Russ during their junior year. Russ had a reputation of being a bit of a hellion and was responsible for starting a food fight in the cafeteria their freshman year. It was also rumored that, in celebration of homecoming, he and his friends- Bob Cleary and Jeff Turner- were responsible for an over-the-top prank in which they stole sanitary pads from the nurses' office, colored them with red magic markers and stuck them on the locker doors of all the stuck-up cheerleaders around Swanset High.

When their Chemistry teacher Mr. Thayer paired them up as lab partners, Nora didn't have much to say to him initially. Russ was always clowning around and soon began to fall behind in Mr. Thayer's class. Nora saw he was struggling and offered to tutor him every Wednesday afternoon in the school library, helping him pass his midterm exam. She found herself attracted to his good looks and sense of humor and knew there was something more hiding beneath his class clown façade. Naturally, her curiosity got the best of her, and she told him she was determined to find out exactly what made him tick. The chemistry between the two of them only grew stronger from that point on.

Lightly brushing her fingertips over her slow healing scar, Nora took her eyes off the war protest happening outside, closed her books and stuffed them into her knapsack. After sliding her arms into her parka, she slung the heavy sack over her shoulder, headed down to the library's first floor and exited the building. She was greeted outside by a small group of silent, student protesters with strings around their wrists and signs reading "Saigon Puppets" draped around their necks. Behind them stood students dressed like Uncle Sam in red, white and blue top hats and fake white beards, controlling the strings. Nora pulled her hood over her head as if to protect herself and avoided making eye contact with the protesters. She then hurried down the brick walkway with her fists clenched inside her coat pockets as the brisk March winds helped push her along. Given that Russ was actively serving the country, Nora tried her best to avoid the on-campus protests, even when her friends encouraged her to get involved.

As she navigated her way back to her dormitory, Nora thought back to Russ' deployment and began to ruminate about his safety. She had not heard from him since early December and, being concerned, had called the Ayers' residence to ask if there had been any news of his whereabouts. The telephone conversation with Russ' mother, Martha, only made her feel worse as they had not heard from him either and were concerned that he may be missing in action. Nora became uneasy, stopping momentarily to catch her breath, as she made her way up the four flights of stairs to her dorm room, feeling like a heel for having been leaning on Brant Judge for comfort behind everyone's back.

Brant had been filling a void in her heart by spending time with her, easing the feelings of emptiness and depression that she had been harboring since Russ' deployment. He had secretly visited her on campus earlier in the month when Becky went home to observe Purim with her family. She was also filling a void in his heart as his former girlfriend, Libby, had told him she wanted to take a break the previous November. Nora was cautious not to give her heart away, as it was already spoken for, and continued to anxiously wait for another letter from overseas.

When she arrived at her dorm room, Nora opened the door only to find Becky Lieberman curled up in bed, crying.

"Becky, what's wrong?" Nora asked, dropping her bag, its contents spilling out onto the floor.

"Everything," Becky sobbed into her pillow.

"What is it, Beck?"

"How could I have been so stupid?" Becky asked, lifting her head and wiping her eyes.

"Becky, what's going on?"

"I'm pregnant, Nor," Becky confessed.

"Oh boy. Does Carl know?"

"I didn't tell him. I don't want him to know."

"Why wouldn't you want him to know?" Nora asked.

"Because I'm going to get rid of it."

"You can't mean that, Beck."

"Yes, I can, Nor. Carl is in no position to take care of me, or a baby, and I want to go to law school."

A sudden knock on the door disrupted their conversation. Nora opened the door to see Josie, wearing a braided headband around her forehead, holding the strap of her overnight bag in her hands.

"Hi, Jo," Nora said, a wan smile appearing on her face.

"Hi, Nor. I know I'm a bit early, but I wanted to beat the rush hour traffic on Route twenty-four," Josie stated.

"That's okay. I just got back from studying at the library," Nora replied.

"There are so many dreamy guys around here. Oh, hi, Becky," Josie called out.

"She's really upset about something so she may not be up for socializing much tonight," Nora informed her.

"Hi, Josie. I don't mind if you tell her, Nor," Becky said between sniffles.

"Tell me what?" Josie asked, removing her coat and hanging it on a hook on the back of the door.

"Becky just found out she's pregnant," Nora stated, biting her bottom lip.

"From the look on your face, I take it you're not too happy about it. Didn't you use birth control?" Josie asked, taking a seat on the floor beside her bed.

"We usually do but I ran out. The clinic on campus is so overbooked that I couldn't get another appointment. I don't want anyone else knowing. Promise me that this does not go beyond this room. Carl doesn't need to know."

"Promise," Nora and Josie said in unison.

"My parents would kill me if they found out. I need to get rid of it," Becky said, sniffling.

"How far along are you?" Josie asked.

"About six weeks."

"You have lots of options," Josie, who was well versed on women's issues and deeply involved in the Pro-Choice movement sweeping the country, replied.

"Becky, you could always place the baby up for adoption. There are plenty of couples who are unable to have children and could provide your baby with a good home," Nora suggested.

"But then everyone would know that I'm pregnant, Nora, and I'd have to go through the birthing process," Becky replied.

"You're from Long Island, right?" Josie asked.

"Yes."

"Well, Governor Rockefeller signed legislation last year legalizing abortion in New York," Josie told her.

"I know, but how do I find a place to perform the procedure? And how long do I have to get it taken care of? I want to be sure it's safe," Becky said, her eyes focused on Josie.

"If you wait too long you would have to have the procedure by saline," Josie said.

"What does that mean?" Becky asked, squinting her eyes.

Nora sat listening intently to what Josie was saying.

"It's salt poisoning and means that you would have to deliver a dead fetus," Josie said.

"Oh gosh!" Nora blurted out, feeling as though that would be her worst nightmare.

"That sounds terrible. I don't think I could put myself through that," Becky said.

"You're very early in your pregnancy so you still have time to schedule your appointment and figure things out. There's a hospital I know of in New York City where you can have the procedure done. I'll get you the information," Josie replied.

"That would be great. How much does it cost anyway?"

"It varies but I've read that its around one hundred fifty dollars."

"One hundred fifty dollars!" Becky exclaimed.

"Don't worry, we'll figure out a way to help you pay for it. I can pitch in some of the money I saved from my work-study job," Josie said.

"And I can give you the money that my Aunt Gert sent me for Christmas," Nora offered.

"Thank you. I don't know what I'd do without you both to confide in," Becky said.

"That's what friends are for, Beck. There are no secrets in this room," Josie replied.

Nora bit her lip, keeping her own secret suppressed, grateful that she wasn't in trouble like her friend.

"Becky, why don't you get yourself dressed? Dennis is coming to pick us up at seven o'clock to see that band you like play at the brewhouse off campus," Josie stated.

"I don't feel like going. I'm just going to hang in tonight," Becky said, rolling over onto her back.

"I understand. We'll catch you later. Nor, are you coming or are you going to bail on me too?"

"I'll go, unless Becky wants me to stay here with her," Nora said.

"I just need some time alone. Go ahead without me," Becky replied.

"Is anyone else going?" Nora asked, turning to Josie.

"I think Brant Judge is coming along too. You remember him, right?"

"Yes. I. . . remember him," Nora sheepishly replied, feeling herself blush and quickly bending down to pick up her spilled books from the floor, all the while hoping she hadn't given her secret away.

10

Russ flicked the ash off the end of his cigarette before crushing it in the ashtray in front of him at the Rest and Recreation center's smoke-filled bar. He ran his hand over the unpolished wood bar top, finding it sticky with the residue of spilled drinks. Wiping the palm of his hand on the leg of his pants, he thought of what a far cry this bar was from Lance's Pub back in Weaver Falls. The pub's owner, Lance, was cool to work for and had hired him to work as a bar back while he was still in high school, long before he was ever concerned about being drafted.

"You're a good worker kid. Just don't let me catch you sneaking any of the hard stuff," Lance would often tell him.

"Don't worry. I won't," Russ would reply while enjoying a cold draft beer that Lance allowed him at the end of each shift.

Russ thought about how much he had enjoyed mingling with patrons and listening to the local musicians who performed there on Friday and Saturday nights. He also enjoyed the work rituals of wiping down the varnished oak bar top and neatly arranging the clean highball, rocks and shot glasses on their appropriate shelves after closing time. Inspired by the musicians at Lance's, Russ recalled walking into the Weaver Falls Music Shoppe just a few doors down from the pub. It was there that he picked up a second-hand acoustic guitar and, before his deployment, managed to teach himself a few chords. Back in the hootch he felt lucky to find an old six string lying around. It belonged to another GI who was killed in action before Russ' arrival and now provided a welcome distraction from the violence and bloodshed that had become a way of life.

Picking up a cold can of beer, he took a swig and devoured the eye candy that surrounded him. Russ observed as silky-haired Vietnamese girls, appearing hungry for work in short, slinky dresses, circled the bar soliciting their services. They had descended on him and Harry like flies on shit as they entered the bar. Harry had wasted no time, diving right in and running off with the first prostitute with good teeth and a tight ass who offered herself to him. Russ was tired and his enthusiasm had dwindled as the war went on. All he wanted for the moment were a few beers to quench his thirst and calm his nerves.

He had been eagerly awaiting his monthly R&R time, having earned a few days off after weeks of grinding away hunting Viet Cong in the dark, vast network of underground tunnels, armed with only a flashlight, a knife and a pistol. *Non Gratum Anus Rodentum*, or *Not Worth a Rat's Ass*, was their slogan and Russ thought it was an appropriate phrase for a war that sucked the life out of him and the other tunnel rats sent to fight in it. The sultry voice of an Asian woman, wearing a sequined dress and standing on a small stage in the corner of the bar, filled the air as she sang a song in her native tongue. She sounded nice enough Russ supposed, as she attempted to get GIs in the mood, seductively swaying her hips and luring them toward the stage. Russ brought the beer can to his lips, unable to understand a word she was saying, longing for some good rock music like he would hear at Lance's. He took a few more swigs of the ice-cold beer, allowing each one to saturate the inside of his mouth before swallowing them down.

Russ knew he was a good guy, but not that good, as he opened his bi-fold wallet and counted the bills inside. He had managed to survive so far and, although he had some close calls with Charlie, as far as he could tell, he wasn't dead yet.

"GI want love?" a petite girl, sporting a crusted-over cold sore on her upper lip, asked in broken English as she caressed his thigh.

"Not now, Sweetheart," Russ said, brushing her scrawny hand away, knowing that he would most likely catch a sexually transmitted disease from any of the prostitutes on the premises.

"I treat GI nice. Later I come back?" she asked.

"I don't think so," Russ replied.

"I do what GI want. I love GI," the girl persisted.

"No! Understand? Now go away," Russ ordered, annoyed and waving her off.

As he tried to relax, he observed the sights and sounds around him, still finding himself on high alert as his eyes scanned the bar, never knowing when Charlie would appear. He knew the stress of his job was getting to him, and he often reminded himself to stay focused and not get sloppy down in the tunnels. His confidence was waning too as the continuity of leadership had been lost, with battalion officers who seemed unskilled to effectively do their job and with the constant rotation of GIs in and out of his company. There were daily replacements sent for those who were lucky enough to finish their tour and for those killed in action, and Russ knew that many were arriving unprepared to work as a team.

Russ reached into his pocket and pulled out Nora's picture. He traced her loose flowing hair with his fingertip, recalling its silkiness. As he studied her face, he felt a fleeting sense of joy. She was a head-turner, with golden hair and bright green eyes, unlike the working girls all around him. He knew he should probably write to her but had been so wrapped up in simply trying to survive and keeping his head straight, that he hadn't gotten around to it. He could feel the hold that his vicious cycle of pep pills, antipsychotics and numbing agents he had been swallowing had on him. Things that he used to prioritize, such as writing to Nora and his parents, had become the least of his concerns in recent months. As he downed another cold beer, he wondered whether Nora would wait for him as promised with all those draft dodging college boys and protesting hippies around campus. He had reluctantly respected her wishes to wait until they got married before having relations, a decision he now regretted.

He had less than ninety days left of cutting his way through the jungle and navigating the tunnels of Cu Chi. The intense mental pressure had been making him feel like he was going to break again, just as he did the day Davis was killed and, though he wasn't sure, he thought that maybe he already had. He took another swig, savoring the cold amber brew, knowing he would have to be ready to persevere after his R&R weekend was over. He had seen too many short-timers, some with only days left in their tour, killed in action because they failed to stay alert. Russ finished his beer, crushed the empty can in his hand and placed it down on the sticky bar top before thumbing through the bills in his wallet one last time. Ninety days still felt like a lifetime away and, for two dollars and fifty cents, he could buy three hours with a spot-checked prostitute of his choice in the brothel next door, which catered to horny GIs just like him, without the high risk of catching a venereal disease. It was well known the girls in the brothel were also vetted, so he could be sure he wasn't spending his time with undercover Viet Cong informants who would try to gather information from him. While in the thick of war, women, dope, booze and cigarettes were the only pleasures he had to look forward to. As he got up from the barstool, Russ knew it would be money well spent and what Nora didn't know wouldn't hurt her, especially since his return home was not guaranteed.

11

Nora stared blankly ahead, feeling melancholy, as jovial party guests around her feasted on a New England clam boil in celebration of Josie's twentieth birthday. More than a year had passed since she last saw Russ. She recalled that just as the crocuses were starting to peek through what remained of the winter snow, she had been forced to say her painful goodbyes to him after he was inducted into the U.S. Army. Neither of them had known exactly what lay ahead and they were left with just memories of times shared together and hopes of the future to grasp onto. As winter gave way to spring, Nora had lost hope, having sent out four letters to Russ since the previous December, all of which had gone unanswered.

"Hey, Nor, can you pass me a few napkins?" Josie asked, her fingertips saturated with the broth and melted butter she had been dipping her steamers into.

"Here you go," Nora said, her thoughts returning to the present and placing a small stack of paper napkins next to Josie's plate.

"I still can't believe I didn't catch on to this surprise party. This beer is so good, isn't it?" Josie asked with a smile after taking a sip out of the open, aluminum can on the table in front of her.

"It is," Nora replied without emotion.

"You've hardly touched yours. Nor, are you okay?"

"I don't know, Jo," Nora somberly replied.

"I know things have been hard for you, Nor, but you need to move on with your life. Look at everyone having fun all around you."

"I know, Jo. I don't mean to be a drag."

"Why don't you go over there by the horseshoe pit and talk to Brant?" Josie said as her older brother, Ted, who had just returned home from New

Hampshire after graduating with a degree in Forestry, took a seat at the picnic table beside them.

"Are you girls talking about that tall guy over there? Because I think he's diggin' you, Nora," Ted said, nodding his head in Brant Judge's direction.

"Very funny, Ted. We're just friends for your information," Nora replied.

"Just friends? Don't you see how he keeps looking over here at you?" Ted teased.

"I've noticed too," Josie chimed in, nudging Nora with her elbow.

"Don't be silly," she replied, shrugging off their observations, yet knowing they were right, as she glanced over to the horseshoe pit where Brant was immersed in a game with Mr. Henson.

Nora's thoughts were interrupted as Josie's mom approached the table with a huge, chocolate frosted cake, adorned with twenty flaming candles for Josie to blow out. The partygoers stopped what they were doing and gathered around the table. Nora saw Brant make his way over and position himself in her direct line of sight. As everyone sang "Happy Birthday", Nora tried her best to block out what Josie and Ted said, keeping her feelings in check and avoiding eye contact with Brant Judge. She hadn't seen Brant since the night he and Dennis picked up the girls to see the band play at the off-campus pub and he told her he wanted a steady relationship with her. Nora was confused by her own feelings, afraid to act on them as she had the night she went bowling and found herself alone with Brant at Swanset Beach. She had decided that avoiding him would be the best thing to do until Russ returned home, as she still hoped he would.

After the cake was served, Nora mingled for a while longer before saying her goodbyes and discretely exiting out the side gate of the stockade fence. She took a seat behind the wheel of her old clunker, closed the door and let out a sigh of relief, having managed to slip away from the party without Brant noticing. She then turned the key in the ignition, only to be greeted with silence.

"Come on girl," she said, turning the key a few more times, hoping the engine would start up but getting the same result.

"This is just great. Your timing couldn't be worse," she said aloud, slapping her hand on the steering wheel and hearing a sudden tap on the driver's side window.

She turned to see Brant standing there, gesturing for her to roll the window down.

"Hi," Nora said, after cracking the window open.

"I've been wondering when you were planning to say hello."

"Sorry, I was busy helping Josie's mom out and I have to get going. My mom is expecting me home by nine o'clock," Nora said, hoping her excuse sounded credible and glad to have the glass barrier between them.

"Nine o'clock? But its only seven thirty," Brant replied, checking the time on his wristwatch.

Nora, caught in a fib, shrugged her shoulders.

"So, it looks like the old girl is acting up again. Pop the hood and I'll check it out for you," Brant said.

"That's not necessary."

"It is if you want your car to start. Let me see what's going on," Brant said, walking around to the front of the car.

"Okay," Nora replied, popping the hood open as he had asked.

"Try to start her up again," Brant called out.

Nora did as he ordered and turned the key in the ignition one last time. With the engine still failing to turn over, Nora laughed to herself at the irony of the lucky rabbit's foot dangling from her key chain.

Brant closed the hood, sending a shudder through the vehicle and Nora's entire body. As he walked back around the car, she took notice of the outline of his broad shoulders and firm chest underneath his blue T-shirt. As he approached she reached for the handle and rolled the window the rest of the way down.

"It looks like you're going nowhere fast," Brant replied, crouching down to her eye level.

"Why not? What's wrong?" Nora asked.

"Your battery cables are all corroded."

"What does that mean?"

"It means that the charge can't make it to your starter. That's why whenever you turn the key, your engine won't turn over."

"Great," Nora replied, fed up with the old clunker.

"Come on. I'll give you a lift."

"That's not necessary. I'll call my dad."

"I'm going that way. It's really not a problem. Now come on," Brant replied, waving her out of the car.

"Okay," Nora said, rolling up her window, grabbing her macrame handbag and following him over to his car which was parked nearby.

Once at his vehicle, Brant opened the passenger's side door to let her in. Nora caught the mild scent of his musky cologne as a refreshing breeze filled the early summer air and he closed the door behind her. Dusk had fallen and Brant switched on the headlights and stereo. He adjusted the

FM radio's dial as he drove away from Josie's house, eventually settling on a rock song.

Nora looked out the side window and rolled it down, letting the wind whip through her hair as Brant put the pedal to the metal.

The car slowed as they approached an intersection where they were met with a red light. They waited for the light to change and Nora laughed as Brant played his air guitar.

"The party was fun," Nora said, allowing herself to relax.

"It would have been even more fun if you hadn't been avoiding me."

"Sorry about that."

"No harm done. Hey, did you see the look on Josie's face when we yelled 'Surprise!'?" he asked, turning the volume down and making a bug-eyed face.

"I know! She looked like a scared rabbit," Nora replied, giggling and feeling her mood lift.

"Wow! Look, it's a full moon tonight," Brant said, leaning over the steering wheel and catching a glimpse of the huge glowing orb through the car's windshield.

"Don't you usually go to Swanset Beach to see the full moon?"

"You remembered that?" Brant asked.

"Let's go see it before you take me home," Nora replied, feeling her cheeks getting warmer and glad it was getting dark so he wouldn't notice her blushing.

"Far out! Here we go," Brant said.

As the traffic light changed from red to green, Brant stepped on the gas, turned left onto Riverside Drive, and headed toward Swanset Beach. A cool Atlantic breeze was blowing when they stepped out of the car and Nora, wearing a mini skirt and halter top, caught a chill. She watched as Brant walked around to the back of the car and grabbed a blanket out of the trunk.

"There you go," Brant said, draping the blanket over her shoulders.

"Thanks," Nora said as their eyes locked.

"Anything for you. Now come on," Brant said, taking off running toward the shore.

"Wait for me," Nora called out, sliding off her sandals and running after him with sand squishing between her toes.

Out of breath, Nora stopped when she caught up to Brant and gazed out toward the bay alongside him.

"It's spectacular as always," Brant said, admiring the moon's reflection in the tranquil waters.

"It sure is. Here, let's sit down," Nora said, still trying to catch her breath, removing the blanket from her shoulders and spreading it out on the sand of the dimly illuminated shoreline.

They sat silently, listening to the sound of the waves and observing the lights of a fishing vessel off in the distance. Nora lay on the blanket, allowing the moon's beams to radiate down on her and feeling energized as she took notice of stars overhead. Brant's hand lightly brushed against hers. The spark between them intensified as he tickled her palm with his fingertips. Nora caught herself smiling and intertwining her hand with his. She closed her eyes, welcoming whatever was to be between them to flourish. She sensed Brant's closeness and felt the warmth of his breath on her cheek. The light feeling of his lips brushing against hers enlivened her senses. She noticed Brant pause, his lips lingering momentarily, as if waiting for an invitation. Nora's thoughts wavered as she had grown weary of waiting for word from Russ, her mother's rigid views, her sister's absence, the protesters on campus, the never-ending news of the war, and the anxiety and loneliness that seemed to invade her very being in recent months.

"Brant . . . I . . .,"

"I'll stop if you . . .,"

Nora parted her lips and pulled Brant closer. Enough had been said. As they kissed she helped him remove his T-shirt, exposing his muscular torso. The chill in the air dissipated as Brant kissed the side of her neck and slid his hand under her skirt, exploring her body. She happily accepted all that he had to offer and found herself reciprocating his every move, unzipping Brant's jeans and pushing them off his hips. She could not deny herself this moment with him as she felt his warmth and weight on top of her. Brant then pushed his body into hers, taking her breath away. They moved together rhythmically, wildly, and in unison with the tidal forces on the shore in front of them and Nora knew that she would never be the same.

$$12$$

R uss observed the dog-tired faces of other grunts, just like him, around the congested out-processing area. They were all lucky enough to still be standing as they anxiously awaited their instructions at the U.S. military's final processing point fifteen miles outside of Saigon. His Date of Estimated Return from Overseas had finally arrived and he would soon be going back to the United States and out of the warzone. His trip would take close to twenty hours and, after a brief refueling stop in Guam, his chartered aircraft would land at the Oakland Army Base in the San Francisco Bay area. Once there he would step onto home soil for the first time in a year. The alternative, which he was happy to have managed to avoid, was to fly home from DaNang. Russ understood leaving from DaNang would mean he'd be lying down in an aluminum case, alongside the bodies of other soldiers killed in action, where cargo handlers would load him in with his head pointing toward the front of the aircraft, in accordance with the military's regulations.

Tomorrow another fresh crop of Cherries would arrive in-country and, as their feet hit the tarmac in Cam Ranh Bay, they would stare at his tormented face as he passed by them, just as he himself had done twelve months ago.

"Charlie just loves himself some Cherries," seasoned GIs said as they passed by and prepared to board the plane.

"You better watch out. Charlie will hang you from a tree and cut you open like a farm animal until your intestines spill out," another warned.

It was common for guys returning home to heckle those who had just arrived as they were disembarking from the aircraft. As twisted as it was, Russ now understood that their razzing and sick humor were just part of their excitement to be leaving Vietnam. He knew they weren't kidding though, and heeded their warnings, having heard stories of the torturing of GIs by Viet Cong guerillas.

It was an understatement to say that he was grateful to be among the living who would soon be returning home, as he stood in the slow-moving line and waited impatiently to be issued his Class A uniform. He thought back to February of the previous year when he passed his military physical and was deemed officially able to serve. He shook his head and silently laughed to himself as he recalled how some of the draftees arrived wearing women's underwear, instead of briefs, so that they would be perceived as queer and be deemed exempt from serving. Russ told himself he would rather die in combat than dress up in girl's panties with pink lace and the word "Thursday" embroidered across the front as he had made peace with, and bravely accepted, the fact that his country needed him, no matter the outcome.

Eventually making it to the counter, Russ gathered up his crisp uniform and headed over to the back of the next line to have his haircut checked by yet another intense sergeant.

"Keep your military issued items on your person and keep the line moving along if you want to make it home tomorrow," the sergeant yelled out to the group being out-processed, his face such a bright shade of red that Russ thought his head would explode.

Cool your jets, man, we've all been through enough hell already, Russ thought to himself as the sergeant continued barking orders to move the men along through the out-processing procedure with military precision. As a GI at the head of the line had his haircut inspected, Russ recalled the cold, dreary day when he left Swanset and headed to boot camp in western Louisiana after receiving his draft notice. Stepping off the bus at Fort Polk as a receptee, he was greeted by a large sign, attached to a white painted lattice, which screamed "Welcome Soldier to the United States Army. Stand Proud!" Another grueling eight weeks of Advanced Individual Training had followed his graduation from basic, during which he had been trained in search and destroy tactics, defusing bombs, ambush trails and navigating the tunnel network, an area in which he excelled. The drills and training he received in the simulated swamps in the dark of night at Fort Polk's Tiger Land were pure hell but proved to be crucial for his survival.

He was proud of having excelled in his training and the fact that he had stayed focused and successfully completed his missions during his tour of duty, regardless of how much self-medicating he had done. He thought of the hell he had managed to survive while in Vietnam, including hand-to-hand combat, ambushes and the loss of his friend and point man, Johnny Davis. Russ caught himself grinning at the thought of passing Nixon's Operation Golden Flow's urine screening test, having paid another GI, who was drugfree, ten dollars to piss into a cup for him.

"What are you grinning at, Private?" the sergeant inspecting his military buzz cut asked as he reached the front of the line.

"Nothing. I'm just happy to be heading out of this hell hole, Sergeant," Russ replied, feeling his shoulder involuntarily twitch and knowing his last hit of heroin was wearing off.

The sergeant waved him on, and Russ knew all he had left to do was securely pack up his footlocker. After that, he would be home free and flying high on the wings of the Freedom Bird back to the United States, the land that he loved.

13

Leaning against the railing on the top deck, Nora removed her floppy hat and allowed the wind to sweep through her hair. She watched a small cutter, with its headsails raised, pass by the ferry boat's starboard side. As they departed New London and proceeded on their course across Long Island Sound, Nora could overhear Josie briefing Brant Judge's cousin, Jack, about Becky Lieberman.

"Becky is cute. Isn't she, Brant?" Josie asked, hoping to pique Jack's interest.

"She is," Brant replied.

"Tell me more about her," Jack said, seeming to fall for the bait.

"She's quite smart and is looking into applying to law school," Josie added.

"Law school? Wow! She does sound smart," Jack said.

"Becky is down to earth too," Josie added.

"I can't wait to meet her," Jack replied with a boyish excitement in his voice.

Nora caught the smell of Brant's musky cologne being carried toward her by the sound's winds, a scent she had grown fond of. She soon felt Brant's arms encircle her from behind as he got up from his seat and joined her alongside the bow rail.

"Our secret is out," Brant whispered into her ear, his lips brushing her temple.

"I should have known Josie would catch on to us," Nora replied, having come clean about her relationship with Brant after Josie noticed a small hickey just under her earlobe a few days prior.

"I'm glad she did. Now we can enjoy our weekend without faking it," Brant said, discretely kissing the side of her neck.

Nora felt a rush of energy course through her body as Brant sensually stroked her forearm, basking in his affections as the ferry picked up speed, pushing them onward toward the hamlet of Orient Point.

Becky, who was grateful for Nora and Josie's support in terminating her unplanned pregnancy, had invited them to her parents' opulent home on the North Fork of Long Island for the Independence Day weekend. Guilt-ridden since having had an abortion, Becky had found herself pulling away from her boyfriend, Carl. By the end of March, feeling too much strain in their relationship, she had broken things off with him completely.

"Get a room you two," Josie called out from her seat as she played with the strings of her crocheted top.

"Mind your business and let us be, Josie," Brant replied.

Nora turned her head and gave Josie a smirk.

"Just kidding," Josie said before giving Nora a wink.

"Look, there's the Orient Point Lighthouse. It sure is in rough shape," Brant said, pointing ahead.

"It's kind of sad to look at," Nora replied, studying the dilapidated structure's tower as they passed by and thinking that it reminded her of the sad state of the nation.

"I read that the Coast Guard wants to tear it down, but the locals are fighting to keep it," Brant said.

"I hope they win and can bring it back to its old glory," Nora replied.

As Long Island came into view, Nora thought back to the previous April when Josie had found herself happily free once again. Josie had told her that she does not allow herself to get too attached to anyone and that she shouldn't either.

"Date around a little and have some fun until Russ comes back, Nor. Just make sure you don't give your heart away," Josie had urged.

Josie hadn't missed a beat when Dennis Blake received his volunteer corps assignment and was sent off to Senegal to spend the next two years working on agricultural projects with locals there. The way Josie looked at it, they both got what they wanted out of their time together. In the end, Dennis got the draft deferment he had been waiting for and Josie got her freedom back. It had been Josie's idea to have Becky extend the invitation to her parents' place to Brant Judge, and his cousin, Jack. She had high hopes of setting Becky and Jack up, believing they'd be a good match since they were both baseball fans and had both recently attended New York City's first Earth Day Celebration.

When the ferry docked in Orient Point, the group disembarked along with the other passengers, and found fresh-faced Becky, wearing wide rimmed sunglasses, a bikini top and denim cut off shorts, waiting for them at the end of the dock. It was evident, as introductions were made, that Jack and Becky immediately hit it off, just as Josie had planned.

"Follow me guys. I parked my parents' car over here," Becky said as they weaved through the crowd toward the sun-drenched parking lot.

"Will you be able to fit all of us or should we get a taxi, Beck?" Josie asked.

"Believe me when I say there will be plenty of room. This thing is a beast," Becky replied with a chuckle as they approached a brand-new station wagon, its exterior painted red with wood paneled sides.

"Just toss your things in the back. I figured we could head straight to the beach. It's just a hop, skip and jump from here. I brought a cooler and filled it with ice and beer and also made some sandwiches," Becky said, opening the wagon's rear door.

"Good thinking," Brant replied.

"Cool," Jack added.

"I brought some grass too," Josie said, with a sideways smile.

"Sweet," the guys said simultaneously.

"You always come prepared," Nora added, giving her a nudge.

After loading their bags into the back of the wagon, the group settled into the vehicle. Jack, unable to take his eyes off Becky, volunteered to ride shotgun while Nora, Brant and Josie climbed into the back seat.

Once at Orient Beach State Park, the group spent the day swimming, playing frisbee, sunbathing, eating sandwiches and drinking cold beer from the ice filled cooler. Later on, Josie took out her camera, draped its strap around her neck and began snapping pictures.

"Brant come over here. Let me get a picture of you and Nora," Josie said.

Brant hurried over and Nora let out a giggle as he scooped her up in his arms and they smiled for the camera.

"That was cute. Brant, can you take one of us girls?" Josie asked.

"Sure," Brant replied.

"Beck, come get in the picture with us," Josie ordered, waving Becky over and handing the camera to Brant.

"Let's all lie out on the blanket," Becky suggested.

"Good idea," Nora said.

"Let's all put our sunglasses on too," Josie added.

As the girls donned their sunglasses, fussed with their hair, and posed on the blanket, Nora caught Brant watching her. Easy smiles instantly spread across both of their faces.

"Okay girls. Everyone smile now," Brant said.

"Nora already is," Josie teased before the click of the camera shutter was heard.

Later in the day, as the sun began to set, Brant and Jack lit a fire with scraps of wood they had collected during their afternoon walk along the rugged beach. Tired from a day in the sun, Nora took a seat in a nook of a large driftwood log. With her toes in the coarse grains of the Long Island sand, she watched the fires flames dance and flicker. She glanced around the rocky shoreline, out onto the bay, and then back at her group of friends, old and new, who were enjoying the summer night. The scene playing out before her reminded her of summers in Swanset when Russ would strum his six-string around the bonfires with their Swanset High friends. She thought of Russ and all the other servicemen who were sacrificing their lives this very night so that she and her friends could enjoy their freedom this July fourth weekend.

I hope you're okay, Russ, wherever you are, Nora thought to herself, getting teary eyed and hating herself for the situation she had fallen into. She thought of all that had happened in the past year since Russ' deployment, in her heart, in her mind, in Swanset and in the world in general. It seemed like there was turmoil everywhere she turned, including in her own heart. She had made a promise to Russ, which she was unable to keep, and knew she would eventually need to address the fallout from her choices. Nora rubbed her upper arms with the palms of her hands as the fire died down and a chill filled the air. A moment later she felt the weight of a blanket draped upon her shoulders. She turned to see Brant standing beside her once again with a comforting smile and she reminded herself not to give her heart away.

The group of friends spent the next day at Becky's house where Mr. and Mrs. Lieberman hosted a Fourth of July barbeque for their family and friends. Late in the day Josie disappeared and, as much as Nora and Becky tried to track her down, she was nowhere to be found. As night fell and the fireworks started, Josie magically reappeared, taking a seat next to them on the blanket in the Liebermans' backyard, unable to stop smiling as the bright displays of light illuminated the sky.

"Where the heck have you been?" Nora asked.

"We've been looking all over for you," Becky added.

"I was at your neighbor's house," Josie said.

"What neighbors? Do you mean Mr. and Mrs. Cohen across the street?" Becky asked.

"No. I was at the good looking, single attorney's house next door."

"Alex?" Becky asked.

"Yes, Alex. I met him this morning while I was out walking Hampton," Josie said, referring to the walk she took with the Liebermans' Irish Setter.

"He's twenty-five years old," Becky said.

"Twenty-six to be exact," Josie corrected her.

As Nora and Becky listened, Josie continued with her confessional.

"I heard you guys calling my name earlier, but I was in his pool and couldn't find my top. Don't look at me like that. He invited me over and I didn't want to be rude," Josie said.

"Is that so?" Becky asked with her hand on her hip.

"Yes. We smoked a joint and fooled around a little," Josie said with a mischievous smile.

"Josie!" Nora exclaimed.

"What?" Josie asked, shrugging her shoulders.

"You just met him," Becky said.

"I really don't get why this is such a big deal. You can all relax now that I'm back," Josie said with a chuckle.

"Hey, there she is. Where were you?" Brant asked, as he and Jack approached with cans of cola in their hands.

"Don't ask. Let's just say Josie was having a little adventure for herself," Becky said as the three girls giggled amongst themselves.

Jo is certainly living her life on her own terms, Nora thought of her friend, whose strength and free spirit she envied. When the fireworks were over, Nora felt Brant lean in close to her.

"Are you up for a little adventure yourself?" Brant whispered.

"What do you have in mind?" Nora curiously asked as the partygoers began to disperse.

"How about a little boat ride?"

"A boat ride? We don't have a boat."

"We don't, but Mr. Lieberman has a nice little skiff tied up to the dock down there."

"Oh no, you're not really thinking. . ."

"Yes, I am."

"Brant, we can't take his boat out," Nora said quietly.

"No one will know. We can't let everyone else have all the fun. Can we?" he asked.

"I suppose not," Nora said with a giggle.

"Let's hang here a bit. Once everyone is inside, I'll grab that bottle of wine I hid earlier, and we can head down to the dock. What do you say?"

"Okay," Nora replied, with a twinkle in her eye, ready to let loose and be spontaneous.

When the coast was clear, Brant walked over to the arborvitaes that bordered the Liebermans' property. Nora saw him reach into the branches to retrieve a half-filled bottle of vintage wine that he had snuck from an outdoor table earlier in the day. He then gestured for her to join him. Nora giggled as she picked up her tote bag and they ran, hand in hand, through the soft, manicured lawn of Becky's backyard.

"Do you have towels in that bag?"

"I do," Nora replied.

"Good, because we're going to need them."

Once down at the dock, Brant started up Mr. Lieberman's thirteen-foot skiff and snuck it out for an evening ride. The two young lovers took turns sipping the Bordeaux blend straight from the bottle, savoring its silky richness and hints of ripe cherry. After finding a sheltered spot, away from any houses and light pollution, Nora and Brant cautiously undressed one another and took a dip in a shallow area of the secluded cove.

"Earlier today you said the wine you stole had good legs, but I think I just lost mine. I feel like a mermaid out here," a slightly inebriated Nora joked as the salt water covered her naked body up to her shoulders.

"Let me come over there and see if you have a mermaid tail," Brant said as he waded over to where she was and began running his hands over her buttocks.

"Did you find it? A tail that is?" Nora flirtatiously asked.

"No, but I found something even better. I found you," Brant replied before kissing her lips and running his fingers through her long, wet hair.

"Get away you sea pirate! This mermaid wants to swim a bit more," she said laughing, splashing water at Brant and taking a few back strokes away from him.

After returning to the boat Brant wrapped a towel around Nora's wet body then dried himself off with a towel of his own, loosely folding it and laying it over the wooden bench seat before sitting down.

"Come here my mermaid girl," he said as only the outline of his naked body was visible in the moonbeam's shadows.

"Why?" Nora asked, carefully taking a few steps toward him.

"Because. . . I want you. Tonight, you're in charge," he whispered in her ear before kissing her dewy, bare neck and loosening her towel, exposing her nude body.

Nora lowered herself down to join him on the bench. A rush of excitement coursed through her as she soon found her body in sync with his once again.

"Oh, Brant," she cooed, feeling herself full of his pleasure as the skiff bobbed, sending ripples through the once still waters.

Nora basked in his affections as their unbelievably long finish mimicked that of the aftertaste of the fine wine on the back of their tongues. The two lovers grabbed each other tightly and held still until the violent swaying of the boat settled.

"Jack and I are heading back tomorrow. I have to be at the gas station by four o'clock to cover the last shift."

"Josie and I are staying for a few more days. We won't be home until Wednesday. Can't you stay for one more day?" Nora asked, running her fingers through his damp hair.

"I wish I could. I don't want this weekend to end but, before it does, I need to tell you something."

"What is it? You sound so serious all of a sudden."

"I love you, Nora Thompson."

"I . . . love you too," Nora replied, unable to hold back the words that seemed to jump off her tongue.

"You do?" Brant asked, as if surprised.

"Yes, I do," Nora assured him as she parted her lips and kissed his mouth, so that he could feel she meant it.

As they made their way back to the dock they laughed in hushed tones, keeping as quiet as possible.

"Darn it! I lost one of my earrings," Nora said, rubbing her earlobe.

"It must have fallen off when we were skinny dipping," Brant replied while securing the vessel's lines to the dock cleats.

"I hope we don't get found out," Nora stated.

"Don't worry. We'll keep our late-night rendezvous to ourselves," Brant said, helping her out of the boat.

"My lips are sealed," Nora replied before letting out a giggle as Brant tickled her waist and pressed his lips against hers again.

You weren't supposed to give him your heart, Nora reminded herself, all the while knowing it was too late. The thrill of being with Brant felt like a fast-moving rip current, whose pull she had fought but was unable to escape, quickly sweeping her off her feet and carrying her away from the safety of the shoreline.

$$14$$

Russ' soul radiated with joy as he held Nora's hands in his. A crown of daisies adorned her cascading hair, and a simple, white dress hugged her body. He gazed into her green eyes, sparkling like peridot crystals, and he knew she was his everything. As a distant rumble of thunder roared out its unsettling warning, a sudden feeling of uneasiness washed over him. The once clear sky began to turn foreboding shades of deep grey and black, harkening a sense of gloom and uncertainty on the sacred day.

"What's happening, Nora?" Russ asked as he gripped Nora's hands tighter.

As a pelting rain began to fall, Nora let go of his hands.

"I have to go now," she stated.

"Don't go, Nora. Stay here with me," Russ pleaded.

"It's not safe for me here, Russ," she whispered, lowering her gaze, turning her back to him and calmly walking away.

Russ then realized that he had mistaken machine-gun fire coming from the neighboring trees for heavy rain. When he looked back again, Nora was gone. The crown of daisies now lay on the mud-soaked ground at his feet. Russ stood paralyzed with disbelief, surrounded by a sea of his fellow GIs bodies, bloodied by bullets and shrapnel.

"Nora! No!!!" Russ cried out, loud enough to startle the passengers in and around row fourteen.

"Sir. Sir, wake up. We hit some turbulence. I need you to please fasten your seat belt," the stewardess sternly ordered, reaching over and shaking his forearm to rouse him out of his sleep while deploying her required fake smile.

Russ gasped for breath as he opened his eyes and looked cautiously around the cabin. As it was ingrained in him, he instinctively reached for his gun and realized he was unarmed. Wide-eyed and feeling clammy, he locked eyes with the stewardess and did as she instructed. *It was just that dream again,* he thought to himself while catching his breath and wiping droplets of perspiration from his brow with his sleeve. The stress of combat made him irritable, plaguing him with frequent, recurring nightmares and episodes of insomnia just a few months into his tour. He felt like he was losing himself even though the military had prescribed him an antipsychotic to ease his symptoms of combat fatigue.

I'm in Row 14, seat D, Russ thought, reading the square, metal plate on his arm rest.

Wait, I just heard gunfire, didn't I? The stewardess said it was turbulence. Maybe she's lying and working undercover for the Viet Cong, Russ thought to himself as he cautiously glanced around the airplane's cabin again, noticing everyone around him sitting calmly and chatting amongst themselves. Some passengers were reading advice columns and sports sections of newspapers they had picked up from their previous destinations before boarding. Others looked out their small, oval windows at the scenery below, sipping coffee out of disposable cups. The descending plane bumped along in midair as it suddenly hit another pocket of turbulence. Russ quickly slid the window shade open, anxiously gripped his armrest and squinted his eyes as he looked out the window.

"What the . . .? Is that Saigon? Did the pilot turn the plane around while I was sleeping or something?" Russ mumbled to himself, his body tensing up and feeling disoriented as he caught details of the city buildings below.

A warm, gentle touch on top of his hand interrupted his agitated thoughts, causing him to turn his head toward the frail, silver-haired woman sitting to his left.

"You seem a bit troubled. Everything is going to be just fine. You're almost home, dear," she told him reassuringly with a warm smile, as she gently patted his hand.

"Thank you, ma'am," Russ humbly replied, nodding his head in agreement, glancing at the newspaper she was reading and noticing the date, July fifth, printed at the top of the page.

Like many other GIs returning home from Vietnam, Russ Ayers knew he was different from before with his face now hardened, his guard up and his temper quick. He would often wake up in the middle of the night and swear his hands were still stained with the blood of his fallen comrades and the unlucky Viet Cong that had crossed his path. It was kill or be killed, just as he had learned during his Advanced Individual Training at Fort Polk, Louisiana's Tiger Land, the birthplace of combat infantry for the Vietnam War. He didn't have physical scars like some of the GIs who were sent home for being injured in combat. Those veterans became mailmen, or were given other cushy government jobs, and were able to settle back into civilian life with relative ease. Russ' scars were deep and invisible to most people. During the day, his scars played tricks on his mind. At night his scars kept him awake, haunting him and clouding his mind and his ability to decipher what reality was.

"We are now beginning our decent into Boston. We hope you enjoyed your flight. Thank you for flying with us today," the captain announced from the plane's cockpit.

The first leg of the journey back to the states had already proven to be a nightmare and, as the final leg of his flight touched down, Russ felt an immediate sense of relief.

"You made it home. Now try to leave all those horrors of war behind you and make a good life for yourself," the old woman sitting next to him said with a reassuring smile, seeming to somehow understand the hell he had endured and his current state of mind.

"I will, ma'am," Russ replied, smiling back at her.

Unbeknownst to him, that would be one of the last acts of kindness he would receive from a stranger for quite some time.

Russ stepped off the plane dressed in his grey-green, Army issued, Class A uniform and entered the airport terminal with his large duffle in tow. Glancing around, he saw a frenzy of airport patrons, some running to catch their flights and some frantically checking departure boards for their gates. Others waited impatiently, listening for flight updates from overhead speakers, to board planes that would take them to summertime destinations like the Jersey Shore, Virginia Beach and Lake Tahoe.

He made his way through the terminal, habitually scanning the crowd and frequently looking over his shoulder for any potential threats. Although he was surrounded by his fellow Americans in civilian clothes, he felt very much alone without his buddies from his company. He could feel tension in the air as many of the airport's patrons turned and stared at him as he walked by. *Almost home*, Russ thought to himself as he shifted his focus, realizing he would finally be able to see his family and Nora again. He left the states as an immature kid, but grew up fast over the past year, now valuing his loved ones more than ever. Although he had not yet reached his twenty-first birthday, Russ was ready to get on with his life and create a love nest with his girl. He remembered he had safely tucked away his late grandmother's ring in his top dresser drawer before leaving for his tour and was planning to propose to Nora as soon as he returned.

His happy thoughts were abruptly interrupted when a young boy approached. The towheaded lad, appearing to be no more than six years old, stood in front of him with his arms crossed, blocking his path and curiously looking over his uniform. Russ gave him a smile and waited, thinking that maybe the boy would salute him for his service. Instead, Russ watched as the boy took a step back, swung his leg forward and, with all his might, delivered a hard kick to Russ' shin.

"You little turd!" Russ exclaimed.

"My mommy said you're a baby killer!" he yelled.

"Is that so?" Russ asked, his forehead wrinkling.

The boy ran off to rejoin his mother who sat glaring at Russ with a look of disgust that would make most people turn away in shame. Russ was stunned and felt a sharp sting inside, not from the kick in the shin he had received, but from the harsh words that had rolled off the boy's tainted tongue. At one point in time, he could have shrugged off the behavior of that kid with the cute freckles sprayed across his nose. He would have too, if it weren't for the eyes of all the strangers now upon him and for the disapproving glare of that brat's mother following him as he walked by. *Who the hell does she think she is?* Russ angrily thought to himself, doing a quick about-face. As he approached the pair, he could hear the mother whisper something to the boy while they appeared to hide behind an open copy of Beantown's favorite newspaper. *What cowards, hiding behind that rag,* Russ thought. The kid and his prim and proper mother nearly jumped out of their seats as he dropped his duffle bag down hard on the floor beside them.

"Is that how you're raising your boy?" he calmly asked.

"Pardon me?" she exclaimed with a huff of her voice and a flutter of her eye lashes as she looked up from the paper.

"Don't bat your eyelashes at me. You heard me. Your boy kicked me and ran . . . and called me a baby killer," Russ sternly replied, waiting for her response.

"Isn't that exactly what you are? How many innocent civilian lives have you taken. . . , soldier?", the woman asked, offering no apology.

"You don't know shit about my job in Vietnam. Where does a boy his age learn the term 'baby killer' anyway? He certainly didn't think that up on his own."

The woman remained silent.

"Lady, I'm sure the only reason your husband put a ring on your finger was to dodge the draft while I went off to serve this country. You should know that thousands of GIs gave their lives so that people like your husband could enjoy their freedom to settle down and buy a house surrounded by a white picket fence. I suggest you teach little Suzie there the real facts," Russ said, picking up his duffle bag.

The woman's mousy brown hair and unremarkable facial features appeared to be as bland as her personality. She remained speechless and continued to glare at him with her runt of an offspring clinging tightly to her arm, quivering with fear.

"One more thing. When you go home tonight and bake your coward husband and that rodent child of yours a lemon chiffon cake, think about all the GIs whose last meal was a military ration before having their heads blown off for the likes of people such as yourself," Russ added before turning around, leaving her speechless.

As he walked out of the terminal, surrounded by chatter of the airport patrons in ear shot of his tirade, he did not feel one ounce of guilt for setting that bitch straight. He was taught to be respectful and to abide by the commandments and, most days, he tried his best. When it came to the female sex though, he learned from his father that they need to be put in their place when they get out of line. Seen and not heard, barefoot and pregnant! Forget those bra-burning feminists who were marching on Washington and college campuses around the country. The only ones fighting for true freedom from his perspective were the men being shipped out by the plane-full to go kill the yellow man in the jungle.

Russ breathed in, taking in the fresh New England air and thinking about his fellow GIs, including his tunnel buddy Johnny Davis, who never made it back. *I'll never forget that tough bastard*, Russ thought as he took out a cigarette, needing something to help calm his nerves. He had purchased the cigarettes from a vending machine at the airport in San Francisco during his layover. *San Fran was a shit show too*, Russ thought back to earlier in the day where he had landed on the first leg of his journey back to the states. There, he and other GIs were greeted with a large crowd of tomatoe-throwing war protesters. Some GIs had changed back into civilian clothes just to avoid the confrontation. Russ managed to dodge the tomatoes and other projectiles. He decided he would keep his uniform on until he arrived home in Swanset, as he was no coward. Vietnam took a lot out of him, but he wasn't about to let the peace-loving hippies and leftist intellectuals take his pride too.

While taking a few drags of his cigarette, Russ waited on the concrete sidewalk for a taxi to arrive. *I'm not going to miss those cheap cigarettes from my C-Rats*, he thought as he inhaled, allowing the flavorful smoke to travel deep into his lungs. Letting out a long exhale, he watched the airy grey plume of smoke get whisked away by the summer breeze. When the cigarette burned down, he tossed the still smoking butt onto the pavement and stomped it out with the toe of his polished boot.

A yellow taxi, with its painted white bumper and a stripe of checkered-patterned paint decorating its side, pulled up to the curb. The triangular sign centered on its roof read "Vacant" and Russ flagged down the driver, a stocky guy with salt and pepper hair and a scruffy beard.

"Where to kid?" the cabbie asked in his gruff, South Boston accent.

"Swanset," Russ replied.

"Swanset? That's about a forty-mile trek. It's going to cost at least thirty bucks to get you there," he said, grinning back at him and looking his military uniform up and down.

"I don't care. Just get me home," Russ said as fatigue wash over him.

"Put your bag in the back and get in then."

"Thanks," Russ replied, tossing his duffle into the open trunk and settling into the back seat.

"I felt the same way when I got home from Japan. Where'd they send you?" the cabbie asked.

"Southern Vietnam. Cu Chi District. I'm Russ," Russ replied, now feeling a sense of camaraderie with the cabbie.

"The names Herbie," he said.

"It was hell," Russ added.

"War always is! Cu Chi, huh?" Herbie asked, pulling away from the curb.

"Yup, northwest of Saigon."

"You're not a big guy. I bet they sent you down into those tunnels," he said, looking Russ over through his rearview mirror.

"I volunteered," Russ corrected him.

"A Tunnel Rat hey? Tough job you had there kid. Army 27th Infantry Division," Herbie said, pumping the thumb of his fisted right hand toward his chest and stopping at a red light.

"You don't say."

"Battle of Okinawa in forty-five. Operation Iceberg. Landed April ninth," Herbie said, looking straight ahead, seeming to see something far off in the distance.

"Wow!" Russ exclaimed, noticing the reflection of Herbie's eyes darting back and forth in the rearview mirror, as if he were seeing the battle play out right in front of him.

"The General sent us to hold the right flank of Kakazu Ridge. The Japanese hid too, just like the Viet Cong, and came out of their caves throwing grenades at us as we tried to cross. We blasted their asses out of those caves with flame tanks though," Herbie chuckled, shaking his head and letting out a long breath as the traffic light changed to green and he proceeded through the intersection.

"Good for you. We used those too," Russ replied.

"You know you caught me in a good mood. Boston just beat New York as I pulled up to the curb."

"Cool! What was the final score?" Russ asked.

"Twelve to seven. Sounded like the crowd at Fenway was all fired up. Ah, but that's just a game . . . unlike war. What we did kid . . . well . . . if we can survive that, we can survive anything. Life is full of tough breaks. Hell, I'll take you home for twenty bucks."

"Thanks, man."

As the taxi came to another stop, Russ could have sworn that someone driving alongside them flipped him off. When the car passed them, Russ noticed a large peace sign painted on its rear window and the realization suddenly hit that he most certainly was the intended target for that public display of repulsion. *Damn hippies with their long hair and rimless granny glasses*, Russ thought to himself. He had wrongly imagined being back on home soil would feel way better than this. For the moment though, he was just grateful to be in the company of another combat veteran and for the taste of the cigarette still lingering on his tongue.

15

"I'm so glad you girls were able to stay for a few extra days. Too bad the boys had to head back so soon," Becky pouted as she rubbed suntan lotion on Nora's back.

"I knew you'd like Jack," Josie stated, adjusting the straps of her bikini top while the trio enjoyed one last day at Orient Beach State Park.

"He was so dreamy. Thanks for bringing him along. You seem to really be digging Alex too. I just don't know if I can look him in the eye again and keep a straight face knowing that you fooled around," Becky said with a chuckle.

"Nor, why are you so quiet?" Josie asked.

"She's probably daydreaming about Brant," Becky joked.

"Can't a girl just relax at the beach without being interrogated?" Nora asked while lying face down on her beach towel.

"C'mon, Nor. We've told you all about Jack and Alex," Josie said.

"Yes, now it's your turn, Nor. We want to hear everything about you and Brant. Spill it," Becky added.

"There's nothing to tell," Nora replied, lifting her head and hoping to fend off any more questions from her friends.

"I've known Nora a long time, Beck, and she doesn't like to kiss and tell," Josie stated.

"She doesn't have to tell anything. You can see it on her face. If I didn't know better, I'd say she's in love with him," Becky teased.

"I think he's the one in love with her. He can't take his eyes, or his hands, off her," Josie added.

"I don't want to talk about it," Nora said, putting her face back down on her towel so that Josie and Becky wouldn't see her blushing.

"Well, we want the scoop," Josie insisted.

"Yes, and I'd also like an explanation as to why my father found this inside his boat this morning," Becky said.

Nora lifted her head again and turned to see Becky holding up the gold hoop earring she had lost on the evening of July fourth. *I thought I lost my hoop while Brant and I were skinny dipping. It must have fallen off while we were making out in the skiff,* Nora thought to herself.

"Interesting," Josie said giving Nora a sideways glance.

"Do tell," Becky urged.

"I don't know how that ended up in your father's boat," Nora fibbed, hoping to sound convincing and accepting the earring from her friend.

"That's funny because he also found an empty wine bottle, and an expensive one at that," Becky said.

"Oh my gosh, I bet you and Brant snuck away in the boat to be alone together," Josie exclaimed.

"Sorry, Beck. It was just . . . a little boat ride," Nora confessed, feeling her face flush.

"Sure, it was," Becky replied, her tone implying she wasn't buying Nora's story.

"I bet that boat was rockin'," Josie said with a chuckle.

As Josie and Becky laughed together, Nora felt her face growing hotter with embarrassment. "Stop it! I don't want to talk about it. Why can't the two of you understand that?" Nora said before getting up and running off down the beach, guilt-ridden for having snuck the skiff out without permission and for having fallen for Brant Judge.

"Where are you going, Nor?" Josie called out.

"Nora, come back!" Becky yelled.

Nora felt her heart beat fast and kept running in hopes that all her problems would disappear. As her calf muscles grew tired, she stopped along the rocky shoreline and gazed out over the tranquil waters of Gardiners Bay.

"Nora, we were just teasing," Becky said after catching up to her.

"Why are you so upset?" Josie asked as she tried to catch her breath.

"Because . . . don't you see? I gave my heart away, Jo. I know I shouldn't have, but I did. I never hear from Russ, and I've been so lonely that I couldn't fight it anymore. I don't even know if Russ is alive or . . . I'm a bad person and a terrible friend too. I'm sorry Beck. I'm sorry we took the boat out without asking," Nora said as her eyes welled up.

"It's okay, Nora. My father wasn't upset," Becky assured her.

"Please don't cry, Nor. You're not a bad person. You're an amazing friend and everything you're feeling is normal. This was such a fun weekend. You're allowed to have fun, Nor, and have nothing to be upset about," Josie stated.

"But I still love Russ. So how can I justify falling in love with Brant?" Nora asked, searching for an answer to ease her worry.

"You can't help how your heart feels," Becky replied.

"She's right, Nor, and you can't beat yourself up for being human," Josie said.

"Things like this happen all the time," Becky added.

"Not to me," Nora said, placing her hand on her stomach and feeling it twist into a knot.

"Nothing happens to you because Viviane has sheltered you too much. Now that you're out in the world, you can experience everything it has to offer as you should have been doing all along," Josie replied.

"My mom is so overbearing. I feel like I'm being suffocated," Nora said.

"Now you can understand how your sister felt. Just remember that it's your life, Nor," Josie replied.

"How does Brant make you feel when you're with him?" Becky asked.

"Why do you want to know, Beck?" Nora asked, puzzled by the question.

"Just give us one word that sums up how you feel when you are with him, Nor," Josie said.

Nora's eyes were suddenly drawn up toward the sky where a lone osprey, whistling its sharp call, soared freely high above them. "Free! When I'm with Brant, I feel free. Free and alive," Nora said as she watched the sea hawk swoop down and grab a fish out of the bay with its taloned toes before flying off.

"There we have it. There's nothing wrong with feeling free and alive now is there?" Becky asked.

"No," Nora meekly replied.

"I have to be honest with you, Nor. All the time I've known you, I have never seen you this happy other than when you got those new roller skates for your tenth birthday," Josie said.

"I second that. You've been smiling all weekend," Becky agreed.

"What do you say we head back to our blanket and enjoy our last day here before we have to go home?" Josie asked.

"Okay," Nora replied, turning around, following a few paces behind her friends and looking out onto the bay as she walked, lost in her thoughts. "Ouch!" Nora suddenly cried out, feelings something sharp under her foot, bending down and retrieving an object from the sand.

"What happened, Nor?" Josie asked, stopping and turning back to look at her.

"I stepped on something," Nora replied.

"What do you have there?" Becky asked, watching her pick up the object.

"It's a strange looking shell. I've never seen one like this before," Nora said, brushing off the sand and holding up the thick, grey, irregular shaped shell in her hand.

"That's an oyster shell, Nor. They grow here in the bay," Becky said.

"Cool. We don't have oysters in Swanset Bay, just clams, quahogs and periwinkles. Look at all the lines on it," Nora replied, holding the shell in the palm of her hand and running her fingertips over its bumpy surface.

"The changing tides and storms that come through the sound have a big impact on their growth. The imperfections on its exterior can tell you a lot about what it has been through. The color of the shell tells you the environment and conditions it grew in, and the rings show you how old it is," Becky stated.

"That's interesting," Nora replied, running her fingertips lightly over the scar above her eyebrow, absorbing Becky's words, and finding a shared commonality with the imperfections on the shell's outer surface.

"Every once in a while, you'll open one up and find a pearl inside. It's hard to believe that something so beautiful could come from something that's weathered so many storms," Becky added.

"Far out. I'm going to keep it as a reminder of our special time here on Long Island," Nora replied, loosely closing her hand around her newly found memento.

16

It appeared as though time had stood still as Herbie drove his taxi down Main Street and through the center of Swanset. Russ glanced at his wristwatch and saw the second hand actively keeping time as they passed the familiar red brick exteriors of the Swanset Town Hall, Swanset Public Library and other municipal buildings. With each tick of his watch, Russ could see that, even though everything looked the same, time was marching on.

"I can't wait to go to Swanset Diner. They make the best milk-shakes," Russ said, pointing out the town diner and glad to be back in his old surroundings.

"Something to look forward to. Hey, don't forget to try to connect with your local veterans organization so you have the support of your comrades. They'll give you direction and will stand by you when no one else does," Herbie urged him, making a few more turns and pulling up to Russ' house.

"Thanks. I will. Good talking with you, man," Russ said, reaching for the door handle.

As he stepped out of the taxi there were no signs screaming, "Welcome Home Russ," hanging from the fence and flapping in the mild July breeze. "Welcome" and "Home" were two words he could not recall the feeling of anyway. The two blooming, blue hydrangea bushes flanking the sides of the rusted front gate were the only things greeting him upon his arrival. The chain link fence that surrounded his parents' front yard reminded him of simpler times, having climbed and jumped over it with his neighborhood friends as a young boy.

Russ felt the hairs on the back of his neck stand up and, out of nowhere, was overcome with an eerie feeling. The summers of his youth, spent in the backyard swinging his baseball bat and hunting for garden snakes with his neighborhood friends, were long gone. His elementary school days, when he was a scout and proudly earned his badges for knot-tying and other outdoor skills, were also a distant memory. The carefree snow days during the cold winter months, spent building snow forts in his yard and shoveling the driveways of his elderly neighbors, were replaced with a season of bloodshed and destruction of human lives. As Herbie's taxi pulled away, Russ saluted him and proceeded toward the side door of the house thinking to himself, *I made it. I'm home.*

Russ looked up and saw his mother, Martha, peering out the kitchen window. He walked up the driveway, running his hand along the blue paint on the body of his car. A few seconds later, he saw Martha hurrying out the back door to greet him, dropping her dish towel on the walkway in the process.

"My boy! Let me look at you. How I missed you!" she exclaimed as she squeezed him tightly and kissed him on the cheek.

"I missed you too, Ma," Russ said as he wrapped his arms around his mother's thick waist and embraced her.

Martha was a caring mother who was supportive of him in every way. He was all Martha had left to live for and Russ knew he could do no wrong in her eyes. *Thankfully, Ma doesn't know what I had to do in the tunnels*, he thought.

As they entered the house Russ glanced around the small, tidy kitchen. Martha had been busy and the delicious smell of a freshly cooked roast wafted through the air. Dropping his duffle bag on the kitchen floor, he caught a glimpse of Ann Marie's first communion picture hanging in the adjacent hallway. He often pondered why his little sister was taken from him and still found himself looking for reasons to make some sense of her passing. The thought had crossed his mind that maybe her passing had somehow prepared him for the bloodshed and death he witnessed in Vietnam. He would probably never know, but swore he had felt her presence with him, helping to protect his life throughout his tour, even though his officer thought he may be cracking up when he mentioned he had seen her. She had visited him in his dreams too with her index finger over her lips, signaling him to stay silent, and pointing him in the safe direction so that he could make it home alive. Her favorite game had been hide-and-go-seek and it was as if she had guided him in his deadly game with the Viet Cong. It was something he couldn't explain, he just felt she had been there with him while hiding in the dark tunnels and on the day his friend was killed in action. Russ felt it best not to share his experience with Martha and Fred as it would surely reopen the wound.

"Where's the old man?" he asked, his father nowhere in sight.

"Oh, you know your father. He was grouchy and fell asleep in his easy chair. He had a rough day at the factory. I know it's a hot day, but when you called to let us know you were on your way home, I just had to make your favorite meal: roast with potatoes and carrots," she replied.

"Shucks, Ma. I had a hankering for more of that rationed canned spaghetti with ground meat sauce," Russ joked with a roll of his eyes as they both laughed and made their way into the dining room.

"I'm glad you haven't lost that sense of humor. Your friends will be glad you're back. I'm sure they miss your antics, and Nora too," Martha stated.

"Nora doesn't know I'm home yet. I'm going to surprise her," Russ said with excitement in his voice.

"I'm sure she's looking forward to seeing you," Martha replied sincerely.

"Have you seen her around town much since I was deployed?" he asked.

"She's been away at school, but I did see her a few months back when your father and I were getting some burgers. The poor dear, that injury left her pretty face all scarred up," Martha said, shaking her head.

"Injury? What happened to her?" Russ asked.

"Didn't she tell you?"

"Maybe she did in one of her letters, but it must have been lost in the mail," Russ replied with concern.

"Well, last December she was struck with a sign during a campus protest and got a gash on her forehead. The doctor fixed her up good and all, but it's not in a place where she can hide it. It's a crying shame. She's such a pretty girl."

"Thanks for letting me know, Ma."

"Nora did ask if I had heard from you but, at that point, I had no news for her. She said her schoolwork has been keeping her busy. She was with Josie and Mary Judge's boy. I think his name is Brad. No wait. It's Brett . . . or maybe its Brandon. Oh, I don't remember. You know the boy that works over at the gas station on Read Road? He's a friend of Josie's and they were celebrating the girls finishing their second year of college. Nice girl, that Nora is."

Martha continued rambling innocently about how her hairdresser was gossiping with Mrs. Judge. Mary was telling everyone in the salon about the nice girl named Nora that her son had brought home for dinner. Since Martha's head had been in curlers and setting under the hair dryer, she thought that surely Mary must have said "Norma" or maybe "Cora" as there is only one "Nora" in the entire town of Swanset that she knew of.

Russ began to perspire and could feel his rage building. Although he could see her lips moving, he couldn't hear any other words coming out of his mother's mouth. He could only feel fire coming from deep in his core, up the sides of his neck and finally settling on the top of his head.

"Russell? What's wrong? Didn't you hear a word I said?" Martha asked.

"What, Ma?" Russ asked, feeling heated.

"Oh, dear! I know. You must be hot. It's been so humid."

"I'm used to it," Russ mumbled.

"What did you say?"

"Nothing, Ma," Russ replied.

"I'll get you some lemonade," Martha said as she made her way back into the kitchen.

Russ' mind raced as he became consumed with anger. His mother had a knack for being oblivious to things right in front of her. Martha soon returned with a cold glass of lemonade and a heaping plate full of his favorite home-cooked meal.

"Be sure to eat everything on your plate. You're looking a bit too thin," his mother ordered as she set the plate down on the tablecloth in front of him.

Russ picked at the tender roast as he glanced around the dining room. *Exactly as I remember it,* he thought, studying the busy, floral-patterned wallpaper and sheer, summer curtains with ruffled edges. For the better part of the past year, he had eaten his meals outside, exposed to the elements, deep inside the jungle. He had never found the meals in the bush of Vietnam to be enjoyable since he and his buddies were always on high alert, anticipating an ambush. They had survived on a diet of mainly dehydrated meals and salty canned meats from their rations. To wash it all down, Russ often drank stale water from his canteen or, on more than a few occasions, whatever remained of his fifth of whiskey he liked to carry with him. It felt awkward to now be sitting in a dining room, at a set table, enjoying his mother's cooking off of a clean plate. *I forgot what it feels like to be civilized,* Russ thought, itching in his own skin.

As his train of thought drifted, Russ got thinking about his platoon buddy, Harry Blake, who was two years older than him. Harry had arrived in Vietnam shortly before he did and had recognized Russ' face from around town. While it was not very likely for two soldiers from the same hometown to end up in a platoon together, the two were happy to be in one another's company. They kept an eye out for each other and often exchanged news from back home. They had also made a pact that if either one of them was killed in action, the other would see to it that their families knew they had been brave in battle and did not suffer, whether it was true or not. The two were nearing the end of their tour when Harry decided to sign on for another year. He felt he had nothing to return home to after his fiancé broke things off with him in her last letter. Harry had also told him about a letter he received from his younger brother, Dennis, one night while they got high back in the hootch. Dennis had written him saying that he had started dating a girl named Josie and had gone bowling with her, his friend Brant Judge and a girl named Nora. Russ recalled asking to see the letter which stated his friend Brant was smitten with Josie's friend with pretty green eyes.

"Don't worry, Little Spud. I'm sure it's not your Nora. Maybe the girl was from another town. Maybe from Weaver Falls," Harry assured him.

"Yeah, I'm sure it's another Nora," Russ had suspiciously replied.

Russ put down his fork, finished chewing one last bite of roast beef, and took a few swigs of the tart lemonade before slinging his duffle bag over his shoulder and heading upstairs to his bedroom. Rage began to fire through every fiber of his being. Just a few days prior he was crawling out of a tunnel in the Cu Chi district of Vietnam for the last time not knowing what would be waiting for him when he emerged. He had that same feeling now that he had arrived back home, unsure of what to expect next. As he reached the top of the staircase, it suddenly dawned on him that time had moved on without him and things were not the same as they initially appeared to be in Swanset. He kicked his duffle under the bed and tossed his combat boots into the back of the closet, just because he could, now that he no longer had his sergeant breathing down his neck about keeping his things orderly. Russ opened his dresser drawers and pulled out a pair of broken-in jeans and a T-shirt and changed into them before taking a seat at the foot of his bed and sliding into his favorite sneakers. His feet were still itching from a mild case of jungle rot and he felt relieved to finally be out of his restricting boots. He thought about what to do next as he tied the laces, realizing he was now free to let the ends dangle if he wanted to. He no longer needed to be concerned with wrapping or tucking the strings in as the Army had required him to do. *You're free to do whatever you want. They don't own you anymore*, he reminded himself. He had forgotten what it was like to wear civilian clothes and the loose-fitting material felt good against his skin, allowing him room to breathe. Russ glanced up and took notice of the sun beginning to set outside his westerly facing window. Before making his way back downstairs, he opened the top drawer of his dresser to be sure the engagement ring, which he had set aside for Nora before he was deployed, was still where he had left it.

"Be back later, Ma. I need to gas up my car," Russ said as he grabbed his keys off the hook underneath the kitchen cabinet.

"Right now? But you just got home . . . and you haven't finished your roast," Martha scolded as he let the screened door slam behind him.

Russ lit up a cigarette before getting into his car. He rolled the windows down to cool the interior and let the smoke escape before turning the key in the ignition. As the engine purred, he thought back to his time in Vietnam when he longed to take his car for a spin. Russ put the car in reverse and backed out of the driveway. He had a mission to fulfill and, knowing this one was personal, put the car in drive, stepped on the accelerator and peeled out with a battle-ready screech.

17

"Dad, did anyone call while I was away?" Nora asked as she sat at the breakfast table drizzling maple syrup over her hot pancakes.

"No, not that I'm aware of," Richard Thompson said, looking up from his morning copy of *The Weaver Falls Herald*.

"Mom, did anyone call while I was in Long Island?" Nora turned and asked, before picking up her fork and taking a bite of her pancake, secretly hoping that Brant had left her a message.

"Nora, I'm barely awake and have not even had a sip of my coffee yet. Your father just said no one has called for you but, I'm sure Josie will call before noon as she always does," Viviane complained, pouring her coffee into a ceramic mug.

Swirling a piece of her pancake in the pool of maple syrup on her plate, Nora replayed her trysts with Brant Judge in her mind.

"That's an awful lot of syrup. You better start watching your waistline young lady. You still haven't lost your freshman fifteen yet," Viviane said, sitting her svelte body down on the chair beside Nora.

"Leave her alone, Viv, and let her enjoy her pancakes for goodness' sake," Richard said, looking up from his newspaper again and coming to his daughter's defense.

"I'm not hungry enough to finish the rest and need to take a shower anyway," Nora truthfully replied, suddenly feeling nauseous, pushing her plate away and excusing herself from the table.

After exiting the kitchen, Nora made her way up the staircase. *Why hasn't Brant called like he said he would?* she thought to herself as she reached the top step and the telephone started to ring.

"I'll get it," Nora yelled down to her parents, hurriedly picking up the extension in the upstairs hallway. *It's got to be Brant. I just knew he would call*, Nora thought, anxious to hear his voice.

"Hello?" Nora excitedly answered.

"Nor, thank God you picked up," Josie said with desperation in her voice.

"Jo? What's going on? Why are you calling so early?" Nora asked, disappointed that it was not Brant as she had hoped.

"Brant is in the hospital, Nor," Josie said.

"What? What happened, Jo?" Nora asked, the feeling of excitement now replaced with worry.

"I ran into Brant's neighbor when I was picking up sweet bread at the Portuguese bakery this morning. You know the guy whose family is fresh off the boat from the Azores?" Josie asked.

"Do you mean Jamie? The guy with the Virgin Mary statue in his front yard?" Nora asked.

"Yes. That's him and I bet he's praying a novena for Brant right now. He told me that Brant got jumped while working at the gas station the other night."

"Oh, no!"

"When Jamie pulled up to the gas pump, he found Brant lying on the ground, all beat up with a tire iron beside him."

"Is he going to be okay?" Nora asked, beginning to tremble.

"All I know is that Jamie kept saying 'Muito sangue. Muito sangue'."

"I don't understand Portuguese. What does that mean, Jo?"

"He was saying there was blood, a lot of blood, covering Brant's face. Jamie somehow managed to get him into his car and drove him to Teasdale Memorial Hospital," Josie replied.

"Do they know who did that to him?" Nora asked.

"I'm not sure, but you should go see him. I think the visiting hours end at five o'clock."

"I'm going to take a quick shower then go right there," Nora replied, her hands now shaking.

"What are you going to tell Viviane? I'm sure she'll ask where you're going."

"My parents are leaving this morning to go to a weekend marriage-building retreat on the Cape. God knows they need it. I'll take off to visit Brant as soon as they leave."

"Good plan. I'd go with you, but my parents and I are going to my grandma's house. She just got out of the nursing home since having her stroke. Just be sure to call me over the weekend to let me know how things went, okay?"

"Okay. Thanks, Jo," Nora replied before placing the telephone back on its cradle.

Suddenly, sick with worry, Nora ran into the bathroom as fast as she could, locked the bathroom door and vomited into the toilet bowl. The wretched smell of last night's half-digested pasta dinner mixed with bile acids filled the room, causing her to vomit a second time.

"Who was that on the telephone?" Viviane called from the bottom of the staircase.

Nora flushed the toilet, got up from the floor and cracked open the bathroom door.

"It was just Josie, Mom," Nora replied as she rubbed her hands on her neck and swallowed to ease her burning throat.

"See. I told you she'd be calling soon," Viviane replied with a huff, seemingly satisfied she had accurately predicted Josie's incoming telephone call.

After pushing the bathroom door shut and locking it again, Nora slid the window open to allow the foul odors to escape. She then reached for the shower faucet and turned the water on to drown out her mother's voice. Waving her hand under the stream of water until it ran warm, she was relieved to find that Viviane took the hint and was no longer flapping her lips at the bottom of the staircase.

Nora showered, got dressed, and waited impatiently for her parents to leave for their retreat. She checked the time and noticed it was nearing noon when the coast was finally clear for her to head out. Once inside her vehicle, she prayed it would start.

"That's a good girl," she said as the engine turned over and she gently patted the steering wheel.

Once at the hospital, Nora went straight to the information desk to find out Brant's room number, got into the elevator and pressed the button to take her to the third floor. Stepping out of the elevator, she timidly approached the nurses' station.

"Hello. How may I help you today?" a nurse behind the desk asked.

"I'm here to visit someone. Can you tell me where I can find Brant Judge's room? The receptionist at the information desk downstairs told me he is in room three twenty-five."

"Just one moment please. It's been a busy day around here. Let me check the room assignment log to confirm that," the nurse replied as she put her reading glasses on, picked up a clip board and started flipping through its pages.

"Ah, here we go. Judge, Brant. He was admitted for head trauma and observation. You are correct and will find Mr. Judge in room number three twenty-five, but first you need to sign the visitors' log. Please write your name, your relation to the patient and the room number that you will be visiting. It appears he already has a visitor so you'll have to wait your turn. Only one guest is allowed in at any given time. See here?" she said, handing her the clipboard and pointing to a signature on the page with the tip of the pen.

"Okay," Nora replied.

As other visitors before her had done, Nora added her name to the list and took notice of the guest's name that preceded hers.

"Libby Vincent . . . girlfriend?" Nora read aloud, feeling the skin around her scar pulling tight as she squinted at the cursive writing above her own signature.

"Yes. Once Miss Vincent leaves, you can go in. Mr. Judge's room is on the left side of the hallway. Just go through those doors to the waiting area," she instructed, pointing to a set of double doors.

"Thank you," Nora replied, nervously stroking the scar above her eyebrow.

With trepidation she proceeded through the set of doors, bypassing the waiting area. *Girlfriend?* Nora thought as she headed down the hallway, suspecting that Libby had an agenda of her own.

The bright overhead lighting, the strong smell of surface disinfectants and the sight of sick patients sitting in their hospital beds as she passed by their rooms, made her stomach churn. As she walked further down the hallway, she softly read the room numbers posted outside of each room aloud.

"Three nineteen. Three twenty-one. Three twenty-three. Three twenty-. . .," Nora read, stopping as the sound of a young woman's perky voice caught her ear.

Standing outside the open door of room number three twenty-five, Nora discretely peered inside and saw a slender, young woman, with long hair pulled into a tight ponytail, sitting on the edge of Brant's hospital bed. She observed the woman's upper body leaning in toward Brant who lay in a semi-upright position with a bandage wrapped around his head. She watched closely as the woman stroked the side of his head with one hand, while her other hand was intertwined with his.

"Oh, Boo Bear. I came as soon as I heard what happened to you," she said.

"Thank you," Brant replied, his voice hoarse.

Nora hid herself from their sight, pulling herself away from the door frame as a doctor and nurse hurriedly pushed a patient on a gurney down the hospital's corridor.

Once they passed, Nora leaned in again and continued to eavesdrop on their conversation.

"I'm so glad you're here," Brant said with a mild slur in his speech.

"I've missed you so much, Boo," Libby cooed.

"I'm so in love with you," Brant replied, quieted as Libby pressed her index finger against his lips.

"Shh now, Boo. You need your rest. But first I have just what the doctor ordered to cheer you up," Libby stated, leaning in closer toward him.

Nora watched in disbelief as Brant and Libby's lips met. The seconds that passed seemed like an eternity as Libby and Brant playfully, then passionately, kissed one another. Nora felt her stomach twist up, the pang causing her to jump back and instinctively turn and run. She found herself bolting down the hallway, weaving her way past a group of candy stripers in pink and white striped uniforms. With her eyes filling with tears, she caught a glimpse of the glass window of the nurses' station up ahead and a restroom sign just beyond it. Now frantically running and trying to avoid bumping into a slow-moving old woman with a walker, Nora's arm hit a room service tray that was sitting on a cart outside of room three nineteen. The covered plate of a partially eaten chicken dinner crashed to the floor, its metal cover spinning like a top in the middle of the hallway. Nora's momentum slowed as she glanced at the silverware, gravy and peas and carrots scattered about. Not paying attention to where she was going, she suddenly collided with a large figure in the hallway.

"Ugh," Nora said, coming to an immediate halt.

"Whoa! Slow down young lady," a uniformed Swanset Police officer said.

"I'm . . . I'm so sorry officer. Excuse me," Nora meekly replied as she briefly looked up and then continued her sprint toward the restroom.

Bursting through the door and into the first open stall, she fell to her knees, sickened by what she had witnessed and overheard. Feeling tears on her cheeks and her stomach retching, Nora leaned her head over the toilet bowl. She hated herself for having given herself to Brant Judge. The betrayal that pierced through her heart was like nothing she had ever felt before.

"He lied to me. He lied to me all along. I knew I shouldn't have given him my heart," Nora whispered to herself while getting up from the floor, exiting the stall, and making her way over to the sink.

As she washed her hands, she studied her reflection in the restroom mirror, her focus landing on the scar above her eyebrow once again. *You are a stupid fool, Nora Thompson. That's what you are, an ugly, stupid fool.* Her body trembled as she exited the restroom and noticed the clipboard still on the nurses' station counter, directly in front of her. She walked over, picked up the pen and furiously scribbled over her name on the visitors' log until it was completely obliterated.

"You look a bit pale. Are you okay, Miss?" the nurse asked, peering curiously over the rim of her glasses.

"Yes, ma'am. I just . . .," Nora began to say.

"You just what?"

Never again Brant Judge. I will never let you into my life again, Nora thought as she swallowed hard, straightened her shoulders and brushed a loose strand of hair off her forehead.

"I just . . . changed my mind. I have to go," Nora said, calmly walking toward the elevator and out of Brant Judge's life.

18

Hearing a loud crash coming from the hallway outside his room, Brant struggled to fully open his heavy eyelids. Now alert, he was stunned to find himself face to face with his ex-girlfriend who was teasingly tracing his lips with the tip of her index finger.

"Libby?" Brant asked, his eyes widening.

"Yes, Boo?" Libby replied, coquettishly.

"Stop that! Get off me," Brant exclaimed, his thoughts unjumbling and pushing Libby away.

"What's wrong, Boo? My kisses have always helped you feel better in the past," Libby pouted, her eyes wide with surprise.

"My head hurts," Brant said, ignoring her statement and rubbing the side of his head which was wrapped in a sterile dressing.

"Oh, Boo," Libby said comfortingly.

"Stop that too," Brant ordered.

"Stop what?" Libby asked, straightening up.

"These pain pills are making me loopy," Brant stated, rubbing his temple.

"Shall I page the nurse?" Libby asked.

"No. No and stop acting like we're still together. Stop kissing me . . . and once and for all stop calling me Boo. I hate when you call me that," Brant firmly said.

"But, Boo . . .,"

"But nothing. Libby, it was nice of you to come visit me, but you should know that I've been seeing someone . . . someone very special."

"Then why did you act so happy to see me and why did you kiss me back? And why did you tell me that you love me?" Libby asked, her eyelids fluttering at an unusually fast rate.

"Lib, these pain medications are making me so groggy that I thought you were her."

"Who is she? What's her name?" Libby asked, firing her questions in rapid succession.

"It's none of your business, Lib. I didn't question you when you broke things off with me for that Ivy League guy now did I?"

"No but . . . well, where is she from?" Libby continued pressing.

Brant turned toward the window and shook his head out of frustration.

"I was hoping we could get back together, Boo. I miss you," Libby said, caressing the side of his head again.

"It's time for you to go, Lib," Brant said as he caught sight of someone in the doorway in his peripheral vision.

"Judge junior! How the heck are you?" Officer Peter McMillan asked in his deep, authoritative voice.

"Mick, my man! Come on in. She was just leaving," Brant said, perking up when he noticed his father's friend, an officer of the Swanset Police Department, enter the room with his polished badge displayed prominently on his chest.

"Bye, Boo," Libby said disappointedly, looking back at Brant one last time before exiting the room.

"Later," Brant replied.

"Wow! I bet she cheered you up," Mick said as he bobbed his head in the direction of the doorway where Libby had just exited.

"She tried to," Brant replied.

"This place is crawling with attractive women today. A pretty, young girl bumped into me just a few doors down from here. She was in such a hurry that she knocked over a room service tray and crashed right into me," McMillan said.

"That must have been the commotion I heard a few minutes ago," Brant replied, sitting more upright and adjusting the pillows behind his back.

"I heard you got into a scuffle of some sort," the officer continued.

"Yeah, Mick, it's no big deal. Just an angry GI who just got back from Vietnam."

"So, you're scheduled to start the academy in a few weeks, and you know how word gets around in this town. Chief caught wind of your altercation while having breakfast at Swanset Diner and asked me to stop by on the hush and get your side of the story. Care to tell me what happened?" McMillan asked.

Tread carefully, Brant told himself. He had a squeaky-clean record and was aware even a small misdemeanor could be detrimental to his entry into the police academy.

"Sure, Mick. I was getting ready to close the gas station the other night when a customer pulled up. I started to fill his tank, not making much small talk since it was closing time, and he started telling me how he just got back from Vietnam. I told him I'd give his windows a quick wash while he was waiting for the tank to fill."

"Okay. Then what happened?" Mick inquired.

"He got out of his car and started coming toward me. I could see he was hiding something behind his back. I told him to back off, but he just kept coming at me. He had this crazed look in his eyes and got right up in my face. He was so close that I could smell his stale cigarette breath."

"Sounds like he was looking for trouble," Mick replied.

That's when I threw the first punch, but I'm not going to tell you that, Mick, and possibly ruin my chance at going to the academy, Brant thought.

"Then he started swinging a tire iron at me and clocked me in the head. Once I was on the ground, he started punching me and was yelling crazy stuff about killing Viet Cong. When he saw the headlights of another car approaching, he took off. I must have passed out after that because next thing I knew, I was here in this hospital bed," Brant said, concluding his story.

"Did you happen to get a good look at the guy's face or get his license plate number?" McMillan asked.

"No, it was getting dark."

"But you just said that he had a crazed look in his eyes, didn't you? You could see his eyes but not his face?"

"I guess I got fixated on his eyes. Sorry I don't recall his other facial features, Mick."

"How tall was he?"

"He was shorter than me . . . I think."

"How about his race?" McMillan probed.

"Remember it was getting dark and I passed out Mick, so I can't be sure."

Brant was fully aware of the half-truths he was telling Mick. He had never met Russ Ayers before, that much was true. However, he was one hundred percent sure that it was Russ who was responsible for putting him in the hospital.

"So, you're the prick who's been making moves on my girl while I was in 'Nam," Russ had said.

"Hey, I'm not looking for trouble," Brant had replied.

"The way I see it is that's exactly what you were looking for. You shouldn't have messed with Nora," Russ had told him as he gripped the tire iron in his hand.

"Whoa man! What the hell are you doing?" Brant asked with his hands out in front of him.

"I'm going to make sure that you forget all about her," Russ stated, taking a few steps closer.

"You think so? Let me tell you something. I love Nora and I'll never forget about her. Let's go," Brant replied, fired up and swinging his clenched fist at Russ.

Brant decided to play it cool with Mick and not give him Russ' name. If he did, he knew it was possible he would only be making matters worse for himself if an investigation followed.

The thought of Nora reminded him that he had not seen or heard from her since he was admitted to the hospital. She was nowhere to be found and hadn't stopped by to check in on him, nor had she rung him on his hospital room telephone. *Maybe her car is giving her trouble again,* Brant told himself. *She's probably tied up doing chores for that demanding mother of hers,* he thought, shrugging it off.

"Well, there's not much more I can do other than wish you a speedy recovery. I'll let Chief know that things are alright here," Officer McMillan said as he started toward the door.

Phew, I'm glad that's over, Brant thought to himself.

"Oh, one more thing before I leave," Mick said.

"What's that?"

"Good luck at the academy, kid," the officer said, giving him a wink.

"Thanks, Mick," Brant replied as Mick disappeared into the hallway and the door closed behind him.

"Ah, shit!" Brant said aloud, the throbbing in his head intensifying.

He closed his eyes to escape the brightness of the fluorescent overhead lights, resting as the nurses had encouraged him to do. *How the hell did Russ find out about me and Nora?* Brant wondered. As he pondered his altercation with Russ, he concluded that their fight in the parking lot seemed to mimic the state of discord throughout the country, and around the world for that matter. There was a lack of harmony in the universe, with the world being divided into hawks and doves, when it came to the conflict in Vietnam. That imbalance spilled over into small towns across

America, including Swanset. Brant thought he couldn't really blame Russ for reacting how he did as it was hard not to love a girl like Nora. Now that everything was out in the open, Brant felt a sense of relief that he and Nora would be able to continue their relationship without further interruption. A wave of exhaustion from a morning of visitors washed over him and Brant soon found himself lost in a daydream of his future, with his soulmate, Nora Thompson. He hoped that when he opened his eyes, he would find her there by his side. Nothing, or no one, mattered more.

19

The repetitious chiming of the front doorbell irritated Nora as she wiped her eyes and made her way downstairs. She had tried her best to ignore it, in hopes that whoever it was would leave, but their persistence got the best of her. Her parents were still away at their marriage retreat and she was grateful to have a few days to herself and not be disturbed by Viviane's prying eyes. Her heart was aching from Brant's betrayal and from the sight of Libby Vincent in his hospital room. She had decided, after crying enough tears to fill Swanset Bay the night before, that she would never be his fool again.

"I'm coming. I'm coming," Nora mumbled as she slowly made her way downstairs, dizzy from having not eaten, her stomach still twisted in a tight, nervous knot.

"Viviane already has enough of whatever it is you're selling. I'm sure she must even have some snake oil somewhere in the house too," Nora continued mumbling aloud.

When she reached the bottom step, Nora took a few more paces toward the front door. Reaching for the doorknob, and noticing the ringing had finally stopped, a strange feeling washed over her. Goose bumps covered her arms, and she was unsure whether it was her intuition sending her a warning or her imagination running away with her. She opened the door only to see the backside of a lean man walking away from the house. Nora realized the fine hairs on her arms were standing straight up, like small antennas gathering waves of information. She rubbed her eyes and assessed the scene, noticing something familiar in his stature and gait. As the screen door hinge creaked, and Nora stepped out onto the front porch, the figure suddenly stopped. Standing momentarily still, she gasped as the man turned toward her. His face appeared weary, and his deep brown eyes were lusterless.

"Russ? Russ, is that you?" Nora asked.

He smiled and, as a sunbeam lit up the side of his face, Nora found herself running down the porch steps and into his arms.

"There's my green-eyed girl," Russ said.

"It's really you!" Nora exclaimed, embracing him and unable to believe that he was there, in the flesh.

"Gosh, it's good to see you," Russ replied, lifting her up, spinning her around and planting a kiss on her lips.

"I haven't heard from you . . . in so long. I thought you were . . .," Nora began to say but stopped herself, at a loss for words and grateful for his presence.

"I'm sorry I didn't write like I said I would. It's been hell, Nor, but I'm here for you now."

"So much has happened since you've been gone," Nora said, trembling and her face wet from the tears trickling down her cheeks.

"It's okay. Everything is okay now," he said, his fingertips gingerly touching the scar above her eyebrow and his thumbs brushing away her tears.

"But it's not, Russ. Can't you see that I'm different than before? Can't you?" Nora asked, losing control of her emotions as she gazed into his eyes.

"So am I, Nor," Russ replied, kissing her again.

"Russ I . . .," Nora hesitated.

"What is it, Nor?"

"I need to tell you something. I thought you weren't coming back when I didn't hear from you, and I began seeing someone while you were away. It's over now, but I need you to forgive me. Will you forgive me, Russ?" Nora asked, confessing her wrongdoing.

"I know all about him," Russ said.

"You do?" Nora asked, stepping back and sniffling.

"I took care of him, Nor. He won't bother you again."

"I don't understand."

"I went to gas up my car and we had an exchange of words."

It all makes sense now. That's how Brant ended up in the hospital, Nora thought to herself.

"An exchange of words? He's in the hospital," Nora replied, scratching her head and trying to piece things together in her mind.

"He asked for it, Nor. He swung at me first. You see, just like you, I've done things I'm not so proud of," Russ replied.

Nora's thoughts raced back to the hospital, and she recalled overhearing Brant and Libby's conversation. She pondered the moment when Brant and Libby's lips were locked together in a passionate kiss, as a lump formed in her throat.

"Nor? Will you forgive me too?" Russ asked, looking down, then looking back up at her, waiting for her to answer.

I will never be Brant Judge's fool again, Nora thought.

"He deserved what he got. Of course, I forgive you," Nora heard herself say, determined not to waste another care on Brant, wanting him to hurt as much as he had hurt her, as she rushed back into Russ' arms.

Nora realized the distance and circumstances had made it next to impossible for her and Russ to communicate on a regular basis and forces beyond their control created an unwanted wedge which fate filled with new experiences. Yet here they were. They were both changed, yet they were together once again. Restored and whole just as they were before the war tore them apart. It was a second chance to make things right, to pick up where they had left off and to forget about meeting Brant Judge the day her tire went flat. She desired nothing more than to forget about making love to Brant, his passionate kiss with Libby Vincent and all the sweet talk and lies he had spoon-fed her.

"Would you like to come inside?" Nora asked, hoping to make things right in her heart and longing to reclaim the time with Russ she had been robbed of.

"Your mother may not want me to."

"Too bad for her. My parents are out of town," Nora replied.

"No Viviane?" Russ asked.

"Nope. We have the place to ourselves," Nora said, tenderly kissing Russ on the lips again, taking him by the hand, and leading him up the porch steps.

"When will they be back?"

"Not until Sunday," Nora replied with a smile.

"We have a lot of lost time to make up for, don't we?" Russ asked, leaning in and kissing the scar above her eyebrow.

"Stay with me tonight, Russ," Nora whispered into his ear, not wanting to let him go and feeling that his return home couldn't have come at a better time.

"Are you sure?" Russ asked, his brow raised, and eyes fixed on hers.

"I need you, and I've never been more certain of anything in my life," Nora replied before letting Russ in and closing the door behind them.

20

"I've been trying to get ahold of you all morning. Where have you been, Nor?" Josie asked over the telephone line.

"Well . . .," Nora said, biting her lower lip and smiling to herself as she twirled the telephone cord around her index finger, having ignored the ringing of the incoming calls earlier that morning.

"Well, what? Nor, what's going on?"

"Russ is back. . . and we spent last night together. He just left," Nora replied with a giggle, his scent still lingering in the air around her.

"He's back and he spent the night? What am I missing here, Nor?"

"What do you mean?" Nora asked, taking a sip of orange juice from the glass on the kitchen table and feeling her tastebuds perk up as its acidity hit her tongue.

"I mean, what about Brant? I thought you were going to visit him at the hospital yesterday."

"I tried," Nora replied.

"You tried?" Josie asked, sounding confused.

"Jo, so much has happened in the past few days. Russ somehow found out about me and Brant. I didn't even know Russ was home, but they got into a fight and that's how Brant ended up in the hospital," Nora replied as she played with the cold, uneaten remnants of scrambled eggs on her plate with her fork.

"Jamie said Brant was really roughed up. Maybe you shouldn't jump right back into things with Russ. You really don't know what he's capable of."

"Maybe Brant deserved it," Nora replied, matter of factly.

"Maybe Brant deserved it? What's gotten into you, Nor? Why would you say something like that?"

"Because Brant isn't who I thought he was."

"What do you mean?" Josie asked.

"Jo, when I went to the hospital, a girl was in his room visiting him."

"What girl? Who was she?"

"His old girlfriend."

"That stuck-up priss, Libby Vincent?"

"Yes, and she wasn't just visiting him. She was sitting on his bed, cozied up to him and they were kissing. He was telling her that he loves her."

"That jerk! Maybe you're right. Maybe he did deserve it. I'm going to call Jack and . . ."

"No. Please don't, Jo."

"But he hurt you. You told me just a few days ago that you were in love with Brant."

"Jo, Russ is home now and Brant . . . well . . . Brant was just a summer fling I suppose."

"Nor, are you sure of what you saw?"

"Of course, I'm sure of what I saw and what I overheard. It made me sick to my stomach, Jo, but I'm going to do just as you said. I'm going to move on now that Russ is home."

"Maybe you should take some time for yourself. You need to sort through your emotions and figure things out. It's okay to think of yourself first," Josie encouraged her.

"I have things figured out already, Jo, and besides, Russ needs me. He told me that I'm the only thing that got him through his time in Vietnam. He kept my picture in the pocket of his jacket the whole time he was there . . . the one you took of me on your campus last fall," Nora said.

"Ultimately, you need to do what's right for you, but don't let these men manipulate you, Nor."

"I won't. You know, it's not like Russ to do something like that. He must have been feeling threatened. He told me last night that, through his training and time in Vietnam, he can sense when someone has it out for him. He said he could tell Brant was a dirty rat, just like the enemy in Vietnam. Russ' eyes looked empty too, like something was missing from them. He said when his airplane landed in San Francisco, there was an angry group of war protesters throwing things him and the other GIs. When he landed in Boston, some lady sent her bratty kid over to kick him and call him an awful name. He was so hurt. These anti-war protesters have gone too far, and I'm worried about him, Jo."

"You know a lot of guys are coming home from Vietnam messed up, Nor. I read an article in the *Globe* about a condition they're calling combat fatigue. Some of the GIs still think they are fighting in the war when they get back," Josie stated.

"Combat fatigue?" Nora repeated, not having heard the term before.

"Yes, but that still doesn't make what he did okay," Josie said.

"I know, but Russ did say that Brant threw the first punch," Nora replied.

"Still, it sounds to me like Russ flew off the handle. You need to be careful."

"I know, Jo," Nora replied.

"My mom's calling me. I've got to go, Nor. Call me later."

"Okay. I will. Goodbye, Jo," Nora said, hearing a click on the other end of the line and returning the phone to its receiver.

Nora sighed and began to clear the breakfast dishes from the table. Seconds later, the telephone rang again and she placed the dishes back down to answer it.

"Oh, Jo. What now?"

"Nora?" a male caller on the other end of the line asked.

"Yes?" Nora replied, recognizing the voice and feeling her body stiffen.

"Hey, where have you been?" Brant Judge asked, his voice weary.

Stay cool and don't let him manipulate you, she thought to herself as she nervously played with the curled telephone cord.

"Nora? Are you there?"

"Yes. I'm here," Nora replied.

"Where have you been?" Brant asked.

Busy trying to forget about you and Libby, Nora thought to herself.

"I've been busy and a bit under the weather," Nora replied, being intentionally vague.

"Busy?"

Not as busy as you, Nora thought.

"Yes. Busy," Nora quickly answered.

"What's been keeping you so busy that you wouldn't be concerned about the fight your old boyfriend started with me? I guess by now you know he's back in town and I'm in the hospital," Brant said with obvious agitation in his voice.

"Yes, I'm aware he's home and I couldn't be happier about it," Nora snarkily replied.

"Is that so?"

"Yes, and he needs me . . . to help him," Nora continued.

"He needs you to help him. Help him what?"

"To help him adjust back to civilian life. Something happened to him," Nora said.

"I don't know what happened to him, but I need you. Nora, I love you. What happened to you telling him it's over and that we are together now?"

Libby Vincent, sitting on your lap in your hospital bed is what happened, Nora thought as she bit her lip, determined not to play his game.

"Russ and I have a long history together and I promised him that I would wait for him. I owe him another chance," Nora firmly stated, steering the conversation in the direction she intended it to go.

"You don't owe him anything, especially after he put me in the hospital. Or did you forget about that? Let me get this straight. Russ shows up at my place of employment, starts a fight with me, puts me in the hospital and you feel you owe him something. Do I have that right?"

Yes, you've got that one hundred percent right and you can have Libby Vincent all to yourself too, Nora sarcastically thought. "Russ would never act that way unless provoked. That's not like him," Nora responded, keeping her composure.

"Well, I never provoked anyone. You know me, Nora. I thought you trusted me. I thought you wanted a future with me," Brant replied.

I did until I saw your true colors and heard you telling Libby that you are so in love with her, Nora wanted to scream out.

"Brant, I still love Russ. What you and I shared together was nothing more than . . . a summer fling," Nora said, hearing the sting in her words.

"A summer fling? What are you saying? Is that all I was to you?"

"I won't argue this with you," Nora replied, standing her ground.

"It wasn't a summer fling for me. I love you, Nora, but I'm not willing to wait until you hash things out with him. You need to decide, is it him or me?" Brant asked sounding impatient.

"Brant, don't you understand? It's too late."

"What don't I understand?"

Nora remained silent on the other end of the line.

"Oh. . . I understand clearly now. I hope you're happy, Nora Thompson. It's been . . . fun!" Brant angrily replied before the phone went silent.

Nora hung up, gathered her thoughts and turned to see the large mess of dishes still waiting for her in the kitchen sink. They were a small mess compared to the mess she had just cleaned up with Brant Judge and Nora watched as her tears dripped into the sudsy water below.

21

The sign on the office door read "Mr. Roland Edmunds - Manager" in bold black letters. *Well now isn't he Mr. Important. Another big shot mid-level manager*, Russ laughed to himself. It was his fourth job interview in the past two weeks, and he was anticipating another rejection. With each interview came schmoozing and small talk, ultimately culminating in rejection when the managers learned he had been in Vietnam. Russ was growing discouraged and found it less than coincidental that the vibe of each interview, and the attitude of the hiring managers, drastically changed every time the word Vietnam was uttered. It was as if he had a black mark on his forehead or a sign around his neck reading "Proceed With Caution: Baby Killer." After leaving the fact that he had been in Vietnam off his job application, Russ had made it through to the second round of interviews with this latest company.

Russ ran his index finger inside the collar of his starched button-down shirt. The dress shirt gave him the polished look he knew all the managers wanted to see, but it itched like hell.

Mr. Edmunds' secretary, wearing a snug wrap dress that accentuated her trim waistline and full bosom, sat behind her desk looking into her compact mirror and applying red lipstick around her open mouth. Russ took notice that her lipstick appeared to be a shade similar to that worn by the prostitutes in Saigon and he tried not to stare. The nameplate on her desk read 'Darlene – Secretary' and Russ wondered if she was as cheap and easy as she appeared to be as she turned her head in his direction and caught him watching her. Russ quickly looked away, then looked back to see she had removed her large framed eyeglasses. After placing the tip of the arm of her eyeglasses in her mouth, Darlene bit down, exposing her white front teeth as she seductively looked him over. She had hinted that meeting Mr. Edmunds was the final step before being offered a position at New England Underground Cable Company.

"Mr. Edmunds is my uncle. He's a bit of a bigot but if he likes you, you're in. I can put in a good word for you if you'd like, Russell," she said softly, giving Russ a wink and a sultry smile.

"I'd appreciate that," Russ replied as the secretary flirted with him and softly giggled to herself before putting paper into her typewriter and getting to work.

I need this job, Russ thought to himself as he tried not to let Mr. Edmunds' niece distract him any more than she already had. Since he was unable to finish his program at Providence Tech after being drafted, he knew he would have to charm the interviewing manager in order to win him over. One thing Vietnam had taught him was that it's all about survival and he was willing to do whatever it took to land this job.

Russ sat, impatiently shaking his knee up and down, in the rigid reception area chair. *Don't blow it. Don't talk about Vietnam*, he repeated to himself as he looked down at his polished loafers, placing the palm of his hand on his knee to stop it from bouncing. *Just listen and stay calm before you say or do anything . . . just like they taught you to do in the tunnels*, he thought. He knew if he remained calm, he would be able to outsmart this Mr. Edmunds guy, just like he did Charlie, and land the job.

Russ remained still and listened as Darlene tapped the keys of her typewriter. Soon his reflexes took over, and he felt his body stiffen, as a faint sound of the knob to the manager's office door turning caught his ear. *It's showtime*, he thought as from behind the door stepped a round man with a bad comb-over who was wearing a brown plaid suit and a red tie that matched his ruddy complexion.

"Russell Ayers?"

Isn't it obvious that I'm Russell Ayers? I'm the only one waiting here you blowhard, Russ thought, being the sole candidate in the waiting area.

"Yes, Sir. That would be me," Russ said, flashing a smile and turning on the charm.

"I'm Roland Edmunds. Please step into my office," he instructed, ushering him into the room.

"Good luck, handsome," Darlene whispered as she twirled a strand of her silky brown hair around her red-polished fingertips, her gaze fixed on him.

You certainly didn't get your looks from your uncle that's for sure, Russ thought, as he passed by Darlene's desk. Upon entering Mr. Edmunds' office, he was greeted with dark paneled walls, tall metal filing cabinets, a spider plant in a macrame hanger and a plethora of certificates of achievement hanging about the room.

"Good to meet you, Sir," Russ said. *Not really*, Russ thought, as he extended his hand and shook the manager's plump, sweaty palm.

"Have a seat," the manager directed him, exhaling a hint of coffee-scented breath in Russ' direction and pointing to another stiff chair in front of his cluttered, steel, tanker desk.

As he took a seat, Russ observed the desktop, littered with stacks of seemingly important papers topped with glass paperweights. In the center of the desk, sat a mug half full of coffee along with the remnants of a jelly doughnut. A framed photograph of Mr. Edmunds, standing in front of the Grand Canyon with his unattractive wife and their three pudgy offspring, sat at an outward facing angle on the left corner of the desk. Russ became distracted and shifted in his seat as he imagined the names of Mr. Edmunds' children to be Greed, Gluttony and Sloth. Sitting on the corner of the desk to Russ' right was a small American flag on a cheap plastic stand.

This guy is living the dream, Russ thought to himself. "Nice office you have here, Sir," Russ lied.

"Thanks. My wife decorated it for me," Mr. Edmunds replied, wiping a drip of jelly off his necktie with a paper napkin.

Well now, of course she did, Russ thought as the manager stated the obvious.

"So, let's get started. As you probably already know, our company manufactures components and cables for use in the industrial sector. We rely on government contracts to keep this place up and running," he said picking up the small American flag and waving it from side to side before placing it back on its stand.

"I understand," Russ replied.

"The cables we manufacture are placed underground. You see . . . there are tunnels that are dug deep into the ground and our cables are run through them. Some of our cables are for underwater use and placed on the ocean floor. Do you know much about that sort of thing?"

"Yes, Sir. I'm somewhat familiar with that technology."

I'm more familiar with tunnels than you'll ever know, Old Chum, Russ thought.

"I see here that you are a graduate of Swanset High School and attended Providence Tech."

"Yes, Sir. That's right. I was enrolled in their electronics program."

"Have you finished all your courses there?"

"No. Not yet, Sir," Russ replied, feeling himself starting to perspire.

"Why haven't you finished?"

"Well, Sir . . . you see . . . I had obligations on the home front to tend to," Russ replied, trying not to offer up too much information.

"Obligations? Okay, well now that's . . . understandable . . . I suppose," the manager replied giving a hearty laugh and flipping through the pages of Russ' application.

"I need someone reliable. Someone who can show up on time and catch on quick. Time is money, so I need someone who can accomplish the tasks he is handed. You look like a sharp enough kid. You're clean cut and you don't speak broken English. Do you think you have what it takes?"

"Yes, Sir. Yes, I do."

"I'll need you to start within the next few weeks. The starting salary is modest, but we offer a good benefit package and mediocre coffee in the breakroom every day," he joked.

"Okay."

"There's no smoking allowed except in designated areas outside . . . and no drinking on the job," he said, handing Russ the company handbook and information on the position's compensation package.

"Sounds good to me," Russ eagerly replied.

"You should know that you were in the right place at the right time, Robert."

"Russell. My name is Russell, Sir."

"Yes. Of course. Russell. Anyhow, we just won a new government contract with strict deadlines to meet. When your application came through, you were the only candidate who didn't have tits, a language barrier, or some other impediment. Damn greenhorns here in Weaver Falls. Is there anything else I should know about you, or do you have any questions for me?"

"You seemed to cover all the bases, Mr. Edmunds."

"Well then, the job is yours, Robert. Welcome to the New England Underground Cable Company family," Mr. Edmunds said, getting up from behind his desk, extending his hand with its thick, sausage-like fingers, and offering him another clammy handshake.

"Thank you, Sir . . . and the name is Russell," Russ replied, feeling the sweat from Mr. Edmunds' palm.

After wiping his hand on the leg of his trousers, Russ exited the interview with his new employee handbook and documents in tow, glad to have secured a job, yet peeved. After locating his car in the parking lot, he settled into its driver's seat. Striking his lighter and taking a drag of his freshly lit cigarette, Russ felt his tension ease. His mind momentarily drifted to the sultry secretary who had come on to him and walked him to the door to see him out, smiling as he replayed watching her applying her lipstick. He then pondered why it had been necessary for him to conceal that he had honorably served his country in order to land a menial job that served mediocre coffee in the breakroom. The irony of the stars and stripes that flew on the flagpole outside the building's entrance, representing valor, purity and justice, made him smirk. Russ let the cigarette burn down and took one final drag before putting it out in the ashtray. He revved the engine, releasing tension with each press of the pedal under his foot, and gave Old Glory a military salute before putting the car in gear and exiting the premises.

22

Russ felt his heart pump fast and hard, as he made his way up the porch steps. Behind his back he held a bouquet of fresh daisies, tied with a green satin ribbon. Letting out an audible breath he knocked on the front door. He ran his fingers through his thick hair, happy that it had finally grown back in since receiving his last military buzzcut. *I sure hope Viviane doesn't answer the door*, he thought to himself. When the sound of footsteps caught his ear, Russ stood up tall, at attention, his military training ingrained in him. A turn of the doorknob revealed Mr. Thompson, in his reading glasses, with the daily newspaper in his hand. *Phew, good to see you, Rich*, Russ thought, dropping his shoulders and relaxing.

"Russell!" Mr. Thompson exclaimed.

"Hello, Mr. Thompson," Russ replied, reaching out and shaking his extended hand.

"I was wondering when you were going to come by. I'm sure you've been busy since you've been back. How are you?"

"I'm fine, Sir," Russ replied, knowing that he really wasn't.

"Come. Come inside," Mr. Thompson said, stepping aside.

"It's okay, Sir. It's such a nice day. Too nice to be inside," Russ said, feeling an unquenchable desire for fresh air and open spaces after having had a restless night dreaming he was trapped inside the Cu Chi tunnels and being hunted by Viet Cong.

"Okay. I'll let Nora know you are here then. Feel free to have a seat on the porch while you're waiting," Mr. Thompson replied with a nod, glancing at the bouquet of flowers in Russ' hand.

"Thank you," Russ politely replied.

Russ took a seat on the porch swing and admired the lush baskets of Boston ferns hanging from the ceiling. With his tactile senses still sharp from his time in the tunnels, he detected a rough surface under his palm. He lifted his hand to see the paint had worn off the swing's armrest, leaving a patch of raw wood exposed. He soon found himself mindlessly peeling at the paint's loose edges with his fingernail as he anxiously waited for Nora to join him outside. In recent weeks, he had become overwhelmed by the internal strife dwelling just beneath the surface of his rugged exterior. As he exposed more of the raw wood, he realized that, sooner or later, he would need to peel back some of his own layers and expose the truth to Nora about his struggles since returning home.

Startled by the sound of the screen door opening, Russ jumped up from the porch swing. As he looked up to see Nora emerging from the house, he felt his breath momentarily swept away at the mere sight of her, in awe of her natural beauty. Her flare-legged jeans hugged her hips and her gauzy, embroidered blouse swayed as she moved. Nora's long hair was neatly hanging down with a center part and she wore a braided, suede headband around her forehead, concealing her scar. Her glossed lips sparkled, and Russ longed to kiss her right then and there but knew Viviane was probably spying on them from behind the drapes of the front window. Nora's eyes, with their soft green irises, glistened as she stepped out onto the porch, instantly putting him at ease.

"Hi, Nor," Russ said.

"Hi," Nora replied, as a smile crossed her face.

"I got these for you," Russ said, handing her the bouquet of daisies.

"Thank you. They're beautiful," she replied, stepping closer and brushing her lips against his.

"Just like you."

"You know they're my favorite," Nora said, stroking the soft white petals with her fingertips.

"So, you said you wanted to talk?"

"Yes, but not here. My parents are just inside. I hope you didn't eat lunch yet. I made us a picnic and thought we could take a walk over to Ashen Park."

"Sounds good to me."

"I'll be right back. Let me put these in a vase and grab the picnic basket."

Russ took the basket from her when she returned, and Nora reached for his free hand as they proceeded down the sidewalk.

"I think I saw your mother peeking out from behind the curtain when you went inside."

"I saw her there too. She pretended she was measuring for new curtains, but I know she usually has my father do that," Nora said, shaking her head.

"I see she hasn't changed," Russ said with a chuckle.

"Unfortunately, she hasn't," Nora replied.

"Do you ever hear from Emily?"

"No. You know my mother has a way with words and dissuaded her from coming home the last time she called. I miss her very much but find myself angry at her sometimes for leaving me to deal with Viviane alone."

"She'll be back someday."

"It would be nice but I'm not banking on it. I'm just glad you're back, Russ," Nora said as they entered the park.

"I'd never leave you, Nor," Russ said, stopping in front of a large oak tree.

"Promise?"

"I promise," he replied, putting down the picnic basket and embracing her.

Russ observed his surroundings and saw the park was filled with kids playing on the merry-go-round and monkey bars. Anxious parents stood cautiously nearby, watching and coaxing their children out of potentially dangerous situations on the playground. Sounds of cheering spectators echoed past them, as a lucky kid hit a home run in the youth baseball game being played in the corner field. Although the sights and sounds told him that his environment was safe, Russ found himself gazing beyond the ball field toward the tree line, on alert for potential threats.

"What are you looking at?" Nora asked, spreading out the blanket she had been carrying.

"What did you say?"

"You looked lost in thought. I asked what you were looking at."

"I was just thinking about something."

"Obviously. Could you elaborate a bit?" Nora asked, letting out a giggle.

"Well, I was thinking about . . . when I used to play youth baseball. That's all," Russ fibbed.

"Oh, that's sweet," Nora replied.

"No, it's not."

"It's not sweet?" Nora asked, opening the picnic basket.

"No. I mean it's not what I was thinking about just then," Russ replied.

"Okay. So, why did you say that if it wasn't true?" Nora asked, handing him a sandwich wrapped in waxed paper.

"Because I was afraid to worry you."

"Russ, you're confusing me. Please explain what you mean," Nora said, unscrewing the cover of the thermos and pouring lemonade into plastic cups.

"Nor, I have a lot of stuff going on in my head. Things you won't understand."

"Russ, what's going on? I know it has to do with Vietnam. What happened to you over there?" Nora asked, empathetically.

"It was screwed up, Nor. I saw my buddy Davis get . . .," Russ hesitated, afraid to scare Nora away if he revealed his experiences in the tunnels.

"You mentioned him in your letters. You were supposed to go to the U.S.O. show together. What happened to him?"

"I can't tell you, Nor. I can't bring myself to say it."

"Oh, Russ. He didn't make it, did he?"

Russ looked down and shook his head.

"Nor, I saw things there. I had to do things . . . things I didn't want to do . . . to a lot of people," Russ told her in a hush tone.

"Russ . . ."

"I can't tell you anymore, Nor. You'll think I'm a monster, if you don't already," Russ added.

"I don't think that," Nora assured him, appearing to sense his distress.

"It was the only way I could get out . . . alive. I feel like . . . I'm not right, Nor. I'm not sleeping . . . I can't remember things . . . and the things I can remember are all screwed up. There's so much static in my head and . . . these pills they gave me . . . I don't know if they're helping or making things worse. I've been drinking and smoking dope just so I can get some relief from my own thoughts."

Russ looked up at the branches of the large oak tree, searching for clarity amongst its rustling leaves and feeling as though something inside him was broken. He felt his face become wet with perspiration and tears, as his cheeks flushed with embarrassment that Nora was seeing him in a such a confused state of mind.

"I'm sorry you went through all that. I've been reading a lot about combat fatigue. Have you heard of it?" Nora asked.

"Yes, that's what the doctors in the Evac hospital were treating me for."

"Have you been to the doctor since you've been home?"

"No. I don't want to see any more doctors."

"It may help to find one. I could help you if you'd like."

"You would do that for me? Really, Nor?" Russ asked, trying to still his trembling hands.

"I'll try, but I need to ask you one more question. I didn't want to bring this up, but I need to understand how things got so violent that night at the gas station. I'm not blaming you, but you did strike Brant with a tire iron."

"I was angry. He was trying to steal you from me, Nor."

"It was as much my fault as it was his, Russ. You're lucky he didn't press charges against you. You need to be sure you don't lose control like that ever again, because that's not the Russ Ayers I know," Nora said, her gaze steady and giving his hand a firm squeeze.

"Nor, you're the only thing that got me through that hell in Vietnam. I know it wasn't right, but I couldn't control myself. I've been fighting to survive for so long. Even now, every day is still a fight to survive."

"We'll get through this," Nora said, giving his hand another squeeze.

"How? I don't know how. Nothing is making sense."

"I'm not sure. But maybe it will help to talk about it."

"I'm not sure that I'm strong enough, Nor."

"You're going to have to try, Russ. I'm going to have to try too."

"Try what?"

"We'll both have to try to be strong and forgive one another. We've both done things we aren't proud of, and those things can't be undone," Nora replied.

"I'll do anything to hold onto you, Nor."

"We both need to heal from what we've been through. Maybe we can do that together."

"I like the sound of that. Where do we begin?" Russ asked, looking to her for direction.

"Let's just sit here for a while, fill our lungs with fresh air and enjoy our picnic. How does that sound?" Nora asked.

"Sounds good, Nor," Russ replied, feeling his inner turmoil momentarily stilled.

23

Russ entered Swanset Savings Bank's marble-floored lobby and was met with a long, slow-moving line. He saw that only three tellers were working and resigned himself to the fact he would probably be there for a while.

"Ayers? Ayers, is that really you or are my eyes playing tricks on me?" Jeff Turner asked as he turned around and noticed his friend standing further back in line.

"Turner!" Russ exclaimed as Jeff made his way over to him and gave him a firm handshake and pat on the back.

"Hey, I heard you were back in town."

"Good to see you. I've been back for a few weeks, but I've been busy looking for work. I just got hired over at New England Underground Cable."

"Hey, congratulations!"

"Thanks. I start next week. How are things going with your father's business?"

"I've been learning a lot from my old man. He's quite the carpenter. We've been busy with some new construction on the outskirts of town by the old ball field."

"Far out."

"Next in line," a teller called out from behind her window.

"I'm next. Hey, Sherry and I are heading over to the Swanset Fair. You and Nora should meet us there."

"We were already planning to go too. After I'm done here, I'm going to pick her up and head over there. We'll catch you later."

"Alright, man. Let's meet by the entrance at noon. Glad you made it back alive," Jeff said, before heading over to the window to complete his transaction.

As Russ waited in the slow-moving line, he recalled that Jeff had an asthmatic condition and had been issued an official waiver, disqualifying him from military service. While in high school, Jeff began working for his father's small contracting business and had been honing his finish-carpentry skills over the past year. Russ' train of thought was suddenly broken as he felt someone tap him on the shoulder.

"Hey, did I hear that guy say that you just got back? Were you in Vietnam?" a nasal voice behind him asked.

"Yeah, man. What's it to you?" Russ asked, startled and swiftly turning around to see a teenaged boy staring at him.

"My grandfather served in World War I and said Vietnam isn't a real war."

"He said that?" Russ asked, feeling his face begin to flush.

"He said it's just military policing and has never been declared an actual war."

"Is that so? Tell me, kid, do you do well in school and do you like history class?"

"History is my favorite subject," the boy eagerly replied.

"I'm going to let you in on some United States history that they won't teach you about at Swanset High or any fancy university. Are you listening?" Russ asked as the two migrated up the line.

"I'm listening."

"Listen real carefully now," Russ instructed.

"Okay. I said I'm listening," the boy replied as the line began to move forward again.

"Vietnam isn't just policing. It's a God damn war regardless of what our government says. It's a combat zone where the enemy uses guerilla tactics to kill smart aleck kids such as yourself. What they don't tell you is how American GIs bleed out and take their last breaths as their buddies airlift them out of that godforsaken jungle. All this happens while you're sitting in sophomore history class with your nose in a book, getting your first hard-on. Don't ever forget that Mr. Smarty-pants. While you're at it, be sure to tell your old grandpa to take his head out of his ass too."

The teenager stood speechless with his mouth hanging open, exposing his metal braces and red, swollen gums. Russ did an about-face, finding himself now at the front of the line.

"Next in line," the teller called out again, cautiously looking Russ over.

"Hey, are you okay?" Jeff said, returning to where Russ now stood after completing his transaction, sounding concerned after overhearing his friend's rant.

"I'm cool," Russ replied.

"Remember you're home now. Don't sweat it," Jeff reminded him.

"I know. Catch you later," Russ replied as Jeff turned to leave.

Whispers of other bank patrons, seemingly appalled by the conversation they had just overheard, filled the lobby. Their mumbling voices descended on Russ like a thick fog, surrounding him, and making it impossible to see a clear way out of the hell he had returned home to. Exiting the bank, Russ spit on the ground, hoping to eliminate the sour taste in his mouth. Settling into the driver's seat of his car, he lit up a cigarette and thought that a fun day at the Swanset Fair with Nora and his friends was just what he needed.

24

Russ knew how much Nora loved attending the Swanset Fair each year and she was eager to join him for a day of games, rides and carnival food. Russ smiled as Nora seemed genuinely happy when he told her he had been offered a job at New England Underground Cable.

"That's great, Russ," Nora said, rubbing his shoulder.

"Thanks, Nor. It's not a lot of money though," Russ replied.

"It's a start and you can work your way up the ladder. Russ, before I forget, I wanted to give this to you. Its Dr. Perkins' telephone number. He's nice and I think you'll like him. I told his secretary, Miss Hargrove, to expect a call from you," Nora said, handing him a folded piece of paper. "He's very trustworthy and can help you to get your medications straightened out," Nora added.

"Thanks, I'll be sure to call there soon. Look, we're here, Nor," Russ said, pulling into the dirt parking lot of the fairgrounds.

"I see Jeff and Sherry there by the ticket booth," Nora said, pointing toward the entrance.

"Well let's go!" Russ replied, opening his car door.

After exchanging hugs with Jeff and Sherry and purchasing their tickets, the group of friends walked through the fairgrounds. The two couples joked like old times, ate cotton candy and tried their hands at carnival games like darts and ring toss. Russ tried to focus on having fun with his friends but couldn't help feeling uneasy as he became engulfed in the crowd. The noises coming from all directions were putting him on edge and Russ found himself pulling away to light up a cigarette.

"Step right up. Hey, you! Try your luck and win a prize for that pretty girl standing next to you," the man behind the booth called out to Russ.

"Go ahead, Russ. Go try to win something for Nora," Sherry urged while holding a blue, plush dog in the crook of her arm.

"Yeah, man. What are you waiting for? I bet you're a better shot than anyone here. Even I won that for Sherry, and I'm a lousy shot," Jeff said encouragingly.

"No. It's okay. Really, Russ. You don't have to," Nora interjected.

Russ, constantly scanning the crowd, tried to tune out the noise around him as his heart rhythm increased in the dense mass of fair patrons. He was feeling like his senses were overloaded as his friends tried to coax him into playing the carnival game. Russ took a drag of his cigarette as his eyes focused on the gun lying on the counter under the carnival booth's striped awning. His mind transported him back to the last time he held a gun in his hands, vividly recalling the VC's lifeless body that took the bullet.

"C'mon, Ayers," Jeff urged again.

"What's up with him?" Sherry asked Jeff under her breath.

"Look at me, Russ," Nora said, pulling him aside, her gaze steady as if trying to get him to focus his thoughts.

"What is it, Nor?" Russ replied, stamping his cigarette out in the dirt.

"Russ, I see how you're looking at that gun. It's just a toy. You don't need to play that game and I don't need a silly stuffed animal."

"What do you say? Do you want to win the lady a prize or not?" the impatient worker called out again.

"Hold your horses!" Russ yelled back.

"Russ, you have nothing to prove here today. It's just a stupid game," Nora told him again, her voice shaky.

"Nor, I'm not afraid. My gun was my lifeline and I always carried it with me. You've never seen me shoot and I want to show you what a good shot I am."

"Are you sure?"

"Yes, I'm sure. Now what stuffed animal do you want me to try for?"

"Gee, I don't know."

"How about that dumb looking monkey over there? You see that big yellow one? It's your favorite color."

"It's technically a gorilla, not a monkey. But sure. Go for it," Nora giggled.

"Okay. I'm ready," Russ said as he approached the booth and handed over his tickets.

"About time. You get only three tries. If you get a bullseye on all three targets, you'll be able to pick one of those giant plush animals from over there on the left."

"I'm going for the big yellow monkey my friend."

"Gorilla. It's a gorilla, Russ," Nora corrected him.

"Okay. It's a gorilla. Nor, are you ready to watch this?"

"I'm ready."

Russ ran his hand over the body of the cork air gun, trying to get a tactile read on its exterior. He had not fired a shot since the day Davis died. Instead, he relied on his knife and his bare hands to get the job done for the remainder of his time underground, gruesomely taking out the pain he felt from Davis' death on his enemy. As he picked up the air gun and gripped it firmly, images of Charlie suddenly appeared in his mind and he was brought back to the foreign land for a fleeting moment. With his eye on the target, he fired the cork gun once, twice, three times in rapid succession. Each pull of the trigger provided a quick release of pressure. When he was done, he returned the gun back to the counter and wiped sweat from his brow.

"Wow!" the carnival worker exclaimed.

"Shit, Ayers. Three bullseyes!" Jeff cheered.

As his mind snapped back to the carnival, he turned to see Jeff and Sherry jumping up and down with excitement. Nora stood still, looking as if she were aware he had just gone someplace else in his mind. Russ breathed in the aroma of roasting hot dogs and buttery popcorn that enveloped him. The sounds of kids laughing and carnival music filled the air around him. At that moment, Russ realized where he was, safe at the carnival, and took a few steps over to where Nora was standing.

"Nor . . .," Russ said, his eyes wide and alert.

"I know, Russ. It's okay. It was just a game," she said, wrapping her arms around him.

Her hug grounded him and reminded him that he was safe.

"What prize did you say you wanted?" the worker called out.

"The big yellow monkey. I mean gorilla!" Nora yelled back to him.

The carnival worker reached back, picked up the large plush gorilla and handed it to Russ.

"He's all yours, Nor. What are you going to name him?"

"Well, he's so . . . yellow. It looks like he just ate a bunch of bananas. I think I'll name him Bananas?"

"Ha, ha. That's a great name," Russ replied, placing the giant, plush toy on his back.

"You have a wicked good shot, Ayers," Jeff complimented.

"Better than you, that's for sure. All I got was this dinky little thing," Sherry joked, as she tossed the tiny stuffed dog into her purse.

"Look, Sherry. It's The Tunnel of Love," Jeff said, squeezing Sherry's waist as they walked.

"Every year we've come to this carnival together, this ride is always Jeff's favorite," Sherry joked.

"That's right it is. Let's get in line. I could use a little loving, Sher," Jeff said, urging Sherry along.

"You guys are too much," Nora said.

"Aren't you coming with us?" Sherry asked.

"We'll sit this one out. I think I want to try a different ride. We'll meet up with you lovebirds later," Nora told them.

"Okay. Catch you later," Sherry replied as she and Jeff hurried over to the line.

"I figured we could sit that ride out," Nora said, turning to Russ.

"That's probably a wise idea."

"Because of the tunnel part. Not because of the love part," Nora explained.

"I've seen enough tunnels for one lifetime."

"I know you have."

"What did you mean just now?" Russ asked.

"About what?"

"When you said it's not because of the love part."

"Just what I meant. I thought of you a lot while you were away and prayed for your safe return. I never stopped loving you, Russ. Let's go and see what kind of rides are over here," Nora said as Russ followed behind with Bananas on his back.

"Hey look, Nor. A Ferris wheel. Do you want to try it?" Russ asked.

"Uh, I don't know."

"Why not? C'mon."

"You know I don't like heights."

"It will be fun. Besides, you have me and Bananas here to keep you company up there," Russ convincingly said as they walked toward the giant wheel.

Once through the ticket line and the turn-style, Russ and Nora climbed into the bench seat and secured the safety bar. Russ took a seat on the right side, leaving Nora in the middle, sandwiched between him and Bananas. As the wheel moved slowly, allowing other fairgoers to take a seat, Nora gripped the safety bar tightly.

"Are you okay, Nor?" Russ asked, sensing her apprehension.

"I don't think this is a good idea, Russ."

"Just hold on. You're going to be fine."

"I don't know if I can do this."

"Of course, you can, Nor. I know you can," Russ said, putting his arm around her.

"Thank you," she said, turning her head and looking directly at him.

Russ felt his heart skip a beat as her eyes locked on his.

Suddenly, the wheel began to move, taking them to new heights as it rotated in the late afternoon sky.

"This reminds me of the rides in the Huey. They would take off with the doors wide open," Russ said, enjoying the freedom of being off the ground and surrounded by the cool air.

"I've only been in an airplane, never a helicopter. Oh gosh. . . I've never been up this high before," Nora said anxiously, looking down at the top of the tents scattered about the fairground below.

Their seat lightly swayed back and forth as the Ferris wheel continued turning. Soon it brought them to the highest point in its rotation.

"Look, Nor. There's Swanset High," Russ said, pointing to his left.

"Where?" Nora asked, squinting her eyes to try to make out the details of buildings off in the distance.

"Right there. See the cupola and the flagpole?"

"There it is. I see it now!" Nora exclaimed, turning her head toward him.

"That's where it all began, Nor."

"Where it all began," Nora reiterated.

High above Swanset, surrounded by the sounds of the carnival emanating from the fairground below, Russ leaned in and pressed his lips against Nora's. Her lips welcomed his and, as she kissed him back, he felt an exchange of love between them that was true and unspoiled by the cruelty of the world beneath them. Russ then felt his heart skip another beat, reminding him that he was still very much alive.

25

Nora brushed her damp hair and directed the blow dryer's warm stream of air around her head while thinking about the items she needed to purchase for her dorm room for the upcoming semester. She was eager to return to campus and start her junior year. *I'll be happy to get back to school and put this summer behind me,* Nora thought.

The fast-approaching September deadline for completing her college physical had slipped her mind amidst all the recent changes in her life. Luckily, an appointment came open at the end of August and Dr. Perkins' medical secretary, Miss Hargrove, was able to pencil her in. Dr. Perkins was a sweet man who had been her family's doctor her entire life. Viviane, who was always looking to rub elbows with the right people, had become friendly with his wife while doing charity work and serving as members of Swanset's garden club. Nora reflected on how, during her office visit, Dr. Perkins questioned her about her general health. She disclosed the episodes of stomach upset she had earlier in the summer and felt herself blush when he asked her if she was sexually active. She could not bring herself to tell him the truth, afraid that word would get back to Viviane. *Maybe Dr. Perkins can sense I'm being dishonest,* she thought to herself as he recommended running what he referred to as "a few extra tests," taking both a blood and urine sample.

Nora ran her fingers through her long locks to check for dryness and looked out the bathroom window at the gloomy sky. According to the local news station, stormy weather was expected through the weekend. She hoped to get out the door before the inclement weather arrived to enjoy lunch with Josie but was determined to intercept Miss Hargrove's telephone call with her test results before leaving the house.

Nora turned off the hairdryer and was struck with a sudden wave of panic as she heard the telephone ringing. *Quick! Answer it before Viviane does*, she thought, dropping her brush on the bathroom floor and sprinting down the hall. Picking up the hallway extension, she heard Viviane's voice on the line. Nora stayed as quiet as possible, putting her hand over the telephone's mouthpiece so that Viviane wouldn't suspect her to be listening in.

"Hello, Miss Hargrove. How can I help you?" Viviane asked.

"I'm calling to let you know that Nora's test results are in," Miss Hargrove replied.

"Test results? Nora simply saw Dr. Perkins for her college physical earlier this week," Viviane informed her.

"Mrs. Thompson, Dr. Perkins also ran some tests. I don't know any easy way to tell you this but your daughter's pregnancy test came back positive."

Nora stood paralyzed in disbelief as the reality of the situation set in. *I can't be*, Nora thought.

"Pregnant? You are surely mistaken, Miss Hargrove," Viviane said, sounding shocked by the revelation.

"No, Mrs. Thompson. I have the results right here in front of me. Dr. Perkins asked me to call you right away."

"That cannot be right. Let me speak with Dr. Perkins right this minute," Viviane insisted.

"I'm sorry, but Dr. Perkins is busy with patients. I can have him call you back later if you'd like," Miss Hargrove offered.

"Of course! Yes. Please have Dr. Perkins call me as soon as he has a moment. Thank you for calling," Viviane said, sounding as if she was trying to keep her composure.

Nora hung up the hallway extension and hurried to her room, locking the door behind her. Absorbing the news, she nervously paced back and forth, creating a matted path on her bedroom's shag carpet. She then glanced at the calendar hanging over her desk and began to flip through its pages. Her finger landed on June ninth, where she had written "Josie's Surprise Party" in the box. *That was the night of the full moon . . . when I lost my virginity with Brant on Swanset Beach.*

"My nausea started shortly after that, but I thought it was just my nerves. Could I have been . . .?" she whispered to herself, biting her lower lip and trying to make sense of it all.

She then flipped the page of the calendar to display the month of July. *Sunday July fourth. That's the day Brant and I snuck down to the dock and made it in the skiff.*

"I started having nausea in early July. I remember because I was feeling sick right after I got back from Long Island . . . the same day I saw Libby and Brant in the hospital kissing," Nora whispered to herself again, scanning the calendar one last time, frantically flipping the pages back and forth, repeatedly counting the days and in denial that what Miss Hargrove said was true.

"Then Russ came home . . . and we . . . maybe its . . .," Nora said to herself, before covering her mouth with her trembling hand.

A moment later, she heard a screaming match erupt downstairs and knew that this was one argument between her parents that she would have to take full credit for.

"Nora Thompson, get yourself down here right now. Your father and I need to talk to you!" Viviane angrily yelled from the bottom of the staircase.

Reluctantly emerging from behind her locked bedroom door, Nora made her way downstairs, dreading the fallout from her actions, and from the telephone call she failed to intercept. Her parents' shouting continued to get louder as she proceeded toward the kitchen.

"That's enough, Viviane. I will not allow you to talk about her like that," Richard Thompson yelled to his wife, his cheeks flushing.

"I would have expected this from Emily, but not from her. If she had abstained as she was taught, we wouldn't be in this predicament!" Viviane screeched.

Both Richard and Viviane turned their heads in Nora's direction when they noticed her standing in the doorway. Seeing the disappointment in their faces, Nora was overcome with shame and swiped her hand against her cheek to catch a tear that had trickled out of her eye.

"Oh, there she is! Save your tears, young lady. You're going to need them in nine months when you're sitting in the delivery room with your legs in stirrups. Dr. Perkins' office called today to inform me that you, Nora Thompson, are pregnant. What do you have to say for yourself?" Viviane prodded.

"I'm nineteen years old and it was unrealistic of you to expect me to abstain."

"What did you just say?" Viviane asked through gritted teeth.

"It's true. All the girls I know at Bridgegate go to the campus health clinic for contraceptives. Now that I'm out of school for the summer, I couldn't get a diaphragm or birth control pills because the doctors in private practice will only prescribe them to married women," Nora replied.

"Well, that's why I told you to abstain. Instead, you chose to be a tramp and get yourself pregnant," Viviane screeched.

"Stop right now, Viv, or I swear . . .," Richard began.

"You swear what, Richard? Well? The whole town is going to be talking about us if they aren't already. We raised you in a good home and this is the thanks we get."

"Viviane!" Richard interjected but was once again interrupted by Viviane's harsh tongue.

"You will not shame this family, young lady. Do you hear me?" Viviane screamed, inching her way closer to her daughter with each syllable.

"Mom, women have options now. I have options," Nora said, becoming silent as Viviane approached her and raised her arm. Seconds later Nora felt the sting of her mother's hand across her face.

"Do not lay another hand on her, Viviane!" Richard yelled, grabbing his wife's arm.

"Do not tell me about options. You will not have a child out of wedlock and abortion is not an option in this household if that's what you have in mind. I suppose that promiscuous friend of yours put those ideas in your head. I always knew that Henson girl was trouble," Viviane hollered, not allowing Nora to speak.

Nora looked with desperation to her father for help.

"Daddy, please. I'm not ready for any of this. I want to finish my degree. I'm supposed to go back to school next week. Daddy, I . . . I don't know what to do," Nora pleaded, unable to control her emotions a moment longer.

"I'm going to tell you what to do," Richard calmly assured her, lovingly wrapping his arms around her.

Nora had a special bond with her father and was grateful she had at least one parent she could rely on. She knew deep down she was one of the causes of her parents' marital problems, as she was the apple of her father's eye. Viviane, who always needed to be the center of attention, was not good at hiding her jealousy very well when her husband showed his affection for Nora. She had also figured out that her parents only got married because Viviane herself had become pregnant with Emily. With her dreams derailed and a baby to care for, Viviane had grown bitter through the years. As sad as it sounded, Nora knew it was true. It now appeared that history was repeating itself and Mr. Thompson knew he needed to regain control of the situation since Viviane was obviously too angry to think rationally.

"I had bigger dreams for you, Nora," Viviane blurted out.

"You mean you had bigger dreams for yourself. Don't you, Mother?" Nora replied, holding her gaze.

"Stop it now! Both of you stop it. Viviane, do not say another word. Nora, I want you to call Russell and ask him to come by for dinner tomorrow night. He and I are going to have ourselves a talk," Mr. Thompson said.

"But . . .," Nora sobbed, unable to admit to her father that she had not always been the good girl he thought her to be.

"Do as I say. Give him a call. Please, Nora. Everything is going to be fine," Mr. Thompson reassured her.

"Okay. I'll do as you say. Thank you," Nora said, kissing her father's cheek.

Feeling Viviane's seething glare follow her out of the kitchen, Nora made her way up the staircase and thought about what she was going to say to Russ. She picked up the hallway telephone and heard its agitating hum in her ear. She hesitated dialing Russ' number, slammed the phone back down on its receiver and took a few steps back.

She was aware the phone call she was about to make would be life altering and reflected on how she had already put the nail in the coffin when it came to her and Brant's relationship. *He would want no part of me now after the things I said to him and besides, he can't be trusted. Libby Vincent can have him for all I care*, Nora told herself. *Russ has been sincere. I can see he is struggling but he said he needs me*, Nora thought. She was certain of only two things- that Viviane felt abortion was not an option and Russ still needed help adjusting back to civilian life. *He's troubled. Am I strong enough to take that on? Maybe we'll be okay and can succeed in raising the baby together*, Nora pondered. *Just continue to put your feelings for Brant aside. I promised Russ that I'd help him, and I don't want to break anymore promises*. Nora was torn but hurriedly picked the telephone back up and, with a trembling hand, dialed Russ' number. It seemed to her that everything was in slow motion as each turn of the dial felt like an eternity. Nora drew a deep breath in, dialed the final number, and waited. As the telephones connected, and the line began to ring, Nora knew there was no turning back.

"Hi, Russ," Nora said, her voice quivering.

"Hi, Nor. I thought you were going for lunch with Josie today?"

"I was but I had to cancel our plans."

"You sound upset. Is everything okay, Nor?" Russ asked with concern.

"I know you have a lot on your mind, Russ, but I have something to tell you."

"What is it, Nor? Did I say or do something to upset you? If I did, I'll try to fix it," Russ replied.

"Dr. Perkins ran some tests last week during my college physical."

"Tests? Are you sick again?"

"No. I wasn't feeling well earlier in the summer, but now I know why. Russ, I just found out I'm pregnant."

"Pregnant? Are you sure? How?" Russ asked, seemingly caught off guard.

"Yes, I'm sure and I think you can figure out how."

"How do you know the results are accurate? Maybe they got your test mixed up with someone else's," Russ replied, appearing as shocked as Viviane had been.

"It wasn't a mix-up, Russ. The doctor ran both a urine and a blood test to be sure. I don't know what I'm going to do."

"Shit, Nor!"

"Russ, what should I do? My father wants you to come by for dinner tomorrow to talk to you," Nora waited, hearing nothing but silence on the other end of line. "Russ, are you there? Please say something," Nora pleaded.

"I'll take care of you, Nor . . . and the baby."

"I don't have to keep it. My mother is against abortion, but I don't care. There's still time to get rid of it. I can go to New York like my friend Becky did. No one needs to know."

"Don't talk like that, Nor."

"This came at a bad time."

"Marry me."

"Marry you? Russ, you just got back and are still readjusting and I'm going back to school in a few weeks," Nora replied to the daunting proposition.

"I want to spend my life with you, to build a life together. That's what I've always wanted."

"Everything is happening so fast. I don't know if I'm ready."

"Nor, if there's one thing Vietnam taught me it's that sometimes you just have to go with the flow and let life take you where you're supposed to be. I'd like to ask your father's permission to marry you."

"But how do I know where I'm supposed to be, Russ? I want to finish my teaching degree."

"I know you do, Nor, but we can figure that part out later after your father and I talk."

Nora then took her turn being the silent one on the other end of the line, at a loss for words and thinking about what say next as she anxiously traced the surface of the raised scar above her eyebrow.

"What do you say, Nor? Can I ask your father's permission to marry you?"

"Yes."

"For real? You aren't pulling my leg, are you?"

"For real, Russ," Nora replied, still unsure of herself and feeling as though she were taking a deep plunge into uncharted waters.

$$26$$

The face of her wristwatch read 10:07 a.m. as Nora backed her car out of the driveway to run another one of Viviane's errands. The previous day's exhausting fiasco with her parents left her depleted and wanting to curl up into a ball like a pill bug, rather than face the unforeseen effects of the choices she made.

She called over to Josie's the day before and left a message with Mrs. Henson, cancelling their lunch plans. When she got off the phone, she found her parents sitting outside on the front porch swing. Nora tiptoed over to the open dining room window and carefully listened in on their conversation through the screen.

"There's no sense in grounding her," Richard told his wife.

"I suppose it doesn't make a difference. She's already in trouble, or should I say already knocked up? Things can't get any worse now can they, Richard? She is just going to have to marry that Ayers boy. She could have done so much better," Viviane ranted.

"Unruffle your panties there, Viv. He's coming for dinner tomorrow night. We'll figure this out."

Good old, unsupportive Viviane. I can always count on her to make matters worse, Nora thought to herself as she drove toward Josie's house. She knew she would have to make her meeting with Josie quick as Viviane had instructed her to go directly to Swanset Village Grocer to pick up a dozen eggs and then come straight home. Viviane would surely have a fit if she knew she was stopping at Josie's after yesterday's rude comment, *"I always knew that Henson girl was trouble."* Josie, of course, had no idea of the bomb that Nora was about to drop on her.

"Jo was right again. I should have listened to her and taken a pregnancy test sooner," Nora said to herself as she turned down Josie's street.

Josie was sitting on her front steps and ran over to Nora's car when she saw her pull into the driveway.

"What's going on, Nor? Why couldn't you talk on the phone and why did you have to cancel lunch yesterday?" Josie asked with an urgency in her voice.

"Get in!" Nora replied.

"What's wrong?" Josie asked, immediately running around to the passenger's side of the car and climbing in.

"Let me roll up my window. I don't want anyone overhearing us."

"There's no one around, Nor. Turn off the car and let's talk."

"I can't stay long but I need to tell you something."

"What is it? Is it Russ. . . or Brant?"

"Yes and no."

"What does that mean? Spill it, Nor."

"You were right, Jo."

"Right about what?"

"I'm pregnant," Nora confessed to her friend.

"Oh boy! I wish I wasn't right for once," Josie replied.

"I found out yesterday morning. That's why I had to cancel on you. Dr. Perkins ran a pregnancy test on Wednesday and his secretary called with the results."

"Do your parents know?"

"Of course, my mom picked up the phone before I could. Miss Hargrove told her while I listened in on the hallway extension."

"That must have gone over like a fart in church."

"That about sums it up, Jo. My mother is furious. My dad is just disappointed in me."

"How far along are you?" Josie asked.

"I counted back on my calendar, and I think I'm probably about eight weeks. Or maybe ten weeks," Nora replied.

"Holy crap, Nor! Well, which is it eight or ten? Two weeks makes a big difference."

"I don't know. Jo, I don't know what to do," Nora said with a quiver in her voice.

"Are you going to call Brant? There's a possibility that it's . . ."

"No, Jo! I'm not calling him."

"Why not? It could be his. Couldn't it?"

"The same reason Becky didn't tell Carl. We are through and I don't want him to know. Please promise me you won't tell anyone about this. Not Brant, or Russ, or anyone. . . ever. Promise me!" Nora pleaded.

"I promise, Nor."

"We'll be back on campus in a few more days. Jo, do you think it would be too late to consider an abortion at that point?"

"Not too late, but the further along you are, the more likely you are to have complications. Are you sure that's what you want to do?"

"I'm not sure, but Becky seems fine since she had hers."

"She's been struggling a lot emotionally since she terminated the pregnancy. This Pro-Life movement is gaining momentum and guilting women into going through with pregnancies they don't really want. I guess you need to ask yourself if you could live with yourself if you ended the pregnancy."

"My mother screamed at me and said abortion is not an option for me. I know it's not legal here yet, but I could go to New York City to get one without her knowing like Becky did."

"Viviane is from a different generation. It's your body, not hers. You're in charge of your reproductive life, Nor, not Viviane," Josie said firmly.

"Yes, but she would disown me if I chose to terminate it. You know how strict my parents are, Jo. Just look how she treated Emily, and she wasn't even pregnant. She doesn't want me shaming our family by having a baby out of wedlock," Nora said.

"Okay, so what does she expect you to do? Get married or something?" Josie asked with a chuckle.

"Yes."

"What? Is Viviane seriously expecting that of you?"

"She is, Jo. How else do you think someone with her mindset would remedy a situation like this? She married my father when she got pregnant after all, although I pretend not to know that."

"You're caught between a rock and a hard place."

"Russ is coming for dinner tonight to talk to my dad. He offered to take care of me and the baby. He wants to marry me, Jo."

"What did you say to that?"

"I told him I would but I'm still thinking about it. He wants me to keep the baby and be a family. He said he'll support me."

"That's all well and good but he has problems of his own that he needs to work on. What do you want? Your life will never be the same after having a baby, Nor. What about school? I know how important your education is to you. As I've told you before, you matter too. If you're thinking about terminating the pregnancy, you need to do it soon because you're a lot further along than Becky was. You'd have to have the saline procedure too because by the time you make an appointment and have the procedure done, you'll already be at the twelve-week mark," Josie informed her.

"I'm not sure what the right thing to do is, Jo. I'm planning to go back to school next week. If I do eventually marry Russ, he would help support me and the baby and I could continue to help him with his struggles. Isn't that what being married is all about, navigating life with someone by your side?"

"You know how I feel about marriage, Nor. I'm not the one to ask about that," Josie replied with honesty.

"Okay, Jo. If I decided not to marry Russ and were to terminate the pregnancy by saline, I'd still have to go through with delivering the baby right? I'd be giving birth to a dead baby, wouldn't I? I don't know if I could go through with that."

"You better prepare yourself and decide soon, Nor. I have a bad feeling things are about to get even messier, and I'm not referring to the thunderstorms in today's weather forecast either."

27

"Be sure to roll up your car windows. The storm is getting close," Martha Ayers warned her son.

"Sure, Ma. I'll check dad's windows too while I'm at it," Russ replied.

The local news station issued a severe thunderstorm warning, just as it had the previous day. The storm had crossed Long Island Sound and was predicted to soon pass over Swanset.

Russ stepped his bare feet out onto the back steps and looked up at the ominous clouds overhead. It had been a dry New England summer and the earth was thirsting for a good rainfall.

With crossed arms, he stood observing the atmospheric changes. It seemed as if a black cloud had followed him home from Vietnam last month and was now manifesting directly above him. *It's about time you show yourself,* he thought. He had been carrying a heaviness around with him since his return, but this was the first time that he was able to lay his eyes directly on it. The darkened sky and distant rumbles of thunder seemed to be coaxing him back to the place where he suffered his own moral death.

"Okay, you're all set," Russ said aloud, patting the hood of his father's pickup truck, confirming that its windows were secure.

More loud rumbles of thunder erupted from the darkened sky as he walked around the passenger side of his car, checking to be sure its window was closed. Circling around the front bumper, a loud crackle of lightening lit up the sky and Russ noticed a reflection as he stood in front of his driver's side window. At first the reflection was his own, but after blinking his eyes, he saw a VC staring back at him. Russ jumped back, gasped for breath and wiped his eyes as he tried to figure out if what he was seeing was real or not. Charlie continued glaring, watching, and waiting. BOOM! Another loud clap of thunder. He blinked again only to open his eyes and see that Charlie was gone. Russ, now on high alert and ready for action, knew he had to hide and get Charlie before Charlie got him. *Kill or be killed*, Russ reminded himself as he made his way to the unkept patch of woods bordering his parents' property just as a downpour started. He could hide there. *Stay low and keep an eye out for tunnel entrances and booby traps*, Russ thought to himself as he got down on the forest floor and began to belly-crawl across the dirt and fallen leaves. *Its rainy season again. Maybe the Air Force put Operation Popeye back into action*, Russ told himself, recalling a recent episode of the world news revealing that the U.S. Air Force conducted a series of cloud-seeding missions to extend the North Vietnam monsoon season, attempting to disrupt their ability to move supplies along their dirt roads. Russ thought this could explain the heavy rain that was now saturating him and the earth. Another loud crack of lightening shot from the sky. *They're getting close, get your grenades ready*, he told himself as he began to frantically search for his rucksack. Feeling around the wet ground, Russ found two of his grenades and clenched them tightly. Rolling clouds of thunder passed overhead as he realized he was being fired upon. It started with a strike on the back of his calf, and he soon felt his entire body being pelted by enemy fire. *They found me! Where are they? I can't see Charlie. I don't see Davis. Maybe Charlie already got to him. Stay calm. Where the hell is he? Think. Quick, throw your grenade.* Russ threw one of the grenades over his head and instinctively covered his head and, with his forearms, braced for the explosion. BOOM! *I must have got a few of them,* he thought as he lay curled up in fetal position, to shield himself from enemy fire. He was alone, ambushed and outnumbered. If he moved, he might be killed and never make it home.

"Russ!" someone called from off in the distance.

Maybe that's Davis looking for me. Maybe he's okay after all, Russ thought to himself.

"Russell, come inside!" Martha's voice echoed through the trees.

"Russ, where the hell are ya?" his father's voice called to him.

I must be hearing voices in my head again.

As fast as it started, the gunfire suddenly ceased, and the ambush was over. *The Viet Cong gave up. They must have retreated*, Russ told himself, carefully assessing the scene to make sure there were no VC around. He got up from the ground, loosened his grip on his grenade and opened his hand to reveal a round, grey rock sitting in his palm. He began to pat down his body to see where he had been hit, surprised to find no blood or bullet holes on his torso or extremities and his skin perfectly intact. Emerging from the trees, Russ looked up to find the sun breaking through the remnants of the storm clouds. He could see what he thought were his barracks not far away and made his way slowly toward them in a catatonic stupor.

"Russell! Why didn't you come inside? Where did you go?" Martha exclaimed, opening the back door and watching her son approach, his face and clothes covered in mud.

"I was in the jungle, Ma. . . looking for Charlie," Russ responded in a monotone voice.

"What? Don't you mean the woods? Who's Charlie?" Martha asked, appearing dumbfounded as her forehead wrinkled.

"You know . . . Charlie. I saw him," Russ reiterated.

"You're covered in mud. Come inside and get in the shower. That was a bad storm. I thought the windows were going to break from that large hail," she replied.

Russ recognized worry in his mother's voice and sensed her confusion.

"What the hell happened to you?" Fred exclaimed, looking his disheveled son up and down before taking a swig of beer from the open can in his hand.

"Nothing," Russ replied, unable to look his father in the eye or make sense of what had happened outside.

"You're supposed to be having dinner with the Thompsons tonight at seven o'clock. I already ironed your shirt and its hanging in your closet with your sport coat. You should go get cleaned up so you aren't late," Martha suggested.

Once alone in his room, Russ shut the door and leaned up against it. Stretching his neck back and staring at the blank ceiling overhead, he tried to make sense of the ambush in the woods. *What just happened out there?* After a few minutes of unsuccessfully trying to piece things together, he proceeded down the hallway to the bathroom. There he slipped off his muddy clothes and let them fall onto the squares of the black and white tiled floor. He looked down at his bare, dirty feet, and realized they were itching a lot less. He had been regaining sensation now that his case of jungle rot was improving. A few of his platoon buddies had bad cases and one GI from Missouri was even sent home when the infection set in and required amputation. Russ could still smell the decaying flesh. *At least I came home with both feet on the ground,* he thought to himself as he ran the water, adjusted the temperature, and stepped into the bathtub. He felt his feet sting as they hit the water and he pulled the vinyl curtain shut. Russ ran his hands along his naked torso and extremities, again searching for bullet wounds. Again, he found none. He felt a pain near his temple and rubbed the left side of his head as a throbbing headache set in. *I know I saw Charlie out there*, he tried to convince himself. *Ma mentioned something about a hailstorm.* Russ put his face directly under the shower head, trying to wash away the stress and feelings of terror. *And where the hell were Davis and Harry . . . and the rest of the company? Davis always has my back*, he thought to himself, placing his palms over his face as his head pounded harder. Confused by what had just occurred outside, Russ held back his tears. He tried to wrap his head around what had happened in Vietnam and around events that took place since returning home. There was the incident at the airport with that bitch and her little spawn of the devil, at the gas station with Brant Judge, and in the woods just now. There were other things too, like conversations he overheard when waiting in line at the post office and the bank. He would see people look at him and whisper while others treated him as though he was invisible. During a few of his job interviews, all of which he was qualified for, things had gone sour once they asked about his employment gap and found out where he had been for the past year. After one interview, while waiting for the elevator, he overheard a conversation between two managers walking by in which one said, "It isn't even a real war so those returning GIs don't deserve any special treatment." As hard as he tried to adapt to civilian life, he could not seem to lose the heavy cloud that hung overhead. He continued to be plagued by night terrors and would often wake up not knowing where he was. He was especially bothered by crowds of people and loud noises. His guard was always up and his eyes always on the lookout for the enemy. It was as if the darkness from inside the tunnels had somehow latched onto him. The enemy, it seemed, was everywhere.

"I don't want to be this way. I just want to feel . . . like myself again," he cried aloud. Reaching out and turning the dial all the way to the right, he allowed the now frigid water to shower down on him, waking him and washing the filth from his face and body. *If only I could free my mind*, he reasoned with himself. Russ knew the war had poisoned him. Although he was ready to leave Vietnam behind him, Russ knew Vietnam was not yet ready to leave him, and maybe it never would.

28

Russ gnawed on the inside of his cheek while thinking of how Nora called the previous day sounding distraught and adding a bit of melodrama to his otherwise dismal week. He now sat upright in the stiff wingback chair, swirling a glass of whiskey on the rocks in his hand. Each swallow of the amber liquor relaxed his nerves, just as it had in the bush of Vietnam. It was just what he needed to kill the edginess he was feeling from his episode out in the woods a few hours prior and from the current situation he found himself in.

Moments earlier, Mr. Thompson slid the pocket doors of the parlor closed, trapping him inside. While Nora and Viviane busied themselves in the kitchen, Richard Thompson paced the polished oak floor with his own whiskey glass in hand.

"Now, we are not happy about the timing of this, Russell, but, as we all know, these things do happen from time to time. We also know your parents raised you properly and you will do right by our daughter," Mr. Thompson stated, stopping in his tracks with his eyes glued on Russ.

"Mr. Thompson, I was just as surprised as you were," Russ replied, lifting the glass to his lips, indulging in a large gulp of the single malt scotch and letting the fact that Nora really was pregnant seep in some more.

"Tell me, Russell, how do you plan to remedy this situation?"

"Well, Sir, I've loved your daughter since our high school days and I take full responsibility. With your permission, I would like to ask Nora to marry me. I brought something with me. It belonged to my grandmother," Russ said, pulling a small box out of his sport coat pocket and opening its hinged cover.

Mr. Thompson reached into the breast pocket of his crisp, button-down shirt and donned his reading glasses. He took the box and carefully inspected the sparkling, pear shaped diamond engagement ring.

"Nora will surely be pleased," he said, looking at Russell and the ring approvingly.

"I sure hope so."

"Marrying Nora is the right thing to do, and Viviane and I would expect nothing less from you. Of course, Viviane had always hoped Nora would marry a doctor or lawyer to secure her financial future and place in society. She likes to brag you know. However, I've always liked you, Russell. You have a good work ethic and even served our country when you were called to do so and . . . well, that's good enough for me."

Russ nodded his head in acknowledgement of Mr. Thompson's statement.

The idea of Viviane being my mother-in-law makes my stomach churn, Russ thought to himself.

"We haven't told Nora yet, so as not to upset her, but we also feel that its best she does not return to school in her . . . delicate condition. We plan to set aside the money that was earmarked for her room, board and tuition at Bridgegate and use it instead for essentials for the baby. Perhaps the two of you can take a trip downtown to find a crib and a nice baby carriage."

"Thank you, Sir. Nora is not going to take that news well though . . . about her education I mean. I start my new job at New England Underground Cable on Monday, and I've saved all my military pay. I have my eye on a place on Hails Hallow Road, just south of Broad Cove. Its small and needs some work but it sits on two private acres. I'll be able to swing the monthly payments with the money I've saved. The loan officer at Swanset Savings Bank already approved the mortgage."

"Very good, Russell. I read in the *Weaver Falls Herald* that there are layoffs coming at the textile mill where your father works. Viviane and I, being parents of the bride, will take care of the wedding expenses so you kids can have a nice day for yourselves. Your parents won't need to worry about the financial end of things. But the wedding must be soon, before Nora starts to show. That's the only concern Viviane has."

"Of course, Sir. That's very generous of you."

"Well, let's head into the dining room. Viviane and Nora prepared a nice dinner and are surely anxious for us to join them. After you," Mr. Thompson said, extending his arm and gesturing toward the pocket doors.

Russ pushed himself out of the tall wing back and swallowed down the rest of his whiskey before placing his glass on its coaster. As he followed

Mr. Thompson into the dining room, Russ saw Nora sitting at the table with curious eyes.

"Here they are. You can stop fidgeting with your silverware now, Nora," Viviane scolded from across the room.

Russ immediately felt out of place as he glanced around the fancy room. A crystal vase filled with fresh flowers and illuminated tapered candles adorned the center of the table. He noticed that everything sparkled, including the polished cherry wood chairs, the etched wine glasses, and every piece of silverware that was neatly arranged in their appropriate places around each plate. He hoped that he was dressed nice enough as he smoothed his necktie, making sure that it was covering the buttons running down the center of his dress shirt.

"Russ, come sit over here," Nora said, patting her hand on the seat of the chair next to her.

As he settled into the side chair, Nora took his hand, making him feel more at ease.

"How did it go? What took you so long in there anyway?" Nora asked, obviously concerned by the fact that he and Mr. Thompson had been behind closed doors for over half an hour.

Russ felt Viviane's eyes on him and looked up to confirm he was right.

"Good, Nor. All's good," Russ replied as discretely as he could, barely moving his lips as he spoke.

"Excuse me for a moment while I get dinner from the kitchen," Viviane said, getting up from the table.

"It smells so good. I bet you and your mother have outdone yourselves again," Mr. Thompson said.

"Your mother was glaring at me," Russ whispered, leaning in closer to Nora.

"Just ignore her. That's what I do," Nora giggled.

"Here we are," Viviane announced, reappearing from the kitchen a few minutes later carrying a large tray of plated dinner entrees and a wooden bowl overflowing with fresh salad greens.

After putting the tray down on the sideboard, Viviane placed the salad bowl in the middle of the table so everyone could help themselves. She then made her way around the table passing out the plated entrees as Mr. Thompson followed closely behind, pouring red wine into the long stem glasses at each place setting.

"Only a little taste for you, Nora," Mr. Thompson said, pouring a small bit of wine into his daughter's glass.

"This is nice. Thank you for inviting me for dinner," Russ said.

"We're happy to have you back, Russell," Mr. Thompson replied.

"Shall we eat?" Viviane asked.

"Just a minute, Viv. Everyone, raise your glasses. A toast to Russell and Nora . . . and to family," Mr. Thompson said with his glass in the air.

"To family," Nora, Viviane and Russ repeated after him, their glasses clinking together.

"This wine tastes familiar. What kind is it?" Nora asked after taking a sip of the silky wine with its hints of ripe cherry.

"It tastes familiar? Young lady, I can assure you that you have not had this wine with dinner before. I've been saving this one for a special occasion. It's a refined, soft wine from France with a hefty price tag," Richard Thompson boasted.

"Oh, I thought I had tried it before. Never mind," Nora said, placing her glass down and seeming to become agitated, her hand trembling as she began rearranging her silverware.

"Nora, once and for all, please stop your fidgeting. It's not very becoming on you," Viviane scolded again.

"Dig in everyone," Mr. Thompson said.

"Bon Appetit!" Viviane chimed in.

Russ noticed Nora picking at her salad and seeming to half-listen to the ongoing chatter in the room.

"Nora?" Viviane called from across the table.

"Yes?" Nora replied, looking up from her plate.

"Didn't you hear me? I asked you if you could please pass the dinner rolls."

"Of course, Mother," Nora said, passing the woven basket of warm bread across the table.

As Viviane went on about her garden club happenings, Russ noticed that her eyes were upon him again.

"Russell?" Viviane asked.

"Yes, Mrs. Thompson?" Russ asked, swallowing with a hard gulp.

"Would you tell us what the flora was like in the jungle of Vietnam?" she asked, raising her eyebrows.

"Well, ma'am, I suppose you could say that it was very green and lush," Russ replied, not really wanting to talk about Vietnam ever again and hoping he wouldn't say the wrong thing.

"I suppose that would be accurate with the monsoon rains there in the jungle," Viviane replied.

"Yes, ma'am," Russ said, looking down at his plate and recalling the monsoons pouring down on him and his company as they cut their way through the thick jungle with machetes.

"Did you fight during the monsoons?" Viviane prodded.

"Um . . . we um . . . oh shit!" Russ said, tripping over his words and knocking over his glass of water.

"Oh, my tablecloth!" Viviane exclaimed, immediately pushing her chair back and grabbing a towel off the sideboard.

"I'm so sorry, Mrs. Thompson," Russ said, feeling like he was blowing it and craving another shot of Mr. Thompson's whiskey. Russ felt himself perspiring as he recalled a day when the heavy monsoon rains poured down on his company. Two of his fellow GIs, whose vision was obscured by a veil of rain, walked directly into a trip wire. One lost both of his legs while the other lost his life.

"It's okay, Russ. Mom, Russ doesn't like to talk about his time there," Nora said, squeezing Russ' hand under the table.

"Well, why not? I thought it would be interesting to . . .," Viviane rambled, as she sopped up the spilled water.

"Viv, you heard Nora. She knows him better than we do," Mr. Thompson interjected.

"Hmm. I sure hope so . . . considering the circumstances," Viviane replied, pursing her lips and sitting back down in her chair.

"Daddy, are you and Russ planning to let us in on what was said behind those closed doors?" Nora asked.

"Now, young lady, I will let Russell do the talking later," Mr. Thompson said between bites of beef stroganoff.

"Well, Daddy, it does pertain to me. I'm heading back to school in a few days, and I should know. Don't you think?" Nora asked.

The table suddenly became quiet as everyone stopped chewing and all movement ceased. Russ noticed Mr. Thompson appear to almost choke on his food, repeatedly clearing his throat and then sucking down his glass of the vintage wine.

"Nora, your mother and I have been meaning to speak to you about that," he said.

"What about it? I've already packed most of what I need in my trunk, so I'll be ready to go next week," Nora replied, seeming to sense that something was not right.

"What your father is trying to say is that, in your delicate condition, we feel its best that you stay here with us rather than return to Bridgegate," Viviane said.

"As I've informed Russell, your mother and I are setting aside the money we would have spent on your tuition and fees for things the baby may need," Mr. Thompson added, clearing his throat again.

"Daddy, are you saying that I'm not allowed to go back to campus? It's my life and it should be my decision," Nora said, raising her voice.

"In a perfect world it would be. However, as we all know, this is an imperfect situation now, isn't it? You will begin to show soon and can't be seen walking around campus pregnant now, can you?" Viviane asked, with an intense gaze.

"This is my life, Mother. Not yours!" Nora yelled, stomping her foot, throwing her napkin down onto her plate and pushing her chair back.

"Nora Thompson!" Viviane exclaimed.

"Young lady, that is no way to speak to your mother," Mr. Thompson said.

"Nor, it's okay," Russ said, reaching for her hand and attempting to calm her down.

"It's okay? Really, Russ? How can you say that any of this is okay?" Nora asked, pulling her hand away and standing up, her face flush with anger.

"You sit back down right this minute!" Viviane yelled.

"Everyone remain calm," Mr. Thompson said, trying to catch his breath again.

"No! I will not!" Nora said, backing away from the table and bolting out of the dining room.

The house shook as the front door slammed shut, startling the three who remained seated at the table.

"Maybe I should go talk to her," Russ suggested, wiping sweat from his brow and wishing he had a cigarette on him.

"Yes. Yes, go ahead, Russell," Mr. Thompson said, waving him away from the table to go smooth things over with their perturbed and pregnant daughter, before refilling his own wine glass.

Russ gladly left the room and made his way outside. There he found Nora sitting on the porch swing covering her face with her hands.

"Can I sit with you, Nor?"

"You knew my parents weren't allowing me to go back to campus? Why didn't you tell me?" Nora lashed out.

"I just found out there in the parlor. Can I please sit down?"

"I can't believe this. It's like they are punishing me because I made this one mistake," Nora continued.

"Well, your parents want what's best for you and I don't see it as a mistake, Nor," Russ said taking a seat beside her.

"My parents don't know what's best for me, Russ. Look how my mom treated my sister. They want what's best for themselves."

"One thing I do know is that they do want to be sure you're taken care of. I told your father I'm prepared to do just that . . . to take care of you and the baby."

"Russ, they just want to be sure they are spared the shame and embarrassment of having an unmarried, pregnant daughter. I can take care of myself. I've thought about things and think that you need to take care of yourself before you can take care of me and a baby."

"I know and I have been. We've been through a lot together, Nor. Heck, we were just kids when we met. Now there's a baby on the way. We're adults now, with adult problems that we can solve together."

"Russ . . .,"

"Wait, Nor. Please let me finish what I have to say. I know I'm not perfect, but I want to do the right thing. You deserve no less."

Russ then reached into his jacket pocket, pulled out the hinged box and opened it. Nora's green eyes grew wide at the sight of the sparkling pear-shaped diamond ring.

"Nora Thompson, I promise to love you and this baby forever. You would make me the happiest man on earth if you would marry me. Will you, Nor? Please say yes."

As he nervously waited for Nora's response, he watched her eyes dart back and forth, sensing her uncertainty.

"Everything is happening so fast," Nora replied, getting up and pacing the porch floor.

"I know, Nor, but I told you that life is like that. You just have to roll with things sometimes," Russell replied.

Nora sat back down, and her bright eyes continued to dart back and forth between Russ and the glistening diamond ring.

"I need you, Nor," Russ said, anxiously waiting for her response.

Nora's eyes locked with his.

"I made a promise to you long ago, Russ, and I know that I let you down. I didn't keep my end of the deal but that doesn't mean we can't repair things, right?"

"What are you saying?" Russ asked.

"I'm saying. . . yes! I'll marry you," Nora replied.

"Thank you, Nor. Thank you for sticking by me. I love you."

"I love you too."

"Would you like to try on the ring?"

"Yes, please," Nora said as Russ slid the ring onto her finger.

"It's a perfect fit."

"It's beautiful, Russ!"

"Just like you. What do you say we go back inside and tell your parents?" Russ asked, feeling relieved that Nora had accepted his marriage proposal.

"Wait, Russ."

"What is it, Nor?"

"Let's. . . make it a great life. Okay?" Nora said, leaning in and kissing him on the lips.

"We will. We'll make it a great life, Nor," Russ said, taking hold of her hand and leading her back inside the house.

As they entered the dining room, hand in hand, Viviane and Richard perked up.

"Are you kids, okay?" Mr. Thompson asked.

"More than okay, Sir," Russ said.

"Oh?" Richard asked.

Nora held up her left hand, bedecked with the sparkling diamond.

"She said yes!" Russ exclaimed.

"That's wonderful! Viviane did you hear that? What do you have to say, Viv?" Mr. Thompson asked excitedly, jumping up from his seat, as if in disbelief.

Everyone watched as Viviane looked up and, as if thanking the heavens above for answering her prayers, let out an audible sigh. She then reached for the bottle of wine and poured what remained into her Bordeaux glass, taking her time to twirl it, sniff it and observe the legs running down the inside of the tall, broad bowl.

"Well, Viv? What do you say?" Mr. Thompson asked again.

"Richard, I'll drink to that," Viviane replied, raising her glass and allowing the Bordeaux blend to flow past her lips, taming her harsh tongue.

29

The black muscle car, in need of a good washing, came to a stop at the intersection of Prospect Street and Old County Road. Brant Judge waited for the traffic light to change as he sat enveloped in the midday sunlight shining through the car's dusty windshield. It occurred to him that his vehicle's idling engine was mimicking the cadence of his life over the past few weeks since his release from Teasdale Memorial.

His physician had recommended he take it easy for the rest of the summer to allow his body to fully recover. Besides a few follow up appointments to monitor his progress and a routine eye exam, Brant's August calendar had been rather empty. His telephone calls to Nora had gone unanswered and he had come to terms with the fact their relationship was over. All that was keeping him going now was his upcoming training at the police academy on the Cape. Once there, his mind would be occupied, and his days would be full. The academy would provide a much-needed distraction from recent events in his personal life and help him to refocus his mind on something other than Nora Thompson.

He had been totally blindsided when Nora came to Russ' defense after the fight at the gas station. She insisted Russ would never act that way unless provoked. She also claimed to know Russ to be a better person than that. The fact that Brant was the one who landed in the hospital seemed to be a moot point.

"How on earth can you believe him over me? I thought you trusted me, Nora" he remembered telling her.

Nora reminded him that she and Russ had a long history together. She said she owed it to Russ to give their relationship another shot now that he was home. *Sounds like he pulled the old Nam card and she fell for it*, Brant thought to himself. It appeared to him Nora bought into whatever story Russ must have sold her. *I can't believe she did that to me*, Brant thought. He was also surprised that Nora wouldn't see him face to face. Instead, they ended things over the telephone. *What a great way to end a "summer fling,"* he told himself.

Brant wanted a future with Nora and he was certain that, just a few weeks ago, she wanted the same. Her flip-flopping left him baffled. *Maybe I misread her? Something is off here. . . but what? It doesn't even sound like the same girl I knew*, he thought.

The loud blare of a car horn shook Brant out of his engrossed thoughts. He looked up to see the green light summoning him to proceed through the intersection. As he drove through Swanset's town center, Brant stopped periodically to let pedestrians cross the street and eventually found a shaded parking spot on Main Street alongside the Swanset Public Library. His destination, The Chowder Shack, was just a few blocks away and Brant found himself in the mood to be outdoors. He was looking forward to taking a walk as his headaches had become less frequent and, according to his doctor, that was a positive sign. Brant recalled Dr. Schwartz reaching into his pocket and taking out his pen to sign off on the medical forms required by the police academy. Brant studied the doctor's illegible signature. *Things should start moving along now*, he told himself.

Labor Day was approaching which meant The Chowder Shack would be open for only a few more days. He and his parents decided they better get their fix before they closed for the season. Since Mary and Walt were immersed in a Saturday afternoon gardening project, Brant offered to take a ride and pick up their Chowder Shack favorites.

The Chowder Shack was packed, as it always was on weekends. The line of customers was long, wrapping around the corner of the weathered, cedar shingled building. Brant took his place in line amongst the other patrons and waited in the shade under the canvas awning. He pushed around the crushed clamshells on the walkway with his foot and made small talk with an elderly couple, who recognized him from the gas station, to pass the time. A warm summer breeze carried the pleasant aroma of fried clams past those waiting to place their orders as he scanned the menu board hanging overhead.

"Welcome to The Chowder Shack. What can I get for you today?", a lanky teenage boy asked when he finally reached the counter.

"Hi. I'll take two quarts of clam chowder and a dozen clam cakes. Oh, and throw in a bottle of cola for while I'm waiting," Brant ordered.

"You've got it. That comes to $7.75," the boy replied as he placed the beverage on the counter.

Brant handed him two five-dollar bills and accepted his change. He then slipped a dollar into the tip jar by the register.

"Thanks, man! You're number seventy-seven. Lucky sevens! Your order should be ready in about fifteen minutes."

"Okay. Thanks," Brant replied before walking away from the counter, not feeling the least bit lucky.

He took a seat at one of the shacks brightly painted picnic tables, twisted the cap off his soda bottle and took a swig of the ice-cold beverage. While savoring the refreshing flavor of the cola hitting his tongue, he partook in some people watching. The shack attracted lots of families with small children and Brant couldn't help but smile seeing the kids at the adjacent table giggling between bites of French fries dipped in ketchup. It reminded him of the times he and his cousin Jack came to the shack as kids.

The sound of a woman laughing soon caught his attention. It was a familiar laugh and Brant turned to see a girl with long brown hair sitting at the table behind him. Her back was toward him and, even though he couldn't see her face, he knew it was Josie Henson. He had not seen Josie since before his fight with Russ and had been laying low, trying to avoid Josie and anyone else connected to Nora.

"Order up number seventy-seven," announced a girl from behind the counter.

That's me, Brant told himself, getting up and heading over to pick up his order. When he got to the window, the young girl was busy scooping ice cream, so Brant again waited patiently at the pickup counter.

"Brant?" he heard a nearby voice call out.

He turned to notice Josie walking toward him with a tray full of used-up napkins and paper plates to dispose of.

Here we go! Brant thought to himself.

"Hey, Josie. How's it going?" he replied, trying to sound surprised to see her.

"Good. Just grabbing lunch with my brother. He's here visiting for the weekend from New Hampshire. He's in the john currently," Josie snickered.

Brant smiled half-heartedly. "Where in New Hampshire is Ted living now?" he asked.

"Manchester."

"Nice little city. I've stopped there a few times on the way up to North Conway," Brant said.

"He decided to stay up there after graduating and accepting a job offer. Have you heard from Dennis?"

"I received a letter from him last week. He's really digging his assignment."

"That's great! So . . . what are you up to?" Josie asked.

"I'm just picking up lunch for my folks. The shack will be closed for the season soon so you've got to grab it while you can."

"There's nothing like The Chowder Shack, that's for sure," Josie said.

After a long, awkward hesitation Josie spoke up again.

"How are you doing? I've been wanting to check in with you. I left a few messages with your mom," Josie said, getting right to the point.

"I know. Thanks. She told me you called. I've been busy getting ready to leave for the academy and stuff," he replied in hopes of deflecting any talk of Nora.

"That's great, Brant. You'll make a great police officer. I just want to say that I feel bad for all you've gone through . . . with Russ and all," Josie sputtered out.

"Not as bad as I feel," Brant replied, not wanting to sugar coat things.

"Nora has a good heart you know. Sometimes the universe just works in mysterious ways," Josie said comfortingly.

"A good heart? Or a fickle one?"

"C'mon, Brant."

"I hope she's happy," he added, hoping now that Josie would elaborate a bit.

"I'm sure she hopes that you and Libby are happy too."

"Me and . . . Libby?" Brant asked, taken aback.

"Yes, I thought you were back with her," Josie replied.

"Why would you think that?" Brant asked, confused by Josie's assumption.

"You're not? I must have . . ."

"You're mistaken. I'm not with anyone. I've been laid up for weeks and finally got medical clearance to start the academy. I'm sure Nora will be happy to know that, since she only cares about herself these days," Brant said, feeling himself getting agitated.

"I haven't seen her much since Russ got back. But . . . to be honest, Brant, you should know that Nora and Russ are engaged to be married."

"What? Are you serious?"

"Yes. I didn't want you hearing about it from just anyone. I'm sure she wants you to be happy too," Josie added.

"Oh? Did she tell you to say that? Because if she really wanted me to be happy, she'd be here with me right now!" Brant replied, pointing to the ground and irritated by the news that was just dropped on him.

"Brant . . ."

"She made me happy. She talked about a future with me before that hot head came back into the picture."

"Number seventy-seven, your order is ready for pick up," the announcer called again.

"Seventy-seven. That's me," Brant said, signaling to the girl behind the counter. "Josie, I've got to go. I hope you have a great time at the wedding. Be sure to give the bride my best wishes," he sarcastically added.

"Brant, wait."

"I said I've got to go. See you around, Josie," he replied, grabbing his takeout order and navigating back down the pathway of crushed clamshells, hearing them crunch beneath his feet with each heavy stomp he took.

Brant picked up his pace once he reached the smooth asphalt surface of the road, burning off steam from his conversation with Josie in the process. After turning the corner onto Main Street, and passing Swanset Savings Bank, he hurled his empty soda bottle into an alleyway, shattering it and causing a few stray cats to bolt in fear. *I can't believe she's marrying him*, he thought, reaffirming that he had lost the girl he loved. By the time he reached his parked car, his head was throbbing again. His appetite for his favorite summer fare from The Chowder Shack was now lost. *That's enough excitement for one day. Forget about her*, he told himself, knowing it would be hard to do, as he pulled away from the library, leaving a black skid mark, a cloud of dust and Nora Thompson behind him.

30

Nora stood in front of the oak-framed, cheval mirror on an early October morning, searching for the naïve girl in a mini skirt and braided headband that she used to know. A more mature version of herself, three months pregnant and wearing a simple, white wedding dress, now stared back at her.

"Here it is, Nor. Are you ready for me to put it on for you?," Josie asked as she walked over to the mirror with a headpiece made of fresh daisies in her hands.

"I am, Jo. Make sure it covers my scar," Nora said, turning to her friend.

"Okay, just let me center it. That looks good. I'll secure it with a few bobby pins too, so it doesn't fall off. Okay, Nor, turn around, look in the mirror and tell me what you think," Josie instructed.

Nora lightly stroked her loosely curled, golden hair that cascaded down past her shoulders and made a slight adjustment to the crown of daises that now encircled her head.

"I love it, Jo."

"You look so beautiful, Nor."

"I'm so glad you're here with me today."

"Always the bridesmaid and never the bride is my motto. Really, Nor, I wouldn't miss this day for anything. Besides, where else would I be?" Josie joked.

"Hmm . . . maybe visiting Alex on Long Island again?"

"Lucky for you, that's not until next weekend," Josie said with a chuckle.

Nora let out a giggle before turning back toward the mirror.

"I'm nervous, Jo. I can't believe this day is already here."

"I know. Viviane must have been busy expediting things with the church in order to get you and Russ into that weekend Pre-Cana class. I bet they asked for a sizable donation to pull that off and to reserve the church on such short notice," Josie said.

"Well, she wasn't happy that we had to settle for a wedding without a mass but, in the end, Viviane got her way once again. I'm relieved to have a simple wedding though. I find all that pomp and circumstance unnecessary," Nora added.

"It will be short and sweet. Are you ready, Nor? I mean are you sure you're ready to take this on?"

"I think so."

"It's not too late to change your mind. My convertible is parked right out by the side door with the top down. If you want to run, just say the word."

"Jo, don't be silly. I couldn't run out on Russ like that."

"Hey, I just wanted to make sure you're thinking straight. I wasn't sure if you heard from Brant."

"I haven't bothered to return his calls. I think he finally got the hint. I'm trying to stay focused on the here and now and to leave the past behind me," Nora said, placing her hands on her belly.

"I'm sure it's not easy. You know, I did see him at the Chowder Shack a few weeks ago."

"You did?"

"Yes, and it was strange. He said that he and Libby aren't together."

"They aren't? It must not have worked out with her. I can't concern myself with him anymore, Jo. I want to be there for Russ, and I have more than just myself to think about." *But I saw them together. I heard him tell Libby that he loves her.*

"So, you're really ready to do this?" Josie asked.

"I'm as ready as I'll ever be," Nora replied, rubbing her hand over her lower abdomen, which was starting to feel a bit fuller, but still not showing any hint of pregnancy.

"Okay, we better get going. Everyone is waiting for you to make your grand entrance."

Nora turned back to the mirror one last time and ran the palms of her hands over the fabric on the front of her dress. She then took a deep breath and turned toward the door.

"Let's go," Nora said, picking up her bouquet and following Josie into the church narthex where her father was waiting.

Father Meehan stood at the front of the church in his white, celebratory vestments as Josie walked in and took her position to the left of the center aisle. As Nora entered the church, joined arm and arm with her father, she looked ahead and saw Russ and his best man Jeff waiting at the top of the aisle with their eyes upon her. In the rows of church pews on either side of them, stood a small gathering of family and friends to bear witness to their exchange of vows. Viviane, standing tall with her lips pursed, locked eyes with Nora and nodded her head, as if to ensure that everything would go off without a hitch. As the organist played and the notes emanated from the large pipe organ, Nora noticed Russ rubbing the side of his head as if he couldn't wait for the music to cease. He appeared groggy and Nora assumed it was from the lack of sleep and all the drinking he did with Jeff and a few of their buddies at Lance's Pub the night before. He perked up as she approached, looking at her through bloodshot eyes, before a wide smile stretched across his face.

"You look beautiful," Russ whispered, the smell of alcohol expelling from his lungs.

"Thank you," she whispered back, with an easy smile before turning back toward Father Meehan who had already begun speaking.

"Russell and Nora, have you come here to enter into marriage without coercion, freely and wholeheartedly?" Father Meehan asked.

"I have," Russ replied, before letting out a loud hiccup.

"I have," Nora stated after an ever so subtle hesitation, flashing Russ a look of disapproval.

"Are you prepared to follow the path of marriage, to love and honor each other as long as you both shall live?"

"I am," Russ and Nora replied in unison.

"Are you prepared to accept children lovingly from God and to bring them up according to The Law of Christ and his church?"

"I am," Nora and Russ replied simultaneously again.

"Since it is your intention to enter the covenant of marriage, join your right hands, and declare your consent," Father Meehan instructed.

Russ turned and took Nora's hand in his. Nora noticed Russ subtly gasp and hold his breath as if trying to suppress another hiccup that was about to surface.

"Russell, do you take this woman to be your wife? Do you promise to be faithful to her in good times and in bad, in sickness and in health, to love her and to honor her all the days of your life?" Father Meehan asked.

"I do."

"Nora, do you take this man to be your husband? Do you promise to be faithful to him in good times and in bad, in sickness and in health, and to love and honor him all the days of your life?"

"I do," Nora softly replied.

"May the blessings of the Lord be with you. What God has joined let no one put asunder."

The sound of a door slamming shut in the narthex caused a brief distraction and pause in the ceremony as Nora, Russ, and all their guests turned their heads toward the back of the church.

"The wind must be picking up out there," Father Meehan light-heartedly announced, appearing to try to get the guests to refocus their attention, as the familiar roar of a car's engine outside the church faded away.

That sounded like . . .

"Bless, O Lord, these rings," Father Meehan said, sprinkling holy water on the gold bands, which lay upon a square, satin pillow, before presenting them to the bride and groom.

. . . Brant's car.

"Take this ring as a symbol of my love and fidelity," Russ said, as he slid the golden band onto the ring finger of her left hand.

"Take this ring as a symbol of my love and fidelity," Nora repeated, sliding the ring onto his left ring finger.

I made my choice.

The organist began playing again, causing Russ to rub the side of his head, as if trying to quell a throbbing ache, as he and Nora walked to the side of the altar together.

"How much did you drink last night, Russ?"

"Too much," Russ replied.

"Be sure to hold onto this tightly so we don't drop it," Nora whispered to him as she handed him a wooden ring with three strands of rope attached to it.

Nora took the three strands in her hands, each strand symbolizing herself, Russ and God respectively, and began braiding them together in front of their wedding guests, as the organ music continued. Russ patiently watched as Nora worked on the braid and, once completed, carefully passed it to him so as not to let its ends unravel. Nora watched as he appeared to be all thumbs but somehow managed to successfully knot the ends. Together he and Nora passed the cord of three strands, a symbol of their love and commitment to one another and their unity with God, to Father Meehan.

"Though one may be overpowered, two may defend themselves. A cord of three strands is not quickly broken," Father Meehan announced as he joined Russ and Nora's hands and bound them together with the braid.

"I now pronounce you husband and wife. You may now kiss," Father Meehan announced as Nora and Russ' lips met.

"We did it, Russ. We really did it," Nora said, giggling as they walked hand in hand down the steps and out to the courtyard behind the church where their outdoor wedding reception awaited them.

The newlyweds and their guests enjoyed an afternoon in the church's gardens with a spread of crudité, appetizers of clams casino and Swedish meatballs, finger sandwiches, champagne and a tiered wedding cake with raspberry filling.

"It's been a wonderful day, hasn't it?" Nora asked.

"It sure has. Can you wait here for just a second, Nor?" Russ asked.

"Sure. I'll just be right here sipping my champagne," Nora replied with a smile.

"I'll be right back," Russ said, kissing Nora's forehead before making his way over to his best man.

Jeff was leaning against the trunk of an old sugar maple, its leaves already changed to a vibrant orange hue against the early autumn sky.

"Hey, you did it. You really did it. Right after the ceremony Sherry asked, 'When should I expect to see a ring of my own?'," Jeff said with a chuckle.

"She won't wait forever you know," Russ replied before putting a cigarette in his mouth and lighting it up.

"Yeah, I know. So, Nora doesn't know about the house yet, does she?"

"Nope. We managed to keep it a secret. She thinks we're going back to live with her parents for a while, since she doesn't want to move into a tenement in Weaver Falls. There's no way in hell I'm living under the same roof as Viviane. Nora has no idea that I even applied for a mortgage," Russ stated.

"I'm with you there, the heck with living with your in-laws. Imagine trying to get it on with your new bride with that witch, Mrs. Thompson, in the next room listening in. That would be my idea of being in hell. Nora is going to be surprised. It's a nice wedding gift for your new bride and that bun in the oven," Jeff said jokingly.

"Quiet, man. No one knows about the baby except our parents, you and Sherry, and Josie. Old Aunt Gert over there, the one with the cat-eye glasses, she's the motor mouth of the family. If she gets wind of it, I'm toast," Russ said, discretely pointing to the table where Nora's aunt from upstate New York was sitting.

"Let's get you and Nora out of here then. Last night was a late one and you look beat. I'll bring the car around front. Come on out when you're ready so you kids can get on with your lives."

31

"Where are you taking us, Jeff? I can't stand the suspense," Nora said from the back seat as they passed by the marshlands of Broad Cove.

"Just a few more minutes 'til we reach the secret destination, Mrs. Ayers," Jeff said in his best chauffeur's voice.

Nora noticed the sun beginning to set as the car navigated up a hill and down a winding road on the outskirts of Swanset. With Russ' arms wrapped lovingly around her, Jeff veered the car into a dirt driveway where the branches of a large weeping willow tree came into sight. Nora saw that beyond the tree stood a weathered, white picket fence and a quaint farmhouse that was illuminated from within.

"Where are we, Russ?" Nora asked as she peered out the window.

"Home," Russ replied.

"What?"

"Welcome home, Nor."

"Russ, I don't understand."

"It's ours, Nor."

"What do you mean it's ours? Did you buy this place or something?"

"I sure did. It's my wedding gift to you. Would you like to see it?" Russ asked.

"Really? I mean . . . yes . . . of course, I would. Jeff, how long have you known about this?" Nora asked, suspecting Jeff had been in on the secret too.

"Who me? I have no idea what you're talking about," Jeff said with a chuckle.

As they made their way over to the house, Nora admired the window boxes and the hanging porch swing.

"Wait, is this the swing from my parents' house?" she asked running her hand over the peeling paint on its arm.

"It is. Your mother wanted to get rid of it, so I snagged it for us."

"Thank you. I've always loved this porch swing and was so upset when they took it down. Wait, so my parents were in on this too? They didn't buy the house did they? If they did, we will never hear the end of it from my mother."

"No, Nor. I already told you, I bought it. I saved all my military pay and cashed in some savings bonds that my grandparents left me for the down payment. We don't owe Viviane anything. I asked your parents not to tell you because I wanted it to be a surprise. I hope you aren't upset with me, Nor. I wanted to do something special for you."

"It's beautiful, Russ. It really is."

"Would you like to see the inside?"

"Yes!"

Russ waved Jeff away and watched as he pulled out of the driveway.

"Okay, here we go," Russ said, scooping Nora up and carrying her over the threshold through the farmhouse's front door.

"Oh, Russ!" Nora exclaimed, in awe of the newly refinished floors, the open staircase's turned newel post and painted white spindles, and the cozy furnishings of the farmhouse's interior.

"What do you think, Nor?" Russ asked as he gently put her down.

"I think . . . I'm really surprised. How did you find the time to do all this?"

"I had some help. My father and I came here after work and did the interior painting. My mother took the window boxes home, painted them and added the flowers once I hung them back up. Jeff and his dad helped with the carpentry. Sherry was in on it too. She hung all the curtains and organized the kitchen cabinets."

"How about all this furniture? Where did it come from?" Nora asked, running her hand over an armchair's polished wood surface.

"A few pieces are hand-me-downs. I found this hutch and that end table on the side of the road and cleaned them up with a fresh coat of paint. We can get a few more pieces with the money we received from the wedding if you'd like."

"Sure," Nora said, glancing around the house's interior.

"Well, there's more. C'mon I'll show you around. Here's the kitchen," Russ said, leading her into the room.

"It's nice."

"We'll eventually get new appliances, but these work okay for now. I had this new linoleum floor installed and my father repainted the cabinets. I hope you like the yellow paint, Nor."

"You know it's my favorite color," Nora replied with a smile.

"There's more to see upstairs."

"Russ, this railing is beautiful. Every detail is just perfect," Nora said, running her hand over the smooth, oak-stained banister.

"I sanded that down myself and stained it to match the stair treads."

"You did a nice job," Nora said as they proceeded up the staircase.

"Here's the room I like the most. It's our baby's room," Russ said, stepping aside and allowing Nora to enter first.

"Bananas is here too? Wait, how on earth did he get here?" Nora exclaimed as she walked into the room and was greeted by the giant, yellow gorilla that Russ won for her at the Swanset Fair, sitting in a Boston rocker in the corner of the room.

"Jeff picked up Bananas from your parents' house this morning after you left to have your hair styled. He brought him here right before the ceremony."

"Very sneaky," Nora joked.

As Nora studied the wallpaper's whimsical pattern, she imagined their future child spending time in the room. She then walked further into the bedroom and over to the bookshelves flanking the sides of the window and a built-in bench seat with a hinged top. Nora gently lifted the cover to reveal a toy box containing a plastic rattle, alphabet blocks and a few children's books.

"Did you buy these, Russ?" Nora asked, pointing to the items inside the chest.

"Yup. I know the room is bare, other than that old rocker, but your parents want us to go to the furniture store together to pick out a new crib."

"We will," Nora replied, feeling Russ' love for her in every little touch around the farmhouse.

"If you come this way, we have an upstairs bathroom with a clawfoot tub. I still need to install a new light fixture, and it's a bit small, but at least we don't have to go downstairs to use the toilet in the middle of the night," Russ chuckled.

"It's nice, Russ. I like the tile. It's original to the house, right?"

"Good eye, Nor. Yes, it's the original tile from the 1920's. Now I hope you like this room," Russ said as he walked a bit further down the hallway and opened a door.

"This is . . . wow, Russ! It's . . .," Nora became speechless as she looked around their new bedroom, absorbing every detail of the sheer curtains, the light oak headboard adorned with hand carved leaves and acorns, and a wedding ring quilt that covered their marital bed.

"What, Nor? It's what?"

"It's just . . . perfect," Nora said, walking over to Russ and embracing him.

Russ leaned in and kissed her parted lips, sending a surge of longing through her body. Although they had a rocky start since Russ' return home, the months that followed had been healing ones in which they learned to forgive one another and make the best of their situation. Nora knew the only thing they really needed was each other and hoped the joy she was feeling on this day would last a lifetime.

32

1972

Where am I? Russ thought, finding his shirt damp from night sweats as he sat up in the darkened room. Through dilated pupils, he tried to decipher outlines of objects hidden in the night's shadows. His fingertips recognized the familiar, raised stitching of the cotton quilt as his sharp sense of hearing tuned into the sound of the wind-up clock ticking on the bedside table. The sound of Nora gently breathing as she lay asleep in their bed, assured him that he was home. He looked at the clock and saw that it was way too early.

"Two fifteen. Shit," Russ whispered to himself as he turned and let his feet touch the floor, moving quietly so as to not wake Nora.

He pulled his terry cloth robe up onto his shoulders and then made his way downstairs. It was his third consecutive night of waking up from disturbing dreams of being back in Vietnam, as his mind refused to let him rest. While he and Nora were doing well settling into their married life together, he had been keeping his inner turmoil to himself, afraid to appear weak. His prescribed chlorpromazine didn't seem to be helping lately even though he had been taking it as directed. Dr. Perkins suggested he avoid alcohol to prevent weakening the effectiveness of his medication, but he was not about to give up his whiskey, his cigarettes, or anything else that helped to deaden his thoughts. His insomnia was also problematic and the only way he could manage to get a good night's sleep was by taking sleeping pills. Since they made him groggy, he avoided taking them during the work week. Instead, the coffee from New England Underground Cable's breakroom, with its guaranteed grounds at the bottom of each cup, kept him going while on the job. Although he had been finding himself more irritable and with a short fuse, he had somehow managed to hold himself together regardless of how rotten he felt on the inside.

Russ, tired from a long day of Mr. Edmunds' breathing down his neck, had fallen asleep easily for a change. On this Wednesday night, his dream had brought him back to the day when he and Davis discovered a fully equipped operating room down in the tunnels where the VC would care for their wounded. The dream, which began with Davis joking as he always did, soon morphed into a night terror with Davis' headless body lying on the operating room table surrounded by a fresh puddle of shiny, wet blood. Russ knew he should try to get back to sleep but felt too much angst to do so as he was unable to shut off his thoughts. Instead, he checked the thermostat, turning it down just a tad, and walked around the farmhouse's first floor to make sure all the windows and doors were locked and secure. Peering out the window, he noticed a newly fallen snow covering the lawn and tree branches, surrounding the house in a crisp, white glistening blanket. He then opened the basement door, flicked on the light switch at the top of the stairs and made his way down the wooden steps to check the level of the oil tank.

"Half empty. In a few more weeks, we'll need another refill," he said to himself, concerned about the cost of warming the place for the winter, as the cellar's frigid, underground air brought a chill to his bones.

Taking a few steps to the left he pulled on the cord of the overhead light, illuminating the top of his workbench, and reached for the key to his footlocker dangling from a small metal hook. With a turn of the key, he opened the trunk's hinged top, allowing the familiar smells of Vietnam to escape. He took out his combat boots, held them near his nose, and let the odor of the dried mud stuck to their soles permeate his nostrils. He then found his field coat and, after removing his bathrobe, slid it on. Russ reached into the jacket pocket to find his dog tags dangling from their beaded metal chain. The hairs on the back of his neck perked up as he draped them over his head. He continued to sift through the trunk's contents finding his flashlight, letters from Nora and other paraphernalia he had packed for his trip home.

"There you are my old friend," Russ said as he pulled his pistol from the bottom of the trunk and polished its dinged-up exterior with the sleeve of his jacket.

With the gun in hand, Russ was overcome with a sense of security he had been longing for since returning home. He rummaged through the trunk's contents a bit more, recalling a memory with each item he touched. At the very bottom of the trunk sat a box containing a small stack of pictures taken during his time at the Cu Chi base camp. Russ sat thumbing through the stack, feeling as though a part of him remained there. One photograph of him and Davis back in the hootch, struck a chord in his heart. He found himself unable to put the photograph down as Davis stared back at him with his shiny smile full of bright, white teeth. He drew the picture closer and his eyes became transfixed on Davis'. It was as if Johnny was summoning him back. Russ' thoughts began to control him as events from the past flashed in his mind.

A faint noise suddenly grabbed Russ' attention as dust from the floorboards above fell into the open trunk and onto the sleeve of his field jacket. He closed the trunk's lid and got up from the basement floor as suspicion and paranoia set in.

"It's Charlie. He's here," he whispered to himself before carefully loading the handgun with bullets he had stashed in the bottom of his toolbox.

As the floorboards overhead creaked, Russ reached for the string again and turned off the overhead light. He quickly made his way over to the bottom of the staircase where there was an extra wall switch to turn off the light.

Stay still and listen. Kill or be killed, he thought as he turned the switch off and waited in darkness, with keen senses, listening for movement from Charlie and running his open palm over the cold, bumpy surface of the stacked fieldstone cellar wall. After a few moments he quietly proceeded up the staircase, with his loaded gun in hand. Once at the top, he slowly opened the basement door and made his way into the darkened hallway. He knew to be careful not to step on the creaking floorboard in front of the basement door so Charlie wouldn't hear him.

Charlie is close by, he told himself as he leaned his back against the wall, sensing someone was in the living room. Just then, he heard the front door opening and a rush of brisk, winter air rush down the hallway toward him. The sound of footsteps on the front porch followed. *Charlie is outside. Close the door. Be quick*, he told himself as he maneuvered down the hallway, dashed toward the front door, closed it and secured the locks. *Stay quiet. There could be more VC still inside. You need to find Charlie before he finds you*, Russ thought as his mind raced and he tried to decide what to do next. He then heard someone knocking and trying to turn the locked doorknob. *They're trying to get in. They know I'm inside.*

"Russ? Russ, are you in there?" someone called out.

Russ remained still. *They know my name*, he thought.

"Russ, please open the door. It's cold out here."

It sounds like Nora . . . but it can't be . . . she's upstairs sleeping. Charlie is trying to trick me by disguising his voice, Russ thought as he hid along the side of the bookcase in the living room.

"Russ, please open the door. I don't have my coat and it's freezing out here," someone said again while frantically pounding on the farmhouse's front door.

Don't believe them. Don't open the door. It's a trap, Russ told himself as he continued to wait in silence. As the knocking became more forceful Russ made his way into the kitchen, rechecking the back door's lock to be sure that the house was secure. The knocking and disguised voices continued for nearly an hour before finally stopping. After a few moments, Russ made his way over to the corner of the living room and peered through a slit between the curtain panels. It was big enough for him to see through, yet too small to expose him to the enemy who could still be lingering outside. In the moonlight's glow, reflecting off the snow, he could see fresh footprints on the porch that led to the road and eventually faded away. Exhausted from the episode, Russ felt his eyelids grow heavy. *Charlie must have given up. Stay downstairs to keep the house secure in case he comes back,* he told himself as he sat down in the plaid, upholstered secondhand chair. Having managed to scare Charlie off, he closed his eyes, felt his heart rate slow as his body returned to a state of calm and eventually succumbed to sleep.

33

"That's a night for the record books," Officer McMillan said to his fellow officer.

"You can say that again. That guy has issues," Officer Ed Findlay replied as the pair entered the locker room at the Swanset Police headquarters.

"Rough night guys?" rookie officer Brant Judge asked as he suited up for his Thursday morning shift.

"Mornin,' Judge junior. You had to be there," McMillan said.

"Enlighten me . . . and that's, Officer Judge now. Knock it off with that junior shit already Mick, it makes me sound like I'm a ten-year-old," Brant stated.

"Fair enough, Officer Judge," Mick replied, patting Brant's shoulder.

"You better sit down for this one," Findlay interjected.

"A call came in to dispatch around 4:20 a.m. from a resident on Hails Hallow Road. A Mrs. . . . . Fletcher. Yes, Fletcher was her name. Anyway, she called requesting an officer for a domestic issue. When we arrived, I asked her if she and her husband had a spat and she said no. After a brief explanation she led us toward the living room, and we peeked in," McMillan stated.

"What was in the living room?" Brant asked.

"A pregnant girl, asleep on the couch," Findlay added.

"Shut it, Fin," Mick said, throwing his dirty rolled up socks at Officer Findlay's head.

"Hey, those reek," Findlay joked.

"Fin, let me finish the story already. Laying on Mrs. Fletcher's couch is a young woman who is about six months pregnant, wrapped in a blanket and fast asleep. Mrs. Fletcher told us she heard someone frantically knocking on her front door around three thirty this morning. When she opened the door, she sees her neighbor standing there in her bathrobe and slippers, shivering."

"Geez, no coat? It's nearing the end of January and it's freezing out there," Brant stated.

"No coat. No boots. No hat. Just her bathrobe and slippers. So, Mrs. Fletcher takes her in of course, helps her warm up and asks her what she is doing outside. The girl tells her she went out on her porch to look for her husband after waking up and seeing he wasn't in bed and got locked out. She told Mrs. Fletcher her husband had fallen asleep and didn't come to the door to let her back in. Mrs. Fletcher suspected there was more to the story and told her she could stay the night."

"Poor girl. Then what happened?" Brant asked.

"This is where things get real interesting," Officer Findlay chimed in again.

"So, we let the girl sleep and, on Mrs. Fletcher's recommendation, we go across the street. Turns out her hunch was right. We knock on the door and at first no one answered. We knock again and the husband yells out, 'Who's there and what do you want?' I then say, 'Swanset PD. Open up' and the guy responds by asking, 'How do I know you aren't Charlie?' I identify myself and tell him we just want to talk. He then informs us he has a gun and isn't afraid to use it and we see him peek out from behind the curtain," Mick said.

"We didn't know what to expect next knowing that he was armed," Findlay added.

"Armed and potentially dangerous. We urged him to put the gun down, hoping the situation wouldn't escalate, and told him that if he doesn't open the door, we'll have to force our way in. A few more knocks, and a few minutes later, the guy finally decides to open the door and is decked out in a U.S. Army field jacket with dog tags around his neck," Mick stated.

"He had a dazed look in his eyes too. Like his mind was somewhere else," Officer Findlay added.

Hmm . . . I've seen that look once before, Brant thought.

"I tell him we wanted to talk to him about his wife and he tells us that she is asleep upstairs. We ask him if we can see for ourselves, so we cautiously follow him up to the second floor. It's a nice little farmhouse and nothing is out of place. When we get to the upstairs bedroom, he tells us his wife is pregnant and he doesn't want to wake her. When he opens the door, he realizes that she isn't in bed like he thought."

"He was actually surprised she wasn't there," Findlay stated.

"Yes, he was genuinely surprised and then became agitated and says, 'Charlie must have broken in while I was sleeping. I have to find my wife.' We ask who Charlie is and, as suspected, he tells us Charlie is what he and his buddies called the Viet Cong. He tells us that the enemy is everywhere. So, we take a seat and just talk to him for a while. We tell him not to worry, that his wife is safe, and we explain where she is. His eyes fill with tears and he tells us he came back from Vietnam a few months ago and has been having a hard time," Mick said.

"Can you believe he thought we were Viet Cong when he came to the door? I mean two Scots like us," Findlay said with a snicker, shaking his oblong head in disbelief.

"He told us he's on some strong medication, but it doesn't seem to be helping and he's always looking over his shoulder. I suggested he try to get himself straightened out and reminded him he has a beautiful wife and baby on the way who need him. He reluctantly agreed to let us take him to the mental health facility in Weaver Falls for help. He'll get a psych evaluation there and hopefully they'll get him squared away," Officer McMillan said, finishing up his recap of the night's events.

"You said this happened off of Hails Hallow Road?" Brant Judge asked.

"Yes. You'll get the full report later but since your shift is up next, it's probably best you heard this directly from me. The address is seven twenty-three Hails Hallow Road," Mick said, reading his handwritten notes.

"And the name of the occupants?" Brant asked.

"Let me see here," Mick said, flipping through the pages of his notepad.

"Ayers," Findlay said.

"Ayers?" Brant asked, feeling his heart sink with immediate concern for Nora's safety, as he thought back to the previous July when he met Russ Ayers and experienced his violent streak firsthand. *That was about six months ago.*

"Yup. Fin is right for a change. The last name is Ayers. Russ Ayers is the husband and the wife's name is . . . uh . . .," Mick said as he ran his finger down the page of his notepad.

Nora, Brant thought, anticipating what Mick was about to say and hoping that somehow he'd be wrong.

"Nora . . . Nora Ayers. Pretty young thing too, I'll tell you. Even pregnant, she's a stunner. Pretty face . . . and striking green eyes. She looked familiar to me. Maybe I've seen her around town. How does a girl like her end up involved with an unstable guy like that anyway?" Mick asked.

"I have no idea," Brant replied.

Six months pregnant? Six months ago was . . . July, Brant thought, not realizing until now that Nora was expecting, let alone at the end of her second trimester. *I had no idea. I tried to call her before taking off for the police academy and she never returned my calls. Surely Josie would have said something to me if . . ..*

"Enough about that. I need to get home and tackle a to-do list that Janice has been nagging me about. Do you have any questions before I head out, Officer Judge?" Mick asked.

"Just one more thing, Mick. How far along did you say the girl was again?"

"Six months. The girl told us she is about six months along. Clean the wax out of your ears, Judge," Findlay blurted out as he stood in front of his open locker, stripped down to just his birthday suit and his navy-blue uniform socks.

"Why do you ask?" Mick asked.

"I just want to be sure I have all the facts straight," Brant replied, aware that he was once again telling Mick yet another half-truth.

34

"When we spoke to Russ this morning, he told us he thought you were upstairs sleeping last night and that someone was trying to break in. What do you mean he locked you out of the house?" Martha inquisitively asked over the phone line.

"He's confused, Martha. It was so cold last night, and I was on the porch knocking and calling out to him for almost an hour," Nora replied, sensing that her mother-in-law did not believe her.

"Maybe he didn't hear you. Or maybe he fell asleep. He always has been a deep sleeper after all," Martha insisted.

"Martha, Russ has been having trouble," Nora replied, knowing that her husband's sleep, and his mind, had been restless for months.

"So, you had the police come and take him away? As his wife you should be there for him."

"I have been, Martha, but he keeps things from me. Haven't you noticed a change in him since he came back?"

"What are you saying?"

"He's not the same Russ as before. Something happened to him but, since he won't talk about it, I can't help him. Has he said anything to you? Or have you noticed any change in his behavior?"

"Don't be silly, Nora, of course he's the same Russell. He hasn't said anything to me but, shortly after he came home there was . . . an incident," Martha said, appearing reluctant to tell Nora what she knew.

"What kind of incident?" Nora asked, wondering why Martha had not mentioned anything to her before.

"One day last summer . . . it was a stormy day. Remember that big storm that came up from Long Island sound?"

"Yes, I remember," Nora replied, recalling the storm that came through Swanset the same week she found out she was pregnant.

"He was in the woods and he wouldn't come out. When he eventually did, he wasn't . . .," Martha hesitated.

"He wasn't what?" Nora curiously asked.

"Making sense. He just wasn't making sense."

"Well, what did he say, Martha?"

"Something about . . . looking for someone. I don't really remember. Anyway, what does this have to do with last night, Nora?" Martha asked, sounding agitated.

"It has a lot to do with it, Martha. Russ has combat fatigue and needs help."

"Are you saying there is something wrong with my son? There's nothing wrong with him. He is fine and your neighbor shouldn't have overreacted and called the police on him. Now look where he is . . . at some . . . hospital . . . getting asked twenty questions by psychiatrists," Martha scolded, her voice cracking as she spoke.

"He needs our help," Nora insisted.

"Stop saying that. There is nothing wrong with my Russell. Maybe your hormones are getting the best of you, Nora."

"But . . .," Nora began, but stopped herself, knowing Martha was in denial and anything she said was falling on deaf ears.

"Fred and I will pick him up Saturday morning and bring him home as he asked us to. Thankfully, he's only there for forty-eight hours and can sign himself out. He belongs at home, not in some . . . mental institution. You should try to get some rest. That little bundle arrives in just a few more months. Everything will be better once the baby is here, you'll see."

Within seconds of hanging up from speaking to her mother-in-law, the telephone rang again.

Nora took a deep breath in before picking the telephone back up.

"Hello?"

"Good morning. Is this Mrs. Ayers?"

"Yes, it is," Nora replied, not recognizing the deep voice on the other end of the line.

"Hello, Mrs. Ayers. My name is Roland Edmunds. I'm the plant manager over at New England Underground Cable. I understand you called my secretary, Darlene, earlier this morning to let her know that your husband would not be coming to work today."

"Yes, good morning, Mr. Edmunds. As I told your secretary, Russ is not feeling well today."

"Can I speak with him please?"

"He's not home, Sir."

"He knew we have a tight deadline to meet by the end of the week and we need him here. Where is he anyway?"

"Mr. Edmunds, Russ is in the hospital."

"The hospital? Well, gee I sure hope it's nothing serious. We need him back here as soon as possible."

"He should be home by Saturday and will return to work Monday morning, Mr. Edmunds," Nora said, trying not to give too much information and anticipating a discriminatory attitude from Russ' boss if he knew his hospitalization was due to a mental health crisis.

"Saturday? So, he won't be in tomorrow either?"

"No, Sir," Nora meekly replied.

"Please give Robert my best and have him bring a doctor's note for HR. Have a good day now," Mr. Edmunds said with obvious irritation in his voice.

"Thank you . . . Mr. Edmunds," Nora said as the phone line cut out before she could complete her sentence. ". . . and his name is Russell, not Robert, you jerk," Nora said aloud as she hung up the phone.

Nora made her way over to the sofa, draped a blanket over her growing belly and took a sip of hot tea as the television anchor delivered the morning news. She welcomed the relief the tea brought as the added honey coated her sore throat and the liquid warmed her insides. Even though the skin on her ears, face and hands were red and painfully tingled with frostnip, the fluttering sensation of her baby's tiny kicks comforted her, reassuring her that last night's freezing temperatures had not caused it harm. After hours of being chilled to the bone, her core body temperature seemed to finally be returning to normal.

"According to the Associated Press, United States President Richard Nixon has announced he will be cutting the existing 139,000 troops remaining in Vietnam in half. He is expected to pull out 70,000 American troops by May first of this year," the morning news anchor, with a thick mustache, tight necktie and pointy collared dress shirt, announced in an exaggerated, peppy tone.

"It's about time, don't you think?" Nora said.

"Be sure to tune in tonight at nine p.m. eastern standard time for our live coverage of President Nixon's 1972 State of the Union Address, which is said to include a recap of his recent trip to Moscow and a list of his new proposals and legislative items that are in the best interest of our country and for the promotion of world peace," the reporter stated.

"World peace? You've got to be kidding. There's been so much damage done by keeping all those boys in Vietnam for so long and by widening our involvement in the war by invading Cambodia. He should do this country a favor and resign," Nora ranted under her breath, having heard enough and resentful of the policies that seemed to have damaged so many lives, including her own and Russ'.

An unexpected knock at the front door suddenly broke her train of thought. She pushed herself off the couch, steadied herself and turned off the television set. Walking over to the window and pushing the curtain aside, she saw a man with a clipboard outside on the front porch and a van parked in the driveway.

"Good morning. May I help you?" Nora asked when she opened the door.

"Good morning, ma'am. I'm with Weaver Falls Floral Design and I have a special delivery for a Nora Ayers," the delivery man, wearing a navy blue knit hat and matching scarf, announced as white wispy clouds formed from his warm breath contacting the frigid morning air.

"I'm Nora Ayers."

"Today is your lucky day then. These are for you," he said, presenting her with a tall vase full of fresh daises and pink roses.

"For me? Who are they from?"

"You'll have to open the card to find out. Have yourself a nice day now, Miss."

"Thank you. Please be careful. I wasn't able to shovel the snow off the steps," Nora said, accepting the arrangement and the white envelope into her hands.

"I will. Don't you worry about me, miss. You shouldn't be shoveling snow in your condition. Good day to you," he replied before carefully walking down the steps and getting into his van.

After shutting the door behind her, Nora placed the vase on the kitchen counter, opened the envelope and carefully pulled out the card. *I'm sorry I hurt you. Please forgive me. Love, Russ.* Nora lightly bit her lower lip, fighting off tears as a flood of emotion washed over her. She allowed Russ' words to sink in and understood he had not intended to harm her.

"Of course I forgive you," she said as she reread the card and held it close to her heart. She found herself gently weeping at the thought of Russ being evaluated at a mental health facility after having been so caught up in his thoughts that he was unable to separate what was in his mind from reality. She found it astonishing that, even in a moment of deep despair, Russ was still showing concern for her well-being.

Nora wiped her eyes, added cold water to the vase from the kitchen faucet and carried the arrangement into the living room, setting it on a pedestal table in front of the window. She stood momentarily and admired the flowers, before leaning in and enjoying their fragrant aroma, just as she knew Russ would want her to. She also knew Russ needed her now more than ever and she intended to continue to provide her unwavering support and love to help him through his latest ordeal.

35

"Who plowed my driveway?" Russ asked as his father's old pickup traversed the snowy backroad and his house came into view.

"Jeff plowed it for you. Nora called to let us know that Jeff was concerned when you didn't show up at Lance's to play darts on Friday night. When she told him what happened, he came by to clear the snow so we wouldn't get stuck when we brought you home," Martha said.

"Good thing too 'cause my back can't take shovelin' this heavy snow anymore," Russ' father said.

"Jeff knows I was hospitalized?" Russ asked, turning to his mother who was sandwiched between him and his father on the pickup's bench seat.

"Yes. But, as I told Nora when she said that you're different than before, there's nothing wrong with you," Martha said self-convincingly.

"Nora told you that I'm different than before?" Russ asked with concern.

"For Christ's sake, Martha. Nora didn't mean any harm in that. Your wife is just worried about you, Russ. We all are," Fred said, keeping his eyes on the road.

"She said that you're not the same Russell as before you were deployed. I told her that was nonsense. Your wife means well, but I reminded her that her hormones are getting the best of her. Don't listen to that talk. You are going to be just fine, Russell," Martha said, patting Russ' knee.

Russ felt his stomach twist as he absorbed what his mother had just told him. *Nora told Ma that I'm not the same as before. Why didn't she tell me this herself and how long has she felt this way?* Russ wondered.

After saying goodbye to his parents, Russ stepped out of the truck and felt the bite of the cold January air. *Poor Nora was outside for an hour with no coat in colder weather than this,* Russ thought to himself as he pulled the hood of his parka over his head, feeling as though he had failed her.

The crusty layers of frozen snow crunched underfoot as Russ made his way up the unshoveled walkway. Three inches of snow had fallen since he left to go to the hospital with Officer McMillan and Findlay two days ago. He knew that Nora, being as far along as she was, was in no condition to shovel snow. *I'll get to it later,* Russ thought, feeling sluggish, and anxious to get inside to see his wife.

Russ saw movement in the front window and, as he got closer, he saw Nora waving to him, seemingly anticipating his arrival. Being cautious so as not to slip, he made his way onto the porch, hoping that his conversation with her would go well.

"Welcome home," Nora said as she opened the front door, her loving arms and the warmth from inside the house enveloping him.

"Hi, Nor," Russ replied, at a loss for words as he held her in his arms and leaned his head on her shoulder, fighting back tears.

"It's okay. You're home now," Nora told him, seeming to sense his emotions and running her fingers through his thick hair.

"I'm so sorry, Nor."

"I know you are but look at me, Russ. I'm fine . . . and bigger than ever. I think I gained ten pounds this week alone," Nora joked, stepping back and turning to the side to show off her growing belly.

"You look beautiful as always."

"The baby has been kicking up a storm. Here, give me your hand. Can you feel it?" Nora asked as she placed Russ' open palm on her belly.

"I can! Is it okay? Maybe we should call the doctor. I've been worried about you and the baby."

"We're both fine. I think I just need to lay off the coffee. Now, take your coat off and stay a while. I made some soup for lunch to help you warm up."

"Thanks. I missed your cooking. That hospital food tasted like crap," Russ said, grateful to be home with his wife again.

"I've come a long way since my days of making peanut butter and jelly sandwiches in my freshman dorm at Bridgegate, don't you think?" Nora jokingly asked.

"You have," Russ agreed as he took off his boots, hung up his coat, and walked into the living room.

"Sit and relax. I'll bring your lunch to you," Nora told him.

"Okay," Russ replied, turning on the television set, adjusting its rabbit ear antennas and turning the dial to search for something to watch, grateful to be back in his own surroundings and away from those psychiatrists and their probing questions.

"There's mostly just cartoons on this time of day," Nora shouted from the kitchen.

"I think the soap opera you like is on, Nor," Russ called out to her.

"You're right. I guess I lost track of time," Nora replied, glancing at the television and setting a tray with a bowl of hot vegetable soup and crackers on the coffee table in front of him.

While waiting for the soup to cool, the two sat watching the melodrama unfold between the characters on the television screen.

"What a silly story line," Nora said.

"What did you say?" Russ asked, distracted by a vase full of fresh flowers by the front window.

"I said this storyline is so silly."

Russ' gaze became fixed on the vase of flowers.

"They're beautiful, aren't they?" Nora asked.

Where did she get those from?

"Are you okay, Russ?"

"Where did you get those, Nor?"

"The flowers?"

"Yes, the flowers. Who sent them to you?" Russ said, hearing himself raise his voice.

"Russ, you sent them to me."

"No, I didn't," Russ replied, wondering why his wife would make up such a story and glancing back at the soap opera.

Maybe some other guy was here while I was away. Maybe Jeff gave them to her.

"You did, Russ. Don't you remember?"

"No, I don't remember, Nor. Now tell me who sent those to you," Russ demanded, his brow wrinkling and hearing agitation in his own voice as dramatic music emanated from the drama on the television set.

Nora rose from the couch, walked over to the window, and picked up a card that was on the table beside the vase of flowers.

"Here, Russ, read the note inside the card. The flowers and card arrived late Friday morning. It was nice of you to send them," Nora told him as she handed him the card and lovingly rubbed the side of his arm.

"I'm sorry I hurt you. Please forgive me, Nor. Love, Russ," Russ read aloud from the card.

"Did you forget you sent them to me?" Nora asked, looking into his eyes as if searching for something.

"I . . . guess. . . I must have forgot but I think I remember now. The medication they gave me made me really tired," Russ replied, as he gazed into her calming eyes and realized the doctor had him so doped up on tranquilizers that he had lost the memory of sending the flowers.

"Your doctor called earlier and told me that you insisted on sending me flowers and that you wouldn't cooperate until they ordered them for you. He also wanted me to remind you that your body needs to adjust to the new medication he prescribed and that you should expect some side effects. In the long run, it should help you to sleep better though. It's going to be okay, Russ," Nora assured him.

"I suppose you're right," Russ replied, feeling anxious and checking his wristwatch to see if it was time for his next dose of his sedative, unsure if he would ever be able to clear his head and think straight again.

36

When he returned to work on Monday morning after his short get-away to the psychiatric ward, Russ began his day with his usual cup of coffee in the breakroom at New England Underground Cable. Darlene, wearing a tight green sweater that accentuated the roundness of her breasts, with her usual shade of crimson on her pouty lips, pumped him for information as to why he was in the hospital as she twirled her brown locks around her index finger.

"It's none of your business, Darlene," Russ said.

"I was concerned about you when your wife called. She sounds nice. Is she pretty?" Darlene asked, stepping close and reaching over his arm for a coffee stirrer.

"My wife is not up for discussion."

"I bet she's not as pretty as me," Darlene flirtatiously whispered as the side of her breast rubbed up against his upper arm.

"Nice of you to join us today, Robert," Mr. Edmunds said as he entered the breakroom, causing Darlene to jump and step aside.

"It's Russell, Sir. Good morning, Mr. Edmunds," Russ replied.

"Darlene, get back to work and leave Russell and I to ourselves please."

"Of course," Darlene replied, shooting Russ a discrete "catch you later" look, her short skirt moving in sync with her swaying hips as she left the room.

"It appears that you had a medical emergency of some sort. Did you bring in the doctor's note for HR?" Mr. Edmunds asked.

"Yes, Sir. I already handed it in first thing this morning."

"That was bad timing on your behalf. What was wrong with you any-way? Was it a stomach bug or is there something wrong with your ticker?"

"Something like that," Russ replied.

"Well, which was it? Ah, forget it, it doesn't matter. Just know that we really had to scramble to get things done since you left us shorthanded. Your coworkers stayed late and picked up the slack since you didn't show up. Next time, try not to get sick when a deadline is looming. There are plenty of hungry people out there who need a job in this economy. Understand?"

"Yes, Sir," Russ replied, feeling his face flush as he started to perspire. *I understand I'm just a number to you, Edmunds.*

"And remember that I don't pay you to stand around and flirt with my niece. She says you're a good guy, but just know that I form my own opinions around here. Time is money so get to work and make it a productive day," Mr. Edmunds said as a strand of white, ropey saliva stretched between the midline of his upper and lower lips.

I told your niece that I'm married so why don't you tell her to stop coming on to me. "Yes, Sir. I will," Russ replied as Mr. Edmunds stepped out of the room and disappeared into the hallway.

Russ stood alone in the breakroom, taking in a few seconds of peace and quiet before starting his shift. He raised his coffee mug to his lips and took a quick swig, only to get a mouthful of rough, hot grounds.

"This coffee sucks . . . just like this company," Russ mumbled to himself after spitting the coffee back into the mug and dumping it into the sink, wishing he had time to smoke a joint to kill the inadequacy he felt during his lucid state of mind.

In the weeks that followed, Russ felt as though everything that could go wrong, did, as he adjusted to the increased dosage of his antipsychotic medication and his newly prescribed sedatives, which were supposed to help him sleep better at night but didn't. He was also feeling the financial pinch with each bill that rolled in for the home heating oil and repairs to keep Nora's old clunker running. Nervousness set in as Nora's pregnancy progressed and he anticipated the baby's upcoming birth. The only good news that he had received lately was that the draft had been suspended and Nixon had begun pulling more troops out of Vietnam.

During the workweek, he made sure that he always had his cigarettes within close reach, using up his two allotted fifteen-minute breaks each day to quell the frustration he felt with Mr. Edmunds always up his ass. In addition to his prescribed medications and cigarettes, he had a few bottles of whiskey, hidden from Nora, under the driver's seat of his car and locked inside his trunk in the basement, to take the edge off when his medication didn't do the trick. Sometimes, after a particularly rough day, he would pop into Lance's for a couple of quick shots on his way home from work. Now that he was a paying customer, Lance allowed him to have the hard stuff, often pouring him a double at no extra charge.

On the weekends, he had a stash of marijuana to rely on thanks to his high school buddy, Bob Cleary, who had become a talented cultivator of the herb, growing the plants from seeds he had obtained on a trip to the west coast. Bob knew just the right strains for Russ' needs, supplying him with Skunk and Acapulco Gold on a regular basis.

"Weed has so many medicinal benefits. Can you believe Nixon considers this a dangerous substance?" Bob asked the last time they met.

"Hopefully, they legalize it someday and then everybody, including Tricky Dicky, can chill out," Russ replied.

Russ' use of the herb seemed to upset Nora, since Nixon included marijuana on his list of controlled narcotics. What Nora didn't understand, was that the buds of the fan-shaped leafed plant seemed to help him relax better than his prescribed psychiatric medications.

On Saturday afternoons, no matter the weather, it became routine for him to take a walk into the woods behind the farmhouse. Even though he never told Nora or his psychiatrist, it was there that he would find himself out in the jungle with his buddies again. He would canvass the area, picturing Johnny Davis and Harry Blake there by his side, to be sure there weren't any hidden trip wires, trap doors or tunnels underneath the forest floor. He discovered places to hide too, just in case Charlie showed up, like inside the hollowed-out cavity of the large, decaying tree trunk by the brook. After making sure the area was safe, he would sit by the brook's edge and light up a joint in order to escape all the noise inside his head. He always knew this little bit of serenity would be short lived. The drugs were giving him the upper hand to be able to stay focused and, although he wouldn't consider himself addicted to one substance, it did occur to him that he couldn't function well without a combination of them. He managed to do a good job at keeping Nora in the dark about his feelings and she was unaware he felt the need to have something always running through his system. Seeing that he was relaxed whenever he returned from the woods, Nora thankfully agreed to let his marijuana use slide.

On Nora's urging, as springtime approached, Russ decided to stop by the local veterans post after work to fill out a membership application. Through the hall's locked glass entry door, Russ could see a man inside folding an American flag. After hearing Russ' knock on the door, the man stopped what he was doing and made his way over to him with a noticeable limp.

"Hi there. The spaghetti supper is tomorrow," the man said after opening the door as he looked Russ' work uniform up and down.

"Spaghetti supper?" Russ asked.

"Yes. It starts at six tomorrow night. Are you here to purchase tickets?" the man asked.

"No, Sir. It sounds like a fun time but I'm here to fill out a membership application," Russ replied, glancing around the hall, its walls decorated with shiny plaques and framed pictures of former post commanders.

"A membership application? Oh, my apologies. I'm Paul, commander of this post."

"No sweat. Good to meet you, Sir. I'm Russ Ayers," Russ replied, shaking the commander's hand.

"Before I get you that application, why don't you have a seat here and tell me a bit about yourself."

"Sure. Thanks," Russ said as he pulled out a chair and accepted a seat at a round table.

Russ settled into his chair, surrounded by flags of all the branches of the United States Armed Forces displayed in polished, metal stands around the room, feeling as though he belonged there.

"So where are you from? Where and when did you serve?" the post commander asked.

"I was born and raised right here in Swanset, Sir. I graduated from Swanset High in June of '69 and was drafted the following December," Russ proudly stated.

"Drafted in December of '69?" the commander asked, raising an eyebrow.

"Yes, Sir. Then after Basic and AIT, I became an Army tunnel rat in the Cu Chi district of Vietnam."

"And why do you want to become a member?"

"I don't feel I belong anywhere since I came home a few months ago. I suppose I could use some friends to talk to who've been through the same things I have," Russ reluctantly admitted.

"Well, while we do offer comradery and a place for members to come and talk openly about their experiences, we only accept veterans who have honorably served this great country in war overseas."

"Yes, Sir. As I already told you I honorably served in Vietnam," Russ replied, looking directly into the commander's eyes and sensing that something was off.

"Son . . .,"

"My name is Russell."

"Okay. Russell, I'm also an Army veteran. Specifically, I took part in the Battle of the Bulge in Belgium. It was Adolf Hitler's last major offensive against the Western Front in World War II. Did they teach you about it at Swanset High?"

"No, Sir, but I've read about it. It sounded like it was a gruesome battle."

"You're damn right it was. Son, you think these New England winters are cold? You don't know what cold is. In December of '44 and into the following January of '45, I spent six weeks in the frigid cold forest in snow drifts, thick fog and freezing rain being attacked by the Germans. By the time it was over, the entire forest looked like a twister went through it. I lost two toes from the frostbite, but I was lucky. My buddies . . . well . . . my buddies were massacred. Nineteen thousand U.S. soldiers were killed in action, twenty-three thousand went missing and over forty-seven thousand men were wounded in that battle alone."

"I can relate," Russ stated.

"Is that so? You can relate to the guys who died during the Bulge can you? I suppose you can relate to the U.S. troops who died storming the beaches of Normandy too. Am I right, . . . Son?"

"Yes, I can . . . Paul," Russ said resentfully as pictures of the dead bodies of his fellow soldiers, strewn across the jungle floor, flashed through his mind.

"To my knowledge, I'm quite sure that Vietnam has not been declared a war. That means you, and your other little grunt friends who completed your required one year of military police action, are not eligible for entry into this organization," Paul fired back, holding Russ' gaze.

Russ felt his face flush with heat and pounded his fist on the table to let out his frustration.

"Well now, Son, I think it's time for you to go. I'll see you to the door," Paul said in response to Russ' display of raw emotion.

"I can walk myself out. I don't need your help and I don't need to spend another second inside this dive," Russ said as he stormed out of the building, consumed with bitterness for having been made to feel ashamed of his honorable service, and got back into his car.

"Be sure to connect with your local veterans organization. They'll stand by you when no one else will." You were so wrong, Herbie, Russ thought, recalling his conversation with the cabbie who drove him home from Boston the day he returned from Vietnam. Russ slammed the driver's side door shut and noticed Paul watching him from inside the hall. Reaching under his seat, Russ grabbed his hidden bottle of whiskey, loosened its cap, brought it to his mouth and took a large swig. As the whiskey slipped across

his tongue, Russ bid the commander one last farewell with the wave of his middle finger, and the alcohol's warm familiar burn followed.

37

"It's nice to finally meet you, Amy. She's beautiful, Nor," Josie said as she held the newborn baby in her arms.

"It's good to see you, Jo," Nora replied, happy to see her friend who had unexpectantly stopped by while in town.

"Sorry I couldn't get here sooner. I've been so busy on campus and then I flew to California to see the "Womanhouse" exhibit. I just had to see it before they closed it at the end of February. I can't believe it's March already."

"It's okay, Jo. I remember you telling me you were planning to go. How was it?"

"It was so empowering. The art students refurbished an old, rundown Victorian style house in Hollywood and held the exhibit there. One of the artists stuck a female mannequin into a linen closet and had her cross-sectioned body imprisoned in the shelving. Another artist created a "Womb Room" out of crocheted webs. I wish you could have seen it, Nor. It really captured how domestic life is a . . .," Josie paused and glanced around the room.

"What, Jo? It captured how domestic life is what?" Nora asked, cocking her head to the side.

"A tool . . . of oppression . . . for women," Josie replied as her eyes landed on a pile of Russ' wrinkled work shirts sitting on top of an open ironing board.

"I'm glad you enjoyed it, Jo," Nora meekly replied, overwhelmed by her domestic chores and wifely duties, and gaining a sudden understanding that her friend thought her to be oppressed in some way.

"Thanks," Josie said softly.

"Anyway, Amy couldn't wait to meet you. I told her all about you," Nora said, trying to change the subject.

"Oh? What did you tell her exactly?" Josie asked with a curious smile.

"I told her that I hope she's lucky enough to find a best friend like I found in you."

"That's sweet. Amy, I can't wait to tell you all about my adventures with your mom when you get older," Josie said, cradling the swaddled infant.

"Please be choosey as to what you tell her. I don't want her to know everything after all," Nora joked.

"Don't worry, Nor. I'll only tell her the juicy stuff."

"I wouldn't expect anything less from you, Jo," Nora laughed.

"So how are you feeling?" Josie asked.

"Well, I haven't had much sleep since we brought Amy home. She hasn't slept through the night yet. Not even once."

"You do look tired, Nor. Why don't you tell Russ that you need him to alternate nights with you to help with the baby. If Amy wakes up in the middle of the night you could take turns getting up with her. That's what my cousin and her husband do."

"That wouldn't work," Nora replied.

"Why not?"

"Because Russ doesn't sleep well as it is, and he has to be up early for work."

"How have things been going with Russ lately?"

"He just adores Amy and is so affectionate toward her. He's a good father and provider. I think the baby has been a much-needed distraction for him."

"That's good to hear. Has he had any suspicions about the possibility that Amy . . ."

"Jo, please don't go there."

"But maybe Brant . . ."

"Jo, everything is good here so can we please not talk about him?" Nora said.

"Okay, but I read in the paper that Brant was sworn in as a Swanset Police officer recently," Josie added.

"He was?"

"Yes. I guess he decided to stay here in town. Have you run into him at all?"

"No, I haven't, Jo. It's not like I go anywhere. Let's talk about something else," Nora replied, shifting in her seat as old feelings began to surface.

"Wait, I have to tell you one more thing. So, I'm not sure if you knew that Becky and Jack still keep in touch, but I heard through the grapevine that Brant and Libby are officially back on. She thinks she's all that with her impressive pedigree."

"Good for him," Nora replied, feeling as though her friend was rubbing salt on the wound.

"Good for him? Nor, she's a stuck-up bitch."

"Josie!" Nor exclaimed.

"I could have said she's a snob, but bitch is much more fitting," Josie stated with a chuckle.

"I really don't care. I'm just happy to have a healthy baby and to not look like a beached whale anymore," Nora said, shrugging off the news of Brant and Libby's rekindled relationship.

"Okay. I won't mention him again. You look good, Nor, except for those dark circles under your eyes . . . and that skirt you're wearing. Oh, that reminds me, I cleaned out my closet and brought a bag of clothes for you to try on. I know money is tight for you guys."

"No thanks, Jo. I've changed my style a bit," Nora replied, checking the time on her wristwatch, secretly wanting to see the fashionable articles of clothing her friend had brought with her.

"I've noticed! Just because you're married and have a baby doesn't mean you can't be in style. What's with that frumpy skirt anyway?"

"I know that, Jo, but I happen to like this skirt. It keeps my legs warm," Nora said, smoothing her skirt over her knees and trying to deflect Josie's sideways glances.

Feeling uncomfortable, Nora got up and began folding the clothes sitting on top of the ironing board. She thought back to an argument that had ensued with Russ in which he forbade her to wear miniskirts after Jeff commented on what a nice figure she had since giving birth to Amy. She found Russ' request deeply upsetting and confided in Viviane about the matter, since none of her friends were around to talk to about it.

"Well Nora, you are a wife and mother now after all. It's about time you grow up and stop wearing those short skirts anyway. Your job is to keep your husband happy and to keep your marriage together. Do as you're told!" Viviane scolded.

While she did love her husband and continued to support him in any way she could, she found it difficult tolerate Russ' controlling ways. With all of her domestic responsibilities she didn't have time for small battles and fashion had become the least of her concerns.

Nora glanced out the front window and then at her wristwatch.

"Nor?"

"Did you say something, Jo?"

"Yes, I asked why you keep looking at your watch?" Josie asked as Nora checked her watch again.

"Russ will be home from work soon. He doesn't like people being in our house when he's not here."

"Why not? It's just me, Nor. I'm not a stranger."

"I know. He just gets . . . kind of paranoid sometimes. He wants me to keep the doors locked, even during the day."

"That's strange. It must have something to do with his combat fatigue. Is he afraid someone will steal you or something?" Josie said with a chuckle.

"I don't know. Our house is surrounded by woods though. He's just protective and it seems like he doesn't trust anyone lately," Nora replied, looking at her watch again while making her way over to the window and peering out toward the driveway, downplaying the situation while her insides became jumpy.

"Protective? I think it's called being controlling, Nor. I have to get going anyway. I need to stop back home to pick up my clean laundry before heading back to campus. I'm just glad that midterms are over."

"Midterms? Gee, I remember those," Nora replied, realizing that one year ago, she was in her dorm room celebrating with Josie and Becky after finishing up her midsemester finals.

"You have more important things to do now," Josie said, getting up and handing the swaddled infant back to Nora before grabbing the handles of the paper shopping bag full of clothes.

"Thanks for stopping by, Jo," Nora said, catching herself looking at her watch again.

"Remember, I'm just a phone call away, Nor," Josie said as she walked toward the door.

"I know, Jo."

"Take care of yourself and this little bundle of . . . hope," Josie said as she leaned in and tenderly kissed Amy's forehead, seemingly aware her friend's life had become a feminist's nightmare.

"I will," Nora replied, envisioning herself trapped within the shelves of a linen closet.

38

A shiny feathered common grackle, perched in her nest high up in the branches of an eastern white pine, squawked loudly, making her presence known.

"Shut up you stupid bird. I'm not the enemy," Russ mumbled as he trudged through the woods in hopes of silencing his mind and killing his pain once again.

The one place where he could find peace had become a hot bed of activity in recent months as the forest, and all of its creatures, awoke from their winter slumber. The once barren trees were in full bloom, displaying their vibrant foliage. The leaves of the maples, oaks and white birch, combined with the needles of the coniferous trees, now gave the forest a different feel. As he made his way into the woods and headed toward the brook, Russ found himself on high alert, clutching his loaded pistol that was inside the pocket of his field coat. Charlie could be hiding anywhere now that the dense vegetation had filled in around him and he was careful to keep his eyes open for trip wires with each step he took in his polished combat boots with their laces tucked neatly inside.

As he reached his favorite spot, Russ slumped down against the rough bark of a large oak tree. He saw the once semi-frozen brook, and the nearby vernal pools, were now filled to the rim with snow melt and rain from the late spring showers, as the current whisked sticks and other forest debris past him. He took a long toke of his joint as he tried to calm himself down after the argument that had ensued with Nora earlier in the day. He thought back to the previous week at work which had been extra stressful, as the pressure was on to wrap up one of the company's government contracted projects. Russ was there to help the company meet the deadline this time, however Mr. Edmunds still felt the need to give him flak in front of his coworkers.

"Now be sure you don't have tummy trouble this time around, Ayers. No one wants to repeat the last deadline, when everyone had to stay late because you left us shorthanded," Mr. Edmunds had announced.

As his coworkers standing within earshot of Mr. Edmunds' comment laughed, Russ couldn't help but feel belittled and as though everyone was against him. His coworkers didn't know him and, even if they did, they wouldn't understand what he had been through. He had been careful not to divulge much information about himself to prevent management from finding out that he had served in Vietnam. Since Mr. Edmunds had everyone so focused on production, none of them really seemed to care.

Russ took another toke as a cottontail bunny hopped by. He watched as it stopped and briefly looked at him before quickly disappearing into the woods, reminding him of the way Darlene would scurry back to work and make herself look busy every time she noticed Mr. Edmunds approaching. While she was nice to look at, Russ knew to keep his distance. Stories about Darlene's leg-spreading escapades, which eventually led to the firing of a male employee by her uncle, circulated around the plant and validated Russ' first impression of her.

The grackle squawked again and Russ thought about how, on his way home from work the night before, he had stopped off at Lance's for a quick shot of whiskey. Seconds after sitting down on his favorite stool at the end of the gleaming oak bar, he saw Darlene saunter in. He was surprised to learn she had followed him there as she took a seat on the barstool beside him, crossing her legs so that the toe of her high heels rubbed up against his shin.

"Hi, stranger. Can you buy me a drink?" she coyly asked.

"Sure, but I'm not staying long. Lance, can we get the girl a drink?" Russ asked, flagging Lance down.

"What will it be, miss?" Lance asked.

"I'll have what he's having," Darlene said after glancing over at the shot glass in Russ' hand.

"Coming right up," Lance said, reaching for the bottle and filling the glass.

"You like Irish whiskey?" Russ asked.

"I do now," Darlene said before tossing back the shot and licking her red, sultry lips.

"Okay then."

"So why can't you stay? It is Friday night after all," Darlene pleaded.

"You know I have a wife and baby waiting for me at home."

"There's no harm in your wife waiting a little longer. I certainly won't tell her you're here. Besides, my uncle wouldn't want to hear that you were rude to me. You do want to stay on his good side now don't you, Russell?" Darlene asked as she leaned over and wrapped her arms around him.

"Darlene . . .," Russ said as he pulled away.

"What is it, handsome?" Darlene replied, running her fingers through his hair.

"Darlene, I have to . . .,"

"Come home with me? Is that what you were going to say? That you have to come home with me tonight?"

"No, I . . . that wasn't . . . what. . .,"

"I want you, Russell, and I see how you look at me. You're curious about me, aren't you?"

"Another round here, Russ?" Lance asked with a smirk, his eyes darting back and forth between him and Darlene.

"Yes, another round," Darlene blurted out before Russ could say otherwise.

Darlene continued flirting him up in her usual way and, as the alcohol went to work, Russ began to relax in her company.

"Your uncle keeps me busier than a one-legged woman in an ass-kicking contest, Darlene," Russ joked.

"Well, lucky for you, Russell, I'm nothing like my uncle. Now am I?" Darlene asked as she undid a button on her blouse, rolled her shoulders back and brought her breasts front and center.

"Heck no. You have. . .," Russ said, stopping himself and taking a deep breath.

"Gee, its hot in here. You were about to say that I have what?" Darlene asked as she undid another button.

"Darlene, stop that!" Russ ordered, trying his best to resist but unable to take his eyes off her.

"I know you want me. Now tell me what you were going to say," she ordered as she crossed her leg over his.

"I was going to say. . . you have . . . nice assets."

Darlene, obviously flattered, laughed and whispered something in his ear about how she would love for him to come back to her apartment.

"Darlene . . .," Russ said.

"You don't have to be so formal. You can just call me 'Darlin' if you'd like. Now, say you'll come to my place. I promise you won't regret it."

Four shots and three beers later, Russ looked at his wristwatch to find that two and a half hours had passed.

"Shit!" Russ exclaimed, pushing his barstool back and standing upright.

"What's wrong?" Darlene asked.

"I have to go."

"No, you don't. Stay with me. We were having fun," Darlene pouted.

"Darlene, I'm not saying it again. I am going home. . . to my wife. This cannot happen again."

"Party pooper!" Darlene called out.

"Maybe so, Darlene, but remember one thing. I love my wife," Russ said before turning to leave the bar.

"And you remember . . . something too . . . mister!"

"Oh, and what's that . . . 'Darlin'?"

"Remember who my uncle is . . . and that I always get whatever, and whoever, I want," Darlene squawked, just like the common grackle in the tree high above him.

He was glad to have come to his senses and gotten out of there as he certainly wasn't willing to risk ruining his marriage for a floozy like Darlene. It was bad enough that Nora found Darlene's smudged lipstick on his shirt that night and said she'd leave him if it happened again. It seemed as if he couldn't do anything right, and that Nora and Amy would be better off without him. Russ removed his gun from his pocket. It had always provided him with a sense of security and, as he held it, he wondered if it could also bring him the peace he longed for. Russ raised the pistol up to his eye level and stared directly into its hollow barrel. He slowly drew it closer to his forehead, contemplating his next move, before the sound of something rustling in the woods distracted him.

Russ jumped up, took cover behind the trunk of the old oak tree and slid his gun down by his side. The sound of snapping branches and leaves crunching was getting closer and Russ carefully peered out from behind the tree trunk to see a figure approaching.

Don't make a sound. Wait and listen. Charlie must have followed me here.

As beads of sweat dripped down his temples and the back of his shirt became wet with perspiration, Russ could hear his own heartbeat echoing in his ears.

"Ayers?" a voice suddenly called out.

Russ remained still and silent as the figure approached, wondering if he was imagining what he was seeing. His medication had been doing a job on his mind and he often questioned the visions that seemed to materialize out of nowhere. He swore what he was seeing was real but, when no one else around him seemed to take notice, he concluded that maybe they were just figments of his imagination. The lines between what he envisioned and reality itself had become so blurred, he now questioned everything, including this fast-approaching threat.

"Ayers, where the hell are you?" a voice, which Russ thought sounded familiar, called out again.

Where do I know that voice from?

"Come on you Little Spud! I know you're out here somewhere," the voice called again.

Little Spud? There's only one person who ever called me that.

Russ cautiously peered out again to see a man, wearing an army field jacket with the same insignia as his, making his way toward him.

"Ah ha! There you are. Come out from behind that tree."

"Who's there?"

"It's me, Harry! Your wife told me I could find you out here. Heck, don't you recognize me, Ayers?"

"Harry? Harry Blake? Is that really you?" Russ asked, squinting as he struggled to see the man's facial features.

"In the flesh."

"How can I be sure it's really you?" Russ shouted, wondering if it could really be his friend's face that was partially hidden behind a scruffy beard and shoulder-length hair.

"Shit, Ayers, I know I'm missing half an arm and that part of my face got singed, but to mistake me for Charlie? What kind of shit have you been smokin' since you've been home anyway?" Harry asked.

"I can't believe it. Oh my God, Harry. It's really you. You made it back!" Russ exclaimed as he emerged from behind the tree. His hands trembled as he slid his pistol back into the pocket of his jacket and walked over to embrace his friend.

"Somehow, I made it out of that hell hole. We have a lot to catch up on, Little Spud."

"We sure do, Harry."

"Got any weed on you? I could use a hit."

"I have some good Skunk from my friend, Bob."

"Well, what are you waiting for? Light her up my friend and I'll catch you up on everything that's happened since I last saw you."

39

"That was a nice surprise, Russ. It's wonderful that Harry is home," Nora said as she cleared the dishes from the kitchen table.

"It was good to see him again," Russ replied, still in disbelief that he was back.

"It seems like he went out of his way to track you down. You must have developed a good friendship with him while you were away."

"I did. Everyone in our company looked out for one another. We had to," Russ said.

"You guys were out in the woods for quite a while. What were you doing out there?"

"Just smoking and catching up on things. I really don't want to talk about it, Nor," Russ replied, not wanting to disclose the gruesome details of the last few months of Harry's tour.

"Okay. I'm just glad you have someone that you can talk to now. I mean someone who really understands what you've been through," Nora replied as she caressed Russ' back.

"Thanks, Nor. And thanks for inviting him to stay for dinner too. I'm going to retire early if that's okay," Russ replied before kissing Nora's cheek.

"I'm sure this was an emotionally draining day for you. I'll feed Amy her last bottle tonight."

"Thanks. Goodnight, Nor. I love you."

"I love you too, Russ."

After he made his way upstairs, Russ rummaged through the medicine cabinet for his bottle of chlorpromazine. Although he did a good job concealing it from Nora, Harry's surprise visit had caused his anxiety to peak, and he knew he would need all the help he could get in order to get to sleep.

After brushing his teeth, Russ swallowed down his prescribed antipsychotic drug and a couple extra anti-anxiety pills, since one dose hadn't been doing the job lately. As he closed his eyes and his head sank into his downy pillow, turmoil stirred in his mind.

"What happened to the rest of the company after I left?" he had asked Harry as he passed him a joint.

"It got bad. Morale was really low and it became every man for himself. This is some good shit right here," Harry said after taking a lazy toke and passing the joint back to Russ.

"It sure is," Russ replied, taking a couple more puffs.

"Anyway, Charlie kept coming at us with their crafty punji pits, intense firefights and ambushing us left and right. It was man against man and we all had the mindset to just stay alive. Remember how that felt?"

"Like it was yesterday," Russ replied, knowing the nightmare of Vietnam had never left his mind.

"We had to sweep the roads with mine detectors just to get through and that's how my arm got blown off. I swear I can still feel pain in it though."

"I'm sorry that happened to you."

"Hell, there's nothing you could do about it. Consider yourself lucky for getting out when you did. Looking back, I probably shouldn't have stayed on after my first year was up, but when I got that Dear John letter from Donna, everything changed. In the long run, I traded a broken heart for my left arm. Ironic, isn't it?" Harry snickered as he shook his head and took another toke.

"How about the other guys like Blackburn and Lynch who used to lower me down into the tunnels?"

"Ah, you don't want to know."

"Yes, I do Harry. Tell me if they made it out. I need to know what happened to them."

"Okay, but I've got to warn you that Charlie showed them no mercy."

"Go on."

"Let me see. It was maybe about four months or so after you took the Freedom Bird home that our unit began heading north. October . . . no wait. It must have been November because I remember there was talk about Thanksgiving preparations back in the hootch. We had just finished a search and destroy mission in a small village, just like Operation Attleboro back in '66. We turned the place upside down but only found women and children and then we set the whole village ablaze. As we left, the VC came at us with everything they had. Most of us made it out but Blackburn, Lynch and a few others weren't so lucky."

"No, not Lynch and Blackburn too," Russ said, bowing his head and covering his face with his hands.

"The VC were ruthless and, when we went to recover their bodies, we were sickened by what we found. They desecrated them. Shit, I don't know, but maybe it was better than being taken as a prisoner of war and tortured at the Hanoi Hilton."

Russ, barely able to hold his composure, stared at the forest floor feeling lightheaded as a lump formed in his throat and pressure built inside his chest.

"You wanted to know, but now I wish I hadn't told you. Stories like that will keep you up at night. I had to get straightened out before I came back. I was so angry after we found them that I went on a rampage and killed every VC I could find. I got addicted to heroin too and would still be if it weren't for the drug treatment program at the eighty-fifth Evac Hospital in Phu Bai. I took my time coming home to avoid getting spit on at the airport and flew off to Mexico for a few months where I drowned my pain in tequila and the company of all those dark-haired senoritas. I'll tell you, they didn't mind one bit that I'm missing an arm. My family didn't know where I was. I wasn't ready to deal with all the peaceniks, the weird looks and questions from my family and all the closed-minded people in this podunk town. Even my own brother, Dennis, is a conscientious objector. My folks told me he signed on for a two-year volunteer peace assignment of some sort. He always was a wimp. So here we are, Little Spud. Look at you now. You've got all your limbs, a beautiful wife, a new baby, new job and a house of your own. Shit, you escaped unscathed. At least someone made it out without any scars. I'd say you're living the dream. You're living the God damn American dream," Harry said as he wrapped his one remaining arm around Russ' shoulder and let out a cackle.

Those were the last words Russ remembered Harry saying as drowsiness from his self-made cocktail of psychiatric medications set in. He licked his lips to quell the dryness in his mouth and, through heavy eyelids, saw himself walking down a wooded trail. He then saw his little sister, Ann Marie, peek out from behind a tree and point to something further down the path. As he made his way deeper into the woods, he noticed a sign nailed to the bark of a leafless, decaying tree. The sign, in the shape of an arrow, read "Salvation" and beyond it stood Davis, Blackburn and Lynch waving him forward.

40

The aisles of Swanset Village Grocer were filled with customers scrambling to pick up last-minute items for their Labor Day weekend celebrations. Brant Judge despised shopping and was relieved to see that ketchup was now the only remaining item on his list. As he navigated his shopping cart past an endcap stacked high with cans of fruit cocktail, he spotted an overhead sign that read "Condiments." When he turned the corner to proceed down aisle nine, he was met by a woman who was scolding her son for knocking a jar of pickles off the shelf. Brant carefully scooted his cart around the broken glass, pickle juice and kosher dill spears scattered on the floor and, as he looked up, noticed a woman struggling to reach a bottle of salad dressing on the top shelf.

"Let me get that for you, miss," Brant called out, reaching behind her.

"Oh, thank you," the woman replied in a subdued voice.

Brant stood momentarily stunned, as the woman turned around, feeling as though he had been hit by a rogue wave and as if his legs would have certainly given out from underneath him if he hadn't had the handle of his shopping cart to hold onto.

"Nora?" he asked, unable to believe his eyes.

"Hi," Nora softly replied, appearing startled.

"We have to stop meeting like this," Brant said.

Nora stood silent and blushed as she pushed her hair behind her ear and looked down at the floor.

"I . . . sorry I . . . shouldn't have said that. How are you?" Brant asked, stumbling over his own words.

"I'm fine."

"I heard you got married . . . and had a baby."

"I did," Nora replied, seemingly not wanting to engage in conversation or divulge too much information and fidgeting with the label on the bottle of Italian dressing.

"That's great! Congratulations."

"Thanks. Josie told me that you were sworn in as a Swanset Police officer."

"Yeah, it's my rookie year. I'm the one they send out to pick up doughnuts every morning before I start my shift. It's kind of a rite of passage," Brant joked as he nervously smiled, captivated by the sight of the woman he still struggled to forget.

"I've got to get going. Russ is waiting for me outside and Amy fell asleep in the car."

"Amy? Is that . . ."

"Yes, we named her Amy," Nora quickly replied, as she placed the bottle of dressing into the shopping cart.

"Wow, you had a girl. That's great. When was she . . ."

"Thank you," Nora replied, cutting him off mid-sentence as she pulled her pocketbook strap up higher on her shoulder.

"What happened to your arm?" Brant asked, noticing a bruise on her forearm.

"Nothing," she replied, taking a step back and pulling the sleeve of her cardigan down.

"Has he been hurting you?" Brant instinctively asked, concerned once again for her safety.

"I'm fine."

"If he's hurting you, please let me know. You can call me at the station anytime," Brant reassured her, being careful not to scare her away, as he recalled the story Mick had shared with him about Russ' mental breakdown over the winter which left Nora locked out of the house in below freezing temperatures.

Since that incident, although Nora was not aware, he would occasionally drive past her house on Hails Hallow Road at night just to be sure nothing was out of sorts. Sometimes, he would see a light on and wonder what she was doing inside.

"I said I'm fine. I really need to go," Nora replied, her tired looking, yet still striking green eyes, unwilling to look directly at him.

"Wait! I just need to ask if . . . is there any way that I'm . . ."

"There you are, Boo Bear! I've been looking all over for you," Libby Vincent, wearing espadrilles and a crisp sundress cinched tight around her lean waist, called out from the end of the aisle as she sashayed her way toward them.

"You found me," Brant replied, thinking her timing couldn't have been any worse.

"Oh, and who do we have here?" she asked, intertwining her arm with his and studying Nora like an insect with her close-set eyes.

"This is an old friend of mine, Nora Thompson. . . I mean Ayers," Brant replied.

"Well Nora, I just love meeting my Boo Bear's friends. I'm Elizabeth Vincent, Brant's soon-to-be fiancé. Everyone calls me Libby," she said, sticking her nose up in the air.

"Brant and I knew each other. . . a lifetime ago," Nora said.

"A lifetime ago? Well, in case he has not already told you, Brant and I were the "it" couple at St. Pat's. After we graduated, I went off to a prestigious university in Connecticut and Boo went to the police academy. We decided to take a little hiatus so that we could focus on our studies but everything turned out great for us. Isn't that right, Boo?"

"Sounds accurate," Brant replied, his face flushing as Libby repeatedly called him by the pet name she had given him.

Libby continued chatting, not seeming to notice Brant's eyes remained focused elsewhere. He watched as Nora appeared to be half listening and forcing a sideways smile, while repeatedly looking at her wristwatch. He recalled the day he found Nora stranded on the side of the road with a flat tire a few months after Libby had broken up with him. Brant wasn't sure but thought maybe it was the intensity of the overhead fluorescent lighting, or perhaps the distracting noise of the harried customers bustling about the store, that were casting a shadow on Nora. The Nora he knew, with the gleam in her eyes and the easy smile, was nowhere to be found in aisle nine of Swanset Village Grocer on this September day.

"We better get going, Boo. My father said if we don't get to Hyannis by three o'clock, we risk missing the ferry."

"Okay," Brant replied.

"We're just picking up a few last-minute items to take to my parents' home on the Vineyard to celebrate the end of the summer season. There's a rumor going around that some famous news reporter is planning to buy the house next door. I can't wait to find out who it is. Isn't that just far out?" Libby asked, playing with her generously sized, sparkling, diamond stud earrings as if to show off her daddy's money.

"I need to get going too. It was nice to meet you," Nora said as she quickly turned and walked away.

Brant watched as Nora navigated her way out of the crowded aisle and waited to see if she would turn back. He stood still in hopes she would give him an indication that she still felt something for him. A small glimpse from her was all he would need to be satisfied that what they shared was more than just a summer fling before deciding to make a serious commitment to Libby.

"Boo, I said its time to go!" Libby said, sounding perturbed.

Brant thought back to the last time he saw Nora, having snuck into the narthex of St. Leo's almost a year ago. He had pushed the church's heavy oak door open ever so slightly and caught sight of her standing at the altar, in her wedding dress, exchanging vows with Russ Ayers.

"Boo? Are you coming?" Libby asked as she tugged at his arm and pursed her lips.

Brant had not heard from Libby since she visited him in the hospital until one day last winter, when he received a call from her out of the blue. She invited him to join her and a small group of their friends from St. Pat's on a weekend ski trip to her parents' chalet in North Conway. He had fallen so head over heels for Nora that he hadn't even given Libby Vincent a second thought. Ever since the weekend in North Conway though, Libby seemed to be clinging to him like plastic wrap.

"Let's get out of here. I need some fresh air," Brant replied as he turned and pushed the shopping cart to the checkout counter.

Libby flashed him her rehearsed smile and adjusted a bobby pin in the chignon at the nape of her neck as they waited in line at the checkout. After what he had been through with Nora, he decided to just go through the motions as he fell back in step with Libby. Brant thought of the sizable donation her daddy made with his old money to secure Libby's spot at her university. During her time there, where she majored in Art History, Libby became a member of the Glee Club and the women's tennis team. There was no doubt Libby was considered a good catch, but Brant found himself still bothered by the fact he didn't have any of his questions answered by Nora. He figured he needed to accept the fact he may never know why Nora made the choices she did and appreciate what he had with Libby.

After the clerk placed their grocery items into brown paper bags, Brant and Libby headed out of the market and made their way through the busy parking lot. Once at his car, Libby waited for him to open the passenger side door for her before getting in and checking her face in the visor's mirror. Brant then popped open the trunk only to see the folded blanket that he had once made love to Nora on, staring back at him and reminding him what he and Nora shared had been real. Brant carelessly flung the bags of groceries on top of the blanket, as if covering up evidence, before slamming the trunk shut, disappointed in himself for wearing his heart on his sleeve. *Forget her*, he told himself as he got in the car and settled down in the driver's seat.

"We're going to have so much fun together this weekend, Boo," Libby said in a lighthearted, kittenish way, wearing a playful smile.

Brant smiled back at the poised and polished trust fund baby who was once again clinging to his arm.

"We sure are," he replied, pulling Libby toward him and planting a firm kiss on her pale-pink frosted lips.

With a turn of the key in the ignition they were off and Martha's Vineyard bound. Seeing Nora had caught him off guard and her unwillingness to open up to him felt like a door being shut in his face. Nora apparently wanted that door closed, so closed it would be. A weekend between the sheets, making new memories with Libby Vincent, was just what he needed to drown out thoughts of his lost summer love, once and for all.

41

1973

Russ' eyes bulged as a menacing set stared back at him. They were black harbingers of death, like a moonless night sky, there to steal his soul. As Charlie gritted his square, yellow tinged teeth together, a pungent odor seeped out from between their wide spaces. Russ felt himself gasping for breath, having no fight left in him, as he lay pinned to the clay tunnel floor, his windpipe being crushed under the force of Charlie's tight, sustained grip.

Out of nowhere came a faint cry. Perhaps it was the cry of a young child, hiding behind a bamboo hut in one of the small Vietnamese villages. As Charlie's grip became tighter, the baby's cries grew louder, stirring something inside of him. Suddenly, Russ sprang up and opened his eyes to find himself in his bedroom with Nora, asleep by his side once again.

The alarm clock's hands told him it was just after midnight as he heard Amy's cries from her nursery down the hall. Russ wiped his eyes with his fingertips and ran his hands along the sides of his face and down to his collar bone. As he rubbed his neck, he felt the protrusion of his Adam's apple was intact. His dry lips stung, and his mouth and throat felt parched, as he tried hard to swallow.

Russ took a swig of water from the glass on his nightstand, stood up and quietly closed the door behind him as he walked out of the room. Nora had not been feeling well and Russ, as promised, headed down the hallway to take care of Amy. He turned on the dim lamp on the hallway table outside the nursery and, as if on cue, Amy stopped crying when he entered the room. She smiled up at him, her legs kicking excitedly, as he stood over her crib.

"Hello there, kiddo. Is that a stinky diaper I smell?" Russ said softly as he picked up the ten-month-old and took her over to the changing table.

"You save the good ones for me, don't you?" he joked, removing the soiled diaper and crinkling his nose as he cleaned her.

Amy kicked and squirmed as he carefully fastened the safety pins to the sides of a clean cloth diaper, slipped a pair of plastic pants on her and snapped her back into her feet pajamas.

"Do you want to see the moon tonight, Amy?" Russ asked as he carried her over to the window.

"There it is and look at all those stars twinkling for you tonight too. They're pretty, aren't they? Just like you and your mommy," Russ said as he sat on the bench seat and cradled her in his arms.

"Now, there's something I've been wanting to tell you. You must always be careful out in the woods, Amy. The animals won't hurt you. The deer, squirrels and brown bunnies are all your friends. Just be sure to never wander off alone and get lost out there. Understand?" he asked, looking down and seeing her eyelids growing heavy as she sucked her tiny thumb.

Looking out the window into the silvery light, Russ scanned the property's tree line in the shadows of the January moon. "You always have to be on the lookout for Charlie. You see?" he asked her before realizing she had drifted back off to sleep. "Don't ever let him get you. . .," Russ stopped himself. *What the hell am I doing?* he thought, realizing this was not his young daughter's battle to fight.

"Don't ever forget how much I love you, Amy," Russ said, as he gently placed her back in her crib and wiped tears from his eyes with the sleeve of his flannel pajama shirt.

He walked back to the window and blankly stared out for some time, alone in his thoughts. *He's always out there. Isn't he? I can't poison Amy and I don't want Nora to hurt anymore,* he thought as he could see Nora's vibrance slowly dimming over the past year. "This is my battle, not theirs. I'm tired of fighting," Russ whispered to himself as the collar of his shirt became wet from the tears that flowed down his cheeks and onto his neck.

"What are you looking at?" he asked Bananas, as he walked out of the room.

Russ turned off the hallway light, made his way into the bathroom and carefully closed the door behind him. His eyes burned as he flicked on the light switch and stood in front of the medicine cabinet. He leaned in close to the mirror, studying his unshaven face and watching his pupils shrink as his eyes adjusted to the light. The once-faint lines running across his forehead appeared more pronounced than he remembered. Russ saw they made his brow appear heavy as if calling attention to the confusion and jumbled thoughts in his head. They reminded him that his scars from Vietnam ran deep. The pasty pallor of his skin and the puffy bags under his eyes only confirmed his exhaustion from his recurring bouts of insomnia and night terrors.

After turning on the faucet, Russ cupped his hands, filled them with cold water and splashed his face, trying once again to wash away the residue of Vietnam that remained. With his face still wet and hands dripping, Russ slid open the medicine cabinet's door and looked over the vast assortment of his prescribed antipsychotic medications, anti-anxiety agents and over the counter sleeping pills.

His internal strife, coupled with the pressures of civilian life, had become too much to bear. He felt alone and it seemed as if everyone was against him and dissecting his every move. It began on his journey home at the airports in San Francisco and Boston, when he was greeted by the group of war protesters, the young boy and his mother, and the hippies who flipped him off. Then came rejections from one employer after another, followed by the stares and whispers from strangers including passengers on the plane, customers at Swanset Savings Bank, and even from Jeff's girlfriend, Sherry, the day they went to the Swanset Fair. Brant Judge, who had tried to steal Nora away from him while he was deployed, was now a police officer in town and still waiting on the sidelines for an opportunity to pounce. Russ knew he had to stay vigilant in case he started coming around Nora again, remembering he said he would never forget about her. Then there was Viviane, who felt he wasn't good enough for her daughter. The pressure followed him to the workplace too, with Mr. Edmunds seeming to have it in for him no matter how hard he worked, his coworkers who he seemed invisible to, and Darlene who liked to make trouble for him since he repeatedly turned down her unwelcomed, sexual advances. The post commander at the local veterans organization had turned him away, making him feel worthless. He felt himself shutting down at the peer-to-peer rap sessions that Harry had encouraged him to attend, as the memories of the bloodshed and his lost brothers in arms flooded his mind. He was heavy with guilt for simply having survived the jungle while his friends were killed in action. He felt as though he was part of some warped experiment as his psychiatrist and family doctor prescribed him pills that never seemed to work. His head was filled with noisy static that only continued to grow louder and take over the little peace and lucidity that remained in the far corners of his mind.

He knew he had hurt Nora with his words and actions even though he didn't intend to. He recalled the night he unknowingly grabbed hold of Nora's arm as he dreamt that he was fighting off Charlie. He awoke to Nora screaming and trying to break free and he had left a visible bruise on her forearm. He had accidentally locked her out of the house the previous winter too, as he was convinced that Charlie was outside on the porch trying to get inside.

Russ knew he wasn't getting any better, regardless of what his doctors prescribed or how much Nora supported him. He became afraid he would hurt her again, or that he would hurt Amy, as he was unable to control his emotions, temper and urge for any substance that had the ability to numb his incessant pain. Russ knew what he had to do and that the bottles lining the shelves of the medicine cabinet, illuminated by the bright fluorescent lights he had installed, were the ticket to his salvation.

$$42$$

The waiting area of Teasdale Memorial Hospital's emergency room was eerily quiet as Nora checked the time on her watch and waited nervously for word on Russ' condition. She had taken a few sips from the cup of coffee that one of the E.R. nurses had kindly handed her. An hour had gone by, and the coffee had turned cold. It was now 5:30 a.m. and Russ' father, Fred, who had accompanied her to the hospital, had taken a walk to the cafeteria to grab a few fresh cups of joe.

Nora paced the floor, wringing her hands, as she recalled waking up earlier that morning to a loud thud and the sound of breaking glass. When she turned on the bedroom light, she found Russ had fallen out of bed and had knocked a drinking glass off his nightstand. He was lying on the hardwood floor, snoring loudly and unresponsive. When she rushed to the bathroom to get a cold towel for Russ' head, she saw that his prescription bottles were empty and strewn about the counter and floor. She then called the Swanset Police Department to report her husband's medical emergency and get help. She made a second call to Fred and Martha who managed to get to the house just a few minutes after the ambulance arrived. Martha was finally able to see for herself that her son was not well and agreed to stay behind with Amy. In the meantime, Fred helped Nora into his truck and the two followed the ambulance to the hospital.

"Mrs. Ayers?"

"Yes. I'm Nora Ayers," Nora said, turning to see a man in a white lab coat approaching.

"Good morning. I'm Dr. Charles Wheeler and I've been taking care of your husband this morning. Please have a seat," he said with a calm and professional demeanor as he made a gesture with his hand, directing her toward one of the waiting room chairs.

"Thank you, Doctor. Is he okay?" Nora asked after sitting down.

"Yes. We had to pump his stomach and he is responsive now."

"Oh, thank goodness!" Nora replied clasping her hands and bringing them toward her heart, grateful that Russ had pulled through.

"Your husband swallowed a large quantity of pills that are contraindicated to be taken together. This resulted in a near fatal drug interaction. Had you not acted as swiftly as you did, he probably wouldn't have survived."

"He must have been confused. Why would he take so many at once?" Nora naively asked.

"Mrs. Ayers, after I pumped your husband's stomach, we kept a close watch on his vital signs. As I was checking his pupils he started to come to. He was struggling to open his eyes and I called out his name and encouraged him to wake up. He then asked if he was in heaven and if he was dead yet."

"What? Why would he ask you that?" Nora asked, confused and trying to process what the doctor was saying.

"Your husband didn't just take that many pills by mistake. He attempted suicide, Mrs. Ayers."

"He tried to end his life?" Nora asked, feeling lightheaded and nauseous.

"Unfortunately, yes," Dr. Wheeler replied, placing his hand on her shoulder.

"But why would he do that to himself? We all love him, Doctor," Nora said as her eyes welled up.

"I understand it's a lot to take in. He's going to need your support to help him get through this," Dr. Wheeler informed her.

"I'm here for him . . . always," Nora said, letting out a sniffle.

"He's asking to see you. Do you feel ready to go in now or would you like to take a few minutes to process things?" he kindly asked.

"I'm ready to see him but my father-in-law took a walk to the cafeteria to get a cup of coffee and is going to wonder where I am. He's very worried too."

"I'll have the nurses keep an eye out for him. Why don't you follow me," he said, helping her out of the chair.

Nora felt unsteady on her feet and held onto Dr. Wheeler's arm as they made their way down the long, sterile corridor leading to Russ' room.

"If you don't mind, I'd like you to wait here for just a moment please," Dr. Wheeler said as they reached their destination.

"Of course," Nora replied.

As Dr. Wheeler entered the room and disappeared behind a privacy curtain, Nora could faintly hear a conversation between Russ and his doctor, although she was unable to make out exactly what was being said. After a few minutes, Dr. Wheeler reappeared.

"You need to know that Russ is in a fragile state of mind. It's best if you try not to ask him too many questions and not place blame on him. It may help to be subtle and to remind him of the positive things he has to look forward to."

"I understand."

"Take your time with your husband."

"Thank you," Nora replied as she took a deep breath and made her way into Russ' hospital room.

"Is that you, Nor?" Russ called out, his voice sounding hoarse.

"I'm here, Russ," Nora said, hurrying over to his bedside.

"I'm sorry for this mess," Russ said, appearing to be in discomfort as he rubbed his throat and his eyelids drooped.

"You don't have to talk. Just rest. I'm not going anywhere," Nora replied as she tenderly held his hand.

"You don't deserve any of this mess I've created."

"Shh. Everything is going to be okay, Russ."

"You're a good person who deserves so much better than what I can give you. I took those pills because I'm not getting any better, Nor."

"Of course, you are! Aren't you?" Nora asked, now aware that Russ had been struggling more than he had let on.

"You know I love you, right?" Russ asked as he picked up a cup of water from his tray table and struggled to get a few sips down.

"Yes, and I love you too, Russ."

"I don't want to hurt you anymore than I already have, and I don't want to hurt Amy. You'll both be better off without me," Russ said, looking directly into her eyes.

Nora's eyes held his gaze as she absorbed the seriousness of the situation.

"I want you to listen to me, Russ. I will not be better off without you. I love you and I need you. Amy needs you. And someone else needs you too," Nora said as she took Russ' hand and placed it on her belly.

Russ looked down and his eyes opened wider. Without saying a word, as he ever so slowly looked up at her, Nora knew that he understood there were more good things to come, if he could just hold on.

43

Russ gazed ahead pensively, unable to focus on the question he was just asked. *What the hell am I doing here anyway?* he thought to himself as he gnawed on the inside of his cheek. It had been more than six months since his overdose and he was sick of wasting time sitting in his inquiring psychiatrist's Weaver Falls office. Bored out of his mind, Russ had resorted to counting the number of dark hairs protruding from his doctor's nostrils to pass the time. *Five, six. . . I think I see one more. Yup, I do. That makes seven. Looks like it's about time to trim those bad boys, Doc,* Russ thought, trying not to crack a smile.

"Russell, would you like me to repeat the question?" Dr. Warren Jacobs asked after a few moments of silence, peering over the rim of his black-framed spectacles.

"Uh, sure," Russ replied, shifting in his seat and having no idea what the psychiatrist had just asked him.

"Please try to focus. Your answers will help me determine if we should stay on the current course of treatment or if we need to change things up for you. The question was: Have you been having any disturbing dreams or thoughts of your military experience lately?"

Practically every night, Bud. But if I tell you the truth, you'll send me back to the psych hospital. I don't want to go back there, Russ thought to himself.

"No, not really," Russ lied.

"Please elaborate. Do you mean you have them some of the time, a lot of the time or not at all?"

"Not at all. I've been sleeping much better since you adjusted my meds two weeks ago."

"So, no disturbing dreams then?"

"No. Not a one. I've been sleeping like a baby," Russ lied again.

"That's promising. It's a sign that your current dosage of medication is adequate and has been effective. Now, have you had any more thoughts about harming yourself or others?"

I don't want to hurt anyone, other than Charlie. I'm only a danger to myself in case you haven't noticed, but I'm not about to tell you that, you "Freud-want-to-be," Russ thought as he laughed on the inside.

"Only my boss when he gets on my case," Russ said with a chuckle.

"So, you have thoughts of harming your boss?" Dr. Jacobs asked, leaning forward and jotting notes on his legal pad.

"Doesn't everyone?" Russ sarcastically asked.

"No. This could be an area of concern. How often do these thoughts enter your mind?"

Every time I lay eyes on that jerk, Russ thought, picturing his portly boss with sausage-like fingers and the tacky strand of white, ropey saliva that always seemed to be bouncing between his upper and lower lip every time he spoke.

"It was a joke, Doc. Gee, you're so busy trying to psychoanalyze me that you can't even tell when someone is making a joke."

"I take all your answers seriously."

"You need to lighten up, Doc. Maybe loosen that tie and make yourself a Tequila Sunrise or a Harvey Wallbanger. Ever try one? A Wallbanger?" Russ asked with a sideways smile.

"No, I have not."

"You should try one. I think you'd like it," Russ said, trying to take focus off himself.

"That brings me to my next question. Have you been consuming alcohol and, if yes, how much and how often?" Dr. Jacobs asked as he read from his clipboard, pinching the arm of his eyeglasses with his thumb and index finger.

I polish off a fifth of whiskey every other day, Dr. Freud, Russ thought as Dr. Jacobs dissected him with his gaze.

"Just an occasional shot is all, Doc, and even that is only on a rare occasion," Russ once again lied and waited for Dr. Jacobs next probing question.

"Please try to refrain from drinking. As you know alcohol can interfere with the efficacy of your prescription medications."

"Yes, Sir," Russ said, saluting him.

"I'm going to give you a refill on the chlorpromazine as it has proven to be effective for you. You seem to be getting on well with your everyday life and your mood appears stable. You haven't reported any blurred vision or twitching so we will keep the dosage where it is for now. We can make adjustments in the future if needed. Remember to take it only as directed and to stay away from the alcohol. Keep up the good work and I'll see you two weeks from today," Dr. Jacobs replied, seemingly oblivious to Russ' lies.

Once out of the office, Russ hurried down the narrow hallway, eyes wide open and repeatedly looking over his shoulder, until he exited the building. He had learned his lesson and knew he couldn't trust anyone after the night the Swanset police officers escorted him to the psychiatric hospital. The men in the white suits had confined him to a straitjacket after he tried to break out of his room and knocked two of the mental health workers to the floor.

First it was Charlie, then Mr. Edmunds, and now, Russ knew, there were always watchful eyes upon him. He had grown suspicious and knew everyone was out to get him. They were plotting against him and trying to make him mess up so they could lock him away or turn him over to the North Vietnamese Army or the Viet Cong. He wondered why his doctors were so adamant that he take his pills. *Maybe they're trying to poison me. Or maybe they're somehow able to track me each time I swallow one.* Russ got into his car and, determined to outsmart them, tore up his prescription, tossed the pieces into the backseat and rolled down the window.

Russ then reached under his seat and pulled out his whiskey bottle, having the urge for a few swigs, only to find it empty. Letting out a sigh of frustration, he pulled his to-do list and ballpoint pen out of his jacket pocket. Swiping the pen across the paper, he crossed "Appointment with Dr. 'Jerk-obs,'" off his list. Russ read down to the next line item: "Stop at Swanset Savings Bank" followed by "Pick up new hinge for bathroom door at hardware store" and "run to the packy." Although he was annoyed that his thirst for his favorite scotch whiskey would have to wait, Russ was relieved his dreaded follow-up appointment with his Sigmund Freud want-to-be doctor was now behind him.

Russ depressed the eject button of his car stereo, pulled an old eight track tape out and tossed it into the backseat. His head already had too much noise in it since leaving Dr. Jacobs' office and he wasn't in the mood to listen to anything loud. While trying to keep his eyes on the busy road in front of him as he crossed the bridge from Weaver Falls back into Swanset, Russ reached over to the passenger's front seat and grabbed a tape Jeff lent him.

"Here, you can borrow this. It's an oldie but goodie and it's still relevant with all that's going on in this world. The first track on this album will really speak to you," Jeff told him as he handed him the tape.

Russ gave the eight-track tape's label a quick glance.

"This ought to be good," Russ sarcastically said as he popped in the tape and pressed play on the car's stereo.

Continuing down the street, Russ turned up the volume as the first track began to play. He listened intently as the singer's distinct voice spoke directly to him, just as his friend promised it would. Images of the broken road of his life were swiftly whisked away by a sweeping harmonica and Russ knew he had failed in his quest to find peace. As he approached Swanset's town center, he watched people pass by on the busy sidewalk. They were familiar faces of Swanset's locals, preoccupied with their week-end errands and mindless small talk, too busy to take notice of their fellow man's struggles. Whether they knew it or not, they had also failed.

The song trailed off as Russ pulled into a parking space in front of Swanset Savings Bank, feeling hopeless that the locals of Swanset and his fellow Americans, blind to their own hypocrisy, would ever be able to acknowledge their role in the injustices shown toward him and his fellow soldiers. Russ turned off the ignition and, as the engine quieted, knew his personal struggle would be endless and, as long as he was breathing, he would never truly be free.

As Russ looked into his own eyes in the rearview mirror, he wiped tears from their reddened corners and caught a glimpse of a smiling couple, walking arm in arm, out of the Swanset Fine Jewelry store across the street. He turned and looked out the back window as the couple walked happily down Main Street before turning the corner. Russ' mind began to churn as he pulled out his errand list and looked it over. He then thumbed through his wallet, pulled out eight dollars, money that was earmarked for his cigarettes, whiskey and the prescription he had torn up, and set the money on his dashboard. He then slid his hand into the front pockets of his jeans and pulled out four one-dollar bills, a couple of coins and the always-expected wad of lint, adding the contents to the money already on his dashboard. Russ thought for a moment before opening his glove compartment and pulled out the ten-dollar bill that he always kept stashed away in case he ran out of gas or ever needed a tow. Glancing at his errand list one last time, Russ looked over each line item carefully before crum-pling the paper and tossing it into his back seat to keep company with his his torn-up prescription and other items he had grown tired of. He then flipped through the pages of his bank book and was disappointed at its meager balance. After missing an entire week of work due to his overdose and having taken time off for some appointments, he had been trying to play catch up every week. He knew he needed to leave what little money was in there for the next rainy day and concluded that ten dollars was the most he could afford to withdraw. Russ straightened out the wrinkled bills and arranged them in a neat pile before counting them up and heading into the bank to complete his transaction.

With money in hand, Russ crossed Main Street and walked over to Swanset Fine Jewelry, where the happy couple had stood just moments before, and peered into the spotless glass window. The sparkling gemstones and gleaming gold necklaces in the display case screamed "expensive" and Russ, disappointed after not seeing anything in the window that he could afford, shifted his focus onto his own melancholy expression reflecting in the storefront's shiny glass. He looked down and, as he turned away, swung his foot forward at a loose rock at his feet, sending it shooting down the sidewalk. With his head down, he followed his shadow along the sunlit sidewalk until he reached the spot where the rock had landed. Instead of kicking it again, Russ looked up and saw that he was now standing in front of a pawn shop filled with secondhand household items and other cast-offs.

The squeaking hinge of the rusted metal entry door and the smell of the musty carpet mixed with the aroma of a burning cigarette greeted Russ upon entering. As he glanced around the cluttered display cases, he saw an aging man sitting on a stool behind the counter, reading the morning's *Weaver Falls Herald* and sipping coffee out of a dinged up ceramic mug. The man paid him no attention as his nose was buried in the morning headline, "Nixon says he will not testify before Watergate Investigation Committee."

Russ quietly meandered through the dim aisles, passing antique metal toys and collections of bone china tea sets and old coins. He came upon a dusty glass case housing an assortment of cameo brooches, pearl necklaces and cocktail rings from by-gone eras and, as he leaned in for a closer look, heard a voice call out.

"Do you need some help over there?" the shop owner asked, putting down his coffee mug and newspaper and walking over.

"Yeah sure. I'm looking for a necklace for my wife."

"Well, we have lots of necklaces over here in this case. What are you looking for, fourteen karat gold or sterling silver?" the owner asked.

"Gold would be nice. I'm looking for a chain with a pendant."

"Are you looking for a diamond?"

"No, a green stone. But I'm not sure what it's called."

"Is it an emerald you're looking for? Like these over here maybe?" he asked, showing Russ a case containing earrings, bracelets and necklaces decorated with vivid green, sparkling stones.

"No. The stone I'm looking for is a lighter shade of green. I wish I knew what it was called."

"Ah, I bet it's a peridot. I think I have one over here," he said, as Russ followed him to the next jewelry case.

"Is this what you're looking for? Some folks call it the "evening emerald." It's the August birthstone," the shop owner said as he held up a delicate gold necklace from which hung a sparkling, round, peridot stone.

"That's it. That's exactly what I'm looking for. It looks like it's good quality," Russ said, taking a close look.

"It's a real nice piece set in fourteen karat gold. No flaws either. See the setting?"

"I see. How much are you asking for it?" Russ asked, hoping to be able to afford it.

"It's thirty-five dollars. And it's a steal at that price if I do say so myself," the man said as he flipped the tag over and revealed the price.

"Oh, well . . . I don't seem to have enough to cover that," Russ admitted with dismay.

"Hmm . . . it's been sitting here a while. Hold on for just a minute," he told Russ as he walked away from the counter and stepped behind a curtain into the back room.

As Russ waited, he took out his wallet and recounted the bills inside which totaled thirty-two dollars. He found himself checking his pockets for any stray bills that he may have previously missed.

"So, this piece here should have been marked down last month and put in that sale case over there," the shop owner said after emerging from behind the curtain and reading down the page of his inventory logbook.

"Really?" Russ asked, now hopeful.

"How much did you say you have?"

"I have thirty-two dollars and about . . . twenty-seven cents," Russ replied as he slid his hand into the front pocket of his jeans and pulled out some loose coins.

"Well, I guess it's your lucky day. The price was supposed to be changed to twenty-nine dollars. Looks like you'll even have a few bucks left over."

"Cool," Russ said, thrilled to have learned the necklace was now his.

"If you have a few minutes, I'll polish it up a bit more and box it up real nice," the shop owner said after completing the transaction.

"Sure. I'd appreciate that," Russ replied.

As he placed his change in his wallet, Russ found himself unable to control his excitement. He looked up and caught a glimpse of himself in an antique mirror hanging on the wall behind the cash register and saw himself smiling for the first time in a long while.

44

With Amy asleep in her arms, Nora sat on the farmer's porch swing, enjoying a rare, cool mid-July breeze and the melody that Russ practiced playing on his acoustic guitar. It had been two years since Russ returned home from overseas and the months following his overdose had been a trying time for them both. Luckily Amy, and the baby that was now on the way, had managed to keep them both going. Russ, to the best of her knowledge, continued going to his psychiatrist every two weeks, which was an important part of his treatment for combat fatigue. She was also happy to see that Russ developed a few new friendships with other boys who returned home from Vietnam, a small inclusive group that supported him in ways she could not, meeting every week at a church hall in Weaver Falls.

They hit a few bumps in the road too after she confronted Russ about the fact she could smell alcohol on his breath on more than one occasion. He eventually admitted he had become dependent on it and, with her help, Russ was trying his best to stay away from the bottle and from Lance's Pub. Russ continued to go for his weekly trek in the woods behind their house to keep his head clear and had recently dusted off his old acoustic guitar to have an outlet for his anxiety. As Russ strummed the guitar strings, Nora smiled, proud of the progress he was making.

"I like that melody," Nora said.

"You do?" Russ asked, as he stopped playing and looked up at her, noticing the sparkle in her green eyes.

"Yes, it's nice. Did you make that up yourself?"

"No, Nor. I'm not that good. It's a song I was listening to earlier from an eight track Jeff lent me."

"Cool."

"I was just thinking about the time we went to the folk festival with Jeff and Sherry."

"Those were fun times, weren't they?"

"They were, Nor."

"Maybe someday we'll get to go again. For now, it's all about these little people though, isn't it?" Nora asked as she looked lovingly at Amy and gently ran her hand over her loose golden curls.

"It is, but it's also about us, Nor," Russ said as he put his guitar down, leaned it up against the porch railing and took a seat next to her on the swing.

"What do you mean?"

"I mean it's you and me, Nor. It's always been you who has been here for me, more than anyone else."

"Well, I do love you after all, Russ."

"You could have chosen anyone, Nor, but you took a chance on me. You, Amy and our new baby are all that matter to me. You know that, right?" Russ asked as he looked intently upon her.

"Of course, I know that."

"I picked up a little something for you," Russ said as he turned and reached behind the swing's toss pillow.

"What's this? My birthday isn't until next month," Nora stated, surprised as Russ handed her a small white box tied with a lime green velvet ribbon.

"It's a token of my love for you, Nor."

With Amy still asleep in her arms, Nora carefully untied the velvet ribbon and opened the box.

"Russ, it's beautiful. But why? How can we afford this?" Nora asked, as the peridot pendant on a delicate gold chain gleamed back at her.

"You really like it?"

"Yes, its lovely, but how can we afford this, Russ?" Nora asked, concerned with the cost of the piece of fine jewelry.

"It's your August birthstone. Consider it an early birthday gift. It's all paid for so you can wear it without worry. Let me put it on for you," Russ said as he gently placed the necklace around her neck and latched it.

"That was so thoughtful of you."

"Now let me see it on you," Russ said as he circled back around and stood face to face with her.

"The chain is the perfect length. Does it look nice?" Nora asked, looking up at him and feeling the pendant resting just below her collar bone.

"It looks great on you and matches your eyes perfectly, just like I hoped. Promise me you will always remember our good times every time you look at it, Nor."

"I promise, Russ. Thank you so much. I really love it and I really love you. I want you to remember something too."

"What's that?"

"There isn't any storm that we can't get through together. I'm always here for you, Russ," Nora told him, sensing a sadness in him in this otherwise joyous moment.

Russ moved closer, slid his arm around her shoulder and tenderly kissed her forehead, his lips brushing her fading scar.

"Did you notice that the willow has lost a few branches recently?" Russ asked, gazing out at the large weeping willow tree beside the driveway.

"Yes. Maybe we should get it trimmed," Nora replied.

"It could be infested with bugs. Maybe we should have it taken down before a limb breaks off and knocks the fence over," Russ said, appearing to study its branches.

"No, don't take it down. I love that old tree. It's the first thing I saw when we pulled into the driveway on our wedding night. It's our special tree," Nora said, with a look of wonder in her eyes.

"Okay, we'll keep it then. It's now officially our special tree," Russ replied, giving Nora a peck on the cheek.

They sat together for a long while, their legs dangling from the porch swing, watching Amy as she peacefully slept. Nora savored the moment, which was perfect in every way, as dusk approached and the crickets' evening symphony began.

45

The day seemed especially long and fatigue set in as Nora busied herself by tidying up the kitchen and trying to keep dinner warm.

"Cookie?" little Amy asked as she sat on the kitchen floor playing with her wooden blocks.

"Not now, my angel," Nora told her daughter, who was now approaching eighteen months of age, aware that she had given her the last of the homemade teething biscuits earlier in the day.

"Cookie, Momma!" Amy screamed, bursting into a temper tantrum.

"Amy, there are no cookies left. I'll bake some for you tomorrow," Nora said reassuringly, picking her up to sooth her and tousling her soft golden curls.

"Momma!" Amy cried one last time before sticking her fingers into her tiny mouth to ease the pain of her erupting baby molars.

The clock hanging on the wall above the cabinets and the chirping crickets outside the farmhouse's half open kitchen windows validated Nora's feeling of being depleted of all her energy.

"It's already seven thirty. Where's your daddy?" Nora asked, exhausted and annoyed, but not actually expecting her young daughter, with only a handful of words in her vocabulary, to respond.

"Daddy," Amy parroted back.

With the toddler on her hip, Nora tidied the kitchen with her free hand and thought back to the night, just a few weeks after Amy was born, when Russ didn't bother coming home for dinner. When he finally strolled through the door at eight o'clock, Nora's eyes became instantly fixated on a smear of red lipstick on his collar and asked where he had been.

"Nor, you know I stop by to see the boys at Lance's sometimes. I had a hard day at work. Cut me some slack, why don't you?" he had said, dismissing her question.

"Russ, I am always here for you, and I can tolerate a lot. You tell me what to do, what to wear and control all the money, but I won't let you lie to me," Nora replied.

"I'm not lying to you. I told you where I was."

"You did, but the next time you go out to Lance's with 'the boys', be sure not to come home with lipstick marks and the scent of cheap drugstore perfume on your clothes from whoever it is you're carrying on with, or I'm taking Amy and leaving you."

Russ' ears suddenly perked up and he hurried over to the mirror in the hallway.

"Ah, shit. Nothing happened, Nor. I promise I would never do anything to jeopardize what we have. I love you," he said after seeing the lipstick smudge for himself.

"If you love me, you'll sober up and maybe tomorrow will be a better day for both of us," she said, too tired from taking care of the newborn all day to even care to ask whose company he had been in.

Instead, she pushed thoughts of her husband's indiscretions to the side and, determined to create a good home for herself and her family, carried on with her wifely duties. Things improved after that and Russ began coming straight home after work to have dinner with her, helping to put Amy to bed each night and enjoying time together as a family. For a short time, Russ appeared to be doing better and all was calm.

"Okay, my little angel, it's time we get your pajamas on and get you ready for bed."

"I sleepy."

"I know. Momma is too."

Nora walked into the hallway with Amy in her arms, catching a glimpse of herself in the framed hanging mirror which was surrounded by photographs of their family and friends.

"You look beat," Nora told her reflection.

She couldn't recall the last time she had been to the salon or had any time alone for her own self-care. A simple haircut now seemed like a luxury, as she hated to ask Russ for money for anything knowing he was feeling stress over the bills that continuously rolled in each month. Her old clunker, which had been on its last leg, finally kicked the bucket in early summer, leaving her with no means of transportation and relying on Russ to take her wherever she needed to go.

As she swiped her bangs to the side, she saw her ugly scar reflecting back at her once again. She looked away and her eyes landed on a picture of Fred and Martha dancing at their wedding. They were good, hardworking people who had been dealt some unfortunate cards and had taken a shine to Amy, just as Nora suspected they would since losing their own little girl years ago. Martha had disappointed her though, as she was unable to cut the cord and unwilling to face reality, continuing to bury her head in the sand instead of helping with Russ' problems, as if hoping they would magically disappear.

Nora then studied a photograph of her own parents, a mismatch in every way. Richard always wore a warm, jovial smile in sharp contrast to Viviane's expressionless face. Viviane, as expected, continued to think of only herself and her social calendar, taking little interest in Nora's new family. Although her father managed to make up for what Viviane lacked, Nora quickly learned she could not rely on her parents as she had hoped. Due to Viviane's insistence, her parents had decided to drive down to Florida for an extended period to search for a condominium to purchase, with plans of eventually putting their Swanset home on the market.

"Your mother thinks that, since you and Russ are adults, you should not be relying on us for financial help. Don't tell your mother, but I plan to find you a car when we get back from Florida," Mr. Thompson told her.

"It's okay. Really, Daddy," Nora replied.

"Nonsense. Your mother often forgets the lean times we had early on in our marriage. All she's concerned with these days is keeping up with the Joneses. If we can afford to purchase a new condominium in Coral Springs, then we can surely afford to help you and Russ out from time to time, especially since you can't work with babies at home. I know Russ would be too proud to ask or accept anything else from us, so we can just tell him that it's a gift for you to be able to take the grandchildren to their pediatrician appointments and to the playground," her father told her after she had confided in him about their finances being tight without Russ' knowledge.

"Thank you for always being there for me, Daddy," Nora had said as her eyes filled with tears.

"Now there. Why so sad? Is there something else bothering you? Has Russ been having a hard time lately?" Mr. Thompson asked, as if sensing Nora was keeping something from him, having become aware of Russ' struggles after his overdose.

"It's just these darn hormones. They make me weepy sometimes. That's all, Daddy," Nora replied, refraining from divulging the sordid details of her home life with Russ to her loving father.

The next photograph Nora looked at was of herself, Josie and Becky posing on their blanket at Orient Beach. She studied her own beaming smile in the picture, recalling that she had been smiling back at Brant as he snapped the photograph with Josie's camera. *That feels like a lifetime ago,* she thought, shaking her head from side to side.

Josie was always good about keeping in touch with her and frequently called midweek when she was on her lunchbreak and when she knew Russ would be at work. She was no longer nearby though and, after finishing her degree, had accepted a job writing for a new women's lib magazine in New York City. She was now cohabitating with Alex in an old brownstone on Manhattan's Upper West Side which, despite being crime ridden, was in the midst of a renaissance according to Josie.

"I'm always just a phone call away, Nor. If you ever need anything, you can call me anytime of the day or night. I mean it. Don't forget my parents are just across town and their door is always open to you and Amy," Josie had told her.

Becky Lieberman, having taken her reproductive life into her own hands, had been accepted into law school, much to her parents' approval. Life had stayed right on track for Becky, who was now just a few city blocks away from where Josie and Alex resided. From time to time, Josie and Becky would call to check in with her and share stories of their glamorous times in the Big Apple.

Nora, though grateful for all her blessings, couldn't help but feel she was missing out on what would have been a very different life scenario had she been careful in the choices she made. Her derailed dream of becoming a science teacher, while meager compared to that of her friends' ambitious career paths, had to be put on the back burner indefinitely.

Nora glanced at a few more photographs of herself, Russ, Jeff and Sherry at the folk festival in the summer of 1969 before Russ was sent off to Vietnam. There was also a picture of Russ smiling as he played his acoustic guitar and entertained his buddies at his company's camp on the outskirts of Saigon. The pictures warmed Nora's heart as she reflected on the good times in their lives.

The last picture her eyes landed on was the one Josie took of her just a few short years ago before she was caught up in the campus protest and injured. It was a copy of the photograph that Russ had carried in his field jacket for the year he was deployed.

"Do you know who this is?" Nora asked, pointing to herself in the picture.

"No," Amy replied, shaking her head.

"It's Momma. That's me, Amy."

"No. You Momma. You," Amy replied with a giggle as she pressed her little index finger against the tip of Nora's nose.

For some reason, Nora found it upsetting that her daughter was unable to recognize the girl in the photograph as being her. She glanced at the picture again and took another look back at her reflection's waning identity. She seemed to lose another little piece of the girl she once was with each year that went by, with each unplanned pregnancy and each random episode of chaos that ensued within their home due to Russ' internal struggles. Nora then ran her hand over the cord of three strands hanging on the wall and was reminded she and Russ created the braid on their wedding day as a lasting symbol of their unified love. Giving herself one last glance in the mirror, Nora watched as the weary woman with an ugly scar and dark circles under sullen eyes, brushed a strand of ragged hair behind her ear and turned away.

After making their way upstairs, Nora changed Amy's diaper and snapped her into a clean onesie. Thankfully, a light breeze picked up, helping to cool the upstairs bedroom from the warmth the early autumn day brought. She then took a seat on the Boston rocker with Amy in her arms and hummed a lullaby until the little girl fell asleep.

"Time to put you to bed," Nora whispered as she got up from the rocking chair and carried Amy over to the white, painted crib she and Russ picked out together.

She carefully laid her sleeping child down and covered her with a satin-trimmed blanket. Nora stood admiring her little girl and watching her chest rise and fall with each innocent breath.

"It's hard for me to take my eyes off you. I love you so much, my little angel," Nora whispered as she lightly brushed her hand along Amy's warm, chubby cheek.

Nora quietly secured the side of the crib before turning to leave the room. Bananas the gorilla, with his bright yellow fur, sat in the corner sporting his usual silly expression. Nora reached out and gave him a pat on the head as she passed by on her way out. She caught herself smiling at the memory of the day she spent with Russ at the Swanset Fair, a time when she felt strong and full of hope. As she turned off the light and closed the nursery door, Nora's stomach let out a loud growl.

"I know you're hungry too. Time to feed you now, little one," Nora said as she stood in the hallway, feeling hunger pangs and rubbing the bump protruding from her belly with the palms of her hands before waddling down the staircase and into the kitchen.

She was now in her third trimester and, unlike when she was carrying Amy, she was overcome with a feeling of dread. She found herself napping whenever Amy did just to be able to function. Her doctor assured her that everything was fine and she was probably tired from chasing a toddler around all day long. Amy, while a handful at times, brought Nora so much joy that she never gave the possibility of an abortion another thought. Unfortunately, Russ hit a few more bumps in the road causing his combat fatigue to flare up again. Along with it came more restless nights, random chaotic episodes of paranoia and, as Nora eventually realized, hallucinations. She felt as though she was walking on eggshells, always treading lightly so as not to set him off. She found herself constantly trying to cope under dire circumstances with no job, car or money to call her own but continued to persevere, trying her best to support her husband in hopes of holding her family together.

The chicken casserole she rewarmed an hour earlier was now cold again. With her stomach growling and being tired of waiting for Russ to return home, Nora took a lonely seat at the kitchen table. As she poured herself a glass of milk, she imagined herself sitting in a fancy Manhattan restaurant with Josie and Becky, dressed to the nines, sipping a martini out of a gold-encrusted cocktail glass just like she had seen models in magazines do. She picked up her fork and fantasized she was eating Beef Wellington off a bone china dinner plate as she took a bite of the cold casserole.

"A girl can dream. Where the heck is he anyway?" Nora said aloud.

Just then she saw the flash of headlights coming up the driveway. Nora looked up at the clock again which now displayed the time as being eight forty-five p.m..

The sound of the car door slamming and Russ' staggered footsteps, heavy on the floorboards of the front porch, caught her attention. Although he had been sober for a few months, Nora knew from the sound of things that he had been drinking again. Startled by the sudden banging on the front door, she jumped up from her seat.

"Nor, let me in, Baby. I . . . I can't find my . . . keys," Russ yelled from the porch.

"Damn it. He's going to wake up Amy," Nora said, hurrying to the door.

"There you are. So . . . what did you do all day besides . . . nothing?" Russ asked, his speech loud and slurred, and his clothes disheveled.

"Shh! Get inside and keep your voice down so you don't wake up Amy."

"Let me see her. I haven't seen her . . . all day," Russ replied between hiccups before lifting a half empty fifth of whiskey to his lips.

"You should have come home sooner then. She's already asleep. Russ, put the bottle down. Where have you been anyway? It's almost nine o'clock and you have to work in the morning."

"There's still half a bottle left . . . and . . . I'm not done."

"Russ, you have to work in the morning. You could lose your job if you're late again or show up hung over. Please give me the bottle and go take a cold shower."

"Nag, nag, nag. Is that all you do? You sound just like Mr. Edmunds . . . and you're starting to look ugly just like him too with that . . . scar. . . and that . . . big . . . fat . . . belly of yours."

"It's been a long day, Russ, and I'm not getting into this with you. Now give me the bottle," Nora said, swiping at the air as she attempted to grab the bottle out of his raised hand.

"I said I'm not done," Russ argued, taking another swig from the liquor bottle.

"Give it to me right now," Nora said, finally grabbing the bottle away from him.

"Give it back, Nor!"

"No. It's going down the drain," Nora said, hurrying over to the sink and starting to pour out the remaining contents of the bottle.

Russ suddenly lunged at her, almost falling over and grabbing her forearm to steady himself in the process.

"Let go of me. You're hurting me, Russ."

"Give me the damn bottle!" he screamed in her face with bulging, blood shot eyes.

"Drink some water instead and sober yourself up."

"You. . .," Russ yelled, trying to grab hold of the bottle, his fingers getting caught in the delicate gold chain around Nora's neck.

"Stop it, Russ. Just stop!" Nora cried out, trying to put an end to the struggle, feeling her necklace break and seeing the peridot pendant fall to the floor next to Amy's wooden blocks.

Russ ripped the bottle from her hands, causing Nora to lose her footing and stumble backward. With flailing arms, she tried to brace herself before hitting her head and landing hard on the kitchen floor, taking the dishrack full of freshly washed plates and glasses crashing down with her. She instinctively wrapped her arms around herself to protect her growing baby, as sharp pains shot across her abdomen. She lay motionless, feeling as broken as the shards of glass and fragments of dishes that surrounded her. Through blurred vision she saw Russ take another swig of whiskey as the room began to violently spin. Amy's distant cries from the nursery echoed through the house as Nora fought to keep her eyes open and a strong urge to sleep took hold. Her exhausting day had finally come to an end and, as defeat washed over her, everything suddenly went black.

46

Nora's heart felt heavy as she sat on the bench seat in her old bedroom, staring out the front window as she had many times before, contemplating her future. This cozy spot, overlooking the two large sugar maples, was where she could always find comfort and work through her problems. It was in these familiar surroundings, at this pivotal moment, that she hoped to find the answers she was looking for.

Russ had been admitted to the mental health hospital in Weaver Falls, where he was undergoing a weeklong observation and psychiatric care after being unable to cope with the latest blow to his already fractured mind. After learning about her own hospital stay, her parents began their three-day drive home from Florida to comfort her. *I have just a few days to decide what to do,* Nora thought to herself, knowing she did not have much time to figure things out before Russ was released and her parents made it home. She was at a crossroads and, as she sat in this familiar spot, was determined not to let Viviane or anyone else dictate her life from this point on.

A gentle knock on the door got her attention and she saw Josie peeking into the bedroom. Nora waved her in and Josie tiptoed over so she wouldn't wake up Amy, who was asleep in the playpen situated next to the dresser.

"Is there room for me?" Josie asked.

"Of course, Jo. Have a seat," Nora whispered, sliding her legs to the side.

"Feels like old times doesn't it?"

"I suppose so, in some ways. It's strange being back here."

"We've shared many secrets in this room."

"We have. I still can't believe you drove all the way from Manhattan just to be here with me."

"I wouldn't want you going through this alone. Why didn't you tell me that things were getting bad again?"

"You have your own life, Jo. I made decisions that I have to live with and didn't want to burden you with my problems."

"You're never a burden to me. Just because our lives have gone in different directions doesn't mean I love you any less. I'm glad you called my parents to pick you up from the hospital since your parents are out of town."

"I didn't know who else to call. Martha acts like I'm to blame for Russ' problems and only makes matters worse."

"Sounds like she's the typical mother-in-law," Josie said, rolling her eyes.

"Of course my mother was all perturbed they had to come back, but my father put his foot down for once after I told him what happened."

"Viviane will never change. You are your father's daughter, that's for sure. How's your head feeling?"

"I still have a little egg on the back that hurts if I press on it, but my heart hurts more."

"I know, Nor. It had to be awful for you. I mean when you came to, and you were all alone with no one to help you."

"It was the abdominal pain that stirred me awake. I didn't know where I was at first and everything was blurry. When my vision improved, I could see across to the living room where Russ was sitting in his chair passed out drunk. I could hear Amy upstairs in her room crying and that's what motivated me to get up. Then I realized I was hemorrhaging and crawled over to the phone to call for help."

"Gosh, that's terrible. I don't know how you found the strength to get through that," Josie said, placing her hand on top of Nora's.

"Things got worse once the paramedics and police arrived. Russ woke up and was hung over. He became hostile when he saw strangers in the house, and the officers had to handcuff him to get him under control. They put him in the back of the cruiser and tried to talk to him. I'm not exactly sure what he said to them but it couldn't have been good because he wasn't allowed to ride in the ambulance with me. I was so scared because I knew I had lost a lot of blood and was having contractions."

"Oh, Nor."

"I was so grateful that your parents were able to come pick up Amy and keep her with them. When I arrived at the hospital, I knew from the look on the doctor's face that something wasn't right and that it wasn't just early labor. He said my placenta was torn and that the baby was in danger, so they prepped me for delivery right away. My contractions came hard and fast and before I knew it the baby was out," Nora said, choking up and holding back tears.

"I'm so sorry. Let it out, Nor. You can't keep this inside," Josie said encouragingly.

"He was so little, Jo. I mean he was the smallest baby I've ever seen. He had dark hair, and he was just so... beautiful. But he didn't cry... he never cried, Jo... not once. Then the doctors and nurses became so quiet, like you could hear a pin drop. That's when I knew something was very wrong. I felt it throughout my pregnancy and even told my doctor that I had a bad feeling, but he assured me that it was just my nerves and that everything was fine. But it wasn't...," Nora sobbed.

"Nor, I'm so sorry."

"Do you remember when I was thinking of terminating my first pregnancy and you said I'd have to have a saline abortion? I said, 'That means I'd have to deliver a dead baby.' Do you remember I said that to you, Jo? Do you?" Nora asked, now agitated and visibly trembling.

"Yes, Nor, I remember," Josie said, looking into Nora's eyes and squeezing her hand tighter.

"Jo, the thing I feared most... delivering a dead baby... it happened. I don't know how I can ever move forward from this," Nora said, bowing her head and burying her face in her hands.

"I know it's hard, Nor."

"When the doctor handed the baby off to the nurse, I noticed a big bulge on his lower back. The doctor later told me that he had a condition called spina bifida. He said it was so severe that the baby wouldn't have lived very long. He told me that Russ was most likely exposed to a chemical in Vietnam that may have caused the birth defect. Orange something. I can't remember what he called it."

"I think it's called Agent Orange. I read about it in the *Times*. It was a chemical that was sprayed on the vegetation and settled into the soil. Russ was in the tunnels so I'm sure he was exposed without even knowing."

"Why would they spray something so harmful?" Nora asked, wiping her eyes with her sleeve.

"I don't know. Thankfully, our involvement over there is coming to an end."

"Is it really? Because it feels like the war is still going on, to me at least. Look how its affected mine and Russ' life."

"I know, Nor, but you made it through so far, right? Look at how strong you have been this whole time. You've been doing this all alone, but you don't have to. You can lean on others for help. Do you hear me?" Josie said comfortingly.

"I know I need to stay strong for Amy but . . . I also need . . .," Nora began to say before hesitating.

"What is it, Nor? Say what it is that you need."

"I need a break . . . from all the chaos . . . from Russ' problems and this terrible war. I need to think about my and Amy's safety. I love Russ and I feel guilty for feeling this way, Jo."

"Listen to me, Nor. You have nothing to feel guilty about. It's about time you speak up and stand up for yourself. I know you love Russ and want to help him, but you are no use to him, or Amy, if you don't take care of yourself. This is finally your time to decide for yourself . . . to do what you feel is right with no pressure from Russ, Viviane, your mother-in-law, or anyone else. My parents have already offered to put you up at their house and look after both you and Amy if Viviane turns her back on you. You need to think about your and Amy's safety."

Nora sat and tried to absorb what her friend was saying, drained and unable to get another syllable out. She leaned her head back and closed her eyes, only to feel the bump on the back of her head begin to throb.

"Nor, you've been through a lot. It's time you get some rest now," Josie said, taking her by the arm, leading her over to her bed and tucking her safely under the covers.

47

The house was now empty, and in disarray, and each repetitious tick of the kitchen wall clock served as a reminder of the punishment, that time itself, had inflicted upon him. The disorderly room, with Amy's blocks, broken dishes and dried blood smeared on the linoleum floor, reminded him of the struggle that had ensued between him and Nora a week ago.

They poisoned me, Russ thought to himself as he circled his finger around the edge of the empty dinner plate on the table in front of him, remembering his conversation with Nora's doctor. While in the back of the cruiser, he had struck a deal with Officer McMillan and was allowed to be present in the hospital while Nora gave birth before bringing him back to the mental health facility. Russ knew if he didn't cooperate, he would have been driven directly to the facility and restrained in a strait jacket. Instead, he opted for being handcuffed with McMillan standing by his side right outside the delivery room door. After only half an hour, Nora's doctor emerged to give him an update on her condition. As his head pounded, the doctor asked him questions about his time in the service. He wanted to know where he had served and what he did. Still hungover, Russ could not understand why he was so concerned about his time in Vietnam. The doctor then informed him that Nora lost the baby and that it was a boy. He told him that he had a birth defect, a neural tube defect to be specific, that was linked to a chemical called dioxin found in herbicides used in Vietnam. Russ recalled that Operation Ranch Hand, the United States military's aerial herbicidal warfare mission, was ongoing throughout his time in the jungle.

"But they told us it wasn't harmful. They said it was safe," Russ said.

"I'm sorry, but there is now strong medical evidence that suggests exposure to Agent Orange causes birth defects in the offspring of those exposed to it," the doctor said somberly.

"You said it was a boy?" Russ asked.

"Yes. I'm sorry for your loss."

"How's my wife?"

"She lost some blood, but fortunately a transfusion was not required. She's obviously distraught and we gave her a sedative to help her relax. We'll take good care of her," he said reassuringly before giving Officer McMillan a nod, dismissing them.

"I had a son," Russ murmured as Officer McMillan escorted him out of the building and back into the cruiser.

Russ walked over to the stove and lifted the sheet of aluminum foil from the baking dish to find a dried-up chicken casserole that had barely been touched. From the corner of his eye, as the sun beamed in through the farmhouse window, something on the floor next to the sink caught his attention. As he bent down, Russ saw the peridot pendant he had given Nora lying amongst the shards of glass and broken dishes. He felt his heart grow even more weary as he picked it up and noticed the clasp of the gold chain was broken, just as his relationship with Nora now was. His eyes filled with tears as he dangled the peridot stone from its chain, remembering the moment he gave it to her and what it symbolized.

After setting the broken necklace on the countertop, Russ turned on the faucet and let the cold water run. Leaning over the sink he opened his mouth wide and gagged, tasting the saltiness of his fingers as he forced them past his palate and down into his throat. He winced, feeling his esophagus burn, as the stomach acid traveled up into his mouth. The bitter, metallic-tasting fluid flowed out into the sink, ridding him of the pills that he had been forced to take before being released from the psychiatric hospital less than an hour ago. He then splashed water on his face and thoroughly rinsed out his mouth. Russ thought back on how he managed to outsmart the doctors and nurses in the psychiatric ward most days, using his tongue to push the pills into the space between his cheek and upper molars, as he pretended to swallow them. He would later spit them out and flush them down the toilet, determined to get the poison that kept his mind in a fog, out of his system. Russ had been struggling to stay clean since his overdose and stopped filling the prescriptions the doctors continued forcing on him. For a while, he managed to stay sober and Lance tried to do him a favor by refusing to serve him his usual double shot of whiskey after learning of his internal strife. Instead, Lance would pour him a cold glass of cola on the rocks and, when he was finished, would send him on his way.

All was going well until one day last week when Mr. Edmunds arranged for Russ and a few of the guys in his department to take part in an in-house training exercise. An outside trainer arrived that morning to teach them how to run industrial cables underground and the company set up a makeshift tunnel that ran through an unused wing of the plant. Russ could feel himself start to perspire as the trainer gave instructions to the group and handed them each a flashlight and a long length of cable from the giant spool. The mandatory simulation drill was meant to educate the team at New England Underground Cable as to how the cables they manufacture at the plant are laid, connected and installed on the ocean floor. As Russ entered the makeshift tunnel and felt along its walls, his mind shifted and suddenly flashed back to the Cu Chi tunnels.

"Russ, you heard the trainer. Turn on your flashlight so we can see where we're going," said his coworker Al, who he was teamed up with.

"Shh, they'll hear you. Shut up and keep your flashlight off," Russ whispered.

"You shut up!" Al fired back.

"You're going to get us killed, man," Russ said.

"What the hell are you talking about?"

"Charlie . . . that's what I'm talking about. Now stay quiet and follow me."

As Al followed behind, Russ' heightened senses kicked in. After crawling through a long stretch of the tunnel, he stopped in his tracks.

"Russ, keep going and start threading the cable through like you were told," Al said.

Russ froze as he felt a vibration in the tunnel wall, telling him that the enemy was close. A shuffling sound to his right where the two sections of tunnel connected in and L shape triggered Russ to react, pouncing on the figure in the shadows. Russ wrestled with the stranger in the dark. Using all his strength, he grabbed the person from behind. *Kill or be killed*, he thought as he tightened a choke hold on the enemy.

"Russ, what the hell are you doing? Let him go!" Al yelled, turning on his flashlight and illuminating the inside of the tunnel.

"We have to kill him before he kills us!" Russ roared, keeping his arm rigid and steady around the enemy's neck.

"Let Bill go," Al ordered, lunging at Russ and breaking his coworker free.

"You . . . asshole," Bill called out, as he gasped for breath and rubbed his neck.

"What the hell is wrong with you? You could have killed him," Al screamed.

Afraid of what he would face when he emerged, Russ sat with his head down between his knees as his coworkers left him behind in the tunnel.

Russ heard Mr. Edmunds and security being paged over the plant's speaker system as the trainer cleared the workers out of the area. As Russ emerged from the makeshift tunnel, sweaty and disheveled, Mr. Edmunds was there to greet him with crossed arms. Back in his office, Mr. Edmunds read him the riot act and told him that he had had enough of his antics. Due to Russ' assault of his coworker during the training exercise, his many days of missed work due to undisclosed health issues, his semi-frequent tardiness, the lies that Darlene had fed him of Russ' inappropriate come-ons and reports of smelling alcohol on his breath, Mr. Edmunds decided it was high time to take action against his insubordination. He then handed Russ a broom, demoting him to a janitorial position. Mr. Edmunds finished his rant by telling him the only reason he wasn't being fired was because he knew that he and Nora had another baby on the way. He said it was out of the goodness of his heart that he was willing to keep him on the payroll and that, during this probationary period, he would be keeping a real close eye on him.

"Having a rough day now are we, Russell?" Darlene asked as he exited Mr. Edmunds' office and closed the door behind him.

"I have only one thing to say to you," Russ had replied.

"Oh, and what would that be?" she asked as she fluttered her overdone blue powdered eyelids and thickly mascaraed eyelashes at him.

Russ leaned in close, eye to eye with Darlene, and caught a whiff of her cheap, flowery perfume.

"Darlin', you're one conniving bitch. You did say to call you Darlin' now, didn't you?" Russ replied, not caring if there would be any repercussions, before proceeding on his way.

When he punched out of work, after a day of his coworkers' sideways glances and whispering behind his back, Russ headed straight to the packy and picked up two bottles of his favorite scotch malt whiskey. He then drove to the pier in Weaver Falls and drank until he was good and drunk, and his feelings were numb. It had been all downhill from there, and now he was left with nothing but reminders of the pain he had caused Nora as he walked over to the closet, grabbed a broom and attempted to clean up the disaster surrounding him.

48

"Good morning, Judge. Glad to have you back," Officer McMillan said, fixing himself a cup of coffee in the breakroom at the Swanset Police headquarters.

"Hey, Mick," Brant replied, groggy from having just returned home on a red-eye from his two-week long honeymoon in Paris with his new bride, Libby Vincent-Judge.

"So, how was that honeymoon of yours? And what's the matter, did that gorgeous bride of yours wear you out in the sack? She looks like she'd be a fun gal," Mick said, wiggling his eyebrows and nudging Brant with his elbow.

"Hey, that's my wife you're talking about. And no, not in the way you're thinking, Mick, so get your mind out of the gutter. Libby had us running all over Paris, to the Eiffel Tower, the Louvre, Notre-Dame Cathedral and all those other old, gaudy places. I'm so sick of looking at artwork and I swear I'll never eat another croissant for as long as I live. Are there any glazed doughnuts left?" Brant asked, noticing a doughnut box sitting on the counter.

"Oui, oui. Looks like there's one left with your name on it," Mick said with a chuckle as he lifted the cover, peeked inside and slid the box over.

"Come to Daddy, you sweet thing. I'm so glad to be back in the states. You can't find these in Paris," Brant said before biting into the doughnut's shiny, sugary coating.

"That reminds me, I'll be on vacation next week. I'm taking the missus to the Poconos for our anniversary. I made sure I booked a room with a heart-shaped hot tub and mirrors on the ceiling. Janice is going to be really surprised," Mick boasted.

"I'm sure she will be," Brant said, nodding his head as he took another bite of his fried ring of sweet dough.

"Fin is going to be out next week too. He's getting that bum knee of his fixed. That means we're going to be short staffed, so you'll have a bit more terrain to cover during your shifts. You're going to have to make your usual rounds and cover the east side of town too. It's generally quiet out there on those country roads, but you should probably know that we had another incident out on Hails Hallow Road while you were away."

"What happened?" Brant asked, knowing all too well that was the street Nora and Russ' house was on.

"It was that Ayers couple again. Things got really ugly this time. Russ, he and I are on a first name basis now, well he came home plastered and got into an altercation with that pretty little wife of his."

"What the hell happened, Mick?" Brant asked with concern, tossing his partially eaten doughnut into the trash can.

"She got knocked to the floor and went unconscious. Now mind you, she is very pregnant again and she wakes up to find she is bleeding and Russ is passed out drunk while the little tike upstairs is crying her eyes out from all the commotion. Somehow, she was able to muster up the strength to place a call for an ambulance. As Fin and I arrived, Russ woke up, hungover as shit, and starts swinging at us. We had to cuff him and take him outside so the paramedics could get the wife out of there. The kitchen was a wreck with broken dishes all over the place. As he sat in the back of the cruiser, I told him if he could cool off, I would follow the ambulance to the hospital, which I did. I kept the cuffs on and sat with him inside the hospital maternity waiting room. As it turned out, his wife lost the baby. It was awful. The guy's head was already in a bad place and then the doctor told him it was a boy and he had a severe birth defect, most likely due to herbicides he was exposed to in Vietnam. When we got back in the cruiser, the guy cried all the way to the psych hospital and told me Vietnam poisoned him, not only his mind, but his body too. He said how he was trying hard to stay sober and, after having a flashback while on the job, he unintentionally attacked one of his coworkers. His boss demoted him and that's when he turned to the bottle again. He said he feels like everyone is against him. The guy has been trying to hold it all together, but it's like he's shovelin' shit against the tide. I must be getting soft in my old age. I'm usually good at not letting this job get to me, Judge, but if you could see the sadness in this guy's eyes and hear the brokenness in his voice. It brought tears to my eyes, Judge, it really brought tears to my eyes."

"Thanks for the update, Mick. You go and enjoy that hot tub with Janice in the Poconos. In the meantime, I'll be sure to keep a close eye on things over on the east side."

"I've got to get going. Come outside for a minute so I can give you my log notes before I leave," Mick said, placing his coffee cup down and walking toward the door.

"Sure," Brant replied, following Mick outside and feeling unsettled.

"I want to get out of town before that storm gets here. It's supposed to be a doozy," Mick said, pointing up to the sky.

As Brant followed Mick to his vehicle, he looked up and saw ominous clouds off in the distance, slowly rolling their way toward him and casting a dark shadow over Swanset.

49

"It looks like it's going to start raining any second. Are you sure you don't want me to come inside with you, Nor?" Josie asked from behind the wheel of her convertible.

"I'm sure, Jo. I'll just be a few minutes."

"Okay, but if you aren't out in ten minutes, I'm going over to Mr. and Mrs. Fletchers' house to call for help."

"I'm just going in to pick up a few things and see how Russ is doing. He sounded sad when I spoke to him this morning. I've really appreciated your parents taking us in and watching Amy today, but I'm ready to come back home. I just need to be sure Russ is staying sober and following his doctor's orders before I bring Amy back."

"Okay. Hopefully he's been doing his part. Oh, don't forget to take the casserole you made for him from the back seat."

"Thanks for reminding me. I'll be right back," Nora said, grabbing the casserole dish and closing the car door.

Walking up the driveway toward the farmhouse, Nora noticed light droplets of rain pinging off the sheet of aluminum foil that covered the casserole dish. She had been apart from Russ for over two weeks and longed to return home to him. Like her, Russ was mourning the loss of their baby boy and Nora hoped their brief separation would help Russ clear his head. Nora felt more rain droplets on her forehead and wiped them with the back of her hand before stepping onto the porch. When she looked up, she saw Russ standing inside the doorway to greet her.

"Hi, Nor. It's good to see you," Russ said, his hair greasy and uncombed.

"It's good to see you too. I made you a casserole," Nora said, sheepishly smiling, stepping inside and handing him the dish.

"Thanks. That was nice of you," Russ said, peeking under the foil covering and placing the dish down on the side table.

"How are you doing? You sounded sad on the phone earlier," Nora said, looking around the farmhouse's darkened interior with all its shades drawn and then back to Russ' pale skin, scruffy beard and grey, shadow-encircled eyes.

"I could use a hug," Russ replied, looking down at his bare feet.

"So could I," Nora said, wrapping her arms around him and catching the scent of alcohol expelling from his lungs.

Nora sensed Russ begin to tremble and loosened her embrace. Stepping back, she saw Russ' eyes overflowing with tears.

"Have you been getting any sleep?" Nora asked, caressing his damp cheek.

Russ stood silent, shaking his head.

"Russ, tell me what's bothering you."

"Everything, Nor."

"Our son?"

"Yes. We had a son, Nor, and we lost him because of me. I never even got a chance to see him . . . or hold him."

"We did have a son and he was precious, Russ, but it wasn't meant to be. The doctor said even if I had gone full term, he wouldn't have survived. It's not your fault. Do you hear me?" Nora said soothingly, understanding his pain and fighting back her own tears.

"It's all my fault, Nor. Don't you see I've been poisoned?"

"What do you mean you've been poisoned?"

"By the military. They sprayed that herbicide. That's why the baby was deformed. It must have absorbed through the pores of my skin. And by the doctors . . . they're all against me. They keep forcing their pills on me. I think they are trying to track me, so they can know where I am and so Charlie can get me, Nor. When I don't take them, I'm able to see things."

"What things?" Nora asked, feeling her heart beat faster.

"I see my little sister . . . and Johnny Davis too. When I go into the woods . . . they're there. They said its okay if I go with them."

"Russ, your doctor told you that you need to stay on your medication. You know that."

"Did they tell you to say that? Don't believe them, Nor! Mr. Edmunds is against me too . . . he and . . . that bitch, Darlene, have been conspiring with the Viet Cong and set up those tunnels inside the plant to try to get me fired or killed. Can't you see that?" Russ asked, his eyes growing wide.

"No, Russ. I can't see that. Have you been drinking again?"

"No," Russ replied, his eyes darting back and forth.

Nora turned and made her way onto the porch, disappointed by Russ' lie and disturbed by the words coming out of his mouth. As heavy rain began to fall, Nora noticed that Josie was no longer inside her car. *"Okay but if you aren't out in ten minutes, I'm going over to Mr. and Mrs. Fletchers' house to call for help,"* Nora remembered her friend saying as a gusty wind picked up and the porch swing began to wildly oscillate.

"Nora, wait!" Russ called out, following her outside.

Nora turned and stood face to face with her husband, unable to find the man she knew behind the set of lost eyes that gazed back at her.

"I have to go," Nora said, checking the time on her wristwatch.

"Wait. I have something for you."

"Not now, Russ. I need to get back to Amy."

"Don't go. Stay with me, Nor," Russ pleaded, momentarily tucking one arm behind his back.

"We had a deal that you'd stay away from the bottle and follow your doctor's orders. I love you and will continue to do all I can to help you, Russ, but it's not safe for me here," Nora said, turning and calmly walking down the stairs and flagstone path, seemingly undisturbed by the rain saturating her hair and clothing.

"Nora! No!" Russ yelled, hurrying down the porch steps.

"Nor, get into the car!" Josie called out, sounding frantic and running up the driveway.

Nora turned her head to see Russ rushing toward her and, as she took a step forward, felt him grab hold of her arm.

"Nor, please don't go," Russ pleaded as the rain soaked his hair and T-shirt.

"Russ, when you get yourself sober and start following your doctor's orders, I'll come back again."

"No you won't, because I'm not getting any better, Nor. I know I'm not," Russ said adamantly as he pulled her closer.

"Get your hands off of her and let her go, Russ," Josie called out.

"She's my wife so stay out of it, Josie," Russ yelled, tightening his grip on Nora's arm.

"I will not stay out of it. Let her go! You are not going to hurt her anymore," Josie fired back, stepping forward and reaching out to try to grab Nora's free arm.

"Get away! Stand back, Josie, and get off my property," Russ yelled, suddenly grabbing Nora by the waist from behind and pulling her against him.

"You let her go this minute or . . .," Josie began, stopping mid-sentence and taking a step back.

"Or what?" Russ said, pulling out his pistol from the back pocket of his jeans and waving it in his free hand.

"Shit, Russ! What the hell are you doing?" Josie asked as a terrified expression washed over her face.

Nora saw Russ become more agitated and his breathing grow heavy as the sound of sirens approached and a Swanset Police cruiser pulled into the driveway alongside Josie's car.

"Go back to your car and get out of here, Josie," Nora urged her friend, fearful of what may happen next and knowing Russ was not of sound mind.

"I'm not leaving you, Nor," Josie said, shaking her head.

"You called the cops? Are you against me too, Josie? Are you?" Russ shouted, tightening his hold on Nora.

Through the torrential, blinding rain a uniformed officer stepped out of his cruiser and made his way toward them.

"Put the gun down and let the lady go," the officer called out.

Nora could feel her insides stir as Russ squeezed her even tighter. He moved back toward their property tree line, dragging her along with him to a sheltered spot under the canopy of the weeping willow tree.

The unforgiving rain continued pouring down on them and Nora's vision became obscured. As heavy droplets of rain pelted her face, she noticed something familiar in the veiled silhouette of the officer approaching them.

"It's you! You tried to steal her away from me once but I'm not letting you take her from me again," Russ roared.

Nora blinked to rid her eyes of the rain that clouded them and, through the willows wet, whipping branches, saw it was Brant Judge, with his silver Swanset Police badge brightly displayed on the left side of his uniform shirt, who had arrived at the scene.

"I said let her go. Now calm down and nobody will get hurt," Brant instructed.

"You think you are going to come onto my property and tell me what to do? Do you?" Russ wailed.

"I just came here to talk and keep the peace. That's all," Brant replied, his eyes locking on Nora and seemingly willing to fight for her now.

The winds picked up and old memories stirred in the back of Nora's mind. She remembered how much it hurt when she realized she had probably just been the unlucky girl who Brant caught while rebounding from his broken relationship with Libby. She remembered the lies he fed her between sips of the vintage wine. She recalled how she felt when she saw him kissing Libby in his hospital bed just days after professing his love to her on Long Island. She remembered how he seemed to move right on, flitting off to the Vineyard and eventually marrying his on again, off again girlfriend with the trust fund and Ivy League education. He couldn't save the day then and he couldn't save it now. She was disillusioned and he was too late. Russ held her tightly and Nora remembered it was his heart she promised to love, through good times and bad, as she stood with him in this chilling moment.

"You don't belong here. Leave us alone," Nora heard herself cry out, her voice muffled by the wind and the erratic movement of the willow's branches.

"I have a gun and I'm not afraid to use it," Russ said, keeping Nora close.

"Is this how you want things to go down, Ayers? Because my job is to serve and protect and that's exactly what I intend to do here today," Brant said, gesturing for Josie to leave and taking cover behind the back tire of Nora's clunker.

It was the very same tire he had once changed during their chance encounter when he stumbled upon her disabled vehicle along the side of the road, and they instantly fell for one another.

"Nor, look at me," Russ whispered into her ear.

"Drop your weapon," Officer Judge ordered, reaching into his holster for his pistol.

"Please look at me, Nor," Russ pleaded.

"What is it, Russ?" Nora nervously asked, trembling as she saw the barrel of the pistol close to her head.

"I want to look into your beautiful green eyes one last time."

"Russ, I love you. Please put the gun down," Nora said as their eyes locked and hers filled with tears, clouding her vision again as Russ raised the gun up higher, brushing it against her hair.

"I said drop your weapon. This is your final warning, Ayers!" Brant shouted.

"All the pain I've caused you will be over soon, Nor," Russ said, his voice cracking and his lips laying a soft kiss on the scar above her eyebrow.

Nora became dizzy as her heart rate sped up and her legs shook. She gasped as Russ raised the gun yet higher. In the rain-filled sky a deafening shot rang out. Nora's body went limp and collapsed onto the mud-soaked ground, beneath the swaying willow.

50

With her hair pulled back into a low ponytail and wearing a simple black dress, Nora sat alone on the porch swing with Russ' burial flag on her lap. The stars and stripes that had draped his casket had been tightly folded into a triangle before being handed to her at his graveside service that morning. As the last of the family and friends dispersed from the somber, post-funeral gathering inside the farmhouse, everything grew silent. Nora found herself unable to take her eyes off the keepsake flag as she replayed the events of that tragic day in her mind.

She looked over toward her rusting old car where Brant had taken cover, then over toward the tree line where she and Russ shared their final moments together under the willow's swaying branches. The yard was now dry, with vibrant green grass, and the willow was still. There were no signs of the suffering that had taken place there just a few days prior. After fainting, she had awoken to find herself lying on the ground with Josie calling out to her. The blaring sirens of Brant Judge's police backup, and other emergency vehicles arriving on the scene as the rain let up, made her stir and realize she was not dreaming.

"Don't look, Nor. Please don't look," Josie pleaded as Nora lifted her head, turned and saw Russ, lying motionless on the ground behind her, under their special tree. His head was turned away from her and she crawled her way over to him through the sticky mud.

"Russ? Russ, can you hear me? Are you okay?" she asked, as he lay perfectly still.

"Nor, please don't," Josie cried out again.

Ignoring her friend's pleas, Nora reached out to grab hold of Russ' hand, only to find it limp and lifeless. Her hands were shaking and she felt unsettled as she moved closer. Nora saw the side of his T-shirt, still wet from the rainstorm, was covered with what she assumed was mud. As she reached up and touched the side of his face a sudden wave of panic, which immediately turned to hysteria, washed over her when she realized that Russ' dark hair and T-shirt were saturated in blood and a that bullet had struck his head.

"No! No! Wake up, Russ. We can get you better. I know we can," Nora cried out, laying her head on his chest to listen for a heartbeat, only to be met by silence.

"Nor . . .," Josie began.

"He did this, Jo!" Nora cried out, pointing at Brant.

"No, Nor, it wasn't . . ."

"I told him to leave us alone!"

"Nora?" Brant asked, as he cautiously approached.

"Look what you've done. I told you to leave! I didn't want you here! You shot my husband. You killed him and . . . I hate you for it, Brant Judge. Do you hear me? I hate you!" Nora cried out, still sitting by Russ' side.

"I . . . didn't . . . shoot him," Brant said, stumbling over his own words.

"My husband is dead because of you. He didn't deserve this. Why would you do this to me?"

"Nor, please listen to me for a minute," Josie said, seeing that Nora was emotionally distraught.

"Nora, I did not shoot Russ. I never fired my gun," Brant calmly stated.

Trying to make sense of it all, Nora forced herself to stand up, shaking her head as she looked to Josie for understanding.

"He's telling the truth. I was in my car and I watched the whole thing unfold. I wasn't about to leave you. I'd never be able to live with myself if something happened to you, Nor. Brant never fired his gun. I thought Russ was going to shoot you, Nor, but instead, after he kissed you on the forehead, he looked up to the sky. It was as if he saw something calling to him and then he pulled the trigger on himself. After you fell to the ground, the rain stopped. It was as if the universe was speaking and saying that it's over, that Russ' pain is over, and he's finally free. I'm so sorry, Nor. I'm so sorry that this happened to him, and to you," Josie said, holding her friend in a warm embrace.

Nora blinked and, as her thoughts returned to the present, ran her hands over the folded flag one last time before reaching back and untying the ribbon at the nape of her neck to allow her hair to fall down. She then placed her hand on the peridot pendant resting near her collar bone, having discovered it sitting in its box and waiting for her on the kitchen table.

Unbeknownst to her, Russ had repaired the necklace before placing it back in its box along with a handwritten note in which he apologized for all the pain he caused her and asked her to remember him every time she looked at the pendant. If only she had stopped when Russ told her he had something for her, instead of turning away. *Maybe I wouldn't be sitting here with his burial flag in my hands if I had just stayed for a moment longer*, she thought, as all their hopes, dreams and joy were now washed away by the torrential rain.

Nora recalled how, after the storm cleared, the coroner's vehicle and the last of the police cruisers pulled out of the driveway and made their way down Hails Hallow Road. Curious neighbors who came out in their raincoats carrying colorful umbrellas in hopes of getting a glimpse of the action, walked back to their houses, ignorant of their own warped role in the deadly charade that had transpired. Nora knew the information they gathered would later be used to fuel their gossip sessions around Swanset's barber shops, municipal buildings, diners and coffee houses. In the morning, they would feast upon the headlines in the newspaper, scrutinizing the details of the tragedy, word by word and line by line, between sips of coffee and bites of cheese danish and sunny-side up eggs. They would then continue living their lives with the same closed off mindset as before, waiting to devour the next big headline or juicy bit of gossip as a means of entertainment to enhance their otherwise mundane lives in their podunk town. They would repeat this cycle hour after hour, day after day, and year after year, as other veterans, just like Russ, continued to suffer in silence, unless something was done to stop the madness. She was aware that if nothing was to change, then people all over the country, in small towns just like Swanset, would continue the cycle for decades to come. The whispering about each new tragedy . . . without anyone really talking to them, the stares and sideways glances . . . without anyone really seeing them, and the gossip and flashy headlines . . . without anyone really listening to their stories or understanding their pain, would all continue. Nora wondered how long this condemnation without gratitude would go on and prayed the conflict at home would end. Somehow, she hoped peace would be brought to those veterans whose cries for help were being ignored and to the families they left behind.

51

Crisp American flags hanging from telephone poles lining Main Street waved in the breeze as residents of Swanset set up their lawn chairs and jockeyed for prime viewing spots along the parade route. Viviane, who had been complaining about her throbbing bunions and the chill in the November air, followed behind with Richard as Nora pulled Amy along the bustling sidewalk in her little red wagon. She had made amends with Viviane for no other reason other than her father had asked her to, and she was Amy's grandmother. Nora supposed it was the right thing to do as she grappled with the realization her mother was incapable of thinking of anyone but herself, offering Nora little comfort after Russ' tragic death.

Finding an open spot in front of the Swanset Public Library, Nora securely positioned Amy's wagon before taking a seat along the sidewalk's edge. She rolled her eyes as her father opened a lawn chair for Viviane, who had finally caught up with them and continued to fuss and complain about the sun in her eyes and her aching feet.

The town's annual Veterans Day parade, which began every year in the parking lot of Swanset High School before proceeding north on Main Street and through the town center, would culminate at the local veterans post that turned Russ away when he reached out for help. A few weeks prior, Nora stopped in at the post after being invited there by its new commander who caught wind of Russ' struggle, his passing and his membership rejection. Like the past post commander, the new commander was also a World War II veteran but had a different mindset. Nora found him to be kind and apologetic as he recognized the sacrifices of her late husband and his fellow veterans. He had graciously extended the invitation for Russ' friends to march in the parade with a warning they may not receive the warm welcome they were hoping for. At ten o'clock sharp, the parade kicked off, as it always did, with onlookers decked out in patriotic colors and wearing American flag pins on their lapels, ready to cheer on their local heroes who had bravely served their country.

Amy, bundled up in her fall coat and knit hat, covered her ears as a Swanset police cruiser slowly rolled by, its siren going off intermittently as it led the parade and ensured the route was clear. A parade volunteer walked along the side of the road selling small American flags on wooden sticks to benefit the local veterans organizations. As the woman approached, Nora reached into her purse and handed her a small donation. Pulling out a flag from her plastic bucket, the woman kindly handed it to Amy, bringing an instant smile to her ruddy-cheeked face. Amy looked up at Nora, her blue eyes beaming, as she waved her little flag and pointed to the larger flags flying on the poles high above her.

"Amy, you have a flag of your very own now to wave when all our heroes march by," Nora said, kissing her tenderly on the cheek.

"My flag," Amy said, proudly waving it in the air.

"Yes, it's your flag, my love," Nora said, seeing other parade-goers also waving theirs as the first group of veterans marched toward them.

The small group of veterans from World War I, just a fraction of the two million men who were sent to France and bravely fought against Germany and Austria-Hungary, marched proudly along as the crowd bestowed their gratitude with salutes and applause.

As the World War II veterans approached, the crowd grew even more excited. With everyone now standing, relatives, friends and neighbors offered their heartfelt thanks to the large group of brave, deserving veterans who endured the attack on Pearl Harbor, the Battle of Normandy, the Battle of the Bulge, Okinawa, Midway, Iwo Jima and countless other gruesome battles.

The applause continued flowing as veterans of the Korean War marched forward. These brave veterans lost over three hundred men in the Battle of Pork Chop Hill, fought in ground combat in the Battle of Bloody Ridge, and endured heavy fighting during the gruesome Battle of Triangle Hill.

Suddenly, a wave of jeering could be heard as another group approached and Nora instantly felt her heart sink. She was overcome with sadness as, like a row of collapsing dominos, she watched the parade-goers settling back into their aluminum lawn chairs one by one. Peering down Main Street, she caught a glimpse of the black cloth banner that she had sewn for the Vietnam Veterans waving in the wind as Russ' friends, exposed, defenseless and on high alert, as if anticipating an ambush, valiantly marched toward her.

"Nora, for goodness' sake please sit down. Can't you see you're the only one still standing?" Viviane said, her lips pursed.

"I can see very clearly, Mother. For once in your life, could you please do something for me and just shut up," Nora replied, fed up with her mother's distorted views and silly demands.

"Look, Amy, here come daddy's friends," Nora said, helping her daughter out of the wagon.

"Harry?" Amy asked, looking up at her and clutching her flag's wooden stick.

"Yes. Uncle Harry, Ray, Mike and Jimmy are all coming. See?" Nora said, pointing down the street.

"I clap?" Amy asked.

"Yes, we will clap for our heroes, Amy," Nora replied as Amy let out a squeal.

The small group of four Vietnam Veterans were met by uncomfortable glances and name calling, while others chose to flat out ignore them, as they made their way along the parade route. Unlike the other groups of veterans, Russ' friends were not dressed in their military uniforms, instead opting to wear their jungle fatigues and field jackets. Nora could see from the twisted expressions on Ray and Jimmy's faces, friends Russ met at the peer-to-peer sessions he attended, they knew they weren't welcome as they each held an end of the banner, announcing their presence and demanding to be seen.

Harry Blake proudly marched behind them, strutting his stuff and repeatedly crisscrossing the road, displaying the scar running down the side of his face. With the sleeves of his field jacket torn off, he exposed what little remained of his left arm so the crowd was aware of exactly what he sacrificed for the sake of his country. Mike, however, stole the show as he marched a few paces behind. His dark, disheveled, shoulder length hair was as wild as the look in his wide eyes which scanned the parade-goers flanking both sides of the street. He wore a bandana around his forehead and his army field coat was wide open, showing off the dog tags hanging around his neck. He proudly carried the American flag on a wooden pole he made from a branch he found in the woods behind Nora and Russ' house, having shaved down the bark to expose the smooth oak surface underneath before carving Russ' name and rank on it. He told Nora he was carrying the flag in honor of Russ and, as Nora observed from afar, he would have made him proud as he violently waved the stars and stripes, just like the untamed creature, the baby killer and the bottom of the barrel grunt all the parade-goers assumed he and his friends to be. Nora knew he was showing them that it was his flag and his country too, and he and his buddies deserved the same respect and accolades as those that marched ahead of them on Main Street.

Nora took Amy by the hand and guided her along, stepping off the curb into the road. She turned to face Russ' friends as they marched toward them and began to clap loudly, cheering them on as they approached. She was determined to give them encouragement to keep moving forward, with Amy standing beside her excitedly waving her flag.

As the banner drew closer, Nora heard the parade-goers begin to shout and realized that their comments were directed at her.

"Sit down lady!"

"Why the heck is she clapping for these degenerates?"

"She must have a thing for losers!"

"Nora, for the last time, please sit down. You're making a scene," Viviane blurted out through gritted teeth.

Nora turned around, slowly rotating in a full circle, scanning the crowd in disbelief. She saw anger and disgust in all the faces around her and was jolted by a projectile striking her forehead. As the object fell to the ground Nora looked down to see shards of glass land near Amy's feet and cover the top of her tiny, patent leather Mary Jane's.

"Momma!" Amy cried out.

"It's okay, my love. Momma will protect you," Nora assured her.

Feeling warmth on her face, Nora swiped her hand across her brow only to discover that she was bleeding. She realized the scar above her eyebrow had been torn back open, stirring up an animal-like fierceness from deep inside of her. She was tired of the heavy feeling of shame the townspeople bestowed upon her and her family in recent months. She had endured the lack of empathy, pretending not to hear the negative talk about Russ' death or notice the quick turning away of heads when she looked up to see eyes on her every time she walked into Swanset Savings Bank, The Swanset Village Grocer, or anywhere else around town. She now understood how Russ must have felt, always feeling as though he was being dissected and unable to escape his living hell, and Nora found herself stepping into the middle of the road, bringing the parade to a screeching halt.

"You cruel, ignorant bastards. Look at all of you. Just look at yourselves!" Nora screamed, feeling her face flush and certain that her insides would burst open as Officer Peter McMillan and Officer Brant Judge, who were both assigned to police the parade route, approached.

"What's going on here?" Officer McMillan asked as his eyes surveyed the scene.

"They threw a glass bottle at me and my daughter. They're ordering me to sit down. I will not sit down! I will stand up for these men, for Russ and his friends, today!" Nora ferociously replied, feeling her forehead sting.

"Sit down and shut up already!" another angry voice called out.

"I know you've been through a lot, Mrs. Ayers, but you need to get out of the road and go sit down like they said. Maybe you should take your daughter home and bake her some cookies or something," McMillan stated, shrugging his shoulders and gesturing for her to head back toward the sidewalk.

"No, Mick. Let the lady speak," Brant Judge said, appearing to try to take control of the situation.

"What did you say?" Mick asked, glaring at his subordinate officer.

"Everyone settle down. I said let the lady speak," Brant said, loud and clear into his megaphone so everyone around them could hear, looking directly at Nora, as if trying to make amends for all that happened between them.

Brant then reached into his pocket and, as the sun bounced off his golden wedding band, handed Nora a hanky.

"Remember that our scars remind us of where we've been and how far we've come. Go ahead. Say your peace," Brant instructed, handing her his megaphone.

"Thank you," Nora said, accepting the hanky and wiping blood from her face.

With the megaphone in hand, she walked toward Harry Blake, who had waved her over.

"Nora, you don't have to do this," Harry said, with a nervous look in his eyes.

"You're wrong, Harry. I do need to do this, for Russ and for all of you," Nora said before turning back toward the crowd which had grown denser with curious onlookers.

"We came here today as a community to celebrate and honor our nations brave heroes, yet many of you fail to recognize the sacrifices of the four heroes standing right in front of you. They are the bravest of all, being here today like this, yet you see them as worthless nobodies. You spit on their clothes and throw things at them. You call them baby killers and savages. I'm asking you to look at yourselves and your own behavior and attitudes. From what I can see, you are the savages, not them. These men standing before you were just boys when they were deployed. They had their dreams and innocence stolen from them. They were your paperboys, the kids in your neighborhood who shoveled your driveway and mowed your lawn. They were your classmates and your students. They were once scouts and played in Swanset's youth baseball league. They are the same young men who held the door for you as you walked into church on Sunday morning and who carried your groceries to your car for you when you left the market. They never asked to be sent half a world away and many of them didn't want to go. Then, when things got too intense and these boys were beginning to break, they were handed speed and God only knows what other kind of drugs, to bury their fear and keep them in fighting mode. Many of them came home addicted and alone. We sent them there! We did this to them! Don't you see they were following their orders? They did their job and defended the freedoms of others, and this is the thanks they get? The last of our troops pulled out of Vietnam over six months ago and it's about time we start thinking about what we can all do to help these men, our community, and our nation heal from the aftereffects of this . . . unwinnable war," Nora said, feeling a sense of peace and handing the megaphone back to Brant.

Turning to Amy, Nora smiled.

"Hero," Amy said, looking up at her mother and waving her flag.

"Amy, would you like to go see daddy's friends now?" Nora asked, kneeling and brushing shards of glass off the top of her daughter's shoes with her bare hands.

"I go, Momma," Amy replied, nodding her head.

"Where are you going? Haven't you created enough drama here already?" Viviane asked, obviously embarrassed by her daughter's public rant.

"Just shut up, Viviane!" Richard firmly ordered, standing up and giving Nora a wink.

Nora then scooped up Amy and placed her back in the wagon.

"Nora, you're bleeding. They hurt you," Mr. Thompson said somberly.

"Don't worry, Daddy. All their ugliness has only made me stronger," Nora replied, before giving her father a hug, grabbing the wagon's handle and making her way over to Russ' friends with Amy in tow.

"That was something else what you just did. Russ would be proud of you," Harry said.

"He'd be proud of you too. Now, if you don't mind, Amy and I would like to march with all of you. Would that be okay?"

"The more, the merrier," Harry replied taking the handle of the wagon in his only remaining hand and pulling Amy along.

As the parade started back up, the people lining the street chattered amongst themselves, carefully studying her and Russ' friends as they stood united and marched onward. Officers McMillan and Judge stayed close by, walking alongside them as they proceeded down Main Street, ensuring there would be no further problems. With her gaze focused ahead, Nora smiled and stood taller, taking notice of a few townspeople standing in support of the small but determined group. She felt the heaviness in her chest lift and let out a deep sigh upon spotting familiar faces of those whose lives were closely linked with hers and Russ' scattered about the parade's path. She first noticed Jeff and Sherry waving to her as she passed by the Swanset Town Hall, followed by a nod from Russ' old boss, Lance, wearing a broken-in baseball hat and leaning against the trunk of an oak tree in front of Swanset Savings Bank. She turned her head and saw Josie Henson's parents across the way, by the jewelry store, giving her a thumbs up. As the group passed St. Leo's Church, Nora saw Father Meehan standing on the steps, making the sign of the cross, signifying the acceptance of death, suffering and sacrifice. Mr. Thayer, her and Russ' chemistry teacher from Swanset High, gave her a wink from under the rim of his scally cap as he stood outside the pawn shop along with his father, the shop's owner, clapping and saluting Russ' friends to show them the sacrifices they made mattered. It was a small start, but Nora knew that these few people, with open minds and hearts, could have influence over others and provide the foundation for change.

Out of the corner of her eye, Nora caught a glimpse of Amy waving to Brant Judge, who was walking alongside the wagon. Like an iridescent pearl inside a tumbled oyster shell, Amy was untarnished and the one perfect thing that had come from all the storms Nora had weathered. Brushing her fingertips along the wound on her forehead, Nora felt a sharp, fleeting sting shoot across the reopened, jagged imperfection. She continued to watch as Amy's flag fell to the ground and Brant bent down to pick it up. As he leaned in to hand the flag back to Amy, Nora noticed his eyebrows raise and his mouth hang open. From the stunned expression that washed over Brant's face, Nora realized he had seen his own eyes, bright like the glowing full moon over Swanset Bay, looking back at him. The world would always be an imperfect place and Nora knew, that like the rest of humanity, she was imperfect too.

THE END

Acknowledgements

To my mother, the strongest woman I will ever know, who sacrificed everything for our family and showed unwavering love and devotion to my father during his darkest days.

To my son and daughter, the lights of my life, my pride and joy. You are my constant reminder of goodness in this tumultuous world.

To my husband, the love of my life. Thank you for loving me and all my imperfections and for coming on this journey with me.

To my mentor and friend, the late author and poet Janice Indeck, who encouraged me to write my story and saw something in me that I did not see in myself. I know you were with me every step of the way and I will always remember you.

To my friend Arlene Adelkopf, for your line editing services. I can still see your red pen marks on my manuscript. Thank you for your wisdom, guidance and for sharing your Scottish shortbread recipe with me. I am forever grateful.

To the members of The Writer's Café in Parkland, Florida for welcoming me into your group. Thank you for all your encouragement, input and help with the developmental editing of this novel. I am grateful for your wisdom, kindness and, most of all, your friendship.

To SFC William Dickson U.S. Army Reserve Retired Civil Affairs and Psychological Operations Command, Tanya Downs, Lauren Jill Hochman, Cynthia Perry, and Eleanor Nelson-Wernick, Ph.D. for your input, knowledge, support and proofreading. I appreciate you taking time out of your busy lives to help me perfect my story.

To my cover designer Dina St. Andrew for working with me and sharing your talents to bring the vision of my novel's cover to life.

To all the brave heroes who honorably served in the United States Armed Forces. Thank you for your service to our nation and for defending the freedoms of others. Your sacrifices are not forgotten.

Lastly, to my Lord and Savior, Jesus Christ, through whom all things are possible, for giving me beauty for my ashes and joy for my mourning.

Afterword

Survivors of suicide loss experience a unique grief. In the year 2020 alone, there were 6,146 United States veterans who died by suicide. It wasn't until 1980 that Post Vietnam Syndrome, formerly known as shell shock or combat fatigue, was officially recognized and given the diagnostic term we now refer to as Post Traumatic Stress Disorder or PTSD.

Suicide impacts spouses, children, parents, siblings and friends- all of who are left behind to pick up the pieces while searching for answers with grieving hearts. Suicide is not shameful and survivors left behind shouldn't feel like it is. It is also not something for others who haven't been impacted by it to openly joke about, judge or gossip about behind closed doors. In the long run such behaviors only make matters worse for their loved ones. Suicide and mental health are okay to talk about, just as one would any other illness or medical condition, as it does not discriminate and impacts people of all ages, races, genders and socioeconomic backgrounds.

It is my hope that *Beneath the Swaying Willow* will open up discussions, increase awareness and reduce stigma associated with mental health disorders and suicide, particularly among our nation's veteran population. I also hope it will bring comfort to others who have lost a loved one to suicide in knowing that they are not alone.

Peace,
Amily D'Nas